W9-AUJ-021

PENGUIN BOOKS

The Shortest Way Home

JULIETTE FAY's first novel, *Shelter Me,* was a 2009 Massachusetts Book Award Book of the Year. Her second novel, *Deep Down True,* was short-listed for the Women's Fiction Award by the American Library Association. She received a bachelor's degree from Boston College and a master's degree from Harvard University. She lives in Massachusetts with her husband and four children. *The Shortest Way Home* is her third novel.

Praise for *The Shortest Way Home*

"With trademark wit and grace, Juliette Fay portrays a man forced to rescue his family as he reaches for his own freedom. She keeps you turning the pages, even as you want to stop and admire her writing."

—Randy Susan Meyers, author of *The Murderer's Daughters*

"Insightful, funny, and tenderhearted . . . full of truths about family, falling in love, and finding out who we are meant to be."

—Amy Hatvany, author of *Best Kept Secret* and *Outside the Lines*

"*The Shortest Way Home* is Juliette Fay's best yet and shows us that loving the people in your life can be as exciting, as daring, as difficult an adventure as any."

—Marisa de los Santos, *New York Times* bestselling author of *Falling Together* and *Love Walked In*

"A touching and engrossing story about the lengths to which we'll go to avoid where we're meant to be, and the way the heart leads us gently back."

—Nichole Bernier, author of *The Unfinished Work of Elizabeth D.*

"*The Shortest Way Home* is full of heart and of understanding about the often awkward collection we call 'family.'"

—Meg Waite Clayton, bestselling author of *The Wednesday Sisters*

"If you've ever thought you or anyone in your family might be just a bit less than perfect, read this book."

—Nancy Thayer, author of *Summer Breeze*

"A smart, sincere look at the meaning of home, the complicated nature of family ties, and how the things we run from are often what we need the most." —Allie Larkin, author of *Why Can't I Be You*

"*The Shortest Way Home* is as complex and full of surprises as the well-examined life. This is one beautiful novel, rich with depth and heart." —Julianna Baggott, bestselling author of *Pure*

"Heartfelt . . . Juliette Fay does a wonderful job creating this quirky, lovable cast of characters finding their way in life and love."

—Shilpi Somaya Gowda, *New York Times* bestselling author of *Secret Daughter*

"Powerful, beautifully written, and at times heartbreaking . . . a meditation on the impossibility and the inevitability of finding our way home." —Julie Buxbaum, author of *After You*

The Shortest Way Home

Juliette Fay

PENGUIN BOOKS

PENGUIN BOOKS
Published by the Penguin Group
Penguin Group (USA) Inc., 375 Hudson Street, New York, New York 10014, USA • Penguin Group (Canada), 90 Eglinton Avenue East, Suite 700, Toronto, Ontario M4P 2Y3, Canada (a division of Pearson Penguin Canada Inc.) • Penguin Books Ltd, 80 Strand, London WC2R 0RL, England • Penguin Ireland, 25 St Stephen's Green, Dublin 2, Ireland (a division of Penguin Books Ltd) • Penguin Group (Australia), 707 Collins Street, Melbourne, Victoria 3008, Australia (a division of Pearson Australia Group Pty Ltd) • Penguin Books India Pvt Ltd, 11 Community Centre, Panchsheel Park, New Delhi–110 017, India • Penguin Group (NZ), 67 Apollo Drive, Rosedale, Auckland 0632, New Zealand (a division of Pearson New Zealand Ltd) • Penguin Books, Rosebank Office Park, 181 Jan Smuts Avenue, Parktown North 2193, South Africa • Penguin China, B7 Jaiming Center, 27 East Third Ring Road North, Chaoyang District, Beijing 100020, China

Penguin Books Ltd, Registered Offices:
80 Strand, London WC2R 0RL, England

First published in Penguin Books 2012

A Pamela Dorman / Penguin Book

Publisher's Note
This is a work of fiction. Names, characters, places, and incidents either are the product of the author's imagination or are used fictitiously, and any resemblance to actual persons, living or dead, business establishments, events, or locales is entirely coincidental.

ISBN 978-1-62090-670-5

Printed in the United States of America
Set in Granjon • Designed by Elke Sigal

For my sisters, Jennifer Dacey Allen and Kristen Dacey Iwai,
beautiful inside and out

AUTHOR'S NOTE

Both Huntington's disease and sensory processing disorder are conditions with fairly broad ranges of symptoms and challenges. Though I researched extensively, this story is not meant to be a comprehensive review of either subject nor to represent the entire gamut of experience. I hope readers will find the depictions in this novel to be plausible, interesting, and enlightening. For more information, here are two of the many resources I found to be helpful: Huntington's Disease Society of America http://www.hdsa.org and Sensory Processing Disorder Foundation http://www.sinetwork.org.

Think you're escaping and run into yourself.
Longest way round is the shortest way home.

—James Joyce, *Ulysses*

ACKNOWLEDGMENTS

I first learned of Huntington's disease many years ago from my then-housemate, Susan Koehler Arsenault, and I've been pondering it ever since. I'm grateful for her openness about facing this terrifying disease over the course of her life, including her mother's diagnosis, growing up with that loss coupled with the uncertainty of her own status, getting tested, and adjusting to life as a noncarrier but with a sibling who does have HD. This story owes a debt of gratitude to her.

Many thanks to Jennifer Allen and Megan Lucier for sharing their experiences of parenting children with sensory processing issues. Dr. Julia VanRooyen of the Harvard Humanitarian Initiative's Women in War project gave me intriguing, heart-wrenching information about her work in Kenya and the Democratic Republic of Congo. Bridget Anderson and Jeremy Colangelo-Bryan also provided information from their Kenyan experiences. Karen Maguire offered wonderful stories and insights from her career as a massage therapist. Betsy Gemmell Steinberg, RN, gave me the inside scoop on nursing—and so much more—in a middle school setting. I only wish I could have included more from my interviews with these fascinating folks.

This novel has benefited greatly from the close inspection, careful reflection, and sound recommendations of talented writers, readers, and friends: Nichole Bernier, Alison Bullock, Kathy Crowley, Kristen Iwai, Megan Lucier, Randy Susan Meyers, and Catherine Toro-McCue. Eagle Scout Liam Fay gave me the thumbs-up on my depiction of scouting.

Keiji and Kristen Iwai produced another wonderful book trailer to introduce readers to *The Shortest Way Home.* Take a look at www.juliettefay.com. Julia Tanen continues to share her impressive public relations and marketing know-how.

It's a huge delight to be working with editor Pamela Dorman, associate editor Julie Miesionczek, assistant editor Kristen O'Toole, and the great team at Viking Penguin again. In addition to superior editorial acumen, their faith and vision mean the world to me. My agent, Theresa Park, has already given me a lifetime of good advice. I'm grateful for her brilliant mind, her friendship, and her team at Park Literary: Peter Knapp, Abigail Koons, and Emily Sweet.

The muses in my life are five great blessings who inspire me daily: Quinn, Nick, Liam, Brianna, and Tom Fay. Who says writers have to be unhappy, tortured souls? If it were true I could never write a word, thanks to them.

The Shortest Way Home

CHAPTER 1

When the plane took off, Sean didn't experience that exhilarating liftoff surge he usually got when his body, mind, and soul were ejected into the earth's atmosphere. This flight was no prelude to the next adventure. In fact, it was adventure's negative image. It was an anti-adventure. He was going home.

High in the whispery layers of cloud above the Democratic Republic of Congo, Sean had a moment of regret. Maybe he shouldn't have left. Maybe if he'd just hung in there a little longer, the burnout he'd been feeling would've worked itself out—and maybe the knots in his back would've followed suit.

A miraculous healing of mind and latissimus dorsi. He chuckled at the thought, and at his own sudden nostalgia for the hardest, most heartbreaking stint he'd ever taken on. Not that he disliked his work. In fact, he loved it. Recently, though, his plan for his life, his very vision of himself, seemed to be coming unraveled. Threads popping, holes gaping like a poorly constructed sweater. And he had no idea what to do about it.

When he changed planes in Nairobi, Kenya, he downed a quartet of ibuprofen tablets and balled up his old canvas jacket for a pillow, hoping for sleep during the overnight flight to London. Something crinkled when he laid his head down. Paper in one of the jacket pockets.

It was Deirdre's letter. He'd first read it while walking back to his quarters from the hospital a month or so ago and must have jammed it into a little-used pocket and forgotten about it. Or tried to forget about it. He certainly hadn't kept it on purpose. Traveling light was a sort of obsession with him. But somehow, despite his distaste for the letter and for hanging on to stuff, her words had come along for the ride.

Sean,

How's everything. Hope you're well. So, it's great you're over there saving the world and all, but we're having our own little natural disaster here at the moment. Aunt Vivvy's lost it. She brought home a dog. I am not making this up. A big one, some kind of german shepherd or doberman. The thing is huge—scares the crap out of Kevin.

On the upside, I got a part in Joseph and the Amazing Technicolor Dreamcoat at the Worcester Footlight. Just the chorus, but I'm also understudy for one of the leads. Hopefully, she'll develop a facial tic or get incarcerated for criminal lack of talent before the show goes up. Rehearsals start in a month, and I'll be gone a lot. Not as much as I'd like, but a lot.

Kevin's okay, though all he does is go to school, study, and walk in the woods. It's creepy.

I really think you should come home. I know I keep saying that, but I've about had it now, Sean. Seriously.

So happy birthday. 44. Wow. Who'd have thought, huh?

Dee

Actually, Sean wouldn't be turning forty-four for another six months. He guessed it was Hugh's birthday she'd been thinking of, and since their brother had been dead for six years, he wasn't around to correct her. Sean didn't really care if Deirdre knew the actual date of his birth, though she was his sister, and he imagined normal families kept track of things like that.

He tucked the letter into the seatback pocket in front of him, intending to give it to the flight attendant when she came by collecting trash. It was midnight and relatively quiet, the plane's muscular hum obscuring what little evidence there might be of human interaction. Sean closed his eyes, but as he drifted off, the image of the letter peeking from the seat pocket insinuated itself into the landscape of his dreams.

The connecting flight out of London was oversold, and passengers waiting to board were getting unruly. As Sean stood braced against a wall, willing his aching back not to go out on him, he saw a man in a business suit jab his finger toward an airline employee behind the desk. The aggravated drone of his voice rose until Sean heard him yell, "I demand an explanation!"

Sean chuckled to himself. He hadn't set foot in the so-called first world in years. Granted, he'd lived in the poorest, most degraded places on the planet for most of his adult life, so the contrast was particularly palpable. In the tiny hospitals and medical outposts he'd staffed, people were grateful just to be kept alive for another day. They didn't demand explanations.

As the plane began its businesslike descent into Logan Airport, Sean gazed out the window. The city seemed to be posing for one of those tourist postcards with the word *Boston* written in colorful letters across the top. Low humidity, he realized. Weird for June. He could see everything so clearly. The Custom House Tower, Rowes Wharf, Chinatown. He knew that planted awkwardly among the dim sum restaurants and acupuncture clinics was Tufts Medical Center, where his mother had first been diagnosed. It was a genetic coin toss—heads you got it, tails you didn't. She'd lost the toss. Her older sister Vivian had won. Depending on how you defined winning.

In 1980 the whole family—Sean, his parents, baby sister Deirdre, and six-year-old brother Hugh—had moved into Aunt Vivvy's cavernous house in Belham, Massachusetts. Sean's father was a merchant mariner, out at sea for months at a time, and his mother could no longer remember if she'd fed the dog six times or at all. That dog was sent to live with a new family. Sean always suspected that Aunt Vivvy had simply had him put down. She was not an animal lover. Or a lover of anything other than order and gardening, as far as he could tell.

And now she had a dog of her own? Sean wondered if Deirdre had overdramatized the visit of some unfortunate pooch to Aunt Viv's perfect, crabgrass-free lawn. Drama was the currency of Deirdre's life—she was the Warren Buffett of drama—and she was clearly invested in Sean's return. A hostile takeover of his life designed to increase her assets and cut her liabilities.

No one met him at the airport, nor did he expect anyone to. He took the Logan Express toward Framingham. It all looked different from the ground. The Massachusetts Turnpike, a smooth ribbon of roadway, laid itself out submissively before the bus. He'd ridden this stretch countless times in his childhood, but now, after years in places where the roads were little more than rutted, hole-pocked paths—if there were roads at all—the Mass Pike seemed suspiciously unimpeded, as if it were a trap of some kind, leading him docilely toward his downfall.

As the bus sped forward, a strange feeling came over Sean, his heart rate increasing, his breathing oddly shallow. Had he picked up some sort of respiratory bug? The sound of his pulse throbbed in his ears as he gripped the battered straps of his backpack. He had to get off the bus. He had to run from this illness, and though he was sure he was sick, he also felt as if he could run faster than he ever had. He took a few deep breaths and closed his eyes to the Mass Pike racing by. Then it came to him. It wasn't a bug at all, though it was a rare condition, at least for him.

Anxiety.

Deirdre met him at the bus station in Framingham. She was waiting in the drop-off/pickup area, idling Aunt Vivvy's ancient but meticulously maintained Chevy Caprice Classic. He heaved his backpack into the back, got into the front seat, and took a deep breath, hoping the oxygenated blood would soothe his still-constricted veins.

Deirdre watched him for a moment, and then reached over to give him a brief hug. He responded a second late, as she was beginning to release him, making the gesture even more awkward than it normally would have been. *Six years*, he thought. *I barely know her anymore.*

"So, um . . ." She glanced around and spied his pack behind him. "That's all you've got?"

"Yeah, that's it."

"Looks like the one you had in high school."

"It is." He sucked in another oxygen load and glanced over at her as she backed out of the waiting area. Her pale skin was sprinkled with freckles—Irish fairy dust, their mother used to call it. And fanning out from the corner of her eye was a tiny thread of a line. Crow's-feet? How did his baby sister already have crow's-feet? But she was thirty-two now, he remembered. She'd only been twenty-six the last time he'd seen her, after their brother Hugh died.

"Who's at the house?" he asked.

"Viv's there. Who knows where Kevin is—probably in the woods somewhere. School's out next week, so there isn't much homework going on." She glanced at him, dropping her chin so her eyes peeked out over the tops of her sunglasses. *Drama*, he thought, *here it comes. . . .*

"And there's George." Her gaze returned to the road.

Would he take the bait? Hell, why not. "Who's George?"

"Oh, you'll see. Can't miss her," Deirdre said dryly. "Especially when she sniffs your crotch."

He smiled—he couldn't help it. Deirdre knew how to deliver a line.

"Good," he countered. "Haven't had a good crotch sniff in some time."

"She's thorough. You'll be set for years to come."

When they pulled into the driveway, he noticed the grass was long. And was that a dandelion? Was Viv laying off the chemicals? She usually spent the entire spring with a spray bottle of Roundup in hand, ready to spritz even the most delicate weed to kingdom come.

"What happened to Stevie?" he asked.

"She fired him. She said he was cutting it too long so he could come back more often."

"Stevie? The guy would've cut it with nose hair trimmers if she'd asked him."

"Yeah, I don't know. Kevin cuts it now, but he can't always get the mower started."

When they walked up the wide steps to the front porch, a loud bark startled Sean. Deirdre didn't flinch. "Shut your pie hole, you damn dog!" she yelled, turning the knob and shoving her shoulder against the door. The barking intensified. Deirdre heaved her shoulder against the door again and it popped open. The dog (if it could be called that—in the dim foyer, Sean could've sworn he was looking at a Shetland pony) stood on high alert, barking as if it were the last defense against masked intruders.

"Cripes, enough already!" Deirdre said, and the dog reduced its clamor to an annoyed growl. She turned to Sean. "Just stand there a minute till she decides if she's going to take a chunk out of you." The dog stalked forward and stretched its long black nose toward Sean's hand. Then the nose jammed between Sean's thighs so hard he yelped, swatting the dog away. The dog stepped back, apparently satisfied that Sean—or his crotch, at least—posed no immediate threat.

The swinging door from the kitchen let out its muted little screech, an *ee-EEE* sound that Sean would've recognized in any state of consciousness. It soon revealed Aunt Vivian, her wizened arm pressed against it as if she were pushing back the stone from a tomb. Once she'd gotten through, the dog lowered its tail and murmured a low whining plea for her attention.

"Shh, now," she told the dog, her hand running over its back as it slid up beside her. "Deirdre, did you forget to feed this poor creature?"

"Auntie Vivvy," she said, feigning patience. "Sean's home."

His aunt glanced over to him, and for a moment there was no look on her face at all, as if she were seeing a shrub or a bookshelf. Aunt Vivian wasn't given to grand gestures of warmth, even by an orphan's standards, but this seemed colder than usual. Then her eyes sharpened to reveal the relentless intelligence behind them. "Sean Patrick," she said. "Has war broken out here in Belham? Some horrific act of God, perhaps? I must have missed it on the news."

Sean smiled. "Thanks for sending the airfare, and your driver here to round me up."

Aunt Vivvy's gaze dropped to the worn backpack on the floor beside him. "Take that up to your room, please," she said. "And I'd like you to cut the grass. Kevin has yet to prevail over the mower this week."

The oak stairway rose to a landing halfway up the back wall of the house, then did a tidy about-face and continued in the opposite direction toward the front. At the top was an alcove with a cushioned window seat. A circular window looked out over the front yard; Sean remembered imagining that it was really a ship's hatch. On the ship was his father, giving orders, bravely securing lines in a storm, or keeping a lookout for pirates. Sean knew the kind of pirates his father spoke of didn't wear eye patches and striped shirts, but he'd often found it hard to adjust the picture in his mind. Once an imaginary pirate had a striped shirt, it was pretty hard to make him change his clothes.

To the right was Aunt Vivvy's room, and no one but her ever went in that direction. Sean hauled the backpack down the hallway to the left, back aching with the effort. The first bedroom was Deirdre's, the walls plastered with theater posters. Aunt Vivian had often chastised her about the wallboard being shot with thumbtack holes and said that "when the time came," Deirdre herself would be the one to spackle all those marks. Apparently, in the thirty-one years she'd inhabited the room, the time had yet to come.

At the end of the hallway was the room that Hugh and Sean had shared until Sean left for college. It had bunk beds, but these had been un-bunked and placed next to each other when Hugh brought his pregnant girlfriend home to live. Her strict Filipino Catholic parents had disowned her, but as Hugh mentioned to Sean in that offhand way he had, "It really isn't that big of a deal. They've been disowning her since she started smoking weed in the ninth grade. This just made it official."

On the right side of the hallway was his parents' room. It also had twin beds, because their mother couldn't always remember that the man who tried to climb into bed with her at night was actually her husband. "Lila," Sean could remember hearing his father plead when they lived in their old house, just the five of them. "It's me. *Jesussufferingchrist*, it's me!"

Now it appeared that Sean would occupy his parents' former quarters. There was clearly a boy living in his and Hugh's old room. Sean peeked in and saw the strewn clothes, the bed piled high with mismatched blankets, and the odd collection of items on the desk: an old cassette tape, a scratched compass, a short pair of scissors, and a blue plastic whistle.

Sean set his pack on the floor in his parents' room and lay back on one of the beds, but his body didn't seem to remember how to relax. What was he thinking, coming here? That static feeling he'd been having off and on for months came over him again. There was no guidance anymore, no reassurance that he was on the right path. In fact, he was pretty sure he was currently on no path at all. Maybe this had been the case all along.

He had the sensation of being observed, and for a moment it calmed him. This used to happen often—a feeling that there was a presence watching over him as he disinfected a wailing child's suppurating gash or held a baby while his mother's rape wounds were examined. *Yes*, this presence seemed to say, *this is where you should be, doing exactly what you are doing.*

That hadn't happened to him in over a year, though, and after a moment he realized it didn't feel as if he were being gazed upon lovingly. It felt like surveillance. He snapped his head up and looked around quickly. There in the doorway stood the dog, just staring at him.

CHAPTER 2

After twenty-four hours of travel, at least it felt good to lie flat. His back had been hurting for months, maybe longer, though he couldn't really be certain. His days at the small hospital near Bukavu, Democratic Republic of Congo, had been filled with patients whose bodies were so battered that paying attention to his own discomfort seemed absurdly weak. Most of them were victims of brutal tribal warfare, women and children who were relatively lucky enough to have made it to the hospital before their wounds prevented them from walking.

Sean's pain came and went. Sometimes he thought it was improving, and then a simple action—bending to lift an emaciated patient from her cot, perhaps—would bring it on with a vengeance. The sensation was like an unhitching of something that surely ought to have stayed connected, and then the compensatory clenching of the surrounding muscles to keep the unhitched pieces from separating altogether. He should have been able to evaluate exactly what was going wrong. But all he could do when it came over him was squeeze his eyes shut and mutter, *"Jesussufferingchrist,"* against clenched teeth.

It had gotten pretty bad toward the end of his time in Bukavu. It was a wonder he'd stayed so long. He supposed he'd been waiting for that time-to-move-on feeling that settled on him reliably every several years or so, but it never came.

Usually he would hear of something—military attacks on native Indians in Guatemala, for instance. He had gone there right out of nursing school and stayed for a few years, learning the dialect and suturing wounds, staying far enough away from the politics to be ignored.

And then he'd heard of a clinic in the Dominican Republic tending to the slaves of the sugar industry, with an infant mortality rate that rivaled that of the Dark Ages. From there he'd gone to Kenya. In 2001 there had been a devastating earthquake in India, and he had thought to go for a month or two and help out, but stayed for several years. Then the tsunami in the Indian Ocean hit, and there was such widespread need for medical care, it took him a few days to figure out which country to head for and which relief agency to offer himself to. He wrote Aunt Vivvy for travel funds to Sri Lanka. She never said no. She never said yes, either. She just wired the money without a word of interest in his plans or news from home.

Bukavu hadn't been his first stint in Africa. The first had been in a little clinic outside of Bomete, Kenya. He'd loved it there. The staff had been great—hardworking and friendly—almost like a family. It was fourteen years ago, now, but Sean could still see it clearly. Lying there in his long-gone father's bed, it was a relief to focus on the unambiguous past rather than on his throbbing back and undefined future. . . .

He'd only been in Kenya a month, so his Swahili was just slightly better than that of Dr. Yasmin Chaudhry, a newly arrived OB/GYN he was working with.

"She says she feels . . . full of air?" Sean struggled to translate.

"Does that mean she's breathing well, or having trouble?" asked Dr. Chaudhry.

"Imevimba," insisted the girl, and blew her cheeks up like small, coffee-colored balloons.

"Swollen!" said Sean.

"Bloody hell," muttered Dr. Chaudhry. "Of course, she's *swollen.* She looks about ten months pregnant."

Slowly, Sean reached out and took the girl's hand. In the six years since graduating from nursing school, he'd learned that no matter how good his intentions, a tall freckled white man was an oddity in developing countries, and sudden moves didn't do anything to instill trust. He gently pressed his forefinger onto the back of her hand, creating a depression that took several moments to disappear. It was a sign of preeclampsia, a potentially deadly pregnancy complication that could only be remedied by delivery of the baby.

Dr. Chaudhry met his gaze. "Ah," she said, nodding. "Check her blood pressure."

It wasn't only his patients Sean had to prove himself to. He stifled a smile, secretly enjoying the challenge of establishing credibility with a new medical team. It always made coming to a new place just that much more interesting.

The girl's name was Amali, and she was *kumi na sita*, which was either sixteen or seventeen—the two numbers sounded alike, and Sean couldn't remember which was which. It was enough to know she was quite young, though he'd treated pregnant twelve-year-olds in Guatemala and the Dominican Republic. This was Amali's third pregnancy. She and her husband had traveled more than forty miles to the hospital on foot—she wearing a pair of battered bedroom slippers, the soles all but worn through, and he with no shoes at all.

"Your children?" said Sean. *"Watoto?"*

She shook her head and looked away.

Stillborn, he guessed. Sean had delivered as many dead babies as live ones. Most women didn't come to a hospital unless something had gone terribly wrong, and by then it was often too late. Any small complication—even something as common as a breech birth—could trap the baby in the birth canal, causing death. Cervical necrosis could set in, sterilizing or even killing the bereaved mother. Sometimes Sean wondered which was worse. Children were often the only joy desperately poor women had—and the only thing they could offer a prospective husband, without which they lived in the double jeopardy of being female and having no protector.

Amali's preeclampsia was confirmed by high blood pressure and a dipstick urine test indicating an overabundance of protein. Dr. Chaudhry ordered an induction, instructing Sean to manually strip Amali's cervical membrane, and if that didn't kick-start labor, to break the amniotic sac. She hurried off to see another patient, whose terrified screams reverberated throughout the curtained labor and delivery area. Amali's eyes went wide with fear.

Oh, great, thought Sean. *And now a white guy's going to stick his hand in your vagina. Not quite the day you bargained for.*

In halting Swahili, liberally mixed with English and an entire ballet of interpretive gesturing, Sean explained the plan to Amali. Her expressive face changed with every new piece of successfully transmitted information. Skepticism, mild disgust, deep concern as her eyes flicked toward the direction of the ward door, beyond which her husband waited.

He doesn't have to know, Sean wanted to say. *He'll just be happy you're alive.*

Amali looked at him, her face pinched in anxiety. *You really have to do this?* she seemed to be saying with those enormous dark eyes. *Seriously?*

Sean took her hand and pressed his thumb into the bloated skin, showing her the dimple it made. *"Mbaya,"* he said. "Bad for you," pointing to her, "and for the baby," indicating her belly.

She gave the tiniest of nods, turned her head away, and parted her knees. Sean averted his own gaze to give the illusion of some small bit of privacy. As he slid gloved fingers toward her cervix he prayed silently, a habit he'd gotten into back in nursing school. For women he usually said a Hail Mary, but today he heard the Gloria in his head. *Glory to God in the highest, and peace to His people on earth*. He began the painful procedure of irritating her cervix into dilation. *Lord God, heavenly King, almighty God and Father, we worship You, we give You thanks, we praise You for Your glory. . . .* When he'd finished, he pulled the sheet back over her legs and left without a word, knowing eye contact would only compound her embarrassment.

He came back later to check on her and there were no contractions, so he talk-mimed the need to break the amniotic sac. This time he used what looked like his sister Deirdre's plastic crochet hook. During his brief visit home a month before, she'd been crocheting a

1960s-era vest as a costume. He slid the amnio hook into Amali's vagina. The image of Deirdre, whose main worry was whether she'd get the lead in her high school play, was weirdly incongruous as he broke the water of a girl of approximately the same age, who'd already buried two children. *Lord God, Lamb of God, You take away the sin of the world: have mercy on us. . . .*

The induction failed. Amali's contractions were weak, and the hospital carried no Pitocin to chemically force them. Dr. Chaudhry looked tired, and Sean felt himself in that crystallized state of sleep deprivation where objects take on an added glimmer when they move. As they began the Cesarean section, the doctor's face went into a fixed blank state, suggesting intense concentration . . . or that her mind had wandered far away from the understaffed, underequipped hospital on the outskirts of a small Kenyan town.

After anesthesia had been successfully applied, and just before the incision, Amali's blood pressure skyrocketed, and she began to hyperventilate.

"Hold her still," commanded Dr. Chaudhry.

Sean threw himself across the young girl's heaving body and the scalpel was applied. He waited for the duckling squawk of a newborn and felt his own pulse race, adrenaline rushing into all the cracks of his fear. Two young lives would be lost or saved in these moments. And though he knew the final outcome was in God's hands, he felt the rightness of his being there to help. In moments like these, Sean experienced a surge of gratitude for having been guided so clearly to his life's work. And despite everything, he felt immensely lucky.

A baby girl was soon released from the confines of her mother's body. After tending to the baby, Sean went out to tell the father, who had waited all night at the hospital door. The young man shook his hand vigorously and came in to see the baby while his wife was being stitched up in recovery. Slipping his newborn daughter into his shirt to keep her extra warm, he sang quietly to her. Sean had never seen an African father take such an active role in a baby's care. Generally this was considered the sole province of women. He felt an unexpected hopefulness for the future of a baby with such a devoted father, despite their profound poverty.

In the glory of God the Father, amen.

Sean soon learned that Dr. Yasmin Chaudhry wasn't as young as she looked. He was twenty-nine, and she had a solid decade on him. An Englishwoman of Pakistani descent, she was well trained and had a fortitude that Sean came to admire greatly as their friendship grew.

She was also quite clear about her lack of interest in any kind of romantic entanglement. She had a way of physically holding herself apart without seeming cold. Her eye contact was direct but not inviting. This was a relief to Sean, who was generally agreeable if one of the transient health care workers was interested in a casual interaction. He'd had a vasectomy years before and was careful about protection. But he tended to stay away from longer-term staff and older women— not because he wasn't attracted to them, but because they were more likely to hope for an actual relationship.

One evening Sean was walking down the deeply pocked road by the doctors' quarters—small cement bungalows clustered together near the hospital. Yasmin's tiny yard was overgrown with weeds and flowers. She worked too many hours, she said, to trim plants that would only grow back again. It was a warm night and she was sitting in her window and spotted him.

"Come in for a glass of something," she called to him. And he was happy to sit with his friend at the little table by the window and feel the breeze and smell the tangle of roses that sprawled against the house. They drank Rocamar red wine out of scratched glasses, conversation ambling through current patients, wish lists of supplies they would never see, and the various peculiarities and suspected motivations of their coworkers.

She questioned him in her guileless way about how he had come to Kenya, and he found himself talking about his mother's death from Huntington's, an incurable disease passed from generation to generation, characterized by mental and physical deterioration and early death. Symptoms often came on by the victim's early forties. His mother had died at thirty-five when he was fifteen, giving him a 50 percent chance of inheriting the disease himself.

"I've heard about that," Yasmin said. "Isn't there a test for it now?"

"Some people take it, some don't."

She studied him for a moment, her hand resting around her glass. "And you haven't."

He shrugged. "My brother and sister don't want to know, either."

"Why on earth wouldn't you want to know?"

Sean gazed out the window, the hum of insects seeming to grow louder in the silence. It was always so hard to explain it to people. "Put yourself in my shoes," he said. "If I were to tell you that I could say *for certain* when and how you'd die, and that you could linger for years, becoming an enormous burden to your family . . . would you still jump at the chance?"

Yasmin's night-black eyes went vague for a moment as she envisioned his dilemma. Her focus returned and she said, "There's just as good of a chance you'll find out you *don't* have it. You'd be free to marry and have a family. You obviously enjoy the company of women."

He raised his eyebrows at her.

"It's clear as crystal," she said flatly. "No one mistakes you for homosexual."

He laughed at her forthrightness. "Anyway . . ." he said. "For me the trade-off works. Not having to deal with definitive bad news is worth not settling down and working in some small-town American hospital, bandaging lacrosse lacerations. I'm happier than most people," he said, taking another sip of his Rocamar.

And he was.

CHAPTER 3

Twelve years later, Sean had returned to Africa, this time to Bukavu, Democratic Republic of Congo. It had been an entirely different story. The staff had worked just as hard—harder, maybe—but the civil war that raged around them caused a level senselessness to their patients' afflictions that was nearly impossible to bear. Of course, the whole planet throbbed with suffering, but it was hard to out-suffer the women and children who clustered around the hospital, malnourished and homeless, severed from their families and any place in their culture by the unspeakable indecency of their "war wounds."

By this time Sean was forty-one, and he'd been thinking of the DRC as his last stop. Part of him was glad that his final stint would be as hard as any he'd experienced. But things weren't working out as he'd bargained. No tremors in his limbs or saccadic eye movements, no memory loss—at least that he could tell. None of the Huntington's indicators. All he had was back pain.

"Let me help you," a nurse's assistant had offered quietly, when the pain had begun to show on his face more. It was humiliating. At night he'd prayed for relief, or at least for the strength to bear it without revealing himself.

But these days when he prayed, he heard no response. This was new. God had always been with him, he felt, guiding him, injecting him with the fortitude necessary to face such depths of human suffering and provide relief. But now that it was becoming clear that all he *personally* suffered was goddamned garden variety back pain, divinity had hit the high road.

And the pain of others . . . for the first time, it had really gotten to him. He'd be having his daily meal of sweet potato and *fufu*, a porridge made of manioc tubers, and an image would pop into his head. A boy with his arm hacked off at the shoulder. Or a gangrenous foot. His stomach would turn, and he'd give the rest of his *fufu* to whoever was near. There was always somebody willing to take the rest of your *fufu*.

But not eating, it had become a problem. He'd gotten too thin and was losing his musculature. He could tell by how difficult it had become to hold down the bigger patients when they were being treated. Also, the attention he'd always gotten from women seemed to be slowing these days. He was used to getting checked out by the temporary medical personnel who passed through, offering a couple of months of service before they decided to head back to the States and get normal jobs. He'd slept with them occasionally, grateful for his vasectomy.

But the frequency of longing looks and I'm-willing banter had dwindled. He told himself he didn't care, that wasn't what he was here for. But it was a temporary reprieve from the ugliness, and he had to admit he missed it.

"You're pale," one of the African doctors had said to him one day as they'd debrided a toddler's facial burn.

"Yeah," Sean had joked. "I'm not from around here."

The doctor had smiled, but added, "You're too pale even for a *muzungu*." A white guy.

Sean had given a no-big-deal shrug, but inside he'd bristled. *Pale?* he'd thought. *No freaking kidding, I'm pale. Up to my armpits in the blood of children all day, listening to one horror story after another. Can't eat, can't sleep, and my goddamned back is killing me. For the love of Christ, I'm supposed to be resting in peace by now, and all I've got is this shit!*

That's when he knew.

He'd seen it before—people who'd burned out but didn't leave, who brought everyone else down, too. And he couldn't move on to the next place like he always had in the past, because he'd only bring his bad attitude with him, as infectious as any disease.

He'd decided it was time to cash out for a while. Take a little break, get healthy. Maybe travel for pleasure for the first time in his life. He'd always had the idea that when the Huntington's symptoms came, he'd head to Tierra del Fuego and off himself there. It just seemed like a very cool place to see before you died. Now he could enjoy it without the distraction of impending suicide.

He'd considered making a withdrawal from the small trust fund his mother had left him, of which he'd only ever used the interest, to splurge on a trip. He didn't have to figure out where right away. And he'd conceded that he should make a quick appearance at home first, since, as Deirdre had pointed out, it had been a while. He'd written to Aunt Vivvy, who was still the sole trustee of his trust fund, and asked her to wire him the money for a plane ticket. As always, she'd consented without a word.

Resting had improved his back pain somewhat, but Sean's brain still buzzed around the problem of his next move, and he was unable to truly rest. He figured he might as well take care of the lawn—there was no sense getting on Aunt Vivvy's bad side this early in the visit. He went down to the shed and pulled out the rust-pitted mower.

Yanking the starter cord was excruciating, and after a couple of tries his back was in spasms again. He dropped to his knees in the luxuriously long grass and let himself topple over onto his side, easing down until the soft green blades swept against his face. The backyard was bordered by woods, so he had no worry of being spotted by a neighbor. The smell of dirt and growing things soothed him, and he closed his eyes and relaxed for a few minutes.

Apparently it was longer than that, because when he opened his eyes again, he felt something damp on his cheek and realized it was drool. A man was standing a few feet away, and for a second Sean thought it was Hugh. Then the man spoke, and his voice was wrong.

"Should I . . . uh . . . like, call 911 or something?" It was too high to be Hugh's. *Oh, and* . . . Sean's sleep-addled brain reminded him . . . *it couldn't be Hugh.*

"I'm okay," said Sean. "I just needed a quick lie-down." His voice felt sticky, as if he had recently eaten peanut butter.

"Oh," said the voice. "I could call a cab. I've done that before. I know the number."

He thinks I'm drunk, Sean realized and struggled to rise, clenching his molars to stifle a groan. "I live here," he said when he got to his knees. He shaded his eyes against the sun, trying to get a better look at his would-be rescuer. About five feet tall, he guessed.

"Here?" The voice was incredulous. "I don't think so. Auntie Vivvy wouldn't—"

Kevin. But he was huge! He'd been a little bear cub of a five-year-old the last time Sean had seen him. "I'm your uncle Sean," he said, and the boy's eyes went wide. "Didn't they tell you I was coming?"

"They don't tell me *any*thing," he muttered.

"Well," said Sean, rising slowly. "I'm him, and I'm here." He motioned to the mower. "I thought I'd give you a hand with the lawn, but I wrenched my back pulling the stupid cord."

"Shouldn't have bothered," Kevin grumbled, scratching a bug bite on his arm. "Even when it starts, it cuts out after a few minutes."

"Looks pretty old. I think maybe it's the one I used when I was your age."

"She won't buy a new one."

"Nah," said Sean. "She won't."

"Thanks, though," said Kevin.

They stood there, avoiding eye contact but trying to get a better look at each other just the same. Kevin had his mother's silky dark hair—Sean had met her once when Kevin was about two. His skin was a warm tan color with a faint dusting of his father's freckles along his arms and across the bridge of his nose. His eyes were exactly like Hugh's, round and heathery-green. Sean found this both comforting and disconcerting.

He told the boy, "Maybe it just needs a tune-up."

"Okay." Kevin nodded, but Hugh's eyes remained doubtful.

For the most part dinner was silent, interrupted by short bursts of comment from Deirdre. She had skipped rehearsal for Sean's first dinner home, but it wasn't so bad, she said, because it was the only one she'd missed, and some of the other secondary cast members had missed way more. "Mrs. Potiphar, the role I'm understudy for? She has bad allergies, and her eyes get so red she looks high or like she just had a crying fit. I keep hoping she gets a head cold." Deirdre never actually said it, but it was clear to Sean that Aunt Vivvy had made her stay for dinner. She looked like she was sitting in an ejector seat, ready to hit the release button at any moment.

Aunt Vivvy occasionally murmured to the dog sitting by her feet or mentioned some weather pattern and how it would affect her late-blooming lilacs. "A downpour will dislodge the petals before their time," she said, nodding to herself. Never prone to what she had often referred to as "an unfortunate state of verbosity," to Sean she seemed even less talkative than usual.

Kevin said nothing. Not one word. Sean asked him what grade he was in, and Deirdre answered for him. "He's in fifth. He has Mrs. Lindquist—remember her, Sean? She's still there, the old bat. Did you have her? Hugh and I both did. He used to say she sent him down to the principal's office once a week, just for good measure. Then when I was in her class, she told me, 'Miss *Doran*,'" Deirdre mimicked this as *Dooooran* in a throaty twang. "I am delighted to see you don't have your brother's disregard for *authooority*."

Kevin appeared not to notice. He ate the last bite of his mashed potatoes.

"So," said Sean, addressing him. "Middle school next year, huh?"

Kevin gave a resigned shrug and looked expectantly at Aunt Vivvy, who murmured, "You may be excused." The dog lifted its head, and Kevin gave it a wide berth as he carried his plate to the kitchen.

After dinner, Sean helped Deirdre clear the table. "So, what's with the dog?" he asked. "One of her friends get rid of it or something?"

"No," said Deirdre, piling so many dishes into her arms he was sure she would drop them. "She went to a shelter, for godsake. On *purpose*. She went in and chose that monster, and brought her home and named her George after some guy she knew a hundred years ago. The dog is *female*, Sean. You see what I'm talking about now? Viv's losing it."

Pet ownership was hardly "losing it," Sean thought, as he trailed after her with the rest of the platters and silverware. But he had to admit it was pretty strange behavior for Viv. Deirdre let her pile clatter into the sink. Sean had to raise his voice to ask, "What else are you seeing?"

"What *else*? This is completely not her, for godsake!"

"Look, if you really think there's some sort of dementia starting, there'd be other symptoms than suddenly deciding to get a dog. Does she forget things or get lost?"

"Jesus, I don't know. She hardly goes anywhere anymore because she says her joints hurt. And she's got me and Kevin to do all the chores." Deirdre stopped tossing dishes into the dishwasher and turned to look at Sean. "I've had enough. I've done it alone for six years now. Not like Hugh was much help, but at least he kept things interesting."

"You're planning to leave?"

"No, Sean. I'm not planning to leave. I'm *leaving*."

CHAPTER 4

Right, thought Sean. *Because you're such a pick-up-and-go kind of girl.*

Deirdre had lived in that house since she was a year old, except for a couple of months at Emerson College in Boston. She'd gotten into such nasty fights with her freshman roommate that she'd moved out. Emerson was an easy train ride from Belham, and living at home she didn't have to deal with annoying roommates. She did have to deal with Aunt Vivian, Hugh, his loopy girlfriend and baby son. If she hadn't left then, Sean figured, she wasn't going anywhere now.

"Hey," he said. "I'll finish up here if you want to go to the tail end of rehearsal."

Deirdre was wiping her hands on a dishtowel before the last word was out of his mouth. "That'd be *fantastic*." She started to leave, then turned back. "It's good to have you here. I mean, it's a little weird. You were gone so long, I didn't know what to expect. But it's kind of . . . nice."

"Yeah," said Sean. "For me, too. Weird but nice."

Her face brightened artificially. "Okay, well . . . Ciao!"

"Ciao to you, too." He smiled, thinking, *Half Irish, half English, and she's blowing me off in Italian.*

He should have been tired. His body clock was still synchronized with Bukavu, where it was currently about three in the morning. Plus he was worn out from traveling . . . and something else he couldn't quite put his finger on. Maybe Deirdre's jabbering about Viv and the dog, and grandstanding about leaving. She was a walking barrage of words, his sister.

Not like people were silent in the places he'd lived. In fact, they talked all the time, or screamed or cried. He'd often sat dressing the wounds of some young girl who'd been gang-raped by opposition forces, or a woman who'd been beaten to shreds by her husband, as they wailed out every soul-crushing detail of the assault. He'd gotten a reputation of sorts as someone they could talk to—in English, Spanish, or the Swahili dialect he'd picked up pretty quickly. Most of the hospital workers couldn't bear to hear these kinds of stories over and over.

But not Sean. He could listen. And as his patients added to the catalogue of the world's depravity, either with words or with vacant, dead-eyed silence, his mind would fill with prayers.

Lord have mercy, Christ have mercy, Lord have mercy. You wept for your dead friend, Lazarus. Weep now for this poor girl who would welcome death. Comfort her with your peace and nourish her with your love. Have mercy and make her whole.

Or sometimes, when he was rushing from one patient to another, a simple chant would ripple through his consciousness. *Have mercy, Lord . . . Have mercy, Lord. . . .*

But Deirdre's nattering really got under his skin. And praying didn't work—first, because he'd started questioning where exactly all those prayers were going. And second, because he didn't wish mercy or wholeness for Deirdre. He wished for her to shut the hell up.

Early the next morning an alarm went off somewhere in the house, and it woke Sean with the strange precision of its electronic beeping. A door opened and closed. Then he heard water running. The sound emphasized the pressure in his bladder and he got up. When he stepped into the hallway, Kevin emerged from the bathroom. For a moment he stared at Sean standing there in his boxers, then he blinked and slid past, his narrow shoulder skimming the wall.

At the other end of the hallway, George lay in front of Aunt Vivvy's bedroom door. Her head rose and she eyed Sean. She didn't growl, but her steady gaze warned, *Try me.*

Sean tried to go back to sleep, but found himself listening to Kevin's solitary movements: opening dresser drawers in his room, stepping lightly down the stairs, pushing on the squeaky kitchen door. He wasn't loud, but the absence of any other sounds made it easy to track him.

Deirdre was a late riser, and Sean knew she'd barely get up in time for her lunch shift at Carey's Diner. But where was Aunt Vivvy? When Sean was in school, she'd have a four-minute egg and two pieces of rye toast ready for him when he came down to the kitchen. He didn't particularly like slimy-soft eggs or rye bread, but that's what she made and that's what he ate. Was Kevin fending for himself down there?

Eventually the front door closed with a hushed *thunk* and the house went quiet. Cars hummed along a distant roadway. A woodpecker tapped at a tree in the woods behind the house.

What am I doing here? The phrase seemed to have taken up residence in Sean's brain where his prayers used to live. He got up, showered, tossed on some clothes, and exited the house, certain only of his need to leave. The air was warm and dewy, reminding him of Bukavu. But that was the only thing. The well-maintained houses with their freshly mulched flower beds and wicker porch furniture were nothing like any place he'd lived in the past twenty years.

His back ached and he tried to ignore it as he'd often been able to do in Bukavu. But without the activity of the hospital, it was harder to distract himself, and the pain remained in his consciousness like a clinging child he carried piggyback.

As he walked through the town of his adolescence, Sean's mind turned to Cormac McGrath, his best friend from high school. Over the years, Cormac had shown an uncanny knack for finding Sean no matter where he was, often sending goodies from his bakery. The stuff was usually crushed, moldy, or ransacked by the time it arrived, but wrecked or not, Cormac's packages always brought an unexpected reminder of the kindness in the world.

A couple of months ago he'd written to say that he'd gotten

married. It had surprised and, for a brief self-centered moment, depressed Sean. When they'd gotten together during Sean's infrequent visits home, Cormac had always seemed as happy in his bachelorhood as Sean was. Now it was one less thing they had in common.

Cormac had sent a wedding picture—him in a tux, his new wife in a poufy dress. She had blondish hair and lots of makeup that had smeared around her happy, teary face. Sean wasn't used to seeing women with so much paint, other than the occasional celebrity who'd visit the clinic or hospital as an "ambassador" or, as they invariably said, "to experience it for myself." With a photographer to capture it for the magazines and an iPhone so they could tweet about it.

Most of the women Sean knew and sometimes got together with were aid workers or volunteers. They didn't wear makeup, their hair was either very short or in a ponytail, and they were slightly unkempt like everyone else around them. That had become the norm for Sean.

Looking at the picture, he'd chuckled, wondering if Cormac's wife had consented to the wide distribution of this particular picture, with her face all smeary like that. Cormac, though—he looked like the day they'd beaten their tennis rival, Weston, after seventeen straight years of losses. Someone had taken a picture of Sean and Cormac that day, gripping the trophy in their sweaty hands. Cormac had had that very same look, like it just didn't get any better than this.

Sean had kept that picture in a box with a few other things from his childhood. Chrissy Stillman's pink angora glove, which she'd left in the bleachers when they happened to sit next to each other at a football game—she'd allowed him to put an arm around her because she was cold, and everyone thought he had scored. A really bad fishing lure Hugh had made him. A note from his mother. *Sean, I'm taking Deirdre for her one-year checkup. Auntie Vivvy is watching Hugh. Would you please mow the lawn? Love, M.* It was the last coherent thing she'd written him.

Sean had hidden all of this in a box in Aunt Vivvy's basement, behind the camping gear. Probably no one had gone camping since Hugh died. Sean wondered if Aunt Vivian had tossed it all out. She was like that. She hated clutter.

As he walked, Sean remembered that Cormac's letter had been filled with little updates: his irascible father was now working for him at the bakery, making a godawful mess of things and driving Cormac crazy. However, there had been a marked uptick in sales since his father's many, similarly irascible friends now considered the Confectionary their mother ship. His cousin Janie, whose husband had been killed in an accident the previous year, had found someone new, a guy they all liked. Cormac hoped she wouldn't screw it up.

Sean had had a secret crush on Janie when he was a junior, and she'd come to Belham High as a freshman with a newly grown set of boobs. Those boobs had caught him off guard—one minute she'd been flat as a manhole cover, the next she was all curvy and soft. She wasn't a knockout, like Chrissy Stillman. And she had a sharp tongue—he knew that if she'd seen him looking at her rack, she would've verbally sliced him down to a quivering mass of remorse.

Cormac had caught him checking her out once. "You know I'd have to kill you, right?" And that had been the end of the crush.

Sean hadn't laid eyes on Cormac in six years, and he wondered what his own life would have looked like if he had stayed in Belham, too, and maybe gotten a job at a local hospital. He could imagine himself going for beers at The Palace with Cormac after a tennis match or two on Saturday afternoons. But staying in Belham had never been a consideration. From the time he was fifteen Sean had known he would head out and do as much good as he could in the time that was left, while he waited for his mother's diagnosis to become his own.

Thinking about his old friend, Sean adjusted his course—which had been random and no course at all—toward Cormac's Confectionary. Soon he was in Belham Center passing shop windows, one displaying a dozen brightly colored handbags, another brimmed with paint cans, brushes, and rollers. He couldn't get used to how clean and smooth the sidewalks were. It felt as foreign to him as the places he'd lived were to Belham locals.

The Confectionary had a full glass front, ringed on the inside by a high counter. Customers sat on stools and gazed out across the town green, read the *Belham Town Crier*, or chatted amiably, like a silent movie behind the glass. Sean tugged on the heavy door and let himself in. The dry coolness of the air conditioning sent goose bumps up his freckled arms.

He spotted Cormac right away. At six foot five, with the shoulders of a gladiator and a mass of unruly hair, the guy was hard to miss. The overwhelming effect of Cormac's stature was muted, however, by the baker's apron hanging over a faded cranberry-colored T-shirt. CORMAC'S CONFECTIONARY was printed above a graphic of a muffin at the breast. Underneath it said, BELIEVE IN THE POWER OF BAKED GOODS.

Cormac was behind the long display case, attending to a customer. "I'm a big fan of the ginger mousse cake, myself," he was telling a woman in madras shorts and a pink polo shirt. "But it's a personal decision." He bit the inside of his cheek as he waited for the woman to choose, and Sean watched with amusement as Cormac's natural congeniality began to wane. His hand tapped the top of the glass, and he glanced at the other customers in line, as if to remind the woman that she was not the only person in a dire state of cakelessness.

His gaze passed over Sean without a hint of familiarity. It was a strange sensation, as if Sean were invisible, as if he could take a stack of twenties from the cash register without anyone having a clue. He had a momentary urge to say, "Hey, Cormac, it's me!" and an opposing urge to turn around and walk out. *What am I doing here?* That chant had murmured at the back of his mind since he'd landed at Logan a mere twenty-four hours ago. Had it only been that long?

He didn't wave and he didn't leave. He waited. It was a familiar activity—you waited for everything in developing countries, sometimes hours, sometimes months. It was the only thing that had felt normal to him since he'd arrived. Eventually it was his turn, and as Cormac was depositing the bills from the previous transaction into the register, Sean started in with, "Yeah, I need a cake, but I can't decide between the chocolate-glazed, the chocolate-filled, and the chocolate-infused. Can you give me a full description and your opinion of each?"

Cormac glanced up with a look of forced patience. "Well, let's see," he began. "Wait, we don't have . . ." He stared at Sean for a moment, then his face bloomed with recognition. "Spin!" he said, a nickname from their tennis team days. "When'd you sneak into town?" He came around the counter and shook Sean's hand, pulling him into a back-slapping hug.

"Yesterday," said Sean, relieved to be received with such warmth.

"How's reentry? Little weird? You been gone a long time."

"Yeah, pretty strange. My aunt got a dog."

"Get out," Cormac scoffed in disbelief. "Miss Vivian Preston hates animals."

"So I thought. But hey, you leave for six years, anything can happen. Even something as totally unlikely as Herman Munster here tying the square knot." Sean grinned. "Where is she? I'm dying to meet the poor thing."

Cormac laughed. "She mostly helps out on weekends. She goes to photography school during the week. But listen, what are you doing for dinner? We'd love to have you over."

"No plans whatsoever, that'd be great. Hey, where's your dad?"

Cormac went back around the display case and called, "Pop!" And then, "Let Helen finish, there's someone here to see you." And finally, "The mascarpone isn't going anywhere, Pop . . ." Cormac turned to Sean and muttered, "Current obsession: cannolis."

It wasn't hard to see how Cormac had come by his size. Charlie McGrath was a large man. But he'd trimmed down since Sean had seen him last, and his shoulders now stooped a bit.

"Hey, Mr. McGrath," said Sean.

The older man squinted at him as he took the proffered hand to shake.

"Pop, it's Sean," Cormac said quickly. "Sean Doran, my old friend from high school."

"From the tennis team?"

"Yeah, Pop. Sean. You remember."

"Of course, I remember," Mr. McGrath said irritably. "He just looks . . . older."

Cormac chuckled, but his discomfort showed. "Well, we're not eighteen anymore."

"No, you certainly aren't," Mr. McGrath shot back with a grin. "You're on the back nine now, pal-o-mine."

"Yeah, and you're up at the clubhouse, tossing back brewskies and cleaning your clubs."

Mr. McGrath gave Cormac a playful slap to the back of his head and turned to Sean. "How've you been, son? You eating well over in Sri Lanka?"

"Actually, it's been Africa for the past few years. How about you? I hear your new boss is a real slave driver."

They chuckled over this and traded pleasantries for a while. After a few minutes, Mr. McGrath started to worry about his cannoli filling getting dry, and another burst of customers lined up at the counter. Cormac confirmed their plans for dinner, and Sean went on his way.

As he walked back to Aunt Vivvy's, Sean considered the day ahead. *No plans whatsoever*, he'd told Cormac, and nothing could be truer. It was a stark contrast to the constant activity at the hospital, and weirdly disconcerting. But the reliable impatience he'd always felt to get to the next place, the next incubator of suffering, was gone. If anything, he just felt weary. Suddenly Tierra del Fuego seemed very far away. Maybe the thing to do would be to stay in Belham for a couple of weeks and recharge. Summer in New England was beautiful, he seemed to remember. He would read books, mow the lawn, take naps. It would improve his back pain, too—more than staying in run-down hostels and riding third-world public buses, at any rate.

It wasn't much of a plan, but it was something, which was better than the nothingness he'd been feeling for so many months. And it was an answer to that nagging question of what he was doing here. He was resting up for the next adventure.

CHAPTER 5

That evening, Sean drove Aunt Vivvy's Chevy Caprice to the address Cormac had written on a blank cake order form. It was not the same Caprice his friends had nicknamed Old Ironsides for its likeness in size and turning radius to the Revolutionary warship docked in Boston Harbor. That car had eventually been sent to its final resting place by Hugh, who had proven its destructibility with a series of newsworthy crashes.

Aunt Vivvy had gone right out and bought another Chevy Caprice. Around that time, Sean had made a brief stopover for Hugh's high school graduation. One night he'd accepted Hugh's invitation to get high behind the shed. It had been about the only way Sean could manage to get his party-boy brother to spend time with him, and they had gotten into a gasping fit of hilarity over Aunt Vivvy's buying another Caprice.

"I mean why does she have to have a *Caprice*, for chrissake?" Hugh had chortled between tokes as they sat facing the woods with their backs against the shed. "She's like the least *capricious* person on the planet."

"Maybe she's *secretly* capricious, and we just don't know it," Sean had giggled.

"Yeah, like she has this whole secret capricious life! Vivian Preston, woman of whimsy!" They had howled at the very thought.

"She could be a spy," said Sean, eyes watering with laughter. "But like a double agent because she's so freaking *capricious* she keeps switching sides!"

"No, wait!" Hugh could barely breathe he was laughing so hard. *"A stripper!"*

The comment made no sense, but the sheer absurdity of it made them fall into each other, pounding on each other's arms, convulsing with hilarity till their ribs ached.

Good times with Hugh.

Driving through the twilit town in this second Caprice, Sean felt his chest tighten. A little over a decade after the car's purchase, Hugh had died at the age of thirty-two. A bunch of his friends came to the funeral well on their way to the level of inebriation they felt was a fitting tribute to a man who'd shared their wildest, happiest times—at least from what they could remember. And there had been Aunt Vivian and Deirdre and five-year-old Kevin, pulling at the neck of his button-down shirt as he stared uncertainly at the casket. And Sean, who'd never returned after that. Until now.

Cormac and his new bride lived in possibly the smallest house in Belham. As Sean pulled into the driveway, he wondered if it might have started out as a small outbuilding to the much larger house next door. A stable maybe, or a small barn for housing chickens. Sean remembered Cormac's mention of it in a letter several years back, that it was perfect for a guy who lived by himself and spent all his waking hours at work.

It appeared to have been painted recently, the tan clapboards perfectly chipless and the confetti-pink color of the trim not yet faded to a more respectable muted rose. *Has to be the wife.* Sean chuckled to himself as he walked up the flagstones to the front step.

He had gone to the grocery store that afternoon to pick up a bottle of wine, but was quickly overwhelmed by all the choices. One was billed as "an ample yet balanced offering, rich with buttery, woody notes that cozy up just as nicely to mahi-mahi as to mixed grill." It tasted like buttered wood? He wondered if he'd be able to master American culture and dialect as readily as he'd picked up so many others across the globe. Then his back started to throb and he gave up, snatching a pineapple from the produce section as he walked gingerly to the checkout. He now held the pineapple crooked in his arm like a football.

Cormac opened the door grinning warmly and stood there for a second as if he didn't know what to say. Sean had the sense of fast-forwarding through time, from tennis team and high school graduation through occasional get-togethers over burgers and beers, to this moment now when Cormac's bachelorhood, like so many other things they'd had in common, had faded to memory. This was Cormac's new life, this pink-trimmed former chicken coop, and he seemed completely nonplussed as to how to explain it to his old friend.

"Pineapple?" said Sean, holding it out like an offering.

Cormac's smile was tinged with relief. "Love some," he said, and took it from Sean with one hand, ushering him in with the other.

The small front room had a woodstove—Sean assumed it was from before the wife had taken up residence—and a sofa and love seat with matching floral slipcovers—clearly from afterward. Cormac proceeded toward the back of the house, ducking his head under the low doorframe, and Sean followed. They came into a kitchen with painted cabinets and hammered wrought-iron pulls.

"Barb'll be down in a minute." Cormac reached into the fridge and presented two bottles of Schlitz beer.

"You're still drinking this swill?" said Sean.

"Course not—I went out and bought it in your honor!" Cormac popped the tops and handed one to Sean. They clinked them and took long gulps.

"Yeah, still pretty bad," said Sean.

"Nice how some things don't change."

They were starting to go through the names of their old friends—who'd moved away or married young or hit it big—when Barb came down. She was pretty, Sean thought. Tall and narrow, the kind of girl who was likely string-beany and overlooked in high school but had eventually softened and grown into herself by her thirties. She had long straight light-brown hair, nudged toward blondness by highlights, and a silver heart necklace and matching earrings studded with little pink gemstones. Watching them swing as she approached, Sean wondered how old she was. There was a sort of teenage quality about her.

"Hi there!" she chimed as she reached out to shake his hand. "Sean, I've heard so much about you!"

"Great to meet you, too," he said. "So, you're a photographer?"

She shook her head, and he had a moment of worry that he'd botched the one detail he could remember about her.

"Yes, you are," Cormac chided gently. "Stop telling people you're not."

"I take pictures," she corrected him. "When I'm done with school and I get my first paying customer, I'll call myself a photographer."

"Ah, then you're a picture taker," said Sean.

"Exactly!" She turned to Cormac. "See? He gets it."

Over dinner in the tiny kitchen, they caught up on each other's families. Cormac's mother was active with the Belham Garden Club and had risen to the rank of secretary. "She takes it very seriously," said Cormac. "Has an extra cup of tea before the meetings. You wouldn't want to mix up your pansies and petunias in front of the Garden Gestapo."

Sean laughed. "She must see my aunt quite a bit."

"Not very much anymore, since she stepped down. But Mom stops by with a copy of the minutes so Miss Preston can keep current." Cormac gave a wry smile. "Mom says she always reads them carefully and calls the next day with a suggestion or two for improvement."

Aunt Vivvy wasn't in the Garden Club anymore? She'd been president for as long as Sean could remember, and he'd always assumed she would die with a trowel in her hand. He sent up a little prayer for her, but it gave him no sense of having done something actually helpful; it felt like a bubble that popped and dissipated before rising into the sky.

Cormac asked, "Hey, how's your sister's play coming?"

"Good, I guess. She's an understudy, but I'm pretty sure she's planning to slip *E. coli* into the leading lady's smoothie before the first performance."

"Can't blame her—she'd make a killer Mrs. Potiphar."

How's he know about that? Sean gave his friend a questioning look.

"I had lunch at Carey's Diner last week," Cormac explained. "That girl's gonna make it big one of these days."

"That's the plan," said Sean, buttering a slice of sourdough.

"Oh, my gosh, yes!" said Barb. "We saw her in *Wicked*—she was Elphaba. Her voice is unbelievable. I took a picture when we went backstage to congratulate her." She hopped up from the table and left. A moment later she was back, handing Sean a photograph of Cormac grinning widely, his arm around the shoulder of a woman with green makeup and a black wig. The woman stared straight into the camera, her eyes practically boring a hole into the lens. Without her auburn hair and abundant freckles visible, Sean could barely identify her as his sister.

"She played a witch?"

"Ha!" said Barb in mock outrage. "She played *the* witch—the main character. She was onstage practically the whole time!"

Sean stared at the picture. "No wonder she's so pissed off at being in the chorus."

"Well, the Worcester Footlight," said Cormac. "That's like a farm team for Broadway. Competition's a heck of a lot tougher."

Sean took a bite of his bread while he considered this. His sister was more serious about her acting career than he'd thought. Until now he hadn't really believed she *had* a career.

"Hey," said Cormac, "guess who's living in Weston?" Sean hadn't a clue. He glanced again at the picture lying on the table beside his plate. "Come on," said Cormac. "I'll give you a hint." He waved a hand back over his shoulder as if he were flipping imaginary locks. "Oh, Sean," he trilled in falsetto. "I'm *sooooo* cold!"

Sean's gaze came up from the picture and leveled at Cormac. "No way."

"Way."

"Who?" said Barb. "Who is it?"

"Tell her, Sean."

Sean rolled his eyes. "You're really enjoying yourself, aren't you, Herman?"

"Herman?" said Barb, confused.

"Hell, yeah." Cormac grinned. "It's highly enjoyable."

"Jealous," sneered Sean.

"Me and every other guy in school. Except Ricky Cavicchio. He was enraged."

"And I got the scars to prove it!" Sean laughed and ran his finger across a small white line on his elbow.

"Who's Herman?"

Cormac put a hand on his wife's shoulder, his enormous thumb coming up to stroke her cheek. "I'm sorry to have to break it to you this way, honey, but you're married to him."

"Herman *Munster?*"

"Geez." Cormac's face fell in dismay. "Didn't take you long to make *that* leap."

"Man, it's too obvious!" Sean cackled.

Barb wrung her hands in a spot-on Mrs. Munster imitation and said, "Oh, Herman!" Both men nearly fell out of their chairs laughing.

After dinner they sat on the low couches eating ice cream out of porcelain bowls with *Crème glacée* in curvy cobalt script around the rims. So un-Cormac-like. Sean grinned—innocently he thought—but Cormac made sure to mention they were a wedding present.

When Sean rose to take his empty bowl to the kitchen, he miscalculated how much effort it would take to hoist himself out of the squishy cushions. His back clenched in response, and he found himself falling backward into the couch. He was thankful that he made no embarrassing grunt of pain, but his face must have shown it because Cormac said, "Hey, are you—?" and Barb said, "Oh, my gosh, Sean!"

He meant to say, "I'm fine," but what came out was *"Christ."*

Barb rushed to take the bowl out of his hand, which he held aloft to keep from spilling melted ice cream onto the slipcovers. "What's happening? Cormac, get him some water!"

Sean slid slowly down until he lay prone across the couch. "I'm all right," he insisted through clenched teeth. "Just a little back thing."

"Are you sure it isn't chest pain?" She slid a pillow under his head.

"It's better if I'm flat," he told her, tugging the pillow out. "Not chest pain."

"Can you breathe okay?"

"Yeah, it's just my lower back." It was the first time he'd ever mentioned it to anyone. He never imagined that when he finally did, it would be to a perky picture taker with pink heart earrings. Cormac came in with the water, and Sean told him, "She'd make a good triage nurse."

"She's obsessive about keeping her CPR up-to-date."

Barb gave Cormac an annoyed look. Sean patted her hand. "Good girl."

As he lay there waiting for the spasm to subside, Barb peppered him with suggestions about MRIs and osteopaths and physical therapy. Sean politely declined all the advice, but asked for some ibuprofen, which she hurried off to find.

"Spin," said Cormac quietly. "Is this . . . uh, is this related to . . ."

"No. Actually, I'm starting to think . . ." It felt weird to say it out loud. "I think I might have dodged the bullet."

"Wow," Cormac breathed. The two of them sat silently, contemplating the implications. Sean was glad Cormac didn't say something sappy like congratulations. Not having Huntington's would certainly be great news. But while it would solve one huge problem, cropping up in its place would be a whole lot of smaller ones, which generally fit under the heading of *What Now?*

Returning with the ibuprofen, Barb insisted again that he see someone about his back.

"I just need some rest," he told her, downing four tablets with the water.

"But you're in *pain*." She said this as if he needed reminding.

"Yeah. *Back* pain. I haven't had a limb hacked off with a rusty machete, Barb. I'll deal."

Barb flinched as if she'd been slapped.

"Hey." Cormac's face went dark with warning. "She's trying to help."

Oh, shit, thought Sean, as he looked at his only real friend in Belham. He'd come and gone from so many friendships over the years, mostly by virtue of geography, sometimes by waning interest. But with the end of his days now likely far in the future, he had a sudden revelation sitting there in the tiniest house in town: *You can't afford to screw this up.*

"I'm so sorry," he murmured penitently to Barb. "My social skills haven't caught up with my change of address."

She shook her head and flicked a hand toward Cormac as if to brush away his words. "Pain always makes me crabby," she said. "You should see me with cramps—I'm such a bear."

Sean glanced quickly at Cormac and caught the fleeting look of amused admiration.

"Thanks for understanding," he told her.

Suddenly she slapped her hands onto her thighs. "I know! A massage! That's what you need. And I have the perfect person—Missy over at Tree of Life Spa. She's a *miracle* worker."

Sean nodded, feigning enthusiasm. "That's a good idea," he said. "I'll definitely try that."

"Great! I knew we could figure something out. Let me just get the number." Barb bounded upstairs to get her address book.

Sean's gaze met Cormac's, and he imagined his friend thinking, *Nice save.*

"She's great, Herman."

Cormac's face softened, accepting the apology. "One in a million," he said.

CHAPTER 6

Over the next few days, Sean kept himself busy rereading his childhood copy of *The Magician's Nephew* from *The Chronicles of Narnia* and doing minor home maintenance projects. Some were handed down by Aunt Vivvy, and some he came across himself, surprised that no one had yet discovered them. The bathtub drain was slow, the water level reaching his ankles whenever he took even a brief shower. He tried plunging it, but the water still rose like the tide. Down in the boiler room, he found a plumbing snake and wound it into the drain. That seemed to do the trick.

"I snaked the tub, Auntie," he said as he washed his hands at the kitchen sink.

"Snake?" Her teacup clattered into its saucer, her eyes wide with anxiety.

"Not a real snake. I was just saying I cleared the tub drain." It took a moment before she relaxed. He sat down at the old oak table next to her. "How are you feeling?"

"Right as rain." Her standard response. She resumed sipping her tea.

"Deirdre says your joints are bothering you. Have you talked to Dr. Krantz about it?"

"Simon Krantz died two years ago. So no, I have not pestered him with my petty aches and pains."

He took a Fig Newton from the small china plate where she'd laid them out like fallen dominoes. "Who's your new doc?"

Another sip. "I am between health care providers at present."

"Well, let's get you hooked up with someone new and see if

there isn't something they can do for those joints. No need for you to stop doing the things you love if you can get on a good anti-inflammatory."

The teacup went down into its saucer with a clank. "What leads you to believe I've stopped participating in activities I enjoy?"

"Well," he stammered, thrown off by her testiness. "Cormac said you weren't doing the Garden Club anymore. . . ."

She turned to him, eyes narrowed. "The Garden Club has devolved into a flock of chattering flibbertigibbets who'd rather preen about their grandchildren and critique the executive committee than actually *plant* anything. It was no longer worthy of my time."

"But . . . what about all your friends?" Aunt Vivvy's laserlike glare had always had the effect of reducing his reasoning and communication skills to those of a five-year-old.

She glanced away, and Sean felt the relief as if someone had turned off a thousand-watt bulb. "Some have moved to warmer locales or to live closer to adult children." She took a sip of her tea. "And many have passed."

Lonely. He'd never thought of her as someone who needed much in the way of human interaction. She was a doer, not a talker. But even the most independent, unemotional people felt the loss of those they'd come to rely on, if only for their presence. Sean had seen it many times. An imperious, commanding village leader would crumble into incoherence when he learned his subordinates hadn't survived a natural disaster or tribal attack.

That's why she got the dog, he realized. She wasn't losing it. She just wanted company.

A few days later, Deirdre flopped down onto the couch next to Sean and put her sticky sneakers on the coffee table. She pulled a wad of bills out of her khakis and began counting.

"Do they still do the clapping thing at the end of fifth grade?" he asked, closing his book.

"Clapping thing?"

"Yeah, Kevin's last day is tomorrow, and it reminded me how all the families used to line up in the hallways and clap when we left on the last day of elementary school."

"I have no memory of that," she said dismissively.

"Dee, think," he said, a little annoyed that she was unwilling simply to confirm an inconsequential memory of his. "On your last day of fifth grade, your *last day* at Juniper Hill, didn't everyone come and clap for you?"

"And who's everyone, Sean? Dad was gone, Hugh was probably busy getting high and crashing the car, Viv didn't do school events . . . and where were you? Greenland or something? Who would've come?" She picked a flake of dried ketchup off her pant leg. "Assuming the stupid clapping thing even happened, which, as I *said*, I have no memory of." She swung her legs down and rose from the couch. "Besides, I'm pulling a double tomorrow, so unless they're clapping all the way to Carey's, I'm out."

His original question had been an idle one. And yet her evasiveness had somehow made him feel weirdly strident about it. If he were right about this vague memory of his elementary days, and if the tradition still held, shouldn't *somebody* go down to school and clap for Kevin?

Dinner that night was a box of linguine and a jar of marinara that Sean found in one of the cupboards. Deirdre had gone to rehearsal, and Aunt Vivian hadn't yet risen from a brief rest that had begun two hours before.

"Hey," he said, as he and Kevin sat at the kitchen table and ate pasta from cereal bowls. "When I was your age, they did this clapping thing—"

Kevin slurped a strand of linguine into his mouth. "Uh huh," he said. "The Clap Out."

"Okay!" Sean gave the table a triumphant little slap. "I'm not crazy!"

Kevin looked at him as if he most certainly were.

"No, see, I asked Deirdre and she said she didn't know what I was talking about."

Kevin shrugged as if to say, *Why would she?*

"Don't they send notices home about stuff like that?"

"They do it by e-mail."

Aunt Vivvy had a typewriter. Period. "Aunt Dee has a laptop, right?"

"Yeah, but she's not on the parent e-mail list."

"Why not?"

"Because she's not a parent." Kevin wiped his mouth with the back of his hand—the annoyance showed only in his eyes.

Sean nodded, chastened. They ate their last strands of linguine in silence.

As they cleared the table, Sean said, "So what if . . . I mean, would it be all right if I, like . . . came? And clapped?"

Kevin glanced over at him with a sort of bafflement.

"If you don't want me to, that's fine. No offense taken. And you wouldn't have to introduce me or anything. I could just clap and go. You know, like . . . like the Lone Ranger of clapping." He grinned. "Then I'd gallop off on my white horse. . . . Very inconspicuous, I promise."

Kevin rolled his eyes, but Sean could tell he was stifling a smile.

"Or I could take you with me," he offered. "A big white stallion is a pretty sweet ride—great way to impress the chicks."

"Gross!" said Kevin, a faint pink rising under his scattered freckles.

"Okay, no horse. Got it. How about if I just say a quick 'Hi-ho Silver' and trot away?"

"No!" said Kevin, giggling with embarrassment.

"Please?"

"No! You're crazy!"

"All right," said Sean with a dejected sigh. "I'll just stand in the back and I won't even clap very loudly. Come on, give your old uncle Sean something to do tomorrow."

Kevin shrugged, but he couldn't erase the grin from his face completely.

Juniper Hill School seemed to be just as he'd left it. Oh, there were a couple of additional classrooms tacked onto the back, and a fence across the sledding hill where he and his friends had often endangered the integrity of their spines by sliding down on lunch trays. But other than that, it was the same. Same smell of tempera paint as he walked past the art room; same bulletin boards covered with book reports, each stapled onto a different color of construction paper; same sound of children's voices growing shrill with impatience as they ticked down the last moments of the school day. And not just any school day—the *last* day. Summer beckoned from just beyond the heavy fire doors at the end of the hall.

Parents were arriving, claiming space along the hallway like fans lined up for hot concert tickets. Sean thought he had a good spot near the lost and found until the smell of mildewed fleece wafted by him. He maneuvered down toward a drinking fountain installed at the height of his thigh and found himself outside a classroom door with a sign that said MS. LINDQUIST, GRADE 5. Sean peeked through the narrow window in the door. There was Kevin sitting at his desk, eyes fixed on something across the room. The kids around him were poking each other or rifling through their desks. Sean shifted so he could see what Kevin was gazing at so intently.

There was a young woman with thin brown hair and glasses who appeared to be giving instructions of some kind. A student teacher, maybe? But shouldn't old Mrs. Lindquist be the one to give that tiresome end-of-the-year speech that no child on the face of the earth had ever listened to? Sean shifted his position so that he could scan the entire classroom, but there didn't appear to be any other adults in the room.

A bell rang, and like a flock of birds changing direction in unison, all the parents in the hallway seemed to bring out their cameras and video recorders at once. It hadn't crossed Sean's mind to bring a camera because he didn't own one. He didn't even have a cell phone. But he felt a sudden twinge of regret that he hadn't thought to ask Deirdre if she had a camera he could use. He looked around. The parents whose faces weren't covered by electronics all carried various expressions of intense anticipation. A few were teary. This was clearly a very big deal.

Sean wondered if his own parents had felt the same way—he remembered them both being there, his mother holding baby Deirdre, his father's hand tight around Hugh's, who was practically born ready to take off the second he saw an opening. Or maybe by then his mother's mind had already started to wander, so that she really wasn't taking in the weight of the occasion; possibly his father was too distracted by his wife's waning lucidity to care very much that his oldest would momentarily be marking a milestone.

The principal's voice came on over the PA system, straining to enunciate over the rising din in the hallway. He said what a wonderful year of learning it had been for their school community, requested that all parents check the lost and found, and said a few other things to which no one really listened. And then three of the classroom doors opened and a stream of children began to march down the hall. Sean was taller than most of the other adults, but he found himself straining to make sure that Kevin saw him. Suddenly that seemed important.

The line of children spilling from the classroom laughing and high-fiving people as they marched along came to an end, and Kevin still hadn't come out. Sean peered into the doorway and saw Kevin handing the young woman with the glasses a folded-up piece of paper. His face was so red Sean thought he might burst into flames. She smiled at him with great affection, said a few words, took a deep breath and said a few more. Her eyes welled, and she suddenly clutched him to her, pressing her cheek to the top of his head. Then she let him go. She laughed, said one or two more words. Kevin nodded sheepishly and turned toward the door. Sean popped back out of sight before Kevin could catch him.

When Kevin came out, Sean called his name and he looked up, startled, it seemed, to see his uncle there at school. Sean made a show of silent claps, then mimed galloping. Kevin rolled his eyes, embarrassed but laughing all the same. Sean felt an odd surge of happiness. "I'll meet you outside!" he called, as Kevin went to follow his classmates.

When Kevin was no longer visible beyond the sea of parents, Sean turned and found the young teacher looking at him.

"Are you . . . a relative?" she asked.

"Yeah, I'm his uncle."

She thought about this for a moment, pressing her glasses up a little farther on the bridge of her nose. "The one who lives in Africa?"

Sean nodded. "He told you about that?"

"He tells me a lot of things." Her smile had a strangely sad tinge to it. "Boy, I'm going to miss him." She looked down the hallway. "I better get out there. Nice to actually meet you." And she strode away.

Sean followed the crowd to the front of the school. When he spotted Kevin, he was listening patiently to a man with a brightly colored tie. The man patted Kevin's shoulder. From the look on Kevin's face, he wasn't nearly as happy to be talking to this guy as to his teacher.

"There you are," said Sean. "Ready to hit the high road?"

"Yeah!" Kevin's relief was palpable. The man seemed about to introduce himself, but Kevin grabbed Sean by the elbow and steered him toward the street. As soon as they'd put a safe distance between themselves and the school, Kevin's hand dropped back to his side.

"Who was that?" Sean asked.

"Guidance counselor." Kevin continued up the sidewalk and Sean went with him.

"He seemed to like you."

"That's his job."

Sean nodded. The kid had a point. "And who was that lady in your classroom?"

"My teacher." Said like it was ridiculously obvious.

"Deirdre said you had old Mrs. Lindquist."

"She retired a couple of years ago. That's her daughter."

"I guess Deirdre didn't realize a secret switch had been made," Sean joked.

"She doesn't pay that much attention."

True, thought Sean. "So what do you want to do now? Should we go get an ice cream or something to celebrate the end of your elementary career? We could go home and get Auntie Vivvy's car and hit Dairy Queen."

"Um . . ." Kevin squinted in indecision.

" 'Um' to *ice cream*? What kind of kid are you?" Sean teased.

"No, it's just . . . There'll be a lot of people there."

"The line'll be long," Sean conceded. "But we're not in a hurry, are we?"

"No . . . but it'll be really . . . *crowded*." He said it as if the word tasted bad.

Sean didn't know how to respond. How crowded could it be, and what did it matter anyway? "I see," he said, though he didn't. "Well, um. I'm open for suggestions."

"I was just gonna go home and have a Popsicle."

They walked in silence for another few moments. "Popsicles it is, then," said Sean.

As they made their way home, Sean was glad that he'd thought to go to the Clap Out. Even an uncle you hardly knew was better than no one showing up at all. Especially since Kevin didn't seem to have a friend whose parents had taken him under their wing, like Cormac's parents had done for Sean all those years ago. The McGraths had always included Sean, and had hooted and clapped the loudest for him at his high school graduation. Still, he remembered looking into the audience, hoping stupidly that his father might be there, though he hadn't laid eyes on the man for a good two years. He'd heard so many of his classmates complain about their parents' interference and had told himself that at least he could do as he liked. Aunt Vivvy had made sure he was properly clothed and adequately fed, but she didn't stick her nose into his business.

But graduation had obliterated the little fantasy he'd clung to that his father, a merchant mariner, was just on a long trip. He'd felt the truth of his father's abandonment like a gut punch as he took his diploma, shook the principal's hand, and gazed out into the sea of parenthood that didn't include his own. At least his mother had had a good excuse.

It had been hard enough for Sean at eighteen. How terribly lonely must Deirdre have felt at eleven when no one showed up to her Clap Out, not to mention every other parent-invited event? And how must it have sharpened those steely edges she seemed to have now?

"Hey," he said to Kevin as they rounded the corner toward the house. "You spend much time with Auntie Deirdre?"

"Sometimes," he said. "When she doesn't have a show."

"What kinds of things do you do?"

Kevin shrugged. "I don't know. Stuff."

"Like?"

"Well, sometimes she reads to me. She read me the whole Harry Potter series, and she did all the voices and everything."

Sean was happy to hear that Deirdre had shown some degree of normal involvement with the boy. "I'll bet she's good at that."

"Yeah, *really* good. When she did Voldemort it was so freaky I felt kinda sick."

CHAPTER 7

Deirdre was working double shifts at Carey's Diner quite a bit lately, after which she hurried off to play practice. Sean occasionally saw her late at night, physically limp with exhaustion, but her mind still buzzing from the intensity of rehearsal.

"How'd it go?" he asked her one night when they crossed paths in the kitchen.

"Super." She drew a kitchen chair over so she could reach deep into the top shelf of one of the cabinets. "The hack who landed Mrs. Potiphar? She *sucks.*" Her arm came out holding a bottle of Smirnoff Twist Green Apple Vodka. She hopped down off the chair, got herself a glass and filled it with ice. "And I'm watching the director? And he can totally see it. He's trying to hide the fact that he now realizes he made a mistake, but it's all over his face. It's *awesome.*" She poured the vodka, took a sip. "Oh," she said focusing on him briefly. "Want some?"

"No thanks." He got a beer from the fridge and joined her at the table. With Deirdre gone so much and Aunt Vivvy rarely leaving the house, he'd taken to doing the grocery shopping as well, and had picked up a six-pack of Sam Adams.

There was a strange clicking noise coming quickly down the stairs. It approached the kitchen door and then stopped. Sean looked at Deirdre, and she rolled her eyes. "Damn dog thinks she's the man of the house." There was a low growling noise, and Deirdre said, "It's just *us*, for chrissake! We *live* here." The growling stopped. The clicking of the dog's toenails receded slowly back up the stairs.

They sipped their drinks, the quiet disturbed only by the sound of night insects and the occasional rustle of dead leaves out in the woods. A light breeze puffed at the ruffled curtains.

"I went to that Clap Out the other day for Kevin," Sean mentioned.

"Yeah?" Deirdre said. "Wish he'd go to camp—he just wanders around in the woods."

"By the way, old Mrs. Lindquist retired. Kevin's teacher was her daughter."

Deirdre put her sock-clad feet up on the table and let her head rest on the back of the chair. "No wonder he never complained."

"He seemed to really like her."

"She left messages a couple of times. I think maybe Viv talked to her."

"What were the messages?"

"I don't know." She sipped her drink.

Sean put his beer down. "Did Viv say what she wanted?"

"Nope."

"Do you know for a fact that she returned the call?"

Deirdre gave him an irritated look. "What's your point?"

"My point is, the kid's teacher called several times, Dee. Did anyone bother to call back?"

"Well, that's Viv's job, isn't it? She's his legal guardian."

"And Viv's pushing eighty and won't leave the house. You're the one who said she's losing it. You couldn't have checked to see if she closed the loop?"

Deirdre took her feet off the table and leaned toward him. "You know what, Sean? You're right. I should have checked. I should have done that instead of all the time I spent with the kid because he has no friends. In *fact*, I should've quit my job and my acting career and *every other fucking thing I care about* and become this family's goddamned handmaid. But I didn't. And neither, by the way, did *you*. In fact, you've been all *about* you. You haven't given a shit about anyone else your whole life, Sean. So don't come after me for a few phone calls Viv may or may not have answered." She stood, put her glass on the counter, and left.

Sean sat there at the kitchen table, stunned. How could anyone think he'd been all about himself, least of all his sister? He'd spent his entire adult life tending to other people's gaping, gangrenous wounds. He'd had dysentery more times than he could remember and had never owned anything he couldn't carry in a backpack. People commented on his selflessness so often it had almost gotten boring.

He rose slowly, rattled by her attack. He dumped the rest of his beer in the sink and loaded her glass into the dishwasher. Then he went upstairs and got into bed. He tried to pray for her, which was what he always did—after praying for the attacked, he'd send up a prayer for their attackers to turn their hearts. But it didn't work. He couldn't quiet his indignation enough to open the window of prayer in his mind, couldn't make the connection, couldn't feel the sense of peace and oneness. All he could feel was the buzz of resentment in his head and the throbbing angry pain in his back.

A few days later, Cormac called to say Barb had a class on Tuesday nights—did Sean want to go to The Palace for dinner? Cormac already knew the answer. It was what they always did when Sean was in town—hit The Pal, ate greasy bar food, had a beer or two beyond their usual limit, laughed their heads off, got philosophical, laughed some more, then walked home.

The Palace had been built as a fishing lodge on the shore of Lake Pequot, slowly morphing into a bar sometime during Prohibition (because what better time to start serving alcohol?). Rustic and perennially damp, it still felt a little like a fishing hut to which beer taps and bar stools had been added on a whim. The kitchen came later and was of unknown vintage, but certainly not recent.

"What are you doing for money these days?" asked Cormac as he studied the stained and very brief menu.

"I still have that trust account Aunt Viv set up when my mom got sick. I just pull the interest off that. Don't worry, you don't have to foot the bill."

"Hey, I'm honored to buy brews for a guy who's done so much good in the world." And Cormac meant it, Sean knew. But Deirdre's accusation still rattled in the back of his mind, and the comment made him squirm.

"So, how's business?" he asked.

"Pretty damn good, actually," Cormac admitted. "You'd think strong coffee and fresh muffins were the only known antidote to some disease everybody has." He put the menu down. "Hey, um. If you ever wanted to pick up some extra cash while you're home, I could use the help. I mean, I don't know how long you're staying . . ."

"Yeah, I'm not really clear on that, either. I was hoping a little time off would clear up this back thing."

"Which you won't get looked at."

Sean shrugged.

"Okay, well, just to warn you? Barb got a massage yesterday, and she knows you haven't made an appointment. She'll definitely bug you about it the next time you come over." He said this unapologetically, as if his wife's pestering were something Sean would have to endure without Cormac's intercession or sympathy. It was a change for which Sean wasn't prepared: Cormac, a forty-something bachelor, suddenly committing himself so entirely to another person that he wouldn't intervene or even commiserate about her unwanted assistance. "Just go once," he said. "And if it doesn't work, you can tell her you tried."

They ordered a plate of nachos and some beers and chatted amiably about one thing and another. Cormac's cousin Janie was in minor freak-out mode because she was worried the guy she was with was about to propose.

"This is a problem?" Sean remembered Janie well. Her freak-outs were not pretty.

"Nah, the guy's perfect for her. But you know, she really loved her husband who died, and to her it feels like saying, 'I'm so over you, I'm marrying someone else.' That's what she says. But I also think it's a housing issue. She grew up in the house she and her kids live in, and Tug—that's the guy she's going to marry, or so help me I'll kill her—he's a contractor and she met him when he came to build a porch her husband commissioned before he died. So she's attached to it. And Tug lives in the house his grandfather built with his own hands right across the lake over there." Cormac flicked his thumb toward the window. "So *he's* attached to *that*."

Sean laughed. "See, I'm telling you—life is so much easier when you're attached to nothing!"

Cormac smiled and nodded absently. "I don't know . . ." He took a sip of his beer. "I have to admit, I'm getting pretty attached to being attached."

Sean's smile faded a little. But he clinked Cormac's beer bottle with his own and said, "Herman, you big sap."

Several beers later, the subject of Dougie Shaw came up.

"There is *nothing* you can say that'll make me believe Dougie Shaw should be allowed to carry a concealed weapon," said Sean, licking Buffalo-wing sauce off his fingers. "We're talking about a guy who loved whipping balloons full of ketchup at passing cars."

"He only did that twice, and nobody got hurt."

"You're defending him? The guy was insane. How about when he went to the homecoming game in his mother's wedding gown and asked Ricky Cavicchio to marry him at halftime?"

Cormac burst out laughing. "Jesus! Remember that? He looked pretty good in that dress, too—fit him perfectly!"

"Mrs. Shaw was no ballerina, if I recall. And Cavicchio went so mental it took the whole offensive line to keep him from beating the crap out of Dougie right there on the field. What was the point of that, anyway?"

"Come on, you remember," said Cormac. "Cavicchio had been calling him a faggot and slamming him into lockers since junior high. It was the perfect revenge—the guy was so rattled afterward he threw a bunch of interceptions and lost the game."

Sean laughed. "Okay, so Dougie deserves a medal—not a police cruiser."

The subject of unusual childhood behavior eventually turned to Kevin. "I'm a little worried about him," said Sean. "He doesn't seem to have any friends. And he's so quiet. You can barely get the kid to talk under klieg lights."

"He used to come into the Confectionary every once in a while with your aunt," Cormac said, dipping the last celery stick in blue cheese sauce. "But I haven't seen either of them in a while. Bring him around sometime. Get him a piece of pie."

"Pie," Sean smirked. "That's your solution to everything."

"Solved every problem *I* ever had. Hunger, employment . . ." He raised his eyebrows. "Female companionship."

"Pie slut."

"Fruit, sugar, and a nice flaky crust." Cormac raised his beer. "Makes the world a sweeter place, my friend."

CHAPTER 8

Sean drove to Tree of Life Spa, irritable as an overtired child. He didn't believe a massage would help his back, and he certainly didn't want to spend the money. Eighty bucks for the privilege of having his ravaged musculature pummeled and poked? Why would anyone agree to that?

Independence Day, that was why.

Cormac's Confectionary was the one store in Belham Center that would be open. And as fire trucks and antique cars, uniformed Boy and Girl Scouts, and various clowns and elected officials marched by, parade goers would be thronging to the shop for sustenance. It was only two days away, and Cormac was having a heck of a time rounding up the necessary quorum of employees. Even his father had said, "I'll help if I have to, but I'd sure rather sit my ass in a lounge chair and watch from the sidewalk like I've done every year for the past half-century."

In desperation Cormac had called Sean, and what could Sean say? I'm busy? He wasn't. In fact he was bored. He'd been home for more than two weeks now and, other than the odd home maintenance job, trip to the grocery store, or pass over the carpets with the vacuum, he really had nothing going on. He'd logged some hours on Deirdre's laptop researching travel to Tierra del Fuego and, when that failed to inspire him, other distant locales. Nothing grabbed him.

And while slinging scones and smoothies to the tune of off-key marching band music didn't really light his fire, either, he was willing to give Cormac a hand. He was actually a little relieved to have something to do.

Cormac was unnecessarily grateful. "All the pie you can eat! And bring Kevin!"

The downside occurred to Sean as he hung up the phone. Barb. The massage. Jesus, how had he gotten himself boxed into that one? For a guy who'd spent the better part of his life honing a George Clooney–like ability to avoid interpersonal obligations, he'd really blown it.

So here he was, with his seldom-used credit card in his back pocket, driving to a *spa*, of all places. Aunt Vivian had given him the card shortly before his first overseas trip. "What's this for?" he'd asked naïvely.

"Emergencies."

"What kind of emergencies?"

"I have no idea," she'd replied, paging through *The Avant Gardener.* "Whatever you deem emergent."

The credit limit was purposely kept very low in case it was stolen. The statements went to her, and she paid off the balance from his trust fund. Occasionally his meager earnings outpaced his living expenses, and he sent her the excess, which she posted to the fund. She wired him money for big-ticket items like plane fare and reimbursed herself.

Can't wait to see the look on her face when this *bill comes in,* Sean thought.

Tree of Life was located in a strip mall on Route 9, and was distinctly unleafy. Sean slid the Caprice into a parking spot in front of the sooty pink stucco façade and walked in.

"Hi," he said to the receptionist with the Cleopatra eyeliner and burgundy-red hair. "I've got an appointment with Missy at eleven?"

She gave him a look that said, *Maybe you do and maybe you don't,* and gazed apathetically at the appointment book. Then she got up and went down the hallway without a word. He heard voices, then a strange gush of noise, like someone venting a brief wail of exhaustion or despair. Cleopatra slunk back down the hall toward him, lifted a finger as if it were too much of an effort to point in any specific direction, and said, "Room three." Sean took that as permission to search somewhere behind her for it, should it actually exist.

There were four doors: rooms one, two, and three, and one with a sign that said, MASSAGE THERAPISTS ONLY. PLEASE RETURN TO YOUR ROOM. He entered room three, which was taken up almost entirely by a sheet-shrouded massage table. The lights were dim, and it took him a moment to locate the source of what sounded like a running toilet—a miniature fountain with water cascading over a small pile of smooth black rocks that sat on a table in the corner. The sound made him feel as if he hadn't fully emptied his bladder the last time he'd hit the men's room.

The door opened and in walked a woman with wiry blond hair and pajama-like clothing. Her eyes seemed red. "Hi, I'm Missy?" she said. "I'll be applying a deep-muscle massage?" She instructed Sean to disrobe—he could leave his underwear on if he preferred, it didn't matter one bit to her. Then he should lie facedown under the sheet and rest his forehead on the doughnut shaped cushion at one end. She pressed two fingers between her eyes and abruptly walked out. When the door closed, he heard the weird gushing wail again.

Christ, he thought, *what the hell am I doing here?*

He was tempted to leave. But what if this Missy told Barb he'd walked out on her? Barb would not be happy. So Cormac would not be happy. And Sean calculated it was worth just about eighty bucks and an hour of torture not to piss off his closest friend. *But that's it,* he told himself. He wasn't coming back to this loony bin ever again. He stripped and lay down.

Several minutes later, the door opened and closed with a hushed click. With his face resting in the doughnut hole, he couldn't see anything except the industrial-grade carpet, but he could hear Missy's even breaths, and he thought she seemed calmer. Her hand rested briefly on the back of his head, and he could feel her lean away for a moment. The running toilet sound stopped, there was a click, and soft acoustic guitar music filled the room.

Her hands slid gently up and down his back, lightly skimming his skin, and he felt his brittle nerve endings melt just a little under her touch.

"Okay," she said, her voice round and melodious. "Missy's having a little bit of a hard day, so I'm going to do your massage. I'm Rebecca. I'm sorry—I know you requested her."

"It's fine. I don't really know her," he said. "Everything okay?"

"Yeah." He thought he could hear a little sliver of a smile in her voice. "Everything's fine." Her fingers started to press harder, exploring the terrain of his back. "How's this feel?"

"Uh, honestly? It hurts like hell."

"No kidding—your muscles are like cement. I'll go easy, but I do want you to walk out of here with some relief." As she began to press harder, the pain increased, but it was a shifting pain, not the impenetrable anvil type that he generally carried around all day. "Tell me if I overdo it, okay?" she said.

"Don't worry about that. It hurts all the time anyway."

"How'd it get like this, if you don't mind my asking?"

"I'm a nurse," he said.

"On your feet all day, lifting patients, the stress of people's lives in your hands . . ."

"Exactly."

"Are you wearing good supportive shoes?"

"No."

"Why not?"

"Ow! That's a little sore there."

"And why should I be gentle with a person in your line of work who doesn't take care of his one and only body by wearing good shoes?" She said this in a teasing way, but he knew she was also making a point.

So he told her about Africa, and how his coworkers often had only sandals or battered sneakers. He would never have shamed them by sporting high-end shoes, not for all the knots in his entire body. She began to work on his arms, finding pockets of soreness around his elbows and wrists and even in the palms of his hands that he didn't realize he had. She asked about the work he did, and he found himself telling her about the less gruesome cases, careful to gauge how squeamish she might be. She let out little sighs of sadness, an occasional, "Oh, that's *awful*," but he never heard her reach the point of distress.

"And what sustains you?" she asked as she kneaded the backs of his thighs and calves.

"Sustains me?"

"Yeah, you know, what fills your tank so you can keep going?"

The long answer, which involved genetics, terminal illness, his belief in being chosen by God for the task, and the assumption that he'd be dead by now . . . it was a little heavy to get into with someone he'd just met—and hadn't even seen. But she seemed interested and intelligent, and to have magical powers over his pain, so he didn't want to blow it off, either.

"It used to be faith," he said. "But I have to admit, at the moment I'm pretty burned out."

"So you came back to the States to recharge."

"That was the plan."

"It's not working?"

"Not really. At least not yet. Feels more like a holding pen than a jumping-off spot."

She didn't say anything for a moment, just kept working a line of soreness along his inner calf, pressing at it, coaxing it to dissipate.

"That must sound pretty self-centered," he said.

"No," she said quietly. "I was just thinking . . . the only difference between the two is—and I'm referring more to myself at the moment, so please don't be offended—"

"No, of course not."

"The only difference between a holding pen and a jumping-off spot . . . it's you, and whether you decide to jump."

Sean was just starting to roll this around in his mind when Rebecca's thumbs burrowed into the arch of his left foot, and he let out a screech that he couldn't believe came from his own mouth.

"Wow, sorry," she said. "That's a hot spot."

"Holy *shit*," he squeaked, trying to control his volume.

Her hands lightly stroked the bottoms of his feet. "Try to relax," she said, "and I'll be more careful."

"What *was* that?"

"That was your foot, and it's really unhappy, and I'm guessing the other one feels the same." She wrapped her hands around his left foot again and started to squeeze in little pulses. "Okay, we're going to stop talking now and take nice deep even breaths, and I'm going to make your feet happier. So just let your mind roam around off its leash for a while."

Rebecca inhaled and slowly let it out. Sean did the same. Gradually she increased her pressure, working at his heel, then his toes. When he flinched, she backed off, but never completely. It still hurt a lot, but an image began to grow in his mind of the pain in his feet, and how she wasn't really getting rid of it so much as molding it like clay, putting it back into its proper shape. And that seemed about right to him—that while his pain couldn't be completely eradicated, it could be made to behave. This thought was somehow comforting, and he found himself slipping off into a gauzy doze, remaining so even when she told him to turn onto his back. She held the sheet in place as he rolled over underneath it, and he realized it was the best he'd felt in months. Possibly years.

She came around behind his head and began to work at his shoulders and neck again. Suddenly she stopped, and he heard a little inhalation of breath. He wanted to open his eyes and see if everything was all right, but in his state of relaxation, his reflexes were slow. She began to knead his shoulders again, and the impulse to open his eyes passed, as he floated back down into the satiny swirl of semiconsciousness.

He couldn't say how much longer the rest of the massage took. He felt her fingers on his scalp, and across his forehead and around his cheekbones, and the next thing he knew she was massaging around an ankle. At the end she rested her hands lightly in several spots on his chest and stomach, as if her palms were stethoscopes listening to the internal flow of his body. They wavered over him, smoothing the air from his head to his toes and back up again.

"You can get up when you're ready," she whispered. When he opened his eyes she was gone.

Slowly he rose and got dressed. He walked out to the reception area feeling a little like when he used to get high with Hugh, only smoother and less giggly. Like when he used to pray and it worked. He smiled beneficently at Cleopatra as she took his credit card. "Would you mind adding a twenty-dollar tip on there?"

She raised her eyebrows and included the tip.

He looked back down the hallway, hoping Rebecca would appear. He wanted to see her, this phenom who'd molded his aches back into manageable chunks. But no one came.

CHAPTER 9

"You've purchased new footwear, I see," said Aunt Vivvy, lifting a forkful of peas to her mouth.

Kevin leaned off his chair to look but popped up again when a growl came from under the table.

"George," chided Aunt Viv, and the dog quieted.

"Yeah, my back's been hurting, so I went to this specialty store over in the mall. They recommended these."

"Your old ones were all worn down on the bottom," said Kevin. Aunt Vivvy raised her eyebrows. "Well, they *were*," he said.

"How nice to have you join the conversation," she replied.

Kevin kept his eyes on Sean. "You could hike in those."

"I probably could. Not much mountain climbing around here though."

"Jansen Hill," said Kevin. "You can get to it through the woods out back."

"Maybe you'll take me sometime. Hey, how about after the parade tomorrow?"

Kevin shrugged and stuffed a hunk of buttered bread in his mouth.

Later, after the dishes had been done and Aunt Vivian and George had retired to her room, Sean found Kevin watching television in the den off the living room. On screen, a man was walking across sand dunes and apparently talking to himself. His accent was Australian.

"What's this?"

"Man vs. Wild." Kevin's voice was low and reverent. "It's this guy,

Bear Grylls. He gets himself lost in jungles and deserts and stuff on purpose. Then he has to find his way out."

Sean watched as the man talked about the critical importance of keeping hydrated.

"But he's not alone, right?" said Sean. "He's got a film crew."

Kevin frowned. "How else could we see it?"

"True. So, any chance you want to come with me to the parade tomorrow? I have to help out my friend Cormac, the guy who owns the bakery."

"Not really," said Kevin, gazing intently at the small screen. The man had taken off his T-shirt and appeared to be peeing on it, the camera discreetly aimed above his waist.

"You should come. It'll be fun."

"Parades are boring."

"Maybe you could work with me in the bakery."

At that moment, Bear Grylls raised the wet T-shirt over his face and squeezed the liquid—his own urine—into his mouth. Kevin and Sean let out simultaneous groans of disgust.

To their relief, a commercial came on. "Seriously, you should come," Sean said. "Cormac says we can have all the pie we want."

Kevin looked skeptical. "What would I have to do?"

"Just hang with me and help out. Tell you what, I'll even slip you a twenty. Cormac's insisting on paying me, so you can be my subcontractor."

Kevin thought about this for a minute, eyes blinking pensively. "Okay. But if I don't like it, I can leave and you don't have to pay me."

"Deal."

They walked over to the Confectionary the next morning, Kevin recounting the many instances of Bear Grylls eating disgusting things like a fat squirming rhino beetle larva the size of a gummy worm.

"I brought reinforcements," said Sean when Cormac let them in.

"Excellent! Welcome aboard, Kevin my man." Cormac held his

hand out, and Kevin hesitated, then gave it a perfunctory little slap. He stepped back to Sean's side and surreptitiously scanned the bakery. "Smells good," he murmured.

"Hope so," said Cormac. "Otherwise I'm in the wrong line of work."

He showed Sean how to run the register, the shorthand for writing customers' orders on coffee cups, where to find pastry bags and extra napkins. He addressed all of this to Kevin, too. "Because you know your uncle's going to forget something, and you'll have to be his backup hard drive." Kevin glanced up at Sean, a tiny smile lighting his features.

Cormac assigned Kevin the job of retrieving pastries from the big glass display case and putting them in the to-go bags for Sean. "Throw on a pair of these, okay?" said Cormac, handing them both stretchy vinyl food service gloves. He turned to get the coffee started.

Kevin held them between thumb and forefinger. "I don't like these," he whispered.

"What's wrong with them?" Sean donned the tight-fitting gloves, snapping them around his wrists.

"They feel weird."

"They're not that bad. You get used to them."

Kevin pressed his lips together. "I don't want to."

Sean stared at him for a moment. "Kevin, can you just try? Because I think it's a rule."

The boy slid his fingers halfway into one of the gloves, then quickly pulled it off again. "I can't do it." Sean tried to hide his annoyance, but the kid hadn't made much of an effort.

Cormac glanced over. "Not a fan, huh?" he said. "Okay, I have this other kind—they're plastic and kind of loose, so you're going to have to keep tugging at them to stay on." He opened a cabinet and took out another box. Kevin made a face when he put them on, but he didn't complain.

Customers were waiting outside, and Cormac went to open the

door, calling "Happy Fourth of July! Check out the red, white, and blue cupcakes—specially priced to honor our forefathers."

"And mothers," said a voice. "John Adams was just a short guy in a bad wig without Abigail."

"Too right, chickie," said Cormac.

Though he hadn't seen her in many years, Sean immediately recognized Cormac's cousin Janie. She held a little girl on her hip and headed toward the counter. Behind her was a man with thinning auburn hair holding a boy's hand. Cormac shook the guy's hand and said to the little boy, "Hey, where's my hug!" He leaped up and Cormac caught him for a quick squeeze.

When they approached, Sean waited to see if Janie would notice him. Her light blue eyes went wide for a second, and she said, "Spinster! No way!" She came around the end of the counter and hugged him. "Ow!" said the little girl. "You *cwushing* me!"

Janie introduced her daughter, Carly, and her five-year-old, Dylan. "Almost six," insisted Dylan. "Like five and four quarters."

Sean laughed, and Janie said, "We'll work on that one." Then she laid a hand on the arm of the man and said, "This is Tug Malinowski." There was a hint of awkwardness that Sean recognized, having known her in the gawky inelegance of her teenage years. He supposed she hadn't quite figured out what term to use when she introduced the new love of her life. But then she slid her hand into Tug's, and almost imperceptibly both of their faces went a shade happier.

Sean had witnessed this often enough, the way even the mildest physical contact could change a person's visual. A patient would be failing, but then someone close to her would arrive, and her color would immediately improve, her vitals reflecting the uptick. He could almost see Tug's red blood cell count increasing. It seemed to have the same effect on Janie as well.

Sean reached out to shake Tug's available hand. "I've heard good things."

Tug seemed pleased by this, his glance shifting briefly to Cormac. "Likewise," he said.

Dylan pulled him over to peruse the cupcakes. Barb came through the door, and Carly wiggled out of her mother's arms and ran over. Momentarily alone, Sean and Janie took the chance to catch up. After a few minutes he said, "I was really sorry to hear about your husband, Janie."

"Thanks." She nodded. "He was a good guy. You would've liked him."

It caught at him for a moment, the look on her face. Smart-alecky Janie Dwyer with a permanent whisper of pain behind her eyes. "How're you holding up?" he asked gently.

"Better," she said. He suspected it was the way he felt about losing his mother at such a young age and, not long after, his father. You could never really be fine about it, but you could slowly, haltingly learn to feel better than you did when it was freshly excruciating.

Customers started arriving, and Sean had to return to cash register duty. Janie and Tug took the kids to set up chairs along the parade route, Janie calling, "Catch up with you later, Spinster!" over her shoulder.

"Spinster?" said Kevin, when there was a break between customers. "What's that?"

Sean chuckled. "Well, it's kind of a nickname. Cormac used to call me Spin because we were on the tennis team together and I guess I had a pretty good topspin. And then Janie started calling me Spinster as a joke, because it's a word for an old woman who never got married."

"Good one," Kevin nodded, grinning slyly.

"Thanks a lot!" Sean laughed. It struck him how Kevin's round, green eyes could be so Hugh-like when the boy was joyful.

The Confectionary got very busy just before the parade started. Everyone wanted to make sure they were fully stocked with caffeine, carbohydrates, and fruity drinks before settling into their beach chairs along the route. Barb manned the cappuccino machine, and

Cormac handled the big orders while Sean and Kevin served customers. Once the parade was streaming by, however, traffic into the shop dwindled. Kevin wandered over to sit on one of the high stools by the front window to watch the cavalcade of performance groups and unusual vehicles.

"Hey," said Sean, wiping coffee puddles off the counter. "You said parades are boring."

"They're okay."

"You can go outside and watch if you want. Just keep an eye out, in case more customers show up."

"I can see from here."

"Seriously, it's fine. Go on out."

"I like it *here*."

Sean looked up. Kevin's mouth was set, as if he were ready for a fight. "Hey, it doesn't matter to me," said Sean. "I was just thinking you could hear better out there."

Kevin grumbled to himself, and Sean decided to ignore it.

Cormac and Barb emerged from the storage room. Her pink lipstick looked weirdly smudgy, and a sprig of his hair stuck out at an odd angle from his head. *Oh, my God . . . they were making out,* Sean realized. *Sucking face in the back room like a couple of teenagers!*

"So, um," said Barb, tightening her ponytail. "How's your back?"

Sean busied himself with refilling the napkin dispenser to hide his knowing smile. "Pretty good actually. I went for that massage—thanks to you," he emphasized this point. "And I definitely feel better."

"That's fantastic!" Barb clapped her hands together. "Isn't Missy a dream?"

"Oh, uh . . . Missy was having a little trouble of some kind. A woman named Rebecca took over. She was great."

Barb was skeptical that any massage therapist could be better than Missy. Sean finally succeeded in convincing her that, although he'd suffered the misfortune of being massaged by someone else, Rebecca had kept him from feeling completely deprived. "She had this way of . . . well, it hurt, but it was like a useful kind of pain, so I didn't mind it. Also, her voice was very relaxing. Like we'd be talking about something serious, but . . . I don't know. It all seemed good."

Cormac hung an arm over Barb's shoulder and grinned. "Well, fly me to the moon, Spin."

Sean felt his face go warm. "Ah, shut your pie hole."

After the parade there was another rush of customers, but by noon the doors were locked and the four of them were cleaning out the coffee urns and putting things away.

"Kevin," said Cormac. "Come on over to the display case and pick your favorite."

Kevin's face lit up with shy excitement as he went to claim his prize. Cormac put a hand on his shoulder, and Sean saw Kevin sidestep away. He chose a piece of blueberry pie.

"You probably want the smaller slice," said Cormac. "I don't want to burden you with that big slab." Kevin held his breath for a moment. He glanced up at Cormac. "I'm just kidding!" Cormac assured him. "After all your hard work, you can have the whole pie if you want."

"Really?"

"Kevin . . ." warned Sean.

"It's the Fourth of July," said Cormac. "Pursuit of happiness day. Let the kid have his pie."

After they closed up shop, Cormac and Barb went down to Belham Town Beach on the shore of Lake Pequot to meet up with the rest of his family. It was their tradition to picnic and swim until the fireworks were set off at the far side of the lake in the evening. They invited Sean and Kevin to join them, and Sean would've loved to spend the day floating around in the cool lake water with the McGraths.

Kevin wasn't interested. He wouldn't say why, but continued politely to decline all possible permutations of this plan. As they walked home, Sean finally said, "Well, do you care if I go down to the lake without you?" The boy seemed to spend countless hours on his own—maybe he'd prefer to be left to himself.

Kevin shrugged, but his face was set in that pre-angry state Sean was beginning to recognize. "You said we could go for a hike."

"Well, what if we went tomorrow?"

"You said *today*," he muttered, gripping his boxed pie. "You said after I helped at the bakery."

"Fair enough." Sean resigned himself to keeping his word, though he secretly longed to be with the McGraths. He'd spent so much time at Cormac's house in high school, entertained by Cormac's incessant bickering with his father, being spoiled by his mother and basking in the reflected glow of familial warmth. It was a far cry from his own place of residence, where his father came home less and less frequently until he stopped coming home at all, and Aunt Vivvy ran the place with all the warmth of a garden hoe.

After stopping briefly at the house, Kevin led the way across the backyard and into the woods, a backpack hanging from his narrow shoulders.

"What's in the pack?" Sean asked as the trail became a barely visible footpath through the underbrush.

"Water—"

"Water? How long are we going for?"

"Do you have an appointment or something?"

Sean couldn't tell if he was pointing out the obvious—that Sean rarely had any particular plans—or if it was truly an innocent question. In either case, the implication was clear: they weren't on a schedule, and it would behoove Sean to shut up and hike. He consoled himself with the knowledge that Jansen Woods wasn't that big. How far could they go?

They didn't talk much, walking one behind the other, except for Kevin's occasional admonitions to watch that root sticking up in the path, or jump over this puddle. He moved quickly, confidently, and seemed to know every turn and boulder.

"That's the back of the cemetery over there," he said, pointing across a meadow toward a stand of trees. At first Sean didn't see it, but after a few more steps he discerned that the gray shapes sticking out of the ground beyond the trees were regularly shaped and evenly spaced.

"Our Lady's?" Where his mother and Hugh were buried.

"Yep."

"You ever go over there?"

"Sometimes."

Sean wanted to ask more questions, but couldn't quite form them. What exactly did he want to know about Kevin's side trips to the cemetery? Did the boy know his father and grandmother were buried there? Probably. And did he visit their graves? What did it feel like looking at them? Was it weird or sad . . . or just nothing? Lila had died before Kevin was born, so that was unlikely to elicit any real emotion. And what about Hugh? What kind of father had he been? Had he continued to flit from odd job to wild party to chemically induced hilarity to sleeping all day, as he always had? Did Kevin miss him? Did Kevin even remember him? But Sean found no voice for his questions as they moved through the woods.

"You ever go?" asked Kevin.

"No."

"Ever?"

"No." And it seemed there was some explanation required, something more well thought out than *I just never wanted to.* But Sean didn't really have one, and Kevin didn't pursue it.

Soon they were climbing Jansen Hill, which was not particularly steep, but Kevin didn't break his pace, and Sean could feel his heart rate rising and beads of sweat popping out on his forehead. Near the top a huge tree had fallen. Kevin hoisted his skinny body up onto the log, pulled the backpack off, and set it beside him. As Sean situated himself, the boy took out a stainless steel water bottle, unscrewed the top, and drank several gulps. He offered it to Sean.

"Thanks. This came in handy, huh?"

"You have to stay hydrated," instructed Kevin. "You never hike without water, even if it's supposed to be a short one, because you could get lost. And then what? You'd be in big trouble."

"True," said Sean with a smile. "Where'd you learn so much about it—that *Man vs. Wild* show? Oh, God. This isn't"—he narrowed his eyes dramatically at Kevin—"*pee*, is it?"

"Ew, no!" Kevin laughed.

"And where'd you get this stylin' water bottle?"

"REI. I used my birthday money. I wanted to get a new sleeping bag, but I didn't have enough. Plus it would've been hard to carry home on my bike."

"Wait, you rode your bike all the way to REI? There are some pretty busy roads over there. Why didn't Auntie Dee or Auntie Vivvy take you?"

Kevin reached for the water bottle and took a sip. "Auntie Vivvy doesn't drive anymore. That's why she's got you doing the groceries. And Auntie Dee took me once after I helped her learn her lines for *Wicked*. But she doesn't have any lines this time. Plus she's never around."

Sean's heart sank. The kid was basically raising himself. This should've been clear to him before, of course. He should've gotten it that first morning when he'd heard Kevin fixing his own breakfast and getting ready for school, without anyone to so much as remind him to take the lunch he'd made for himself. Sean should've been sure when he saw Kevin's perplexed reaction to having him show up for the Clap Out. And yet Kevin didn't seem to want people around very much. The kid's resourcefulness was impressive. It seemed to suit him, this solitary, self-sufficient way of moving through the world. Sean was a bit like that himself.

Kevin took a deep breath, a hint of contentment settling on his face. "It smells good up here."

Sean inhaled the scent of pine needles and a host of other woodsy things he couldn't name. "Yeah," he said. "It smells like the world is supposed to smell."

Kevin nodded, fully satisfied, it seemed, with his uncle's answer. Sean wondered if he'd ever seen the kid look so relaxed. "What else you got in that backpack?" he asked.

Kevin reached in and took out a plastic container. Inside was a wide, crookedly sliced slab of pie and two plastic forks, purple and sticky with blueberry juice. He handed one to Sean, and licked the handle of his own. "Go on," said Sean. "It's your pie. You first."

Kevin lifted a forkful to his mouth and chewed happily. "What did he call it?"

"What did who call what?"

"That big guy, Cormac—what did he call today?"

"I think he said it was pursuit of happiness day."

Kevin grinned. "Cool," he said and took another bite.

CHAPTER 10

The following week things got a little strange.

It had started so well. Cormac had asked if Sean was interested in another shift or two at the bakery, and he'd said yes. It felt good to meet someone else's needs again, even if it was just pinch-hitting while Cormac's employees took vacation time. Cormac insisted on paying him, and at first Sean had said no way. It ruined that sharp, righteous feel of *helping*. Cormac seemed to intuit Sean's reasoning. "Pal," he said, "I hate to break it to you, but it isn't that much. Considering what you could make at a hospital, this definitely qualifies as volunteer work."

And then it occurred to Sean that it wasn't a bad idea to give his trust account a little nourishment. His back was better—not great, but manageable—and soon it would be time to find something new. Maybe not so far away, somewhere it wouldn't take days to come back to Belham for visits. Because it was clear to him now that he'd been thoughtless to let so much time go by, especially with Aunt Vivvy getting older and Kevin approaching his teen years. The boy didn't seem to have inherited Hugh's proclivity for mischief, but even a good kid could get into trouble on a bad day. Sean would have to stay in better touch. Maybe get a cell phone and learn to text. Maybe even get on Facebook—he'd heard it was pretty popular with kids these days.

Sean started disaster-surfing on Deirdre's laptop again, the familiar time-to-move-on feeling poking at him intermittently. He had the sense that if he could just recapture the purpose and contentedness, and (if he were honest) the righteousness he'd felt earlier in his career, everything could go back to normal. Or some facsimile thereof.

He crossed off several places in Africa right away. Too far. And too much civil unrest. He was still having those flashes of preteen rape victims and severed limbs and wasn't sure he could stomach a return to those kinds of daily visuals. He focused his search on natural disaster relief. At the moment, Haiti was looking pretty good.

The following week, he borrowed Kevin's alarm clock so he could be up in time to walk over to the Confectionary by five-thirty. He felt calm and happy as he strolled through the slanting rays of early morning sunlight. Entering the Confectionary, he smelled the yeasty sweetness of dough rising and the sharp, invigorating scent of recently ground coffee beans. It reminded him of his childhood visits to the McGrath house—the encouraging smell of food.

Aunt Vivvy's house smelled of cleaning products and talcum powder, the latter his aunt's one indulgence. She never baked unless it was compulsory, like a birthday cake. Meals were adequately nutritious and efficiently prepared, in quantities designed to avoid leftovers.

Now wearing a cranberry-colored CORMAC'S CONFECTIONARY T-shirt, Sean stationed himself behind the register. A teenager trudged in wearing a similar shirt, eyes half-lidded in semiconsciousness, and introduced herself as Theresa. "Call me Tree," she mumbled. "You ring, I'll brew. I can't talk to people this early in the morning."

"Tree," said Cormac. "Hair." She let out a dejected sigh and wound her hair into a strangled bun. Cormac leaned over to Sean. "Use as few words as possible," he murmured. "She's a good worker, but her language processing skills don't kick in until about seven."

The first few customers gave easy orders: a large coffee and a cruller. A cup of tea. They were dressed for work, made no eye contact, and were obviously anxious to spend as little time in this particular transaction as possible. Then a woman came in wearing workout clothes—turquoise yoga pants and a matching sleeveless top. She had big white sunglasses with gold letters on the sides: DKNY.

Dinky? thought Sean.

She lifted them up onto her head, pushing back the glossy light brown hair that fell in gentle waves toward her breasts, and squinted up at the menu board. "Medium half-caf iced skinny latte, two Splendas, and a dash of nutmeg, please," she said, never even glancing at Sean. "No, make that large."

There was a flicker of something pinging at the back of Sean's brain, but he was so distracted by trying to get all the right letters written on the cup, he didn't focus on it. He handed off the cup to Tree and rang up the order. "That'll be four-ten," he said, fairly certain he'd gotten both the letters and the cost computation right. Smiling with satisfaction, he glanced at the customer, recognition hitting him with a crackle of electricity.

Chrissy Stillman.

She handed him a five and gave a tiny flick of her wrist to indicate that the change could go in the tip jar, *College Tuition/Harley Fund* scrawled on it. She moved to the Pick Up counter.

"Chrissy?" he said quietly, unsure if he really wanted her to hear him.

She looked up, tilted her head slightly to one side.

"Sean," he murmured. "Sean Doran."

"Oh, my God, *Sean*!" she called out, her long legs quickly striding back to the Order counter. "Wow! How are you? Where've you been? It's been like—what?—over twenty years!"

"Yeah, I know, long time. I've been doing overseas work."

"And now you're . . ." She wiggled her tan fingers toward the register.

"Oh, no," he said quickly. "No, I'm not . . . I'm just here for a few weeks. Cormac needed a little help so I'm just . . . helping."

"That is terrific. Well, hey! We have to get together! I want to hear all about what you've been doing overseas."

Sean's head started to spin just a little. "Sure, that'd be great."

"What's your cell?" She whipped a phone out of her small white purse and began tapping at the screen. "Sean Doran," she muttered. "Okay, shoot!"

"Uh, actually, I don't . . . lots of places I've worked don't exactly have cell service. I'll give you my home number." He blanked on it for a second, recovered, and recited the number.

"Shoot, shoot, shoot," she said. "I'm late for yoga. But I will definitely call you! I can't believe it—Sean Doran!" She sailed back to Pick Up for her latte. Suddenly her face lost its exuberance. "This is supposed to be iced," she told Tree. The girl reached for the cup, cutting her eyes toward Sean to indicate the source of the mistake. "Oh, never mind," said Chrissy, grabbing the cup. She shone a good-sport smile at Sean. "I'll just crank up the AC!"

Later, he took a good bit of razzing from Cormac about it, as he knew he would. He didn't expect Tree to chime in, though. "Shoulda seen it, Cormac," she smirked. "He was like . . ." She wiggled her body like a happy puppy. "Then he was like . . ." She strutted a few steps, nodding her head smugly. "And then he screwed up the next three orders." Apparently Tree's language processing skills had kicked in.

He walked home that afternoon, back throbbing slightly, but with a silly grin he couldn't seem to get rid of. Chrissy Stillman. The unattainable Holy Grail of his teen years. She had his number. She was going to call.

Sean hadn't been home ten minutes when Kevin banged through the back door with a look of undiluted terror on his face. The dog jumped up and began barking homicidally, and Aunt Vivvy dropped her plate of saltine crackers. Sean turned so quickly to see what the commotion was that his back twanged into spasm and he had to hang on to the counter to keep from falling.

"I . . ." Kevin panted, ". . . there was . . ."

"For goodness *sake*, Hugh," Aunt Vivvy chastised, as the dog continued to bark. "Stop this foolishness! Are you in your right mind? Come here and let me look at you."

Kevin's terror turned to confusion, as his eyes flicked from his irate aunt to her irate dog.

With sirens of pain wailing up and down his spine, Sean could barely process the scene. "Jesus! Stop your damned barking!" he yelled at the dog, who downgraded her outbursts to an aggravated growl. "Get me a chair," he said, and Kevin slid a kitchen chair over to Sean, who lowered himself gingerly onto it. "What is going on here?" he demanded.

"I was in the woods . . ." Kevin said tremulously. He glanced to Aunt Vivvy, who stood looking slightly dazed, the crackers and sandwich plate strewn across the floor at her feet.

"Auntie Vivvy," murmured Sean. "Sit down. We'll pick that up in a minute." The older woman moved obediently to a chair. He turned his gaze back to Kevin and tried to focus on the boy, despite the blistering pain in his back.

"I . . . I was up by the big log. I made a . . . a fort up there a couple of weeks ago. But when I went in, there was . . . stuff in it. Not my stuff. And then some kids came . . . older." His chin started to tremble. "They chased me." He blinked furiously but a tear spilled down his cheek anyway. He quickly wiped it against the shoulder of his T-shirt.

"Ah, Kevin," Sean sighed. "Maybe you shouldn't spend so much time up there alone."

"What'm I *supposed* to do, then?"

Sean didn't know. He could barely form coherent thoughts. Kevin trudged out of the room—Sean could hear him clomp up the stairs and close a door. "Auntie," he said after a moment. "We need to do something about the dog. She can't go into attack mode every time one of us walks into the room."

Aunt Vivian leveled a clear-eyed gaze at him. "George is protective," she said. "It is a laudable trait, one that is grievously lacking in the world, and it is not a feature that can be surgically removed like some sort of mole or polyp." She rose and left the room, the dog trotting behind at her slippered heels.

Sean sat there with his back muscles pulsating as if to a crazed rumba. He wished he'd asked someone to get him some ibuprofen before they'd stormed out. And what was that about Aunt Vivvy demanding to see if Kevin was "in his right mind"? Sean pondered this for a moment. Had she actually called him Hugh?

His brain was too busy sounding an alarm about his back to puzzle it out at the moment. He needed to be flat, so he slid off the chair and onto the floor, vowing to carry ibuprofen tablets in his pocket from now on. The spilled saltines lay inches away from his face and looked like delicate little rafts in the churning waters of the pitted linoleum.

Sean was able to accomplish two things the next morning. The first was to confirm that there were no summer camps that fit into the union of subsets that included Kevin's willingness to attend, the camp's having space for him, and being located within a twenty-mile radius of Belham. Kevin flatly refused to go to overnight camp. "What if I don't like it? What am I supposed to do—leave like a homesick baby?"

Comments from Sean like "It'll be an adventure!" and "You'll make some great new friends!" and "This one has horses, a driving range, skeet shooting, and a gourmet selection of desserts after every meal!" held no sway.

"Besides," Kevin muttered about that last one, "it costs six thousand dollars for two weeks."

He was willing to consider some nature-oriented day camps, but they had no openings. There were a couple of sports camps with available spots, but Kevin wasn't interested. Then Sean found one that looked perfect.

"I went there last summer," said Kevin. "They never empty the trash cans. By the end of the week, there's stinky milk cartons and baloney sandwiches falling out and bees swarming all over. And the counselors are mean."

They'd spent three hours on Deirdre's laptop and making phone calls—all for nothing. Kevin took a book on Denali National Park, his stainless steel water bottle, and a Clif Bar out to the backyard.

Sean popped another quartet of ibuprofen tablets and called Tree of Life Spa. Miraculously, Rebecca had an opening at four o'clock.

He arrived at ten to four with the long-odds hope that she had finished early with the previous client and he'd get a few extra minutes. Cleopatra the receptionist disabused him of that fantasy in record time. In fact she claimed Rebecca wasn't available at all. "You wanted Missy last time," she said. "Now you can have her."

"Why's Rebecca suddenly unavailable?" Sean said, barely able to keep the edge out of his tone. "I just called a couple of hours ago."

"Yeah, um . . ." Cleopatra shook her head as if searching for an excuse. "Miscommunication? Missy will be ready for you in a few minutes."

"When *is* Rebecca available?"

"She's pretty booked up."

"Okay, tell you what," he said, irritation rising like high tide under a full moon. "Why don't you just give me Rebecca's first available appointment—whenever that is. Today, tomorrow, next week. I'll take it."

Cleopatra gave a long-suffering sigh, got up, and went down the hallway toward the massage rooms. Sean sat in the little waiting area, which consisted of two vinyl chairs and a tall dieffenbachia plant. He touched the leaves. Fake. No surprise.

He snorted in annoyance. He did not *want* the wailing, pajama-clad Missy to attempt—and fail, he was certain!—to corral his pain into manageable chunks. He wanted Rebecca. And there was a little part of his brain telling him he sounded like a child refusing to drink out of the blue cup because he'd irrationally determined the red cup to be somehow superior. But it had been a hell of a twenty-four hours, and he wanted what he wanted. It was so unlike him, he realized. He wasn't used to caring the least bit whether he got the blue, the red, or any cup at all. It was exhausting, having preferences like this.

An older woman came in and sat down. "Getting a massage?" she asked congenially.

Maybe, he thought. *It's either that or throw a head-banging hissy fit.*

He smiled back politely. "Yes," he said. "You?"

She nodded. "My first one."

"Who's it with?" he asked.

"Oh, whoever they give me, I suppose. I've never been here before. My daughter gave me a gift certificate for my birthday and . . ." She kept talking, but Sean stopped listening.

"*Whoever they give me*"? he thought. *I'll tell you who they're giving you—Wailing Pajama Girl, that's who.*

Cleopatra returned and gave him a momentary glare. "Rebecca is now available in room three," she said, with a tone that implied, *Happy now, you big baby?*

"I'm *so* grateful." He smiled at her, knowing she'd take it to be sarcastic whether he meant it that way or not. Which he most certainly did.

CHAPTER 11

When he walked into room three, a woman stood there with her arms folded across her chest. Her face was calm, framed in layers of wavy dark hair that fell to her shoulders, but also somewhat surprised-looking. Actually one half seemed calm, the other surprised. Her misaligned right eye was slightly bigger than the other, and the cheekbone on the right was also more pronounced than its mate on the opposite side. The asymmetry made it hard to judge her expression.

"Hi, Sean," she said quietly. "How've you been?"

"Becky? Jesus, Becky Feingold!" He went forward to give her a hug, which she received warmly, if a little awkwardly, too. "You're Rebecca now!"

"Yeah." She gave a little smiling shrug. "It's more adult than Becky."

"Wow," he said stupidly, still trying to assemble the previously unconnected pieces of this puzzle. Rebecca the All-Powerful Pain Tamer was really little Becky Feingold, his pal from high school. They'd hung out quite a bit back then, though it was pretty much an established fact that she'd had a widely known secret crush on him since junior high. She'd never made a bid for his affection, though, and after a while he'd forgotten about it, the crush becoming just another tree in the social forest, and not a terribly tall one at that. She was a nice girl, a good listener, and had a sense of humor that was all the more hilarious for its selective use. The congenital facial deformity had created a barrier between her and many of her classmates. She and Sean both felt an outsiderness that had served to strengthen their friendship.

"Okay," she said, taking a little breath. "You're probably wondering why I didn't say anything before, and the whole deal with today's appointment and everything." She crossed her arms again. "I was just . . . caught off guard the last time, when you turned over and it was . . . you. And you were in a deep state, a really healing place—I could feel everything loosening up and starting to hum at the right frequency again. I didn't want to disturb that. You really needed it."

"Yeah, no kidding," he said. "It was amazing. I felt like a new man." He chuckled. "Well, new—I suppose that's a relative term once you're past forty, right? But better than I've felt in months. *Way* better."

A look flitted across her face—pride, satisfaction, gratitude—he couldn't tell which. Maybe a mixture of all three. But then her smile faded. "Sean," she said. "There's another reason I didn't say anything, and I didn't want to treat you again."

What? he thought. *What's wrong?*

She seemed to be forcing herself to look at him. "Back in high school you told me . . . you said you'd be dead by now. Were you lying? Was it some sort of weird joke you were playing? Because if it was . . ." Her mouth went tight, and she looked away. "Well, that's just unbelievably sick, and I can't expose myself to that kind of toxic—"

"No!" he said quickly. "God no, I would never joke about . . . Jesus, no. I just . . . *I thought I had it.* I was *sure* of it. Growing up everyone always told me I was just like my mother. I looked like her, sounded like her. My father used to say 'The image of Lila.' He used to mutter that at me all the time."

Sean stared at Becky, remembering now the times they'd hung out in her basement, and she'd fiddle around on her guitar and he'd just . . . talk. Or at the end of a party, the two of them often the only ones not making out with some random classmate, her driving him home in her beat-to-hell Plymouth Horizon. They'd idle in his driveway for an hour or two before he went in to face the music of curfew breakage and Aunt Vivvy's wrath. He vaguely remembered talking about Huntington's. What a shock it must have been for her to see him after all those years—naked, no less—when she assumed he'd gone to his grave.

"Swear to God, Beck," he said. "It was no joke."

Her expression softened. "So you don't have it?"

"Well," he said, "I don't have symptoms. It could still surface, I suppose, but it's unlikely. Most people start showing signs by their early forties. My mother was thirty-three."

"But there's a test now."

"Yeah." He scratched his arm, looked around the room. Why was it always so hard to explain to people? "I didn't take it. I don't want to know."

"But you thought you *already* knew."

"Trust me, I've had this conversation before," he said. "It just doesn't make a whole lot of sense to people who haven't faced knowing for sure if they're in for a long, slow death."

"Okay," she said, not as if she understood, but with a willingness to be all right with *not* understanding.

"Becky Feingold." He shook his head in wonder.

"Yep," she said with the faintest hint of resignation. "It's me."

He did get his massage after all. It was a little strange at first to be lying naked with nothing but a thin sheet over his butt while little Becky Feingold worked her magical fingers into the angry hard places across his shoulders and down his spine. But it wasn't long before high-school-Becky seemed to recede into the background. With his eyes closed and his body practically levitating in relief, he could listen to her melodic voice—a trait he'd never noticed in their teen years—and believe in this new person, Rebecca the Pain Tamer.

"How's your family?" she asked.

With his face in the doughnut, he noticed she wore clogs now. Blue ones. He told her about Deirdre working at Carey's Diner, never having left home. "Oh, and she's an actress now."

He heard a little chuckle. "She was only about seven or eight the last time I saw her, but she seemed pretty dramatic, even then. Didn't she keep getting into trouble for wearing your aunt's clothes as dress-ups?"

"I forgot about that! You have a good memory."

She dug a little harder into a spot just above his hip bone. "What about your brother—the one who sank that guy's boat in Lake Pequot." The feel of her thumb pressing into a knob of molten pain made him jerk reflexively. "Sorry," she murmured, backing off.

"Yeah, Hugh." Sean had occasionally told people about his brother's death before, of course. But he'd never had to tell anyone who'd actually known Hugh. "He died six years ago."

Her hands stopped moving. "Oh God, Sean," she whispered. "I'm so sorry. I know how much you loved him."

His throat tightened, and at first he didn't know why. Hugh had been gone a long time, and Sean hadn't gotten emotional about it in years. *How much I loved him.* He'd almost forgotten.

After a moment she asked, "Was it Huntington's?"

Sean cleared his throat, willed himself to relax. "No," he said. "Pneumonia."

"Terrible," she murmured. Her hands began to move slowly, carefully across his hips. "You don't often hear about young people dying of pneumonia these days."

"Well, Hugh had a way of burning the candle at both ends. Apparently by the time he got around to having it checked, it was so bad they couldn't save him." Sean felt the familiar swell of anger when he told this detail. Couldn't Hugh have exercised a little caution for once in his life?

"He had a son," Sean added quickly, to move the conversation away from death and lost chances. "Kevin. He's eleven."

"Does he live nearby?"

"Actually he lives with Deirdre and my aunt—and at the moment, me. His mother was . . . well, what's a nice word for it? A free spirit, I guess. She left when Kevin was two. The state tried to find her when Hugh died, but they never did, so they gave guardianship to my aunt."

"What's he like?"

"Nothing like Hugh. It's kind of weird. For one, he's particular about things. Smells and crowds, stuff like that. Loves being in the woods." Sean told her about Kevin being chased by teenagers, and his unsuccessful attempt to get Kevin into camp. "Also, Hugh always had loads of friends—*too* many sometimes, if you know what I'm saying. Kevin doesn't seem to have any."

"Kids don't always turn out like their parents. Or their uncles."

"Hey, I was no Big Man on Campus."

"Maybe not like Hugh . . ."

"Not at *all*."

"Well," she said. "You always had people around you. You had options."

Options? he wondered. *For what? Falling in love? Getting married and having kids? Any kind of a normal life?*

At that moment she started on his feet, and though it wasn't quite as pass-out painful as it had been the first time, it was no walk in the park, either. "Now *you* talk," he said, gritting his molars against the urge to shriek like a twelve-year-old girl at a horror movie. "How are Sol and Betty?" He was pleased that, even with his eyes rolling back in their sockets, he could pull up her parents' names.

"They're happy as clams," she said, though her voice didn't reflect any glimmer of joy. "Living in Florida now. In one of those communities. Shuffleboard, a pool the size of a Ring Ding, all the kvetching you could want."

"They sold the house? What did you used to call it—the split something?"

"The banana split-level."

"With extra nuts, right?"

"Yeah." She chuckled, glad, it seemed, that he'd remembered. "No shortage of nuttiness." She tugged on his toes one by one.

"Actually, I'm still living there. I mean, I left for *years*," she added quickly, "but I moved back when I went to school for massage. And then they moved out, and there didn't seem any reason for me to leave. They don't want to sell, and I pay the utilities and taxes and stuff . . ."

"Sounds like a perfect arrangement." It did sound pretty great, yet he could tell by her voice that for some reason, it wasn't. He realized it could be very revealing to listen to a person without seeing them. You noticed things that would otherwise be obscured by a smiling face.

It was time for him to flip over, and she held the sheet so he'd be in no risk of a coverage malfunction. He still couldn't decide if it was weirder to be so thoroughly explored by a complete stranger or by an old friend. When her fingers scrubbed gently across his scalp, chasing tension off into the atmosphere, he decided he didn't care. The soft pads of her fingers pressed around his eyes and nose and cheeks, and he realized it had been a very long time since anyone had been so intimate with him as to traverse the topography of his face. It felt unbelievably good and a little depressing all at the same time.

CHAPTER 12

The next day was so hot and so dry it reminded Sean of the time he spent in a refugee camp in the Sudan. *Except your mouth doesn't fill with dust the moment you open it,* he thought. By the time the Confectionary closed at four, it seemed the entire population of MetroWest Boston had stopped by in dire need of a frothy, frappy drink.

He walked home enjoying the heat-purified breeze after working in the freezer smell of air conditioning all day. He hoped there would be a message from Chrissy Stillman on his aunt's ancient answering machine. The thing had a microcassette with magnetic tape that wound around tiny spools. Sean wasn't a technology guy, but even he thought it was only about two steps up from tin cans connected by string. Chrissy had taken his number a little over a week ago, and he was beginning to wonder if the machine had eaten her message. Assuming she'd left one.

When he got home, there was no message waiting from Chrissy or anyone else, and he was a little alarmed by how disappointed he felt. To distract himself, he decided they would eat dinner outside in the shade of Aunt Vivvy's prized red maple. He got Kevin to dust off a card table and some folding chairs while Sean sliced vegetables for stir-fry.

Deirdre was barely home long enough to shower and grab her script, so it was just the three of them for dinner al fresco—four if you counted the ever-present George. Sean reached for Aunt Vivvy's hand as she descended the three steps to the yard, but she batted his hand away, her feet searching for each stair as if it couldn't be counted on not to have moved. She made her way across the lawn and sank elegantly onto her chair. Kevin plunked down next to her, serene as a saint under the bower of the maple tree, face speckled by the glittery late-afternoon light.

The disquiet Sean felt about being forgotten by Chrissy—in fact, about anything—dissipated as he surveyed the scene. Aunt Vivvy reached over and handed Kevin his napkin. He put it in his lap, and she gave him an approving little smile. The dog wandered along the edge of the property sniffing at the old stone wall that ran across the back of the yard. Then she trotted over and put her chin in Vivian's lap, eyes half-lidded in pleasure as her head was stroked.

Everyone's happy, thought Sean. *Even the dog.*

Deirdre came home that night with her face lit up like a hundred-watt bulb in a sixty-watt socket. She yanked *The Lion, the Witch and the Wardrobe* from Sean's grasp and tossed it onto the coffee table. She pulled him up and held his arm aloft while she twirled beneath it.

"What?" He laughed. "What is it?"

"A toast!" she sang out, now towing him toward the kitchen.

"To . . . ?"

She slid a chair over to the cabinets, leaped onto it, and pulled out the vodka with a flourish. She looked at Sean. "You want this or a beer?"

"Beer."

"Then *get* it!"

By the time he'd opened a Sam Adams, her drink was sloshing around in a short glass as she danced with herself across the linoleum. He knew she was waiting for him to ask one more time, so he said, "Please, dear sister, reveal the cause of your merriment!"

"Me," she said with a proud grin. "I am the cause."

"You got Mrs. Potiphar," he guessed.

"Damn straight, I did! The stupid hack got into a throw-your-script fight with the director and stormed out." She took a gulp of her drink, then wagged it at Sean, ice cubes clacking. "He actually *clicked his heels*, pointed to me, and said 'It's all about you now, Eve.'"

"Eve?"

"From the movie." She waited for him to get it and rolled her eyes when he didn't. "*All About Eve*? Bette Davis? Oh, never mind."

Sean raised his beer and clinked her glass. "Way to go!" he said. "I can't wait to see it. Cormac and Barb were raving about you in that wicked witch show."

She snorted her disgust at his ignorance. "Anyway," she said. "The show goes up in two weeks, so you won't have long to wait."

"I'm really happy for you." And he was. Truly. He wanted to show her, and though they'd never been a demonstrative family, he'd become used to hugging in his travels. Patients hugged to show their gratitude. Coworkers hugged about their sadness over a particularly pitiful patient or their relief over a life saved. Bodily contact had become the norm for Sean.

He reached out to Deirdre, and for a second she didn't seem to know what his purpose was, but then she stepped into the embrace and put her arms around him. "Sean," she said, her cheek resting against his chest. "It really means a lot to me that you understand how big this is."

He pulled his head back to look at her, and she lifted her chin. There were tears in her eyes. "I'm thirty-two," she whispered. "Mom was thirty-three. Maybe this is all I get."

He could feel his eyes well up, and shame stung at him. Because he *hadn't* really understood—hadn't done the math. In his mind she was still somewhere in her twenties. But that was wrong. She was thirty-two. "Is it . . . are you feeling . . . anything?"

She shook her head. He studied her eyes for telltale flicking motions, wracked his brain for any time he'd seen her twitchy or ungraceful or confused. He couldn't remember noticing anything, but then again, he hadn't been looking.

How could I not have been looking?

"What about you?" she murmured.

He shook his head. "I think I dodged it." She closed her eyes and squeezed him.

They released each other, slumping exhausted into kitchen chairs as if they'd just run for their lives. She reached for the vodka and refreshed her drink. "I told myself that if I got to play Mrs. Potiphar even *once*," she said, "I'd go to New York."

"You should. You deserve a trip like that."

"No, I mean, to live."

Oh, he thought, the gravity of it pressing harder on him with every passing second. *Shit.*

He fiddled with the beer cap on the table. She tapped her fingers soundlessly against her glass. He glanced up, and she met his gaze with a look of intractability too real to be acting.

"How's it going to work?" he said finally.

"They can't live alone."

"Could we hire someone?"

She stared at him a moment, barely controlled disgust in her gaze. "Well, if no one they actually *know* will stay with them . . . I suppose we'll have to. But it has to be somebody good, Sean, not some cheap rent-a-maid. They both need more than you think." She let out an annoyed sigh. "You got anything left in your fund? Because mine's gone. That's why I've been working so much, so I'd have money for New York."

"Did Hugh—?"

"Right," she snorted sarcastically. "A motorcycle, a boat, and a really expensive fishing rod." She snapped her fingers. "Gone before he was twenty."

Sean felt a surge of disgust for his brother's prodigality. But it was just Hugh being Hugh, at the height of his Hugh-ness. "Viv?"

"No idea," said Deirdre. "She could be loaded or she could be broke, for all I know. I contribute every month, but she's still paying the bills." She tipped her glass up, finished off her drink and rose. "I'm going as soon as the show's over, middle of August."

"Dee, you can't just leave me holding the bag!"

"Yeah, I can," she said. "I've earned it, and then some." She put her glass in the dishwasher and left.

Sean hadn't been to church in months. There were times in his life when he'd gone every day. There was always a church of some kind near the clinics and hospitals where he'd worked—not always Catholic but it didn't matter much to Sean. A holy place was a holy place.

But about year ago, he'd found himself feeling irritable during services—especially if it was a Catholic Mass. Either he thought the priest was too young to know what he was talking about or too old to understand today's world. They burned stinky incense or sang songs like "Onward, Christian Soldiers." *Marching as to war?* He'd had enough of that.

Worst of all, he couldn't say the prayers. The Penitential Rite drove him up the wall. Not because he didn't feel penitent about things. Hadn't he been too stern with a parent who should have brought a sick child in sooner? Hadn't he slept with that cute, slightly insecure med student, knowing it meant more to her than it did to him? He had plenty of things to regret.

But, confessing *to almighty God, and to you, my brothers and sisters?* Why should he confess to a God who was giving him the silent treatment? And the majority of his "brothers and sisters" were too busy just trying to survive. What did they care about his petty misdemeanors?

I have sinned through my own fault. Well, fault—it was a matter of perspective, wasn't it? If he hadn't thought he'd only get half a lifetime instead of a whole one, wouldn't he have made other choices? Wouldn't he have lived a less stressful life, where the temptations were easier to withstand? Whose "fault" was that?

In what I have done, and in what I have failed to do. Had he failed to go to the most primitive, dangerous places on earth to tend and comfort the least fortunate? Had he failed to put his own needs last? *Failed, my ass!*

That was generally the point at which he slunk sullenly out the back, eventually deciding there wasn't much reason to go in the first place.

But Sunday morning he woke in such a funk it seemed that drastic measures were called for. It had been two days since Deirdre had confirmed her plans to leave, throwing him into such a stew of resentment that he'd spent half of Saturday in the den on her laptop making plans for his own departure while she was at rehearsal. He'd narrowed it down to three aid organizations when Kevin came in to see what was on TV. Sean felt as if he'd been caught looking at porn.

"What're you doing?" Kevin had asked, searching for the remote.

"Nothing. Just surfing around." He shut down the laptop.

Kevin had given him a look as he clicked on the TV. Sean couldn't quite decipher it—quizzical, maybe? Skeptical? Disapproving in some way? He didn't stick around to find out.

On Sunday Sean woke early, the blinking vestiges of a dream still firing across his brain, the word *Da* unspoken on his tongue. It was what he'd always called his father, in the Irish tradition. Da's given name was Martin, and he was a short, muscular man with wiry red hair and forearms to rival Popeye's. He spoke with a brogue so thick that Sean's friends often needed him to translate when Da spoke to them. The thought of his father could still ring a faint note of longing in Sean, despite the hateful fact of his desertion.

On Sunday mornings, Da would corral everyone for church, saying, "When I lived on the Great Blasket Island, the priest only came across the sound once a year. Here in America we have a lovely church sitting right up the road, and we'll go if we've legs to carry us." They had a car, of course, but that was how he'd say it, as if he were prepared to march them forcibly.

Sean's mother, Lila, had been Anglican but had converted to Catholicism at Martin's request. Her older sister, Vivian, was none too thrilled with the prospect of sweet, lovely Lila becoming a contemptible Papist—and married to a rough Irishman, to boot. But Lila loved the Irishman and didn't mind the Church, so she married him despite her sister's protestations. However, Lila was a bit lackadaisical about Mass when Martin was at sea. There were Sundays when she said, "God can visit with us over a nice leisurely breakfast, and then we'll offer up our prayers and petitions all the more fervently."

Lying there in bed, Sean didn't really want to go to church. But he wondered if it might feel different at Our Lady Comforter of the Afflicted, his home parish. It had been there, listening to the story of Jesus healing his friend Lazarus, and worrying about his mother and his own uncertain future, that he'd had an epiphany. Right then at the tender age of thirteen, he'd decided that if he couldn't live a normal life, never knowing when or if he'd start to lose his mind, then he'd make the most of what he had: an interest in medicine, a willingness to live without the usual comforts, and a strong desire to get far away from Belham.

His father had beaten him to the exit, however, and Sean tried to remember when exactly Da had failed to return from one of his many stints as an able seaman in the merchant marine. He had taken shorter trips for a while when they'd first moved in with Aunt Vivvy, and he'd been home two years later when Lila fell down the steps into the fieldstone basement, knocking her head against the rock wall as she tumbled. Da had discovered her and had screamed up the stairs for Sean to call an ambulance. That desperate, agonized roar was the last time Sean could remember hearing his father raise his voice. His mother was pronounced dead at the scene.

After that, Da's trips at sea were longer. Then one day Sean realized that his father had been gone longer than ever before, and that they hadn't received any postcards from him in a while. "When is Da's trip over?" he'd asked his aunt.

The sympathy in her eyes worried him—it was unlike her. "Sean," she said. "It was over three months ago. It appears that he's decided to move on."

For a moment he couldn't believe it. He was only starting to accept that his mother was truly gone for good, and now his father had left them? But Aunt Vivvy never lied. She never even coated the truth, so it must be true. The cruelty of it hit him like a grenade, and he broke down crying right in front of her. At almost seventeen he was already far taller than her, and she'd had to reach up to cup her hands around his face and gently swipe the tears with her thumbs.

"We'll get through" was all she said. And her word was law, so he believed her.

Sean got out of bed and with no small ambivalence made his way to Our Lady's. He sat in the back in order to have a clear escape route in case he started to get that annoyed, slightly sociopathic feeling he'd been subject to in Mass lately. As the priest, lectors, cross and candle bearers processed up the aisle, he noticed that the priest was fairly young. *Great,* thought Sean sardonically. *Another dewy-eyed homily about how nothing bad can happen if we just believe.*

To his credit, he did try to listen. But the Word of God sounded remote and static-ridden, as if it were the disembodied voice of a subway conductor on the T in Boston. The priest's voice rose and fell with instructions that no longer seemed to apply to him, words and whole phrases drowned out by his indifference, like the passing of an oncoming train.

He watched a baby wriggle irritably in its mother's arms across the aisle, eyes half-lidded and unfocused. The child rested his cheek against her shoulder for a moment, then popped up again. The mother guided his downy head back to the sleepy haven of her shoulder. Then his eyes closed and his body went slack, a chubby leg bouncing once against her belly, a bare foot twitching and then coming at last to rest against her hip.

This serene tableau might have happened in any country in the world; their skin could have been any color from freckled white to root beer black. The reassuring arms of the mother, the child's utter confidence in her love and the safety of sleep. Not long ago the sight would've been heartwarming to Sean. But not today. He felt his nerves twang with envy toward them both.

He hung in there, though, and thought he might even make it to the end. There was a family a couple of rows up, a mother, father, and three boys. The oldest was maybe fifteen, slouching and yawning. The other two were elementary age. The youngest came and went from the pew with the regularity of a flight attendant. *Again?* the mother mouthed when he apparently notified her of yet another trip to the bathroom. The middle boy bit his nails constantly.

At the Sign of Peace the two younger boys shoved each other, the father and mother kissed, the teenager rolled his eyes when his father shook his hand. As everyone was turning their attention back to the altar, the middle boy leaned back and peered behind his father to his older brother, with a look of doubtful hope. The older boy reached out a fisted hand behind the father's back. They knuckle-bumped, and the older one gave a sly smile that said, *You're a pain in my ass, but you're okay.*

Sean felt as if someone had reached into his chest and squeezed. He remembered how Hugh would wear his father out with his fidgeting, and by about halfway through Mass he'd be turned over to Sean. They would thumb-wrestle or pinch each other till it was time to leave.

Hugh, thought Sean. *Goddamn it.*

He went up to take Communion, took the wafer, and left. It was tasteless, and he had to swallow hard to make it go down.

CHAPTER 13

On Tuesday night, Barb had her class, so Sean and Cormac walked over to The Pal. After an order of mozzarella sticks, a plate of potato skins, and enough beer to make them slouch in their seats and talk more freely than usual, Cormac said, "We're trying to get pregnant."

"Hey, that's great," said Sean. "Congratulations."

"Don't congratulate me. It hasn't worked yet."

"Must be fun trying, though."

Cormac picked at the nachos that had just arrived. "Except it's kind of . . . scheduled."

"When she's ovulating."

Cormac looked up.

"Hey, I'm a nurse," said Sean, "a member of the secret society of guys who know about ovulating."

Cormac laughed. "How'd *I* get in?"

"Trying to knock up your wife." Sean made the sign of the cross in the air between them. "Go forth and be fruitful. Lots and lots of fruit. Pumpkins, kiwis. A whole freaking orchard."

They ordered more beers. "Deirdre's moving to New York," said Sean. "After the show."

Cormac studied him for a minute. "Well, that's one hell of a domino effect."

"Yeah, no shit."

"What're you going to do?"

Sean shrugged. "Dee says they can't be alone."

Cormac's eyebrows went up. "You're staying?"

"No! I'm hiring someone."

"Oh," said Cormac, and took another sip of his beer.

Cormac's cell phone buzzed in his pocket during the next round, and he jumped like it'd stung him. "Damn," he said when he read the text. "What time is it?"

Sean squinted at the clock over the bar. "Looks like somewhere around midnight."

"Shit, I got her worried." He texted rapidly, the phone bobbing under his huge thumbs.

They paid the bill, hustled down the stairs, and stumbled across the parking lot, moonlight splashing across the ruffled surface of Lake Pequot like jewelry.

"I have to pee like a racehorse," said Sean.

"Me, too, but I gotta get home." There was a Dumpster at the far end of the parking lot, and they headed for that.

As they unzipped Sean said, "I forgot to tell you! The massage therapist at the place Barb sent me to—you know who it is?"

"Katy Perry? Because I think I had a dream about her doing that 'Teenage Dream' song."

"What? No."

"It'd be pretty cool if it was."

"Okay, can you shut up and listen? It was Becky Feingold!"

Cormac squinted, shadows from the moonlight making dark rivulets around his eyes.

"For chrissake!" said Sean. "Little Becky Feingold!" But Cormac still didn't get it. Sean put a cupped palm up to the right side of his face.

Cormac's squint fell. "No fucking way."

"Serious! I couldn't believe it—"

Suddenly a high-powered flashlight beam hit them as they stood there with their flies open. Steam from their urine curled like smoke in the illuminated air.

"What the hell!" Sean yelled as they hurried to zip up.

The flashlight owner started to laugh. "Cormac, man, you know better than that. And who's with you? Sean Doran! Where the hell'd you come from?"

"Christ, Dougie, can you turn off the beam at least?" said Cormac.

As Sean's eyes adjusted to the darkness again, he began to make out a man in a police uniform walking toward them.

"Public urination, indecent exposure," said Officer Dougie. "You know I have to bring you in, right?"

"Oh, come on!" said Sean.

"He's not serious," said Cormac calmly.

"Nah, man," said Dougie. "Just kidding. So how've you been?"

They stood there talking for a bit, then Dougie drove them home in the police cruiser, which was nice of him. Sean thought it would've been even nicer if he hadn't made them sit in the back like criminals behind the wire mesh. But rules were rules, and Dougie was only willing to bend some of them. They dropped Cormac off first, as no one was waiting up for Sean.

"So, how's that nephew of yours?" Dougie asked. "Hugh's boy."

"Okay, except he's got nothing to do. Won't go to any camps that still have openings."

"Huh," said Dougie, pulling into the driveway. "I've seen him walking up in the woods when I'm patrolling through the cemetery. If he likes that kind of thing, hiking and stuff, you might want to try Boy Scouts. Got a very active troop here in town."

Sean nodded. Suddenly he felt so sleepy he didn't know if he'd make it up to bed. It was tempting to curl up under Viv's magnolia in the front yard till morning. Dougie was saying a name and writing it on a piece of paper. He passed it over and Sean stuffed it in his jeans pocket.

"Hey, um. I know it's long past and all, but I never got a chance to say how sorry I was about Hugh. He was a great guy."

Sean nodded. Hugh would've found that hilarious—a cop calling him a great guy.

"Never should've happened," said Dougie. "And it wouldn't have, except he was such a good dad."

Sean did make it to his bed. And in the twenty seconds before he fell into a snoring torpor, Dougie's words scrolled over and over in his brain.

CHAPTER 14

The next day as Sean walked home from the Confectionary through the sprinkling rain, it was all he could do not to swing around lampposts like Gene Kelly. Chrissy Stillman had come in. They had bantered a bit, and this time Sean had had the presence of mind to notice that she wasn't wearing a wedding ring. *Chrissy Stillman was not married.*

They made plans to have lunch the next day. After she left, fantasies fluttered constantly through Sean's mind, quickly turning him into the most inept employee Cormac had ever hired.

"I love you like a brother," Cormac said, "but if I have to do one more void on this register, I'm gonna can your ass."

"Have pity," Tree taunted. "He's got a crush-induced learning disability."

The two of them laughed their caffeinated hyena laughs, but Sean didn't care. Lunch. Tomorrow. *With Chrissy Stillman.*

Back at the house, Kevin lay slumped on the love seat in the den watching TV, clicking through channels every few seconds. "Can we get a PlayStation?" he asked. Sean wasn't sure what that was, but he didn't like the sound of it. What kind of kid needed a "station" to play at?

Later when Deirdre buzzed in from Carey's Diner, Kevin wandered into the kitchen. "Any syrup?" he asked half-heartedly. She grinned and pulled a couple of tiny bottles from her purse with a flourish. "You remembered!" he said.

Sean gave Deirdre a *what's the deal* look. "If people ask for real maple syrup instead of the corn syrup junk, we give them those," she explained. "Half the time they don't use them all, and he likes to drink them." Kevin was gleefully lining up three little bottles on the kitchen table. He picked one up, unscrewed the cap, and took a sip.

Aunt Vivian came in from the backyard, her straw gardening hat slightly askew on her head. She held the door for George and then turned to survey her kitchen. Suddenly she banged her hand down on the counter and yelled with surprising strength, "By God, I told you if I caught you with that again you'd be grounded for a month!"

Her wrath seemed to be aimed at Kevin, and he stared back at her, his green eyes round with concern. "But . . . it's just . . ." he stammered.

"Don't tell me 'It's just.' I know what nip bottles are, Hugh. I'm not as naïve as you think!"

Sean looked at Deirdre, whose face revealed as much shock as he felt. "Auntie Vivvy," he said. "That's not—"

She turned on him. "And don't try to shield him from a well-deserved punishment, Sean! He'll never learn, if you continue to defend him as you do." She shook her head in exasperation. "Go to your room, both of you!"

The dog started to bark, and Sean was worried his aunt might fall if she became any more agitated, so he took Kevin by the arm and steered him from the kitchen. As the door swung behind them, he heard Deirdre say, "Can I get you a glass of water, Auntie?"

In the hallway, Sean turned to Kevin, hoping some reasonable explanation would occur to him, but all he could come up with was "That was really . . . weird."

Kevin nodded. "She does that sometimes. Calls me Dad's name. Or sometimes Martin. That's your dad, right?"

"When did she start?"

The boy's brow wrinkled in thought. "Um, I don't know. A while ago. But not too long."

Deirdre came through the door. "Jesussuffering*christ*," she murmured.

"Has it happened before?" Sean questioned her.

"No. I mean, she's been off her game for a while. Doesn't always seem entirely with it. But nothing like *that*. Could it be—?"

"Very rare to have it crop up this late in life. And she doesn't have the chorea."

"What's that?" asked Kevin. Sean had almost forgotten he was there.

"Huntington's chorea. It's a symptom of a disease that makes people kind of jerky and uncoordinated." He looked at Deirdre. "It could be anything. It could be Alzheimer's."

"She needs to be checked out." Deirdre gave him a pointed look. Then she glanced at her watch. "I have to go to rehearsal."

Sean sighed. *Of course you do,* he thought.

Later that night he tried to talk to her about it. "Auntie," he said. "Remember this afternoon when you got so mad at Kevin?"

She neither answered nor met his gaze, but he could tell she was listening. "You thought he was Hugh," Sean said gently. He watched her eyes blink as she took in this information. "He says it's not the first time." She glared at the kitchen cabinets as if they were the ones accusing her. It reminded him of a time when he'd had to tell a teenage boy he'd contracted HIV. The boy had been silently furious with Sean simply for saying the words.

"You don't seem surprised," he said. Still she wouldn't respond. "Aunt Vivvy, I think you know you've been slipping here and there."

"Well, I'm seventy-eight years old," she retorted. "In my dotage, as it were."

He smiled. "You've been sharp as a tack your whole life," he said. "Smarter than the rest of us combined."

"Don't placate me."

"My point is, you're smart enough to know that even an elder statesman like yourself doesn't forget who she's talking to for no good reason. We need to find out what that reason is, Auntie. It's time to find a new doctor."

"Not for all the tulips in Holland," she said.

The conversation went on for a bit, Sean attempting to reason, sweet-talk, and intimidate her into a doctor's visit. She held firm, saying only that it was her decision, and she chose not to. Eventually she said, "Sean, the world abounds with calamities much greater than mine, and I know you're nearly ready to run off and find one. You'll go, and I'll have my way. Why don't we save ourselves the trouble of a disagreement?"

"Because Deirdre's leaving, that's why! She's planning to move to New York next month. I'm sorry you have to learn about it like this—she should have told you herself by now. But if Deirdre and I are both gone, who'll take care of things? Who'll be there for Kevin?"

She stared at him unblinking as she analyzed this new information. "Well," she said finally, "apparently you *will* have your way. At some point I'll be too dotty to know if I'm taken to a doctor or not. Either way, Kevin will be your charge. Yours and Deirdre's. The two of you will have to decide what's to become of him."

CHAPTER 15

Lunch with Chrissy Stillman was a welcome distraction from the previous day's debacle. Just looking at her, lithe and bouncy even while seated, brushed the thought of Sean's foundering family from his mind. They ate at a little café in Belham Heights called Milano that served sandwiches on thick focaccia bread.

She and her husband were newly separated, she told him. "You remember Rick, right? Star quarterback, captain of the football team . . . massive jerk?"

Unfortunately, a surprised laugh burst out of Sean before he could suppress it. "You married Ricky Cavicchio?"

His reaction was not well received. She shifted uncomfortably in her seat and raised her chin. "He was ambitious and smart, and *very* . . . well . . . he was everything I was looking for."

"Oh, no, I didn't mean . . . it's just, you know, rare that high school romances actually . . ." He felt like a heel. It wasn't her fault she'd been slow to realize what everyone else had seen all along. Love being blind and all that. Not that he had much experience with the matter himself.

"I haven't been with him since *high school,* for godsake—we broke up freshman year in college!" She seemed even more annoyed by the idea that she'd never been with anyone else. But then she reined herself in. "We got together after our tenth class reunion. It was obvious we still had feelings for each other."

Sean nodded supportively. "I'm sure that happens all the time."

"We were happy for many years," she insisted. "Then he got all midlife-crisis-y." She rolled her eyes and gave her head a little wag. Sean remembered her making just that same face in high school.

"Affairs, big dumb purchases, getting creative with the taxes . . . After a while it's more than you can handle. Finally I served him papers. *That* got his attention." She pointed at Sean. "But hey—too late, is what I said."

They had twin girls who were freshmen in high school. One was the star goalie of her field hockey team, and the other was on the cheerleading squad. "I'm so proud of them," said Chrissy with a little grin. "I hope I'm not gushing too much."

She had been gushing a bit, but Sean found it adorable—and admirable, really. She was a very committed mom. In fact, she'd decided against going back to the legal field—she'd been a plaintiff's attorney before the girls were born—and was searching around for a line of work that would be more flexible so she could be home for them.

"Right now I'm back and forth between Pilates instructor and dog trainer. I don't have any real education in either, but I have loads of experience," she said.

"You have experience training dogs?"

"Oh, heck yeah! You know what I love to do? I go down to Man's Best Friend—that shelter in Sudbury? And I pick the worst-looking, most badly behaved dog. I bring him home and clean him up and whip him into shape. Takes me about two months to turn a bad dog around."

"No kidding! How many dogs do you have?"

"Right now? Let me think." She murmured names to herself like Bowser and Slick, counting them off on her fingers. "Six? Yep. That's right. I give them away a lot to good families. But only if I think they really deserve the dog and can be a responsible master."

"You don't hear people talking about being a dog's 'master' very much anymore."

"Well, then they're probably not a very good one!" She did the head-wag eye-roll. "Dogs don't need us to be their friends. They need us to be in charge, in control, and responsible. Domesticated dogs are not supposed to be the alpha—*we* are. People who can't provide good alpha leadership don't deserve a dog!" Her cheeks got pink as she talked.

"Do you make house calls?" asked Sean. "Because as it so happens, we've got a very problematic dog at our house." He'd never been so grateful for a bad dog in his life. George suddenly went from being a demonic hellhound to a lovable old grouch in his mind.

Chrissy was delighted to work with George. "He can be my first client!"

"You'll have to let me know what your rates are."

"Oh, I couldn't charge you." Chrissy gave a coy little smile. "We'll just call this a portfolio builder."

Sean smiled back. He'd be very happy to help her build her portfolio. Or anything else that needed constructing.

She would come over on Saturday and work with George. Back at the house that afternoon, Sean reached into his jeans pocket for the piece of paper with her number on it to put it somewhere safe. Two slips of paper came out; the one with her name and number, and another with the name *Frank Quentzer, Scoutmaster* scrawled on it. He'd been wearing that same pair of pants the night Dougie Shaw had driven him home in the cruiser.

Kevin was downstairs watching TV again. Sean had stopped by the library a couple of days before and gotten him some books, thinking that at least he could read them outside, away from the dark little den. But Kevin hadn't liked those books—each was declared too hard, boring, or babyish. The TV was now on practically all day.

That kid's doing Boy Scouts whether he wants to or not, Sean thought as he went downstairs to look for a phone book. *Quentzer, Frank.* He dialed the number and introduced himself, explaining that he was interested in Boy Scouts for his nephew.

"We have a real nice group of kids," said Frank. He had a low, quiet voice, and Sean had to listen hard to hear everything he said. "And sixth grade is the perfect time to start. He'll be right on schedule with the other boys his age."

"On schedule?"

"For advancement. Each boy progresses through the ranks at his own pace. You can join any time, but most begin around eleven, and it's nice if he doesn't start out too far behind," Frank explained calmly. "Don't worry about getting a uniform right away. He won't need it till the school year, when we start doing the meetings and ceremonies."

Ranks? Uniforms? Ceremonies? Sean wasn't too crazy about all the soldierly jargon. He'd had about enough of quasi-military organizations overseas. Maybe this wasn't such a great idea after all. "Well," he said, backpedaling. "I'll let you know if he's interested."

"You know," said Frank, "if he really wants to see what it's like, he should come on our next camping trip. We're hiking Mount Frissell this weekend."

Sean agreed to propose this to Kevin, thanked Scoutmaster Quentzer for his time, and went to find his book, in no great hurry to discuss with his nephew what he'd deemed a nonstarter. He was up to *The Horse and His Boy* in *The Chronicles of Narnia*. Eventually Kevin came out of the den, glassy-eyed from long-term television exposure.

"Who were you talking to?" he asked.

Sean described the conversation he'd had with Frank Quentzer. "I don't think it's your cup of juice," he said. "Sounds pretty . . . regimented."

"They're climbing Mount Frissell? That's the highest point in Connecticut."

"No kidding." Thinking the conversation was winding down, Sean glanced back at his book and began skimming to where he'd left off.

"It's not the highest *summit* in Connecticut. That's Bear Mountain. See, Mount Frissell is on the line of Massachusetts, Connecticut, and New York, and the summit is in Massachusetts. But the part that's in Connecticut is the highest you can be in the whole state." Kevin plopped down onto the couch next to Sean, jostling the book in his hand. "Can I tell you something?"

"Sure."

"I have this . . . it's like a *list*. Like all the things I want to do someday?"

Sean gazed at the boy. A list. Probably everyone had a loose idea of the things they wanted to accomplish in their lives. It seemed kind of unusual to start so young, though. "What's on your list?"

Kevin seemed suddenly self-conscious. "I didn't write it down or anything. I don't walk around with a piece of paper or anything stupid like that."

"Got it. It's like a mental list."

"Yeah! And one thing I definitely want to do . . . you know, someday . . ." He took a breath as if he were about to reveal something dangerous and subversive. "I want to climb to all the highest places in every state. Every one. Even Mount McKinley. That's in Alaska."

Sean watched the boy's face glow with excitement. "How many have you done so far?"

Kevin slumped back against the couch. "Mount Washington, but it doesn't count."

"Mount Washington—that's huge. How could it not count?"

"Because we *drove* up. It was so lame." Deirdre had been trying out for a production of *The Sound of Music*, Kevin explained, and she wanted to feel what it was like to be on top of a really high mountain. New Hampshire was the closest she could get to the Alps without taking a plane. "We did it all in one day," he grumbled. "I threw up on the ride home."

"So it sounds like you might want to try Boy Scouts."

Kevin chewed at the inside of his cheek. "What if I don't like it?"

"Hey, I'm not pushing you, trust me. But if you went on just this one trip, you could count it toward your highest places."

"Okay," he said anxiously, as if it were a highly dangerous mission. "I'll go."

That night Sean called Frank Quentzer and told him that Kevin had decided to join them.

"That's great!" said Frank, his low voice rising slightly. "Now we can go." He explained that the other leader had backed out at the last minute, and he was about to call off the trip.

"You can't go with just one leader?" asked Sean.

"No, it's not safe if someone gets hurt, and it's against policy. No adult is supposed to be alone with kids, ever. Have to be two-deep at all times," he said. "It's great you can come."

"Wait—me? You thought I was coming?"

"Well . . . yeah. It's not that Kevin can't come without a guardian—that's fine and all. But I just assumed . . . I mean, you'd send him off with a bunch of guys he doesn't know?" Frank's voice was quiet, but the incredulity came through quite clearly. "You've never even met me."

Shame burned at Sean as if he'd just stumbled into a campfire. "Oh, God, no . . . I just . . . I didn't . . . I wasn't thinking. Of course I'll go. I love to camp." He hadn't technically camped since his teenage years with Hugh, but he was certainly comfortable in rustic conditions.

"Good to have you on board," said Frank. "You're going to love it."

CHAPTER 16

The next morning, Sean remembered that Chrissy Stillman was supposed to come over on Saturday, and he got a little ticked off about being shanghaied into the camping trip. Now he'd have to cancel with her because he'd be 150 miles away at the highest point in Connecticut. Which was sort of like saying he was blowing her off to visit the coldest place in Florida.

Okay, yes, they could reschedule. But she was obviously a busy person—maybe her interest in training George was more of a whim, Sean ruminated, and now that it was postponed she'd get committed to other projects, other dogs.

He called her, but only got voice mail. He left a message, but had a feeling it would be a while before she got back to him. She'd always been like that—sort of . . . *capricious* was the word that came to him.

This, of course, reminded him of Hugh, and how they had howled with hilarity over Auntie Vivvy's "secret capriciousness." It served to dial back his self-pity. Kevin, who for all intents and purposes was a friendless orphan, was more important than a stupid dog-training session. Even if it was with the woman of Sean's teenage—and possibly adult—dreams.

It would have helped to talk to Cormac about it. Cormac was a guy you could count on to commiserate and then tell you not to be an idiot. But he was no doubt at the Confectionary, up to his elbows in cruller dough or butter cream frosting, and not available for a pep talk.

Sean found himself dialing Tree of Life Spa. His back wasn't killing him, but it did ache, accelerating to a solid throb now and then. A massage would help him settle down, find his balance.

Chrissy Stillman had always had a way of throwing him off kilter, which was both intoxicating and exhausting at the same time.

"Rebecca's booked until next Thursday," Cleopatra told him with utter apathy.

"She's got no openings for a *week*?"

"Um, when you call on a Thursday, that's generally what 'booked until next Thursday' means."

Sean was about a nanosecond away from telling her to go—

"It's him," Cleopatra murmured, her voice aimed away from the mouthpiece. "Psycho high school stalker guy."

A distant voice groaned, *"Jesus, Brittany!"*

"Fine, talk to him yourself, then," she said.

Sean heard someone take a very deep breath and let it out. "Hello?" said the voice.

"Becky?"

"Hi, Sean."

"Hey, I was thinking of coming in, but your wacko receptionist says you're booked solid."

"I am. I'm just waiting for my next client."

"Really? You don't have anything for a whole week?"

"Yep," she said. "I have to go now, I'll talk to you later." And she clicked off.

Sean put the phone down. Becky had hung up on him. He didn't even know what to think about that.

A moment later the phone rang and he picked it up.

"Hey, sorry, I had to switch to my cell phone," Becky murmured furtively. "I wanted to tell you . . . I don't have to treat you here. You could come to my house."

"Really? That'd be great, because I—"

"The spa is closed Sundays and Mondays," she murmured. "That's when I see private pay clients."

"Not till Sunday?" Disappointment nibbled at him. He really wanted to see her today.

She didn't say anything for a moment, and he hoped she was

reconsidering. "Sundays and Mondays," she confirmed. "Here's my cell number. Call and let me know what time works for you." And she was gone again.

Sean called back immediately, hoping to convince her to let him come to her house that night, or even Friday night. He and Kevin would be leaving early Saturday morning for the camping trip and wouldn't be home until late Sunday afternoon. Her voice mail picked up. "This is Rebecca Feingold," said her calm, melodious voice. "Please leave a message, and I'll return your call as soon as I can." It still seemed strange to hear her refer to herself as Rebecca.

"Hey, Becky," he said. "If there's any way you could squeeze me in before the weekend . . . But if not, how about Sunday night—maybe around seven?" He hung up and chuckled to himself. It had almost sounded like he was begging her for a date.

The Belham Scout House was a nondescript little brown cabin tucked into the woods near the Town Beach. There was a gray Suburban SUV parked in front, and a bald guy with a slight paunch standing by the open rear gate. He wasn't actually doing anything himself but seemed simply to be watching the boys do the work of loading gear into the back of the vehicle.

Sean looked at Kevin. "Ready?" he said.

Kevin's face had that squinched-up look he got when he was anxious. "I only know one of those kids," he muttered, "and he's a jerk."

"I bet the others are really good guys."

"Doubt it," said Kevin.

"Hey," said Sean. "You wanted to come, remember? Highest peak in Connecticut and all that. Don't start off with a bad attitude."

Kevin lowered his chin and bit at the inside of his cheek.

Sean softened. "Besides, if they really are all jerks, you'll hang with me, we'll make the best of it, and the whole thing will be over tomorrow afternoon. You never have to come back."

Kevin cut his eyes toward Sean.

"Piece of cake," said Sean.

They took their stuff out of the Caprice and walked toward the group.

Sean went over and introduced himself. "Glad to have you with us," said Frank, though he didn't actually look all that glad. He had one of those faces that barely moved when he spoke. Sean wondered if he might have a mild case of Bell's palsy. Frank called to a boy of about fourteen who was heaving a cooler into the back of the Suburban.

"This is Jonathan," he told Kevin. "He's your senior patrol leader for the trip. That means he's in charge of all the boys."

"Hey," mumbled Kevin.

"Hey," said Jonathan. "That your stuff? Let's toss it in back." The two boys loaded the packs, and Jonathan took Kevin up to the scout house to get more supplies.

Once they had finished packing up, all six boys climbed into the back of the Suburban. Jonathan sat in the middle behind Frank and Sean, and Kevin sat to his left behind Frank. Sean could just see him out of the corner of his eye, staring out the window as they left the familiar confines of Belham behind.

"We've got a lot more kids in the troop than this," said Frank, apropos of nothing, as they pulled onto the Massachusetts Turnpike heading west.

"Oh?" said Sean.

"Yeah, but in the summer a lot of them are in camps or on vacation. Trips during the school year are bigger."

"That's good to know," said Sean, though he didn't really think Kevin would be around to experience these more populated expeditions. He wasn't sure if he was supposed to make conversation or just let Frank drive in peace. The boys wiggled and laughed in the back. Kevin continued to stare out the window.

"You like to camp?" Jonathan asked him.

"Um, yeah," muttered Kevin.

"Where've you gone?"

Kevin said something, but Jonathan couldn't hear him. "Where?" he asked again.

"*No*where."

"This your first trip?"

Sean could see Kevin deflate even further into the seat back. "Yeah."

"Excellent!" said Jonathan. "It's an honor to go with a guy on his first campout, you know. Hey!" he yelled to the others. "It's Kevin's first trip. Tell him what's good about camping."

"Food!" one of the guys yelled. "Yeah!" the others concurred. "Meatballs!" screamed another. Then there was a cacophonous chorus of all the foods the scouts liked. Pancakes with tons of syrup. Stew cooked in aluminum foil over the fire. Reflector-oven brownies.

"All right, settle down," said Jonathan. "He's gonna think we're a bunch of pigs."

"We are!" yelled a thin little voice.

"You need to work on that one, Ivan," another guy teased.

"Knives!"

"Yeah, whittling! Cutting stuff!"

"You got a knife?" Jonathan asked. Kevin shook his head.

"Good. You can't use a knife until you get your Totin' Chip. It's a badge that says you know all the safety rules and stuff. But you can get that pretty soon if you want."

Kevin's green eyes went round. "I can?"

"Yeah, you can use an axe, too."

Sean saw Kevin smile, and for a moment he looked just like Hugh.

The boys continued to call out the things they liked. Fires, fishing, magic cards. They laughed and teased and poked one another. Jonathan did a good job of keeping Kevin in the mix.

"It's important not to help too much," Frank said out of the blue.

If he thinks I'm the type to hover, thought Sean, *he's got another think coming.* Sean had never been fully responsible for another person his whole life. He'd never even babysat, other than for Deirdre and Hugh.

"Jonathan knows what to do," Frank went on. "They're supposed to go to him with problems or questions."

"Pretty big job for a kid his age."

"That's the point. Boy-led troop. If there's something they truly can't handle, they come to us. Or if something's getting out of hand. Otherwise we hang back." Frank nodded, and a hint of a smile emerged on his granite face. "Best management training program on the planet."

They pulled into Bash Bish Falls State Park around ten in the morning and began to unpack the gear into two side-by-side campsites. Frank's and Sean's stuff went to one site, the boys' to the other. Jonathan and a stocky round faced boy named Bodie, who was Frank's son, coordinated the setup of the three tents on their site. Kevin's tentmate was Ivan.

"He's the jerk," Kevin whispered to Sean, when they happened to head to the latrine at the same time. "He was in my class last year."

"Tell them you want to sleep with someone else."

"I'm not gonna do *that*," Kevin said with disgust. "I'll look like a baby!"

"Well, can you handle Ivan for one night?"

"Guess I'll have to," he grumbled.

When the tents were pitched and gear organized, Jonathan called them all over to a clearing in the trees for opening ceremony. He had hung a flag from a tree branch. The boys straggled over, talking and bumping each other.

"Signs up," said Jonathan. Everyone quieted and held up three fingers. Kevin looked over at Sean, mild panic on his face. Sean gave an almost imperceptible shrug, as if to say, *I have no idea, either.* He held up his three fingers, and Kevin followed his lead.

They said the pledge of allegiance, saluting the flag with three fingers extended toward their temples. Then they began to recite an oath. *On my honor I will do my best to do my duty . . .* Kevin watched the others intently, as if he could join in if he concentrated hard enough . . . *To help other people at all times* . . . Finally it ended. Kevin's relief was palpable.

But then they started something new! *A Scout is trustworthy, loyal, helpful, friendly,* they droned, *courteous, kind, obedient, cheerful, thrifty, brave, clean, and reverent.* They said it so fast it was hard to hear individual words.

"Okay, guys," said Jonathan. "I just want to remind you of the Leave No Trace policy, so I better not see any wrappers and stuff lying around. Bodie'll supervise lunch prep, so pack a sandwich, two snacks, fruit, some cookies, and lots of water. Full water bottles, okay? It's not too hot, but you're still going to need all of it on the hike."

Bodie had the boys line up by the picnic table to make themselves sandwiches. Ivan's only had grape jelly in it.

"You're gonna be really hungry if that's all you're bringing," warned Bodie.

"That other stuff's disgusting! It's highly processed," insisted Ivan, as he watched Bodie make himself a ham, turkey, Swiss cheese, and potato chip sandwich.

"Least I'll make it to the top without fainting," said Bodie. "But don't worry—if you pass out, I'll just fold you up and put you in my pack." He raised a hand and another kid slapped it.

They filled their water bottles, packed up their day packs, and got back into the car. After about twenty minutes they were on a dirt road, rocks spitting out from under the tires. Sean looked back to check on Kevin. He was staring out the window again, but this time he didn't look as if he were being hauled off to jail. His eyes glittered with the sunlight filling the car.

CHAPTER 17

The hike started off easily, and some of the boys raced ahead. Frank told Jonathan and Bodie to stop the group. He murmured something to the two older boys, and when they started again, Jonathan was at the front, setting a brisk but maintainable pace, Bodie at the back keeping the stragglers moving. Sean and Frank hiked a few paces behind Bodie.

The trail grew steeper. At some points they had to use their hands to help pull themselves up. Sean was a little worried about Frank. He was older, carrying some extra pounds, and his breathing seemed labored. Sean began to remind himself about CPR compression rounds.

"How you doing?" said Frank when they stopped to catch their breath about halfway up.

How'm I *doing?* thought Sean. *How're* you *doing?* "Good," he said. "Really gets the old ticker pumping, huh?"

"Yeah. Seriously, though, if you need a break, just take one," said Frank in that flat way he had. "You done much hiking?" he said. "You're looking a little pale."

"Yeah, it's that pasty Irish skin of mine," Sean quipped to hide his annoyance. "I always look like I just came out of hiding."

Frank gave the smallest possible chuckle in response. "Okay," he said. But he didn't seem completely convinced.

They reached the summit to find most of the boys digging through their day packs for snacks and water. Ivan said, "We made it!"

"No, we didn't," said Kevin, unwrapping a granola bar. The whole crowd of boys seemed to stop and look. It was the first time Kevin had spoken loudly enough for them all to hear. "This is just

Round Mountain," he explained, looking a little uncomfortable with all the attention. "It's on the way to Frissell."

"He's right," Jonathan confirmed. "Eat your snack, Ivan."

Ivan dropped down next to Kevin and pulled out a bag of pretzels. They didn't say anything to each other, but when Ivan had gone through about three-quarters of his pretzels, he held the bag out to Kevin. "Want the rest?" he said. Kevin took it and said, "Thanks."

The trail wound down off Round Mountain and into the valley between the two summits. Soon they were climbing straight up the southeast slope of Mount Frissell, the troop's pace slackening to account for the added difficulty. Sean climbed behind Frank, hoping the stocky man wouldn't slip and fall back onto him. But Frank was keeping up with the boys, and Sean found he had to struggle more than he'd expected to keep pace. He was ashamed to admit that without the daily exercise of lifting or holding down patients, carrying supplies, and constantly being on his feet, he wasn't in the best of shape.

They reached the top of their climb and took a little side trail to the summit of Mount Frissell, in Massachusetts. Then they hiked until they came to what looked to be a little greenish copper pipe sticking out of the ground. The plaque around it said MASSACHUSETTS CONNECTICUT STATE LINE, 1803, 1906. The boys each took turns balancing on the end of the little pipe.

"This is it," Sean murmured to Kevin. "Your first highest point."

Kevin grinned up at him. "Thanks for taking me," he said.

"Glad I could be part of it." And he was. He was proud of Kevin, and even a little envious—the boy had goals, which was more than he could say for himself at the moment.

The rest of the kids were getting bored and started back onto the trail.

"We're leaving?" Kevin looked slightly panicked.

"What's the matter?"

"I don't have any, like . . . proof." He looked around anxiously, as if there were something he could take with him that would serve as evidence of his accomplishment.

Frank hadn't seemed to be paying them any attention, but suddenly he was in front of them with his BlackBerry. "How about a picture?" he said. "You get in there, too, Uncle Sean." His phone camera made its artificial snapping noise, Frank studying the picture each time until he was satisfied. "That's a beaut," he said. Sean gave him Deirdre's e-mail address, and Frank sent the picture to her. It was the only way Sean could think of to take possession of it.

He looked at the picture in the tiny screen of Frank's BlackBerry. Kevin was grinning like he'd just won the lottery, his heathery green eyes twinkling with satisfaction. Sean glanced at himself and was a little taken aback. He *was* pale. And thin—his eye sockets seemed just a little too big for his eyes. There were threads of silver in the auburn hair by his temples. He hadn't seen a picture of himself in a long time and never spent much time in the mirror. He was middle-aged. There was no doubt about it.

And yet, despite all the obvious wear and tear, in the picture he looked happy—a proud accomplice to Kevin's momentous achievement.

The highest place. One down, forty-nine to go.

Back at the state park, Frank puttered around their campsite, setting up a camp stove, pulling things out of a cooler. He declined Sean's repeated offers to help, so Sean sat at the picnic table and watched the goings-on at the boys' campsite. Jonathan was supervising dinner preparation, while Bodie worked on "advancement."

"Who still needs cooking to get their Tenderfoot rank?" Bodie bellowed. Two boys raised their hands, and he shooed them over to Jonathan. He turned to Kevin. "You wanna be a scout?"

"Yeah," said Kevin nervously. "I guess."

"Okay, it's totally easy. Get your dad to get the forms from my dad. He has them in a folder in the car. Then come back to me." Sean saw Kevin flinch at the mistake and felt the same minor shock wave ripple through his own nervous system. Kevin mumbled something—Sean assumed it was a correction about their relationship—but Bodie didn't seem to notice as he turned to help another scout with a mess of rope the boy was struggling with.

Kevin approached. "Bodie says you have to fill out the forms."

Sean leaned forward. "Kev," he mumured. "You really want to do this? Because I don't have to fill out any forms unless you're definitely joining the troop."

Kevin chewed at the inside of his cheek. "I can quit if I hate it, right?"

"Yeah, but you shouldn't join unless you actually *like* it."

"I do," he said. "I like it. Most of it."

"What don't you like?"

"The latrines. They're disgusting."

Sean laughed. "That's it? That's the only thing you don't like?"

Kevin thought for a moment. "Yeah," he nodded. "That's pretty much it."

"Just pretend you're Bear Grylls, and pee in your water bottle," Sean teased. "That'll solve half your problem, right there."

Kevin laughed and gave him a little punch. It was the first time Sean could remember Kevin making voluntary physical contact.

Frank got the forms and a *Boy Scout Handbook*. "Take this over to Bodie and he'll tell you what to do." For the next half hour, every time Sean glanced over, Kevin was studying the book, murmuring to himself, or reciting something to Bodie. They worked on square knots. Then there was a safety pamphlet he had to go through with Sean. And that was it. He was a scout.

At the campfire after dinner, they all cheered him, and gave him left-handed handshakes, representing friendship with the hand nearest to their hearts. Then the real fun began.

"Who's got a joke?" called Jonathan; as the senior boy on the trip he served as emcee.

A boy got up. "Two cannibals are having dinner," he said. "One says to the other, 'I really hate my mother-in-law.' The other says, 'Relax. Have the potatoes.'"

They all laughed and heckled him. "Yum!" someone yelled.

Another boy got up. "A bear goes into a bar," he began. "No, wait! A bear goes into a gas station . . ." He started to giggle. "And he says to the guy . . . he says to the guy . . ." The boy began to laugh so hard he couldn't finish the joke. Half the boys began to laugh just because he couldn't stop laughing.

After a few more mostly horrible jokes, the boys performed the skits they'd practiced while Kevin had been studying his *Scout Handbook*.

Ivan got up and began to pace back and forth with his hand in the air. "Brains for sale, brains for sale," he called in a fairly believable German accent. "Who vants to buy Albert Einstein's brain?"

Another boy approached. "How much?"

"A sousand dollars!"

"I'll take it." He mimed taking the imaginary brain from Ivan and carrying it away.

Ivan continued on to sell the brains of Madame Curie, Leonardo da Vinci, and Shaquille O'Neal. Then he said, "Zis is zee most expensive brain of all! It costs a zillion dollars!"

"Why's it so expensive?" asked a skit mate.

"It is zee brain of Bodie Quentzer. It's never been used!"

"Bah, ha, ha! . . . Bodieeee! . . . Good one!" they yelled and poked Bodie, who took it with good-natured fury and raised a fist in mock anger, to the great satisfaction of Ivan.

The skits continued until several of the boys got up to sing a song. "Just a small-town girl . . ." they began. Sean had to laugh. "Don't Stop Believin'" by Journey had come out when he was in high school—about fifteen years before most of these boys had been born. They began to forget the words about halfway through, but he helped them along, belting out the line about rolling the dice, and got a whooping round of applause when it was over.

Eventually, Jonathan led them in "Scout Vespers," a quiet song to the tune of "O Christmas Tree." "Softly falls the light of day, while our campfire fades away . . ." sang the high, low, and changing voices.

They all got up and did a few last things to get ready for bed. Frank banked the fire.

"G'night," Sean said to Kevin.

"Good job with that song," Kevin said with a grin. "Can't wait to tell Aunt Dee."

"You better not!" warned Sean.

"I might have to," he teased.

Sean got to the tent before Frank and slid down into his sleeping bag. It had been a long day, but a good one. He rolled onto his side away from the zippered door of the tent, his muscles loosening into the thin pad beneath him, the gratifying feeling of physical exhaustion pulling him toward sleep.

In the murky hinterland at the edge of slumber, he found himself praying that Kevin was having a good time and that everything was okay at home. That Chrissy Stillman could fix whatever was wrong with George, and that Cormac and Barb would get pregnant soon. He was thankful to have such people to pray for—people he knew, not just random patients for whom his prayers often went unanswered. Then he sent up a prayer for all those who suffer and slipped into the distant forest of unconsciousness.

The ride back to Belham was notably more subdued than the trip to the campground had been the day before. True to their teenagerness, the two older boys slept. Ivan read a book, while the other two played cards. Kevin leaned his head against the window and stared out at the scenery speeding by, face slack with highway hypnosis and mild exhaustion.

When they arrived at the Scout House, parents collected their weary boys, guiding them into cars as if they suffered temporary fatigue-induced blindness.

"Bye, Kevin!" called Ivan as he disappeared into a minivan.

"He's really not that mean," Kevin confided as Sean started up the Caprice. "He just like . . . talks. Like he says whatever he's thinking. And he's super smart so sometimes he sounds like he thinks other people are dumb. It's weird—he hums when he goes to sleep, like he's waiting for his brain to slow down or something. Kind of annoying."

"Hey, I can beat that," said Sean. "Mr. Quentzer uses a CPAP machine. It's this face mask attached to a battery-powered motor that pushes air into his mouth, so he can breathe better when he sleeps."

"You had a *motor* in your tent?"

"Yep."

"I'll stick with the hummer."

Sean laughed. "Good decision."

CHAPTER 18

Pulling into the driveway at Rebecca's house that evening was like stepping into a time warp of his teenage years. Everything was exactly as Sean remembered it, down to the overgrown rhododendrons and the seasick-green color of the shingles.

They must have painted it in the past twenty years, thought Sean. *And they picked that same pukey color again.*

Rebecca answered the door. "Hey, it's Smokey the Bear," she teased.

"Complete with a whole new set of camping-related aches and pains."

Inside, the same oversized brown leather couches crowded the living room, the same heavy brocade curtains shut out what little light slipped around the edges of the rhododendrons. Sean didn't say a word, but Rebecca responded as if he had. "It's like being trapped in a *Groundhog Day* of my childhood," she said, sighing.

He looked at her. She shook her head. "They like it this way, and it's their house."

"They come back for the summer?" he asked.

"No. They actually never come back. They think Florida is the Promised Land, but with better amenities. But it's their house," she repeated. "They don't like to change anything."

Sean flopped down onto an enormous leather recliner. "I've sat in worse," he said.

She slipped into the corner of the couch nearest his chair. "Way worse, I'm sure."

"But it's not about comfort, is it?"

"No." She sighed again and muttered, "I really have to get out of here sometime soon."

"The holding pen versus jumping-off point problem. What's stopping you?"

"Money, for one thing."

This surprised him. He paid eighty dollars for an hour of massage. Admittedly he didn't have much experience with what a normal paycheck should look like, but that sounded like a lot to him. "Tree of Life doesn't cover the bills?" he asked.

She let out a disgusted little hiss. "I know—eighty bucks, right? You'd think I was rolling in dough. But Eden doesn't give us much of a cut."

Sean thought she was making a play on words, but she explained, "Eden's the owner. Her real name's Edna, but she changed it to Eden when she came up with 'Tree of Life' for the spa name. It's a chain now. She's got about ten of them spread out all over New England." A little play of mirth came over her face. "She drives a lime-green Mercedes. Specially painted."

"Come on," Sean scoffed.

"I kid you not."

"Sounds like a piece of work."

Rebecca rolled her eyes. "You have no idea. Missy *hates* her. Apparently she comes in for free massages and doesn't even tip!"

"Why don't you go somewhere else?"

"It's steady. She offers health insurance, which most places don't. It's a bare bones policy, but if I come down with malaria or something, I don't have to pay the whole tab." She shook her head. "I don't know. Sometimes I think it's just inertia." She glanced up at him. "I guess we should get going."

"What did you do before you went to massage school?" he asked, anxious to get to the massage but somehow even more interested in the story of how she'd found an occupation she was so good at.

"I was a copy editor. At the time I was doing medical texts, and I was editing a book on neurology that had some really interesting sections on alternative treatment. The massage thing hit me like a bolt. I started reading books about it." She grinned. "I actually started by practicing on my grandmother. She was the one who pushed me to go to school for it."

"She was your jumping-off point. She must be really proud of you."

"She was," said Rebecca, a soft sadness creeping into her smile. "She died a couple of years ago."

"I'm sorry." He reached out over the expanse of the chair's cracked leather arm to squeeze her hand, a reflex from when news of a loved one's death was a daily occurrence. Rebecca looked down at his freckled hand covering her olive-toned fingers. He withdrew it, feeling suddenly uncertain.

"So," he said, searching for something to say. "You must be pretty exhausted by the end of the day, with all that physical labor."

"Yes and no. I mean, it's work, and it can be tiring. But it's also very . . . it's good for me. I've gotten a lot of clarity doing massage." She started to shift in her seat as if to rise. But Sean stayed put, hoping that she would settle back and say more.

"When you're treating patients," she asked, "do you ever pick up on their mood, or their . . . sense of things? Do you ever feel what's happening below the surface?"

He had to think about it for a moment. He wanted to say yes, wanted to have that talent in common with her. But he couldn't lie. "Not really," he said. "Generally they're just in pain and unhappy. It isn't all that hard to pick up on."

She nodded, but he could tell she'd hoped for more from him. "In massage, we're trained to recognize energy. I know that sounds New Agey, but once you learn to do it, you can't not. It's more than just someone's mood, or how they're feeling in the moment. Our bodies are constantly struggling to achieve balance, and we do that with energy. Does that make sense?"

"Sort of . . ."

"Okay, so if a client comes in and his energy is really out of whack, I can feel it. And I have to be careful to keep my energy in balance, because we affect each other, right? You know how some people just make you feel good because they're calm and clear, and other people bring you down, and you don't even really know why? That's energy."

"Hmm," he murmured. "How's mine?"

"How's your energy?" She was obviously stalling.

"No, my cholesterol," he said wryly.

"Um . . ." She grinned. "I'd say you need to cut down on the fried foods."

The room she led him to, up the half flight of stairs from the living room, had metallic wallpaper with a dizzying pattern of little brown and blue circles.

"Nineteen seventies?" he asked.

She nodded. "It was the guest bedroom. Can you imagine anyone getting any sleep in here?" She had moved the bed into one corner, but the room was still crowded with an oversized chest of drawers, a desk, and a floor-to-ceiling pole lamp with five orange metal shades. The massage table stood in the middle, as incongruous as a sunflower growing in a crowded parking lot. She left him to get undressed and he surveyed the room. It wouldn't take much to make it more conducive to her business. She could take a few things out, maybe take down the wallpaper.

He slid under the sheet, put his face in the doughnut cushion, and, mercifully, the room's décor ceased to exist for him. When she came back in, she turned on a CD of soft instrumental music. "I could help you move some stuff out of here," he said.

"I'd have to get the okay from my parents."

"Maybe not. Maybe we just move it, and if they visit we move it back, no harm done."

Her hands began to swirl across his back, and he felt his body respond, every nerve curling to her touch like a cat around its owner's legs. He barely noticed when she changed the subject without answering the question. "Tell me more about Africa," she said, and he complied, knowing that if she'd told him to rob a bank, he would have done that, too.

The small hospital in which he'd worked had open-air buildings, he told her. "Even the operating room. Flies landed in open wounds all the time." After surgery, if they were crowded and didn't have enough space, which was often, they'd put two patients in the same bed. The families of the sick would often sleep under the bed, especially if it was the mother. The children had to be with her. "Child care is strictly women's work. There's no such thing as a stay-at-home father. A man might be home if he's unemployed, but he doesn't watch the kids."

"What did they think of you being a nurse?"

"The patients usually assumed I was a doctor, just not a very good one."

He didn't mind that, though, he told her. He'd been all over the globe, and generally people found a way to make you fit into their worldview. Once they got to know you, you stopped being a failed doctor and were just the guy they could bring a sick child or injured friend to. "And they could tell me their stories. I think they liked that almost as much as getting fixed up. When I stopped being able to listen, that's when I knew I had to take a break."

"Why couldn't you listen, do you think?"

"I just got burned out."

"Was there anything that triggered it?" She had worked her way to his feet, and he braced himself against the pain he knew would come. "Relax," she said. "You don't have to tell me."

He felt the strength of her hands, though she squeezed only gently at his heels. "How's my energy now?" he said, trying not to grit his teeth.

"Unstable," she said. "How's mine?"

"I have no idea."

She laughed. "Good. Then I'm keeping it in the background, like a good massage therapist should."

Once he'd made it through the ordeal of his feet, he could feel the tension drain from the rest of his body, too. It was time for him to flip over, and she held the sheet for him. She came around behind and began to work on his neck and shoulders, and he found himself gazing at her through half-open eyes. Her oddly shaped face was so familiar to him. Her wavy brown hair bounced slightly as she moved.

"I stopped believing in a God who cared," he confessed to her, surprising himself.

She thought about this. "You lost your faith in the face of all that suffering."

He closed his eyes. It was embarrassing to admit, but it wasn't really the suffering that had gotten to him. "It's way more selfish than that," he said. "I stopped believing in a God who cared about *me*." He felt tension rise in his throat and behind his eyes. Her fingers moved down from his scalp and around his eye sockets, as if they were following the pain across his face.

"Why?" she asked.

"Because I wasn't who I thought I was. I thought God had *chosen* me. Yes, I would die young, but I was called to do something extraordinary. By God. Do you see?"

Her warm fingers pressed at his temples. "And now it feels like God pulled a fast one."

He let out a groan. It sounded so childish and self-centered. But it was a belief born in the self-absorption of adolescence and in the wake of loss. His mother and then his father. An abbreviated future. There had to be a reason for it. God had given him that reason. And now it appeared as if he'd lived a life of hardship and self-denial for no reason at all. A fast one, indeed.

"So now you know why my fucking energy's unstable."

She rested a hand on his chest for a moment. "It's a really good reason," she said. In silence, she continued down his arms, and then to his legs, corralling his pain—his energy—in that way she had. He understood it a little better now.

"You know," she said, as she kneaded his calf. "I think you might be a Jew."

A quick laugh burst out of him. "How d'you figure?"

"We consider ourselves God's chosen people, and look how *that's* turned out. Pure trouble for the entire history of Judaism."

"You've got a point," he admitted.

"But also, your life has been one long mitzvah—an endless good deed. That's very important to Jews."

"So you're saying I should go to Hebrew school now?"

"No." He could hear the smile in her voice. "I'm just saying you're in good company. Isn't it what your patients wanted? First to get fixed up, and then to know they're not alone."

After she left the room and he got dressed, he loosened the screw that held the hideous pole lamp to the ceiling and took it down to the living room where she was waiting. It felt like some kind of post-modern spear in his hand. "You have a closet I can put this in?" he said.

"Sean . . ."

"Consider it a mitzvah."

She sighed and led him to a small storage room near the garage, where he stowed it carefully. "Mazel tov," he said, putting an arm around her shoulder and giving a little squeeze. "Am I saying that right?"

"Yeah, you're practically Rabbi Schechter."

"Who's that?"

She smiled and closed the storage room door. "Never mind."

He didn't feel like leaving. She'd always told him to drink lots of water after a massage, so he asked for a glass and sipped it slowly. They sat in the living room, on opposite ends of the vast cracked leather couch.

"Just one room," he said. "Why can't you have just one room the way you want it?"

"You wouldn't understand."

"How about giving me a shot?"

She shook her head in frustration. "I'm sorry, I don't mean to . . . it's just . . . my situation is the opposite of yours. You never felt the pressure to stay and be what people wanted."

He hadn't thought of himself that way—in fact he'd felt enormous pressure to do what he thought *God* had wanted. But he could see her point. And he remembered her parents. "Your folks were kind of hoverers, weren't they? They kept a close rein."

"Yeah, a little," she said sarcastically. "I guess, in fairness to them, they were just worried."

"Why? You were a good kid. You were smart and never got in any trouble that I knew of."

"Sean, look at me."

"What?"

"Jesus, Sean. Either you're being dense or you're faking."

He was startled by this. Becky was generally so nonconfrontational. But he remembered that she could pack a punch when she felt pressed.

"My *face*, Sean," she said, an index finger twitching up toward the side of her head that swelled out like an unexpected hill on an otherwise smooth landscape. "Kids teased me constantly. I was shy. I cried a lot. And I was their *only child*—there was no one else to take a share of their worry off my plate. Of *course* they hovered."

"All right. But that was a long time ago. You're a grown-up now. They don't still need to control your every move." It was obvious by the look she gave him that he still didn't get it. "Beck, do you feel like you owe them something for taking care of you all those years?"

"Uhh!" she groaned, her hands flying up in frustration. If there was anything to this "energy" theory, Sean could feel it then. Definitely very unstable. Rebecca took a deep breath and let it out. "Look, here's the difference between you and me."

She told him a story. One day back in high school, she had stayed late to work on a science lab and missed the bus. She was walking home in a heavy rain when a car pulled up. "It was your aunt, offering me a ride." Rebecca had been feeling particularly sorry for herself that day. Someone had said something mean. When Aunt Vivian questioned why she hadn't taken the bus, Rebecca had admitted somewhat bitterly that honors chemistry was just too hard.

"You know what she said? She said, 'You're an intelligent young woman. I'm sure you'll find a solution.' Not one ounce of sympathy for the poor, sad deformed girl! In fact, when she dropped me off and I thanked her for the ride, her answer was, 'Consider investing in a raincoat.' It was a total kick in the pants!"

"Vintage Aunt Viv." He nodded. "She never put up with whining of any kind."

"She expected you to manage your own needs, and she didn't ask you to manage hers. You see the difference, right? With my parents we manage each other constantly. Trust me, when your whole relationship is built on it, that's a tough habit to break."

It was late, and though he could have sat there and talked all night like they used to, he knew it was time to leave. He pulled five twenties out of his wallet, glad he'd remembered to cash his paycheck from the Confectionary before he left for the Mount Frissell trip.

"I only charge fifty when it's at my house," she said.

"Why? Are you any less effective here?"

She rolled her eyes at the obviousness of the point he was making. "No. But even at fifty I end up with way more than I'd get at Tree of Life."

"Speaking as your average self-centered client, I really don't care what you end up with. I care that I got a kickass massage, as good as or better than what I'd get at that nuthouse you call a spa."

She narrowed her eyes at him. He took her hand and closed her fingers around the bills. "Tip's included," he said. "And since I plan to have all my massages here from now on, I should warn you that every time I come, I'm taking something out of that room."

On the ride home through the lamplit streets of Belham, he ruminated on what she'd said about the difference between her parents and his aunt. Opposite ends of the spectrum, from "We're involved in every move you make" to "You're on your own." And although as a kid he'd always wished for someone who'd look out for him a bit more, Becky had a point. At least he didn't feel he owed Aunt Vivvy the way Becky seemed to feel she owed her parents. He'd earned the right to go his own way. It was something to be thankful for.

CHAPTER 19

The next afternoon the lights went out. Sean had beat an incoming squall on his way home from the Confectionary, the sky growing heavy and dark as he walked, pelting buttons of rain just as he reached the front porch. He had walked through the house turning on lights and gone up to change his clothes. Ten minutes later, the house was dark again.

"Hey, what's the deal?" Kevin hollered from the den where he'd been watching TV.

George started to bark, and Aunt Vivvy emerged from the kitchen. "I didn't hear any thunder," she said to Sean as he descended the stairs.

"Maybe a limb came down." Sean went out on the front porch to see if the neighbors were also in the dark, but their curtains glowed with lamplight.

"Looks like it's just us," he said. "I'll call NSTAR." He asked his aunt for a recent bill so he could find their emergency number, and she went into the den and pulled open the file drawer of her burled maple desk. She handed him an envelope marked NSTAR.

Sean did not immediately locate the number. He was too distracted by the message in bold capital letters across the top of the bill.

THIS IS YOUR THIRD AND FINAL NOTICE.

Wordlessly, he held the bill out to Aunt Vivian. She squinted at it for a moment, then her gaze locked on Sean's. "I paid that bill," she said.

And though it was the same light-saber glare that had so often reduced him to a stammering child, this time he was able to say, "They don't seem to think you did."

Aunt Vivian stalked out of the room, followed by George.

"Auntie Vivvy didn't send the money?" Kevin said, as if he'd just witnessed something as incongruous as his elderly aunt break dancing.

Sean called NSTAR. They hadn't received payment in three months. "We make mistakes," said the friendly customer service representative, "but not very often. We'll put the power back on as a temporary measure. I'd advise you to check her bank account to confirm whether the checks were written and cashed."

Sean looked though the file folder and found three payment envelopes, all containing checks written in her tight, precise handwriting.

He found her sitting on the edge of her bed. He'd only been in her room a couple of times when he was young and didn't remember many details. It smelled of talcum powder. It had lacy curtains and a cameo brooch sitting on a doily on the mahogany dresser. It seemed like the quarters of a woman whose life had been halted somewhere in the 1940s.

George barked dementedly until Aunt Vivian shushed her. And though she looked as angry as a wronged lover, Sean sat down on the bed next to her.

"I didn't realize," she growled. "I had no idea."

"Of course you didn't. You wouldn't knowingly leave your bills unpaid."

She cut her eyes at him, then quickly looked away. "Well, what do you suggest?" she said. "You didn't come up here without a plan in mind."

"Actually, my plan was to ask you the same thing."

She softened a little at this. He'd shown respect for what was left of her mental faculties, and he could sense her appreciation. "You'll take over the bills," she conceded.

"Or I could sign you up for one of those bill-paying services."

She smiled coldly. "Maintaining a viable escape route, I see."

He didn't answer. They both knew it was true.

The next morning Chrissy Stillman showed up unexpectedly. Her blindingly beautiful smile made Sean blink like a startled baby when he opened the door. "Chrissy! Hi!" he said, sounding weirdly breathless to himself.

The width of her smile narrowed slightly. "You got my message, right?"

There was a rapid click behind him, like the ticking of an overwound metronome, the attending growl growing deeper and more aggravated. Chrissy glanced over Sean's shoulder to the staircase behind him, and a strange look came over her. Like she was about to do battle and could hardly wait to start swinging her sword.

George stood at the bottom of the stairs staring back. She barked once.

A noise came out of Chrissy. *Chtch!*

George barked again. She looked at Sean and back to Chrissy, and though Sean had never before considered that George might have actual thoughts, he felt he could practically hear the dog thinking, *And who in the hell is* this?

Chrissy turned to Sean and put her hands on her hips. "Put the dog in another room, please," she instructed.

Put the dog . . . ? Sean had never even *patted* George before, much less directed her movements. "Let me get my aunt," he said, knowing he had probably just emasculated himself in Chrissy's eyes. He went up and knocked gently on Aunt Vivvy's door, and explained the situation to her. "I thought it would be helpful . . ." he murmured, and "I didn't expect her to come so soon . . ." He sounded like he was trying to avoid being punished.

When Aunt Vivvy came down the stairs with him she eyed Chrissy. "Mrs. Cavicchio," she said. "A pleasure to see you again."

"Vivian Preston!" She turned to Sean. "This is your aunt? *Vivian Preston?*"

"Uh, yeah . . ." he stammered.

But Chrissy didn't wait for his answer, stepping forward to take Aunt Vivian's small weathered hand in her own smooth lotioned one. "Vivian, I still can't thank you enough for the magic you and the Garden Club worked on the median near our house a couple of years ago."

There was a second or two when Aunt Vivian's gaze seemed vague, and Sean guessed that she had no memory of the magically transformed median. But she smiled politely and said, "I'm pleased to accept your compliment on the club's behalf," and slid her hand from Chrissy's.

George had sidled up to Aunt Vivvy and begun to growl again. "Shush now," she told the dog. George leaned her head toward Chrissy and sniffed tentatively.

"Thatsa girl," Chrissy purred. "Figure me out. You'll get the picture soon enough."

She asked a series of questions about the dog: where did it come from, what were its likely breeds, any information about prior masters, and the like.

"She was left at Man's Best Friend Animal Shelter and was about to be euthanized," said Aunt Vivian. "There was no other information."

"A rescue dog." Chrissy gave an approving nod. "German shepherd and Labrador mix, I'm fairly certain," she told them. "Such a wonderful combination of protectiveness and loyalty. Now that she's calm, is there somewhere we can all sit and discuss George's needs?"

They moved into the living room, and Kevin wandered out of the den to join them. The first thing Chrissy wanted to know was who regularly walked the dog. Sean and Kevin glanced furtively at each other.

"No one walks the dog," Aunt Vivian said matter-of-factly. "The dog prefers to be with me, and I am not entirely mobile."

"Ah," said Chrissy, nodding sagely. "You are the queen."

"Pardon me?" A slight edge of irritation rose in Aunt Vivvy's voice.

"Every domesticated dog needs a master, one person she's ultimately devoted to. But George is not a small, inside kind of dog. She's a large dog with muscles that require a thorough daily workout. If her master can't provide that, then we need to involve an additional person who can. I call this the English Monarchy Scenario."

"You are suggesting that George needs a prime minister." Aunt Vivvy's gaze swung almost imperceptibly toward Sean.

A prime minister, he thought. *That's pretty much what the whole freakin' family needs.*

"Exactly," said Chrissy. "Now. My understanding from you, Sean, is that your plans are . . . ?"

"In flux," he said.

"I'm sorry, but that's just not going to work for George." Chrissy said it as if to apologize for disappointing news. Sean mentally high-fived himself. "She needs someone who'll be in her life for the duration," Chrissy went on. "Isn't that what we all need? At least one person we can rely on to be there for us no matter what?" Her voice went just a little quavery, as if referring to something raw and unhealed in her own life. Sean wondered how a woman like Chrissy had ever hitched her wagon to a jackass like Ricky Cavicchio.

Chrissy sighed. Then she glanced over to Kevin, who'd been watching this scene play out like a reality TV show—entertaining but with an outcome on which he had absolutely no impact. "Kevin," she said, a certain amount of pomp creeping into her tone, "would you be willing to be George's prime minister?"

"Uh . . . sure." He looked confused. "Wait, what?"

"It's just like England," Chrissy explained. "The queen—your aunt—is the beneficent figurehead, the emotional leader of her people. *You* are the man of action, the one who calls the shots and gets things done!"

Vivian Preston's laser gaze turned toward her youngest nephew and she said, "I'm quite certain you're up to the task."

There was a search for the dog's leash, which was suspected to be in the garden shed out back. Kevin grumbled to himself as he and Sean dug around empty planters and bags of potting soil. Finally he said, "I don't want to be the prime minister! I just want to be a kid!"

Sean put down the bottles of Roundup and turned to Kevin. "I know," he said. "But I kinda need you on this one. I don't know how long I'm going to be around, so I'm really not the right guy for the job."

"Yeah, I know," Kevin muttered. *"Flux."*

It stung. Just as it was meant to.

"Hey," said Sean defensively, "this might actually work out for you. If you're George's prime minister, she has to obey you. That'll be a whole lot better than having her threatening to take a chunk out of you every time you walk in the door."

Kevin tugged the leash out from behind a bag of Holly-tone, rolled his eyes, and left Sean standing in the shed.

Sean was not invited to any further involvement in George's training—or as Chrissy said, *Kevin's* training—which surprised and disappointed him. The dog thing was all well and good, but his original intention was to have more time with Chrissy. This, like so many other things these days, wasn't working out as planned. He watched from the porch as she helped Aunt Vivvy down the steps to the yard.

"Now, Vivian," Chrissy went on. "We are about to conduct a peaceful transfer of power. George will worry that a coup is taking place, so it's *your* job to assure her that you approve of Kevin's authority." Sean had to stifle a laugh. He'd never seen anyone try to inform his aunt of her duties, and she looked none too thrilled about it.

Chrissy instructed Aunt Vivvy to show George that she was handing the leash to Kevin. They did this several times. To Sean's surprise, George studied the motion with great attentiveness. Then Aunt Vivvy was instructed to take Kevin's hand and guide him to pet

George. The dog started to growl but Chrissy corrected her with the *chtch!* sound.

Sean watched Kevin's face change from fear to interest as he patted the dog. "She's soft," he said.

Once it was clear that the dog would put up with Kevin's touch, Chrissy said, "Vivian, would you please explain to George what's happening, and what you expect from her?"

"Pardon me?" Aunt Vivvy's annoyance was abundantly evident, but Chrissy either didn't see it or chose to ignore it.

"You need to explain to her—in words—that Kevin is now in charge of her daily tasks and that you expect her full compliance."

Aunt Vivvy shot an irritated glance up to Sean on the porch. He offered an apologetic shrug, but what could he do—interrupt the Oath of Office? At that distance he couldn't hear every word, but coaxed along by Chrissy, Aunt Vivvy muttered something that boiled down to "Do as you're told and don't intimidate Kevin."

Then they walked together up and down the driveway, ambling slowly to accommodate Aunt Vivvy's pace. George seemed to tolerate Kevin's holding the leash and his fingers' wandering into the soft fur behind her ears when they stopped for further instructions. Then it was time for what Chrissy called an "I'm the Boss" walk. Aunt Vivvy and Sean watched from the porch as Chrissy and Kevin power-walked down the street with George, Kevin skipping every few steps to keep up.

"That seemed to go pretty well," said Sean.

"I'm surprised she didn't make me tap him on both shoulders with my scepter," Aunt Vivvy said drily. She turned and went into the house.

Chrissy and Kevin were gone for quite some time, and Sean went in when he heard the phone ring. It was Cormac, canceling their standing night at The Pal. Barb had an appointment, and she wanted Cormac with her. Sean didn't ask what kind of appointment, but he assumed it had something to do with their fertility issues.

"But hey," said Cormac, "how about coming over for dinner Thursday night? Barb says it's been too long since she's seen you."

"Great." Sean was a little disappointed, though. He'd been looking forward to talking about Chrissy tonight. Not that there was all that much to say. But still, it was fun to imagine that someday there might be. It gave Sean an idea. "Guess who's here right now." And he told Cormac about Chrissy and the dog training. "What if, um . . . Any chance maybe I could bring her along on Thursday? I mean she's probably not available, but if she was . . ."

"Absolutely! It'll be a mini-reunion. I know—I'll call Dougie and Cavicchio and we'll make it a party!" Cormac laughed dementedly at the idea.

"You're an idiot, you know that?" But Sean couldn't help but laugh, too. A more awkward assembly of characters was hard to imagine.

When the power-walkers finally returned, the prime minister looked sweaty and tired and went immediately to the den to watch TV. George trotted upstairs to Buckingham Palace. Chrissy's skin glowed. "That was great!" she gushed. "Wasn't it? Didn't you think it went just *super*?"

"I never would've believed it," said Sean, trying not to stare at the glistening plane of dampness below her collarbone. "You cast one heck of a spell over the three of them."

She grinned coyly. "Thanks for believing in me. You have no idea how much I need the encouragement."

She seemed utterly fearless to him—issuing commands and achieving compliance from his aunt and her murderous dog as if she were born to be saluted. But he knew that how people seemed on the outside was often very different from how they felt on the inside. And he was honored to be privy to her secret insecurity.

She told him she'd be returning on Thursday to continue working with Kevin and George, and he told her about the invitation to dinner at Cormac's.

"Cormac McGrath," she said, tapping a finger against her full lips as if it would jog her memory. "He was that really . . ." she waved her hands up above her head.

"Yeah, he's pretty big. Great guy—he owns the Confectionary. And his wife is very nice," he said. "I know you'll like her."

"Of course! Cormac's Confectionary. Why didn't I put two and two together?" She laughed. "So . . . I'll see you Thursday?"

"I'll be here."

She gave his cheek a little peck and walked to her car.

CHAPTER 20

When she came back on Thursday and learned that George hadn't been walked, Chrissy gave Kevin and Sean a bit of a talking-to.

"Remember how we said George needs vigorous daily exercise?"

"Yeah . . ." Kevin looked away and chewed at the inside of his cheek.

"Daily means *every day*, not just when you feel like it." Chrissy smiled as she said this, but it seemed incongruous with her tone. She looked up at Sean. "You really have to take more responsibility for reminding him."

"Absolutely," said Sean. "I think we're all just getting in a groove with this whole thing. But we're definitely on the upswing. Right, Kev?"

Kevin shrugged and tried to clip the leash on George's collar. The dog set off a warning growl.

"Chtch!" hissed Chrissy, and the growling stopped. "See, this is what I'm saying. Consistency, consistency, consistency. It's just like with kids. If the rules only hold some of the time, they'll never behave."

She had Kevin do a short walk on his own with George, just up the street and back. "Exercise is the number one thing we need to provide our dogs," she continued to chide Sean. "Without exercise they get all moody and sluggish—just like people! You wouldn't let Kevin sit around watching TV day after day, would you? Of course not."

In fact, that was exactly what Kevin had been doing. For weeks. Ever since the teenagers had chased him out of the woods he'd gone from an outdoor kid to an indoor kid. A wave of guilt washed over Sean. He'd felt so proud of himself for taking Kevin on the camping trip, but it had been one day of fresh air and exercise amid many days of wandering the wasteland of TV.

When Kevin came back, Chrissy accompanied him on a longer walk, and Sean went inside to make a phone call.

Frank Quentzer didn't have any further weekend trips planned for the troop until the end of August. "But there's camp. I didn't mention it because it's a lot to take on when you've only been a scout for a week." The troop was going on their annual week-long trip to Camp Yawgoog, a scout reservation in Rhode Island, he told Sean. There was swimming and hiking and rifle shooting, innumerable badges to be earned and campfires to be built. It sounded perfect.

Frank seemed hesitant. "Has he ever been away from home without a parent before?"

He's lived half his life without a parent, Sean wanted to say. *The kid's practically on his own as it is.* He told Frank he'd get back to him after talking with Kevin.

"Can you come, too?" Kevin asked warily.

"I'd like to," said Sean. A break from the family drama sounded pretty appealing. "But things are a little dicey around here. Deirdre's practically living at the theater these days, and I don't think it's a good idea for me to leave Auntie Vivvy alone for a whole week."

"But *I'd* have to go alone?"

"Hey, it's not like you'd be bushwhacking through the frozen tundra by yourself."

"You don't bushwhack through frozen tundra," Kevin muttered. "There's no bushes to *whack*."

"The point is you'd be with Mr. Quentzer and the troop. You're okay with those guys, right? Bodie and Ivan and everyone?"

Kevin's face went tight with anxiety. "What if I don't like it?"

"It's camping—you love camping!" Sean knew he was overselling, which was confirmed by Kevin's you-don't-get-it look. "Okay, listen," he said. "I know it stinks not being able to go up to Jansen Woods anymore. But you can't sit around here watching TV all day. It's just . . . *bad* for you. So if you don't want to go to Boy Scout camp, I think we're going to have to come up with some serious limits on TV watching. It's your choice."

Kevin gave a resigned huff. "Will you come and get me if I don't like it?"

"Absolutely." He dearly hoped he wouldn't have to load Aunt Vivvy and George in the decrepit Caprice and hazard a five-hour round-trip, but if that's what it took . . .

Kevin's face softened into a wry grin. "And you'll be George's prime minister *every day*—not just when you *feel* like it?" he said, mimicking Chrissy's rebuke.

Sean laughed. "You got it. I'll wear that beast out."

Sean took the Caprice over to the car wash and ordered up "the works": interior, exterior—everything down to Armor All on the tires. It still looked like a bucket of bolts. He considered meeting Chrissy at Cormac's to avoid having her sit on the cracked vinyl seat, but he'd already offered to pick her up.

"What a gorgeous antique!" Chrissy said when he opened the passenger side door for her in front of her triple-bay garage. "You should take it to one of those auto refurbishers so you could drive it in parades."

Why in God's name would I ever do that? was the first thing that came to mind. "That's a thought," he said. "I'll bet my aunt would love that." But she wouldn't. She would find it self-indulgent and undignified, and he knew it.

On the ride over, Chrissy asked about Cormac and the Confectionary and to be reminded of his wife's name. It was clear that she wanted to make a good impression, and the thought of it—her hoping to fit in with his friends—made the air seem to vibrate with his good fortune. Chrissy Stillman was sitting next to him in his car. He was taking her somewhere important to him. Every mile was a teenage fantasy.

"Cormac!" Chrissy threw her arms around him like an old friend when he opened the door. "Gosh, it's great to see you again."

Cormac grinned, his eyes flicking almost imperceptibly to Sean. "Good to see you, too, Chrissy. Been a lot of years."

It wasn't lost on Sean that Cormac had seen her at the Confectionary any number of times, and she simply hadn't recognized him despite his conspicuous stature or the fact that his unusual name was on the sign. But Cormac was on his best behavior, and Sean was grateful.

Sean gave Barb a hug. "Hey, picture taker," he murmured in her ear, and she gave him an extra little squeeze. He introduced her to Chrissy, who greeted her warmly and complimented her on the earrings and necklace with the hearts and little pink gemstones. "I got one of my girls the same set a couple of years ago! Target, right? Or was it Walmart?"

"Um . . ." Barb's smile lost a couple of watts. "Target. I just thought they were cute."

"They're adorable. And such a bargain."

The four of them sat in the tiny living room on the squishy sofas with their drinks.

"I love your house," said Chrissy. "It's so cozy. You can really find each other in a place like this. Want to hear the dumbest thing? At our house we actually had an intercom installed. It's so embarrassing, needing a gadget to find your kids." She sipped her drink. "Or your husband. Actually, I practically needed LoJack to find *him*." She gave a bitter little chuckle.

Barb's and Cormac's eyes found each other. Barb stood up. "Let me just check on that roast," she said, and headed for the kitchen.

Chrissy watched her take the five steps toward the stove. "See, this is nice," she said. "Barb can check on dinner and she doesn't even have to leave the conversation."

The three of them reminisced about high school—teachers they remembered, the few friends they'd had in common. "And can you believe Dougie Shaw is a *cop*?" Chrissy said. "That kid was certifiable. You remember him in the wedding dress at the homecoming game? Seriously, I can't believe he didn't end up in a mental ward somewhere."

"Oh, he just had a score to settle with your ex-husband," Cormac said affably.

"What score? And how do you settle anything by *proposing* to another guy in public?"

"Well . . ." Cormac shifted in his seat, considering how to respond. "Ricky was kind of . . . hard on him sometimes. I think Dougie just wanted to play a little joke to get him back."

Chrissy let out a derisive snort. "Psycho," she muttered, and shook her head.

She didn't know, Sean wanted to tell Cormac. *She had no idea Cavicchio was such an ass. But she knows now, so give her a break.*

Barb called them in for dinner. Sean and Chrissy sat shoulder to shoulder at the kitchen table, across from their hosts. When she moved her head, he could smell her shampoo. She was left-handed—a trait he'd never noticed before—and their arms brushed against each other constantly as they lifted forks to their mouths, a sensation that felt just short of foreplay.

Chrissy led the conversations through dinner, with questions about Cormac's Confectionary and how the baked-goods business was doing in a down economy; Sean's next post, and whether he'd go to Haiti and what celebrities he might see there; Barb's photography, what kind of camera she had, and what kind of camera she'd *like* to have someday.

It wasn't until the end of dinner that Sean realized how subdued Barb was. He'd expected her bubbly personality to mesh so happily with Chrissy's. But tonight Barb was quiet. There were circles under her eyes—not the bluish, one-bad-night kind, but the brownish, chronic kind. It had only been about a month since he'd last seen her. He had a momentary urge to take her pulse.

"How about kids?" Chrissy said. "I know you haven't even been married a year yet, but at your age I'm sure you've considered it already."

Barb flinched. Cormac's arm moved a fraction of an inch toward his wife, and Sean could tell that he'd just taken her hand under the table. "We'll see what the good Lord brings," he said with a tight smile.

"Oh." Chrissy licked a dab of mashed potato from her lip. "I didn't realize you guys were religious. Which is great—I'm all for prayer and everything. But conception doesn't always go smoothly late in life. I've had so many friends who've needed a bit of, you know, help. So don't drag your feet if you think you might—"

"Chrissy!" Calling her name was the only thing Sean could think of to make her stop talking. Barb's chin had dropped lower and lower until it was practically on her chest, and Cormac looked as if he'd just taken an uppercut to the face. Chrissy had unwittingly hit a nerve, and Sean told himself it could happen to anyone. But how had she missed their reactions?

"Hmm?" she said.

"We haven't told them about George."

She blinked at him, surprised by the subject change.

"George?" said Cormac, exhaling a long breath. "What's the deal with him?"

"Her," corrected Chrissy. "She's female."

Sean and Chrissy described George's training—"Kevin's training," Chrissy insisted—tag-teaming each other with details about the English Monarchy Scenario and the designation of Kevin as prime minister. "He's probably the most ambivalent chief of state ever elected," Sean quipped, and Barb actually laughed.

"So how'd you learn so much about dog training?" Cormac asked, apparently happy to keep the conversation away from any further land mines.

"First of all," said Chrissy, "I consider it *people* training. Dogs have excellent instincts. It's people that mess them up. And secondly . . ." A shy little smile played around her mouth. "I don't know . . . I've just always felt so connected to animals, ever since I was a kid. They're so easy to deal with compared to people. And they can read me really easily. I think it's because I'm an old soul. Animals can see what's deep inside us, and they feel comfortable with me."

Cormac nodded and smiled. Barb let out a little cough into her hand.

After dessert, Barb told them she had an early class. "I'm so sorry," she said, "I hope you won't mind if I sneak upstairs. But don't let me spoil the party—you guys stay."

"Stay," echoed Cormac. But Sean could tell he was tired. He wondered how their appointment had gone.

"Yeah," Sean said, "and you're getting up to go to work at—what? Five A.M.?"

Cormac grinned and shrugged. "Hey," he said. "I almost forgot. I told my father about your lawn mower. He'll be over tomorrow morning."

"You sure you can spare him?" Sean had borrowed a neighbor's mower a couple of times to keep the lawn from turning into a meadow.

"Trust me," said Cormac with a smirk. "I'm sure."

They said their good-byes, and Cormac gave Sean an extra little slap on the back.

It had started to rain, and as Sean drove Chrissy across Belham and into Weston, the wind picked up and water buffeted the old car from all sides. It gave Sean a weirdly claustrophobic feeling, as if he were trapped somewhere unpleasant instead of with the object of all his adolescent yearnings.

"That was *so* much fun," she was saying. "What a nice couple. Isn't it the best feeling—when you find another couple you both like to be with?"

Sean, of course, had absolutely no idea. Never having been part of a couple himself, he'd never considered the benefits of finding some other likable pair to hang out with. It was foreign and vaguely disconcerting to hear her suddenly referring to them as some sort of matched set—like those little Dutch salt and pepper shakers, slight differences in the intricate blue design the only indication that they didn't contain exactly the same spice.

"Um . . ." he said, pulling into her driveway. He put the car in park but didn't turn the motor off.

She studied him, and he could see uncertainty grow in her gaze like blood leaking into a perfectly clean bandage. Chrissy uncertain—that, too, was completely foreign.

"Is something wrong?" she asked.

"No," he insisted, shaking his head innocently, his lie mirrored by her disbelief. But for once that evening, she stayed quiet, and her unexpected lack of commentary created a sort of vacuum in the confines of the car that ultimately sucked the truth out of him. "I should tell you . . . in case we see them again. . . . You should probably know they're having fertility problems. It's kind of a sore subject."

Chrissy's hand went up to her mouth, brows furrowed with regret. Her hand came down and gripped his forearm. "I feel *terrible*."

"You had no way of knowing." Sean patted her hand. They murmured about this for a few minutes—Chrissy's regret, Sean reassuring her, what good parents Cormac and Barb would be. As they did, their physical contact increased, and Sean could feel his distaste for her earlier behavior leaching out of him. She leaned slightly toward him, which accentuated her cleavage. Her cleavage was *breathtaking*, for the love of God! She was looking into his eyes and then he saw her gaze drop for the briefest second to his mouth, and all the bells in his head starting clanging *dive, dive,* and he was kissing her.

Her lips were as warm and lush as he'd always imagined they'd be—he'd imagined it so many times in his adolescence, it was slightly startling to feel his old thoughts morphing into real life like some sort of science fiction movie. He slid his hand up her bare arm, in part to reassure himself that she was real and not just a set of fantasized lips.

She made the slightest little breathy sound in the back of her throat, and he almost laughed, thinking there should be a caption over his head that read *Kissing Chrissy Stillman*.

After a few minutes, he pulled back to look at her. Her aggressively red lipstick was smeary, making her appear slightly clownish. But her eyes looked satisfied, and that was good enough for him. He'd kissed her—finally, *finally!*—and she'd enjoyed it. They said good night and talked vaguely about getting together soon, and as he watched her glide up the paving stone driveway to her house, he couldn't help but giggle like an idiot.

CHAPTER 21

Charlie McGrath's hands seemed to be made for tools. Despite the fact that he'd quit his job at the town dump to work in his son's bakery more than a year ago, his hands were still callused. Sean wondered idly if he'd been born that way. George had growled at the older man when he'd arrived, but Kevin gave her the *Chtch!* sound, and the dog slunk back to the shade of the red maple to maintain her surveillance of the situation.

"See, ya got all this crap in the carburetor here," Mr. McGrath told Kevin when the dismembered mower lay in pieces by the shed.

Kevin blinked and nodded. Living with women, Sean suspected he wasn't used to hearing adults use coarse language as easily as if they were ordering lunch.

"Goddamned thing's full of gunk." Mr. McGrath shook his head and eyed Sean.

"Don't look at me, I just got here." Sean laughed.

Mr. McGrath chuckled. "Yeah, well, wherever you're off to next, make sure you get home to maintain your gear occasionally, would ya?"

Sean made a mental note to try to convince Aunt Vivvy to go back to her lawn service.

He and Kevin watched Mr. McGrath clean the crap out of the goddamned carburetor and reassemble the machine. The older man had a gravelly voice and a range of expletives that belied his tenderness. Sean remembered how kind Mr. McGrath had been to him as his father made less and less of an effort to get home. "Door's always open," he would growl at Sean, "even for a young scalawag like you."

In fact, Mr. McGrath often reminded him of his father. They

were both blue-collar guys, stocky, and Irish, though the difference in their heights had to be close to a foot. Mr. McGrath didn't speak with a brogue, but he had a strong Boston accent, the brogue's descendant. Both men valued their toughness. It wouldn't do to be caught getting sentimental. And yet Sean knew them both to shed a private tear over the troubles of others.

Martin Doran had lost the privacy of his tears, though. Gritting his teeth in a vain effort to control himself, he would weep in church after his wife died, head bowed, shoulders shaking. Sean remembered how embarrassed he'd felt.

"Well, don't just stand there," Mr. McGrath told Kevin. "Hand me that wrench." Kevin jumped up to retrieve the tool resting in the grass where the older man had tossed it. "There's a good boy." He grabbed the wrench with one hand and tousled Kevin's hair with the other. Kevin appeared slightly confused by these contradictory gestures, but it didn't keep him from hovering over Mr. McGrath's battle-scarred hands as they performed mechanical CPR on the mower.

"And what are you doing with yourself when you're not lollygagging around, letting others do your work for you?" Mr. McGrath demanded of Kevin.

"Uh . . ." Kevin squinted uncertainly at Sean for a moment. "Well, I'm going to Boy Scout camp in a week."

"Boy Scout camp!" Mr. McGrath exclaimed, and it was hard to know if it was with disgust or approval until he went on to say, "*I* was a Boy Scout!"

"You were? Are you an Eagle?"

"Nah, I only made it to Star, and then I started gettin' interested in girls." He landed a beefy hand on Kevin's shoulder. "Take my advice, don't let some goddamned silly thing get in your path. I'm seventy-four years old, and to this *day* I regret not making Eagle."

After Mr. McGrath left, Kevin was to mow the lawn. But he went into the shed first and came out wearing a set of old headphones, big clonking things the size of cinnamon buns, with the curling cord dangling down his back.

"Where'd you get those?" asked Sean.

"My dad."

It still startled Sean sometimes to hear Kevin refer to Hugh this way. The happy-go-lucky rascal Sean had known, and the man who had brought Kevin into the world and cared for him, were almost two different people in his mind.

Kevin must have noticed Sean's discomposure. "They're not supposed to be for mowing," he said quickly. "They went to a tape player he had. And when everything got too"—Kevin grimaced and wiggled his hands around—"he'd put them on me and play this really quiet music."

"Oh." Sean nodded, as if the headphones had been the question all along. "Where's the tape player?"

"It broke and Auntie Vivvy threw it away. She said I wore it out. But I grabbed the headphones before she went to the dump—they still keep the sound out even if they're not attached to anything." He reached down and pulled the cord on the mower and the engine let out its introductory roar before settling into an aggravated growl. Kevin flinched at the noise. Then he let go of the brake and started across the lawn.

A wave of sadness washed over Sean as he watched the boy, who was not much bigger than the mower he was attempting to control. It surprised him, the intensity of the sorrow seeming to far outweigh the visual. He generally only felt like this when he lost a patient he'd grown particularly fond of.

Viv's getting that lawn service if I have to pay for it myself, he thought, and went into the house to confront her.

She was in the den, papers scattered across the burled maple desk like the detritus of a parade. She looked up when Sean came in, her eyes ablaze with fury. "I can't do it," she said tightly. "I can't remember what I've done, what's been paid . . . any of it."

His anger toward her, the image of the broken tape recorder and the boy with the beastlike mower, receded from the foreground of his mind. "Any of it?"

She remained silent, which was as good as shouting the answer.

"I'll go through it with you," he offered. "Some of it might look familiar if we go slowly."

Her arm came out and with a sudden jerk she swatted the bills away from her, several of them cascading to the floor. He'd never seen her do anything so childish.

Loss of impulse control, he thought. *Sudden outbursts.* Instinctively he put a hand on her shoulder, as he'd done so many times with melting-down patients. It said, *You are not alone* and *You are not allowed to go ballistic* in one efficient gesture.

He half expected her to shrug away his touch with a sharp, imperious comment. That was the Vivian Preston he knew. Instead she put her hands to her face and wept. The only thing that had ever worried Sean more was seeing his father do the same thing.

Holy shit, he thought. *We are screwed.*

CHAPTER 22

He brought her into the kitchen, leaving the papers littered across the den, and made her a cup of tea. He thought about putting a splash of whiskey in it to calm her, but he knew she would taste it and get even angrier. Sean was hard-pressed to know how to manage her—she'd never been one to tolerate managing. But then she'd never needed it before.

Her hand trembled slightly as she brought the teacup toward her mouth. "Stop examining me," she murmured, and took a sip.

He turned his gaze down to his own mug. "I really wish you'd see a doctor."

"If wishes were horses, beggars would ride."

He let out a laugh despite himself. She had a comeback for everything, and yet she couldn't do her damned bills. "Okay, I'm going to make suggestions and you're going to shoot them down, but I can't *not make* them."

"Ever the responsible medical professional."

He let out an exasperated sigh. "Have you always been this difficult?"

It was obviously a rhetorical question, but it stopped her for a moment, and she seemed to consider it. Finally she said, "No, I don't believe so. I don't like this . . . confusion. Some people seem to live their whole lives in a state of befuddlement. But it makes me irritable." She glanced at him briefly. "More so than usual."

Of course it did, especially since she'd had so little to hang on to in life other than her intelligence and grit. Sean dug a little deeper for patience. "It could be caused by an imbalance of some kind, in which case it's reversible."

"That's what Simon hoped."

"Dr. Krantz? Did he run any blood work?"

"He did. He died two weeks later. Lovely man."

"Did he find anything?"

"Not a thing. It's likely Alzheimer's or some similarly ruinous cousin thereof. Certainly not Huntington's. There's no known case of onset at my age. But whatever it is, there's no cure."

"Auntie, there are new drugs now that can slow the process."

"Sometimes they can, sometimes they can't."

"For the love of God, won't you at least *try*?"

She put her teacup down and steadied her gaze at him for the first time that afternoon. There was a gentleness to it that bordered on sympathetic. Sean had no idea of what to expect.

"Did you have a plan?" she asked simply. "If the symptoms came?"

"A plan . . . you mean . . ." he stammered.

"Suicide. Were you planning to kill yourself? Or does your faith preclude that option?"

Catholic doctrine was pretty clear. Suicides are said to share no reunion with their loved ones in the afterlife, no communion with Jesus or the saints. They drift alone for eternity. But Sean could never buy the idea that a loving God would actually cut loose the most desperate of his children. He suddenly felt so weary. "Tierra del Fuego," he said. "I was going to do it there."

"Ah," she nodded approvingly. "Parts unknown. Very fitting."

"You?" he asked.

"When I was at risk for Huntington's, I always thought I would have a nibble at some garden chemicals under the red maple."

"Also fitting."

"Yes, but then all of you children came here to live, and I couldn't very well let you find me foaming at the mouth in the backyard. I never did devise a satisfactory alternative. But as the years passed, it became less and less likely I'd need one."

Until now. Neither of them said it, but Sean knew she was

thinking it, too. They sat quietly as the drone of the lawn mower rounded to the front of the house. It seemed terribly unfair—how much was one family supposed to handle? And yet he'd seen families decimated by disease and violence, mothers watching their children die from something as preventable as dysentery, children orphaned with no relatives left to care for them. He reminded himself that at least his family had a roof over their heads and food to eat, warm beds and clean water.

And one hell of a godawful gene pool . . .

Aunt Vivvy did something completely unexpected then. She reached out and covered Sean's hand with her own, the grip of her gnarled fingers surprisingly strong. And he felt sure he knew the reason she was taking his hand for the first time in their entire history together.

"Please don't ask me to kill you," he said.

She sighed. "You're certain?"

"Yeah, I'd really rather not."

"You may change your mind when things get worse."

"I know. Still."

"Let's consider it an open invitation, then. You'll do as you see fit, with my blessing."

Her blessing. Another first. Had she ever given such glowing approval of any of his past efforts? Apparently in her book, of all his good deeds, murder would be the high point.

She released his hand to bring the teacup to her lips again, but the feel of her tight grasp lingered. Would he change his mind eventually, when she became so lost, so hard to handle, that her death would seem like a gift to them both? He'd seen dementia before, but not very often. In the places he'd stayed, most people didn't get the chance to outlive the functionality of their brains. How bad would it get? And how could he possibly find someone willing to care for an increasingly demented old lady and her slightly odd, orphaned great nephew?

"Sean," she said, interrupting his ruminations. "Is it possible that your father was in the yard today fixing the lawn mower?"

"No, Auntie," he said, startled that her delusion so closely shadowed his thoughts earlier in the day. "It was Mr. McGrath, Cormac's father."

"Brigid McGrath's husband?"

"Yeah, from the Garden Club."

"Hmm," she said. "I might have sworn it was Martin."

Sean waited for Deirdre to get home. He desperately hoped that they could come up with some sort of plan. More than anything he just needed to talk to someone.

When she didn't show up after her shift at the diner, he called her cell phone. She was in her car, headed to Worcester. He could hear the rumble of rush hour traffic on the Mass Pike.

"I'm going straight to practice," she said, sounding slightly annoyed at his intrusion. "What's the issue?"

"Jesus, pretty much freaking everything, Dee."

"Okay, well, I've got a show going up in two short weeks, and it's a part I got ten days ago, Sean, so I can't really deal with *pretty much freaking everything* at the moment. In fact, I can't deal with anything other than this performance, aka the basis for my entire *future*."

"So I'm just supposed to handle all this shit myself."

"Welcome to my world," she said. She honked her horn and muttered, "Asshole!" before hanging up. Sean assumed she was referring to another driver, but he wondered if she'd meant for him to have a small share in the epithet, too.

CHAPTER 23

"Hey, any chance you feel like grabbing a bite?"

"Oh, uh . . ."

"It's all right if you're busy. I just thought I'd give it a shot."

"No, I'd like to." But Rebecca was clearly hesitant. "I just need to . . . there's some stuff I have to do first. How's seven?"

"Great! I'll swing by and grab you then."

She seemed about to say something, but then there was some sort of commotion in the background, and she muttered, "Okay," and hung up. Seven would give him plenty of time to pick up groceries, prepare dinner for Kevin and Aunt Viv, and make sure no one needed anything before he headed to Rebecca's. He'd become increasingly aware of checking things like stove burners, reminding Kevin to brush his teeth, and seeing his aunt safely ensconced in her room with her henchman-dog before he left the house these days.

Still, seven felt like a long time to wait to unload his mounting anxiety about Aunt Vivvy and Kevin, his aggravation with Deirdre, even his unaccountably mixed feelings about Chrissy. He wished he could head to The Pal with Cormac and get it all off his chest. But it wasn't Tuesday, and he was hesitant to bother Cormac. Sean could still see the look of despair on Barb's face when Chrissy had asked if they were planning to have kids.

He had a sudden inclination to fire off a letter to his old friend Yasmin Chaudhry, the doctor he'd befriended in Kenya. They had sat countless times discussing just this sort of thing—her family's dismay over her decision to go to medical school instead of submitting to an arranged marriage, his father's disappearance, both families' inability to understand the choices they had each made to spend their lives among the poorest of the poor. Yasmin had an astute eye for the absurdity of trying to make anyone understand it, and they shared the comfort—now so starkly missing in his life—of mutual commiseration.

The last he'd heard from her she was in Haiti. Who knew if the mail even got through these days, and if so, whether she was still there to receive it? Nevertheless, once Kevin and Aunt Vivian were seated at the kitchen table with their barbecued chicken and baked potatoes, he took a pad of paper and wrote a few lines to Yasmin.

When he drove over to meet Rebecca, her house was dark. After fifteen minutes, he was about to drive to the nearest gas station and call her when she pulled into the driveway, her car coming to an abrupt stop just before hitting the garage door. She didn't get out immediately. Sean waited a moment, then he opened her passenger-side door and got in. "What's up?" he said.

She pushed a clump of wavy brown hair back off her face. "I don't think it's going to work out tonight, Sean. I'm sorry."

"What happened?"

Rebecca stared out the windshield. "Eden came in."

"Your boss?"

"Yeah. We were locking up, and she wanted a massage."

"Man, that must have been annoying—you said she's pretty awful."

"She's Satan."

"Oh, Beck, I'm sorry. That sucks. Let's go grab a beer and some food and you can relax."

She closed her eyes for a second, then looked over at him. "I need to meditate."

"Oh."

"I'm sorry. I would've been done by the time you came if she hadn't shown up. And now I really *need* to. She's a completely destabilizing person."

"No, it's fine. Should I come back later? Or I could just hang out till you're ready."

"Well, I usually do some yoga first, so it might be a while."

"Yoga."

She smiled. "Yeah, Sean, *yoga*. Maybe you've heard of it? Like half the world does it."

"I've heard of it, smart aleck. I've even done it a couple of times."

She surveyed him skeptically. "Really."

"Yeah, really. Maybe I'm not one of those guys who says *'Namaste'* in casual conversation and owns his own mat, but I did live in India for a couple of years. Can you top that, little miss yoga girl?"

She laughed her clear melodious laugh. "Nope," she said. "I cannot top that. So, you want to do some yoga with me?"

"Oh, ah . . . okay. I mean, it's been a while. You'll have to tell me what to do."

They went into the house, and Rebecca put her wavy hair into a short ponytail and changed into a pair of stretchy black leggings and a tank top. Sean would have preferred running shorts to the khaki shorts he was wearing, but they were loose, and he felt he could manage.

She took him down to the basement, which was cool and dark, the waning summer light sifting in through small casement windows near the ceiling. There was an old Ping-Pong table folded up against one wall next to an enormous teak entertainment center. A couch and a rolled-up rug had been pushed to one side.

"Hey, we used to play Ping-Pong down here. Is that the same table?"

"Of course it is." She smiled. "You don't replace things in a shrine. The only new thing is the rug." It was a flat, pale Berber with flecks of tan. "Yoga on a shag carpet is just so *wrong*."

They lay down on their backs, hands palm-up by their sides, and began by concentrating on their breathing. "Now, as you inhale, arch your back. As you exhale, curl your back, pelvis tipping upward."

Her voice was quiet and soothing. He arched and curled, happy to follow her lead, the anxiety of the day's events slipping away as he concentrated on her simple instructions.

He kept her in sight so he could see the positions she described. In the simple, stretchy outfit, her shape was more evident. She was petite, as she'd always been, but there was a muscularity to her now. Her upper arms were firm and defined—from years of giving massages, he supposed. Her legs also seemed strong, and she could balance on one leg in the Tree pose without quivering at all. Sean fell over immediately. He let out a grunt of annoyance.

She glanced over at him. "There's a saying in yoga: 'Find the *repose* in the pose.' Don't try so hard. Let your body find its own balance in its own time." With a little grin she added, "And stop competing with me."

"I'm not!"

"Oh no, not in the least." She came around behind him and placed her hands on his hips. "Shift your weight onto one foot. Okay, now slowly, slowly raise the other foot and rest it against the inside of your opposite thigh. Keep breathing. Let the breath calm your muscles."

He did as she said, and though he was still quivery and unstable, he got his foot planted against the other leg, her strong hands buttressing him from either side. As she guided him to raise his arms upward, his mind remained focused on her hands gripping his hips. He was used to the feel of her touch from the massages she'd given him, but this seemed different somehow.

"You're doing it," she murmured near his ear. "You're a tree."

"Yeah, well, my roots are pretty shallow. A light breeze would blow me over."

"Your roots are fine. You just have to believe in them a little more and let them do their job." She let him go, and he held it for a few seconds before tipping again.

They continued on, his muscles straining to hold him in precarious positions. And when he realized he *was* competing with her, he was able to relax and simply marvel at her gracefulness. When they had finished and were lying on their backs again, Sean still breathing a little harder than he liked, she said, "Meditation?"

"If it doesn't involve being a downward dog or a proud warrior, I'm in."

She laughed. "For a guy who's spent most of his life living in squalor, you're kind of demanding."

He looked over at her and grinned. "Sean Doran, Diva Bush Nurse."

As they gazed at each other and laughed, Sean felt a surge, like his nervous system had just gone turbo. A strange array of impulses crackled across his brain in a mental ticker tape: kiss her . . . squeeze her hand . . . laugh uncontrollably . . . run like hell . . .

"Gotta pee," he said, and rose and went to the bathroom.

When he came back she had put a cotton sweater over her tank top. She didn't look at him. "Ready?" she said.

"Yup. What do I do? Just sit quietly?" He lowered himself onto the carpet several feet away from her.

"Um, yeah, basically. Wait—you said you've done this before."

"Yoga, not meditating."

"Oh. Well, do you want me to do a guided meditation, sort of helping you along?"

"Sure."

She began to talk quietly about clearing the mental chatter, focusing only on each breath coming in and out, counting them to guide attention away from thought. He tried to do as she said, but Sean could not make himself focus on his breathing for more than about six seconds. He wondered momentarily if it was an early sign of dementia, an uncontrollable mind. By the count of four he was starting to see images between each number—Kevin *chtching* at George, how had he learned that so fast? And then five—where was the tape Hugh had given him, had it gotten thrown out with the tape player? Sometimes he got to six but he never got to seven. He was a meditation failure.

"If you find your mind wandering, be forgiving with yourself," Rebecca murmured. "Scolding is the opposite of what meditation is about. When you find thoughts drifting in, release them like a feather into the breeze." The softness of her voice wooed him toward acquiescence. "There is no failure in meditation. It is a practice, not an accomplishment."

Stop scolding yourself, he scolded himself. The thought made him smile. And then he let it go like a feather. He did the same for the next thought, and the next . . . And then there came a moment when he felt . . . suspended . . . a soft nothingness . . . peaceful . . . whole . . . graced.

Then his scalp felt itchy and he tried not to scratch, because wouldn't that break the spell? But of course by the time he was thinking those thoughts, questioning the rectitude of scratching, it was already broken.

He opened his eyes and glanced over at her. She sat cross-legged, back straight, face relaxed. And for a moment he wanted desperately to know what she was seeing behind those olive-skinned eyelids. Was he in the scene? Would that be a good thing or a bad one? Did he even want to be there? Her eyes began to open slowly, and he quickly looked away.

"So?" she said.

He shrugged and gave his scalp a good hard scratch.

They couldn't decide where to have dinner. Neither one would commit to a place they actually wanted to go. "Milano?" she said. It was where he'd had lunch with Chrissy.

"Sure, if you want to." But his tone was unenthusiastic.

"I don't really care."

"How about Country Squire?"

"Great," she said. "If I were elderly and had a yen for creamed corn."

By process of apathetic elimination they ended up at The Pal, plates loaded with fries and bacon cheeseburgers.

"I'm surprised you'd eat this." He wiped a drop of grease from his lips. "It's not exactly healthy."

"Yeah, I can't do all-healthy, all-the-time. It makes me cranky."

He nodded. *Of course,* he thought. *Why can't everyone be so normal?* But suddenly that weird ticker-tapey thing started again and he found himself saying, "So did I tell you I got together with Chrissy Stillman last week?"

The burger in her hands ceased its ascent toward her mouth. "No," she said, studying the burger. "I don't think you mentioned it."

"She came into the Confectionary a couple of weeks ago, then we went out for lunch. She's training George."

Rebecca put the burger down. She reached for the salt shaker and sprinkled some on her fries. "I heard she went to law school."

"Yeah, she was a lawyer, then she got married and had kids. Guess who she married."

"I have no idea." Still salting.

"Ricky Cavicchio."

She glanced up at him, set the shaker down. "Come on."

"I am not making this up. She *married* that jerk."

Rebecca's face warmed almost imperceptibly with some unspoken appreciation.

"They split up, though." He took a bite out of his burger.

Her eyes flicked back to him, the warmth gone.

"You never really liked her," said Sean.

Her gaze tightened like a vise, as if to clamp down on something unpleasant.

"Come on, admit it—you know you didn't."

"No, I didn't," said Rebecca. "She wasn't very nice."

"How can you say that? If anything she was Little Suzie Sunshine."

The look on her usually inscrutable face was unmistakable. She was incredulous. "Seriously," he said, "what could possibly make you think she wasn't nice?"

Rebecca didn't answer for a minute, seeming to weigh her options. Finally she said, "She called me Becky Bubble."

"Bubble?"

She pointed to the right side of her face, the part that bowed out in that strange way. "Bubble," she said.

It took a moment for the gravity of this to sink in; when it did, Sean felt mildly ill. He knew Chrissy could be kind of self-involved, but this was heartless. She must not have realized how cruel it was. "God, that's awful," he said. "When did she say it?"

"What do you mean when? She said it a lot."

"More than once?"

"All the time."

"How old were we? Are we talking elementary school? Because kids that age can be really mean without seeing how much they're hurting people."

Rebecca looked at him, and there was a sadness, almost a pity there. She didn't answer.

"Okay, what—junior high?" he asked.

Still she didn't say anything. She crossed her arms over her chest.

"When?" he demanded. "When was the last time?"

"Remember that party at Dougie Shaw's the summer before we left for college?"

"Yeah . . ."

"Remember how I wanted to leave early and you convinced me to stay? Why do you think that was, Sean—because I was having such a good time?"

"*Then?* She called you Becky Bubble in *high school*? Jesus, why didn't you tell me?"

"What would you have done?"

"I would've told her to shut the hell up!"

Rebecca looked away. "I did tell you once. Junior year. She taunted me in the lunchroom, in front of half our class. You weren't there, but I told you afterward."

"Are you sure? I don't remember that."

"You told me to ignore it." Rebecca's voice got tight, as if she could still feel the sting of humiliation. "You said Chrissy was just playing, and I shouldn't take it so personally."

And then he remembered.

Becky had come out of the lunch room looking pale and shaken. He had asked her what was wrong, and she'd told him. He remembered feeling slightly annoyed by her thin-skinned-ness, and told her to brush it off . . . as if a public humiliation about your facial birth defect could be taken any way other than *personally*.

"Oh, Beck," he murmured, shaking his head. "God, what an ass."

She gave a little shrug. "You didn't get it. No one ever called you names like that."

He was still reeling from retroactive guilt. "Lucky, I guess," he muttered.

"It wasn't just luck. You had this sort of . . . it was like a protective coating. People knew they couldn't get to you, so they didn't bother."

"I was basically an orphan with a terminal disease, what more could they do to me?"

"Plus you made it clear you had one foot out the door—things didn't affect you."

"But they did."

She chuckled. "I'm not talking about things like Chrissy Stillman."

She was more relaxed now. His admission of guilt seemed to have irradiated the little ball of cancerous anger she'd obviously been carrying around all these years. "You know, in a way I should thank you—both of you," she said. "People can be mean, whether you've got a funny-looking face or not. Part of growing up is learning how not to internalize it. And your reaction helped me realize that I *did* take things too personally."

"Who wouldn't take something like that personally!"

"No, but see, Becky Bubble wasn't me. That was Chrissy's creation, not mine. I had to get better at not accepting other people's definitions."

"Like your parents'."

"Like anyone's."

He studied her for a moment, the warm brown eyes, the mildly uncontrollable wavy hair . . . the bubble. He had stopped seeing it, he realized, had stopped registering it when he looked at her, and forgot that every time she met someone new they might reject or pity her. And if they were repulsed, she would know it. Her strength wasn't only in her limbs.

"You hate when I call you Becky, don't you?" he said.

She smiled. "No, it's fine. I just decided I like Rebecca better. It's pretty."

"I'll try to call you Rebecca, but I might slip sometimes."

"It doesn't matter what you call me, Sean. We're friends—I'll love you either way."

Yes, he thought. *Me, too. Either way.*

And he wanted to reach over and touch her shoulder or squeeze her hand. But instead he pushed his plate toward her and said, "Here, eat my fries. Yours have enough salt to make you hypertensive."

CHAPTER 24

On Sunday morning, Frank Quentzer called. "What's your e-mail address?" he asked Sean. "I need to send the forms and packing list for camp."

"Oh. I don't actually have one."

There were about three seconds of silence. "You don't have e-mail."

"Yeah, I don't really need it. I'll give you my sister's address and get it from her."

But when Sean powered up Deirdre's laptop in the den, he realized he didn't have her e-mail password and wouldn't be able to access the documents without it. He went upstairs and knocked on her door. She didn't answer, so he opened it and whispered, "Dee."

A muffled grunt came from the darkened recesses of the room.

"Dee, what's your password?" he whispered.

"What?" she groaned.

"I need your e-mail password so I can get something a guy is sending me."

"What the hell, Sean."

"Hey, it's for Kevin."

"I don't care if it's for Andrew Lloyd Webber. I'm not giving you my password."

"Well, can you get up and do it for me then?"

There was a lot of muttering about having one day to sleep in and lack of consideration. "Seriously," she said, yanking on a robe. "What *grown-up* doesn't have his own e-mail account? Oh, yeah—the same one who doesn't have a cell phone."

She followed him downstairs to the den and printed out the

forms. Then she headed back to her room. As she crossed through the living room, Sean heard George growl.

"Shut it!" Deirdre barked. Then there was only the sound of her aggravated soles hitting each stair as she ascended.

Kevin wandered into the den and saw Sean filling out the forms. "Wait, don't!" he said.

Sean looked up. "Why not?"

"I'm not sure about going."

"What do you mean? I thought you decided."

Kevin slumped onto the couch. "Yeah, but I remembered something. Ivan said the middle school schedules come out next week. I have to be here."

"Can't you just get it when you get back?"

"No, because they come by e-mail, and they sent out this form asking what e-mail to send it to, but I didn't know what to put, so I just wrote in that I'd go to the school and pick it up."

"I can do that."

Kevin considered this for a moment. "Are you allowed to? I mean, you're not, like, in charge of me or anything."

And who is? thought Sean darkly. *Look around, they're dropping like flies.* But he said, "I think it'd be okay, under the circumstances."

"What circumstances?"

"The circumstances of my going down there and saying, 'I'm his uncle, give me the paper.'"

Kevin liked this. "Yeah, give me that paper, or else!"

"And if they won't do it . . . I'll . . . take out a squirt gun and squirt them in the face."

"Yeah, and they'll be all like 'Oh, no! Please stop! We'll give you the paper!'"

Sean laughed. "But I'll keep squirting them anyway, just for fun."

"Yeah, then you'll run out of water, and they'll tackle you and call Officer Doug to take you to jail."

"Dougie Shaw? You know him?"

"A little. He came by sometimes."

"For what?"

"I don't know . . . to say 'Hi, how're you doing?' And he'd bring me stuff from the police station, like a plastic whistle and stuff."

"He was the one who told me about Boy Scouts," said Sean.

"Yeah, he knows all kinds of stuff like that."

The night Dougie had brought him home came back to Sean—the incongruity of seeing crazy Dougie Shaw in a police uniform . . . and saying what a good father Hugh had been. Sean wanted to know more about that. And yet part of him didn't. Like Hugh's pranks and shenanigans, his fatherhood had a sort of a semifictional quality in Sean's mind—an interesting anecdote, but probably only half true. Something inside him didn't want it to be fully factual.

The camp packing list had only a few items that Kevin didn't already have, the most critical of which was a Class A Boy Scout uniform. For this they had to go to the Scout Store in Southborough, about fifteen minutes away. Riding down the Mass Pike in the Caprice, Sean said idly, "So you're pretty excited about middle school."

Kevin gave him a look that would melt rocks.

"No?"

"Have you *seen* it?"

"Well, not recently, but I did go there myself when I was your age."

"It's huge. Like fifty times the size of Juniper Hill. And it's made out of cement with really small windows—and they're *never open*. And you have to use a locker room for gym and change your clothes and everything. It smells so bad in there I thought I was gonna puke!"

"When were you there?"

"They do this stupid tour thing. All the fifth graders go over on a bus and walk around and listen to stupid talks and stuff." Kevin was getting really agitated. Sean didn't know whether to let the boy blow off steam or to change the subject.

"So apparently we have to get this sticky stuff to glue on the patches," said Sean. "I'm pretty good at stitching up cuts, but I wouldn't have a clue what to do with cloth."

"Did you ever eat lunch in the cafeteria when you went to middle school?"

"Um, yeah. Pretty much every day."

"It's so *loud* in there. Kids are screaming, and there's like one teacher standing there telling them to settle down. But they don't!"

"Well . . . maybe there's a corner where it's a little quieter."

"I looked," said Kevin. "There isn't."

Sean took his eyes off the highway to glance over at Kevin. The boy's head was turned toward the window. But Sean could see his chin quivering.

"It's normal to be nervous about going to a new place."

There was a little gasp from Kevin, as if his lungs couldn't expand to take in the air. "I don't like bad smells or loud sounds, and I"—another little gasp—"I *don't* like to be bumped. That's what Ms. Lindquist says. She says it's okay not to want to roughhouse." His narrow shoulders began to quiver. "But that's what they *do*. They bump into each other all the time in the hallways, and bang each other into lockers, and do high fives—I saw it!"

Kevin began to sob, his body shaking against the seat, the reverberation of his pain filling the car. Sean felt sick. He had no idea what to do—the kid had to go to school, and he was right—there'd be a lot of nasty pubescent smells and shrieking and banging into one another.

The next exit was theirs, and Sean almost missed it. The Scout Store was a few minutes down the road, and he pulled into a space in the parking lot away from the other cars. Kevin's crying had subsided a little, the gasps for air coming with less frequency.

"Kev," said Sean. "It'll be okay."

Kevin shrugged off this lame attempt at comfort and pulled his T-shirt up to wipe his face.

"What did Ms. Lindquist do to help?"

"Nothing really. She just talked to me."

"Just talked?"

"Yeah, and sometimes when she knew it was getting too much, she would give me a look, like she understood, and I would feel better."

"Maybe there'll be somebody like that at middle school."

"No," said Kevin. "There won't." He wiped his face again and got out of the car.

CHAPTER 25

"Why don't you call his teacher?" Cormac suggested. The waitress set a plate of nachos on the table, the cheese oozing down the mountain of tortilla chips like an orange mudslide.

"Good thinking. But aren't the teachers gone for the summer?"

"Everyone's reachable by e-mail."

"Except me, apparently."

"Jesus, Spin, why don't you get a Gmail account or something? It couldn't be easier."

"Because I don't want a fucking e-mail account, okay? I like my life spam-free."

Cormac snorted a laugh. "You like your life *complication*-free."

"Be honest. What guy doesn't?"

Cormac took a long pull of his Sam Adams while he considered this. "Maybe most guys *think* they do, until they get to a certain age. Speaking of which . . . Chrissy?"

Sean lifted a shoulder dismissively.

"Hold the phone—Chrissy Stillman gets a *shrug*?"

Sean told him about Becky Bubble. Cormac wasn't surprised. "I heard her say it once."

"You're kidding me. What'd you do?"

"Told her to knock it off. But what did she care? I wasn't anyone she wanted to impress."

"Why didn't you say anything when I asked if I could bring her to dinner?"

"Because that was a lifetime ago, and hopefully she's matured. Besides, what was I going to say—no? You've been in love with her your whole life."

"Infatuated, maybe, not in love. I've never been in love with anyone."

"Okay, tomato, tomahto. Whatever. You had it bad for her, and everyone knew it."

Everyone including Becky, thought Sean. The realization stung, and he felt the shame of his thoughtlessness all over again.

"So that's it?" asked Cormac. "Becky Bubble killed your crush?"

"I don't know—I haven't officially ended it or anything. But, I mean, Jesus. Becky *Bubble*? That's pretty fucking cold."

Cormac took another sip of his beer, but the smile on his lips made it hard for him to drink much. "Know what Barb said?"

"What?"

"She said, 'If you go around telling people you're an old soul—you *aren't.*'"

Sean burst out laughing and clinked his bottle on Cormac's. "Love that girl."

"Back off," said Cormac with a grin. "She's all mine."

The next day, Sean and Kevin were on the front porch playing five-card stud. Deirdre had taught Kevin the game, and it soon became clear that they'd played often enough for Kevin to get pretty good at it. Sean was happy to play, except it annoyed him that Deirdre had encouraged the use of a lot of wild cards. "I can barely keep track of what's a real number and what could be *any* number!" he complained.

"Auntie Dee likes it. She says if you get dealt a bad hand, it gives you more of a shot."

Sean was considering this when Chrissy pulled up. "Geez, she didn't even call first."

"Yeah, she did. You were in the bathroom."

"Why didn't you tell me?"

"I forgot. Plus I thought you'd be happy to see her." Kevin gave a gooey look. "Like you *always* are."

Sean flicked a card at him, and Kevin giggled. "Uh-*huh*," he teased.

"Hey, there!" Chrissy called, strolling up the walk in a pair of tight jeans and a short T-shirt. "Couple of handsome gamblers up on the porch, I see." Her straight white teeth gleamed.

"Hi, Chrissy," said Sean.

"Hi," said Kevin, with an equal lack of enthusiasm.

George picked up her head, ears cocked. She looked at Kevin, then back to Chrissy.

"And there's my Georgie-girl. Come on over here and give me some lovin', girlfriend."

George stood, then looked at Kevin again, clearly confused about what to do. Sean stifled a smile, watching the world's most cocksure dog have a moment of utter uncertainty. Kevin gave her a scratch behind the ears, and George lay her head on his lap.

"Look at that! She knows you're in charge. Great job, Kevin," said Chrissy, but her smile didn't seem entirely genuine. "Want to go for a walk? I can give you some advanced tips."

George looked at Kevin. Kevin looked at Sean. George started to whine. Kevin raised his eyebrows at Sean.

Sean nodded. "Why don't you take George for a stroll by yourself?" Boy and dog rose as one and headed quickly off the porch.

Chrissy put her hand on her hip. "What's this about, Sean?"

"Nothing," he said. "I'm just not sure they need any more training."

"I'm not dumb." She gave the little head-wag eye-roll. "Something's bothering you. Is it last week? Was I too forward?"

"No, not at all. I just . . . I don't think we, uh . . . You're great but . . ."

Oh, what the hell, he thought. "I heard something about you—something mean you said in high school. Repeatedly."

"In *high school*? That was quite a while ago, Sean."

"True. And yet it still really bothers me. Becky Feingold—you remember her."

"No, I can't say I do."

"You called her Becky Bubble."

Sean watched the realization dawn on her. "The shy girl with the face thing," she said.

"Yeah, Chrissy, 'the face thing.' You teased her all through school about a congenital cranial defect. Even in high school, when you should've known better. You made her miserable."

Chrissy's eyes flicked back and forth, as if she were not only remembering, but *seeing* the misery. "I forgot about that," she murmured. "It was pretty mean."

"It was mean? That's all you can say?"

"For godsake, Sean, I'm agreeing with you!" She was on the defensive now. "And I'm genuinely sorry—I wish I'd never said it. If anyone treated one of my girls like that, I'd go after them with a sand wedge. But it was twenty-five years ago! What's the statute of limitations on name calling?"

She had a point, and Sean hesitated. How long *can* you hold someone accountable for something she did as a teenager? As he stared at her, pondering just exactly how much he could reasonably hate her, he watched her posture begin to slump, as if she were melting just a little.

Her body gave a sudden twitch. *"God,"* she muttered. Her eyes, utterly devoid of their signature perky gleam, flicked to Sean. "Do you ever get a glimpse of yourself—not the main part, but some horrible little corner—and you just feel sick?"

He wasn't sure if he ever had. But her self-hatred, however momentary, softened the edges of his righteous anger.

"I was seriously bitchy sometimes," she said. "But you have to believe I would never do anything like that now."

"I'm sure you wouldn't," he conceded.

"We've all grown up, haven't we?"

More or less, he thought.

"Can't you give me another chance?"

How could he say no without seeming just as hard-hearted as she herself had once been? He nodded, and she came up on the porch to wait for Kevin to return. They talked, halting and careful at first, but then she made some little joke about her ex-husband and he found himself smiling, and the storm surge of his aversion to her began to recede a little.

Kevin and George rounded the curve of the street then, side by side, the leash slack between them, as if it were unnecessary, a mere accessory meant to make others feel more secure that the big shepherd-lab was under the control of a sensible human. Sean watched them, the loop of the leash hanging loosely from Kevin's fingers, the dog stopping to sniff occasionally and then trotting to get back in stride with the skinny freckled boy.

A car went by. A man at the wheel. Thick neck and granite-gray hair, head turned toward the house. Sean's glance shifted to him a nanosecond after the man turned away again. The car passed Kevin and George and continued up the road.

CHAPTER 26

"What did you do to yourself?"

"It wasn't on *purpose,* for godsake." Sean gritted his teeth as Rebecca's fingers probed the throbbing almond-sized knot by his shoulder blade. Between groans, he described his day to her: eight hours on his feet at the Confectionary, followed by a hike through the woods with Kevin and George. "And then, because I was feeling so great—*ow!*—I decided to go for a run. I've been trying to exercise more."

"Why were you feeling so great?"

"I don't know. I was just happy. Don't you ever just feel happy for no reason? *Damn* that hurts!" It was hot in the room, and so crowded with furniture, there was no air circulation. Sean could feel beads of sweat forming under his chest.

"Sometimes," she said. "But usually something kicks it off, like beautiful weather, or a really sincere compliment from a client." She moved off the knot, kneading around it with the heels of her palms, which helped to dissipate the agony.

"Okay, well maybe there was something," he admitted. Her pressing stopped for a beat then resumed, her fingers traveling down opposite sides of his spine. He waited for her to ask, but she was quiet. It was as if she didn't want to know.

But he had to tell her, pride nudging him to continue. "Chrissy dropped by yesterday."

Still no word from above. Had she heard him? "Chrissy Stillman from high school."

"Oh, *that* Chrissy," she said, and it felt like she was using something pointy and hard, possibly her knuckle, to burrow up under his ribs.

"Yeah, that Chrissy, and can you try not to pierce my kidney, please?"

She backed off a little, but not completely. Sean took a breath. "I told her off."

"You what?"

"I told her I'd heard how mean she'd been to you. And she felt terrible."

"Jesus, Sean. Are you *kidding* me?" She did not sound happy or grateful. She actually sounded kind of pissed off.

"No, I . . . Hold on a minute—I thought you'd be glad about how sorry she is."

"*Glad?* It was twenty-five years ago! Why would you bring that up with her *now*? Like I'm still crying about it, still . . . still some pathetic little *loser* with a screwed-up face! Are you really that clueless?" The heels of both palms slammed into the small of his back. Sean suspected it was not an entirely therapeutic move.

Then her hands came off his back altogether, and he imagined that they were on her hips, just like Chrissy's had been. "Apparently I *am* that clueless," he said. "Because I actually thought you'd be happy that I finally stood up for you."

That seemed to halt her fury, and her hands returned to rest on his back. "Well, thanks for that," she muttered. "But you can see how it might be slightly infuriating, too, right? How it sort of compounds the patheticness factor?"

"Yes, okay," he said. "But you said it yourself—being pathetic isn't you. That's Chrissy's creation. And I'm going to go out on a limb here, but I hope I speak for *both* of us when I say, who honestly gives a shit what Chrissy Stillman thinks?"

She laughed. Such a sweet, melodious sound.

"And by the way," he said. "Your energy got totally unstable for a minute there. I could really feel it."

She laughed again, and the flat of her hand came down hard on his skin, which felt almost as good as a massage.

After he got dressed, he called to her. "Come back in here for a minute." She popped her head in the door. "This dresser's toast," he said.

"Sean, I can't—"

"Yes, you can. You have more muscle mass than I do."

"Well, I'm *able*," she said, "I just don't think—"

"Then don't think. Do as you're told and pick up that end."

They shuffled the clunky brown dresser into the hallway. After hemming and hawing for a few minutes, with Sean threatening to shove the damn thing down the stairs, Rebecca finally decided the best place for it was her parents' bedroom. They hauled it down to the end of the hallway and into the only room in the house Sean had never seen.

Sol and Betty's bedroom was a study in rusts and greens, with a lumpy satin bedspread beaming its polyester shine from the king-sized bed. The headboard was upholstered in a dizzying geometric pattern of avocado green squares and orange circles.

"Holy mother of God," murmured Sean.

"I know." Rebecca sighed. "It really makes me wonder if I'm adopted."

They went down to the kitchen and Rebecca got out some vegetables and hummus. Sean sliced up celery while she seeded a red pepper. "I used to beg my parents to have another kid," she admitted. "I think they ran into some fertility trouble after I came along. They used to say, 'We have you. Why would we ever want anyone else?'"

"That's sweet."

"Yeah, a little too sweet. And completely transparent. Like I needed to be bolstered up so badly that I would actually believe such nonsense."

"Why were you dying for a sibling?"

"Well, it always looked like families with lots of kids were having way more fun than we were. And I figured siblings would sort of diffuse the intensity—they couldn't watch me every minute of the day because there'd be other kids to hover over. Once I figured out they were too old, I used to beg them to adopt."

Sean dipped a wedge of cucumber into the hummus. "I'm available," he said.

"For what—adoption?"

"Yeah, I don't have parents, you don't have siblings. It's the perfect solution."

"Okay, poof," she said. "You're adopted."

He grinned. "This means I have a say in how we handle the house. I'm calling Salvation Army in the morning to haul half the furniture away. Assuming they'd actually want any of it."

She rolled her eyes. "You're hilarious."

"Don't worry." He patted her hand. "I'll be the one to break it to Mom and Dad."

They snacked on the vegetables, and Sean told her about the trip to the Scout Store with Kevin. "He totally fell apart, and I have no idea how to help him. From what I remember, being loud and slamming into one another is pretty much what middle school is all about."

"Has he always had it?"

"Had what?"

"A sensory integration problem."

"What is that? I've never even heard of it."

"Really? It's pretty common pediatric stuff."

"Yeah, well, the pediatric stuff I'm familiar with is more along the lines of malnutrition, burns from falling into fires, and preventable childhood diseases."

Rebecca described what she'd learned about it in massage school—that it's generally associated with being easily overstimulated, and not much is known about its root causes.

"There are all kinds of interesting ways to treat it," she said. "Massage, chiropractic, various products. For instance, does he sleep with a lot of blankets?"

"Yeah, a ton. Even in this heat."

"Physical pressure is very calming to the senses. You could get him a weighted blanket."

"So this is real, this sensory thing—they have devices for it and everything?"

"Absolutely real. And it looks like Kevin's a clear example."

Sean's assessment of the boy shifted in that moment, from merely odd to someone with a definable medical problem.

"I need to find a cassette player, too," he said. "I guess my brother would play soothing music for him when he got overcooked. Kevin still has the tape, but the tape player broke and my aunt threw it out."

"Oh!" Rebecca jumped up. "We have one! When I was a kid I used to love books on tape, and I know the player's around here somewhere." She grinned at him. "Because as you know, bro, we never throw anything out." She began opening overstuffed drawers and cabinets, without luck. Then she said, "I know where it is." She took the stairs two at a time and was back in a matter of moments with an oversized cassette player. "My mother's a huge Barbra Streisand fan. She would always listen to Barbra tapes in bed."

Sean chuckled. "You'd need something to distract you in *that* room."

Rebecca flipped the switch, and two tiny wheels began to turn behind the clear plastic casing. "Jingle bell, jingle bell, jing-jang-gul," sang Barbra.

"A Jew singing a Christmas song," chuckled Sean. "Very ecumenical."

"Oh, yes. We're open to all creeds, here in the Feingold house," said Rebecca with a smile. "We even adopted a nice Irish Catholic boy."

CHAPTER 27

The hall clock said eleven-fifteen when Sean came in that night. As usual Aunt Vivian had left on the small lamp with the bulbous glass shade that sat squat and homely on a side table. The rest of the house was dark. The phone ringing in the kitchen seemed like a fire alarm in the silence.

"Hello?"

"Hello." A heavy voice, old and cracked like a scratched record. "Who'm I speaking to?"

Sean's heart started to pound, and he didn't know why, exactly. The voice gave him a startled, panicky feeling. And there was something else. Anger. It was as if he were bracing for a fight. "Who's calling?" he said sharply.

"Is this Sean . . . or Hugh? I ask you to tell me."

"Who the hell is *this*," Sean demanded.

"Ah," said the voice. "Is it you then, Sean?"

Sean dropped into a kitchen chair like a bag of rocks. He wanted to hang up. And he wanted to crawl through the phone line toward the voice.

"Sean, it's your da."

"Jesussufferingchrist," muttered Sean. "You're alive."

"Yes, son. And I need to see you. All three of you."

You need . . . ? YOU need?

"I should say," Da corrected himself, "I very much *want* to see you. If you'd be willing."

"Jesus, Da."

"You owe me nothing, son. Not a kind word. Not a welcome. But

I hope you might be willing just to see me, and maybe talk a little. I'll ask no more of ye."

Crazy things ran through Sean's brain. *Hugh's dead!* he wanted to scream. *And Deirdre's leaving! Viv's losing her mind and Kevin's got problems I've never even heard of!*

"Please," he said, feeling weak. "I can't even—"

"I know it, boy. It's a shock. And I've put it off for so long. And then it came to me that maybe it's just what you'd been wanting—for your da to call and ask."

For my da to call . . . Of course it's what he'd wanted. To be somebody's son, cared for and encouraged. To be just a little less alone in the world. It's what he'd been desperate for. . . .

Twenty-five years ago.

And now? After having been abandoned when the need was greatest?

"I don't know," he said. And truthfully, he didn't.

"Okay," said the old man. "I'll give you some time. It's the least I can do."

Sean sat there in the dark, moonlight sifting in through the sheer curtains, the receiver gripped in his hand like a weapon. It wasn't until the line went dead and a steady beep hummed that he was certain his father was no longer on the other end.

Gone again.

CHAPTER 28

Sean woke early to a pounding rain. In the half consciousness of waking he imagined his father standing out in the downpour. Because he didn't actually live anywhere, did he? Had he simply made his life aboard ships for the last quarter century? Or had he bought a house or rented an apartment somewhere? Had he signed a lease or mortgage and looked at the address listed, and said to himself, *This is not where I live. I live in Belham, Massachusetts. I have a family there. They don't live at this address.* And then signed the goddamned paper anyway?

Where the hell on this big blue ball of misery called Planet Earth was he?

Sean couldn't stay in bed, remembering that it had been his father's bed at one time, and feeling as if the mattress would rise up at any moment and attach itself to Sean like some sort of blanket-shrouded succubus. He stood in his boxers, shivering in the dampness that had seeped into the house. At one hip, the fabric of his boxers was separating from the waistband, and he randomly thought about throwing them away. *Or I could go somewhere where holey boxers are the norm—where having boxers at all is a luxury* . . . Yeah, that was looking better and better.

He slid them to the floor, put on a pair of running shorts he'd purchased recently and a T-shirt and sneakers. The hell with his back, he was going for a good hard run. When he stepped into the hallway, he glanced down toward Aunt Vivvy's room. George lay outside the door as usual. She picked up her head and looked at him. He found himself walking toward her. She stood, a barely audible growl in the back of her throat.

"Don't fucking start with me," he muttered at her, and knocked on the door.

"Who is it?" came the weak but aggravated response.

"It's Sean. I need to speak to you."

Sean turned the knob and entered. Aunt Vivvy was drawing herself up to a sitting position in her bed, the faded Lanz nightgown slightly askew around her tiny frame.

"What could this possibly be about?" she demanded.

"My father called last night."

She stared at him for a moment, assessing the veracity of the statement. "Here? You spoke to him?"

"Yes." Sean sat down on the edge of her bed.

Aunt Vivvy looked away. "What does he want?"

"He wants to see me. Actually all of us. Apparently he doesn't know Hugh's unavailable."

A look of mild disgust. "Don't be dramatic. One Bette Davis in the family is enough."

"Forgive me, but this is *actually dramatic*. For all I knew, the guy was dead!"

A whine outside the door from George was shushed by both of them.

"Aunt Vivian," Sean said, trying to rein in his temper. "I need to know what happened."

"He left."

Sean slammed his hand down on the chenille bedspread, which caused no sound, of course, but made the point nonetheless. She narrowed her eyes at him, the glint of the light saber glowing behind them. "Think, Sean," she said. "You know almost as much as I do. The drinking, the crying. He couldn't take it, and he left."

"When. How. What was the precipitating event, Vivian. I may have the gist, but you have the details, and I want them."

"How can you be sure that I'll even remember them correctly?"

"Jesus, I can't be sure of *anything*, can I? Just tell me what you know—what you *think* you know—and we'll start there."

She stared off for a moment, her bony fingers skimming slowly across the white-on-white pattern of the chenille. "How old were you when we told you about your mother's condition?"

"Twelve." He remembered it more vividly than he wanted to. Auntie Vivvy and his father sitting there, his aunt doing all the talking, his father looking as if he'd just been Tasered.

Sean had asked, "Could I get it?"

Auntie Vivvy had looked to his father, urging him with her lightsaber eyes to say something, contribute in some way. "Yes, Sean," she'd said finally. "It's an inherited trait, like your brown eyes, which you obviously got from her, instead of the green from your father."

Da's eyes were the color of sea glass, which Sean had always thought was kind of cool, since his father spent so much time at sea. But those eyes had been lowered, staring at his huge callused hands.

"Could Hugh get it, or Deirdre?" Six-year-old Hugh had been swinging by his knees from a limb of the magnolia tree. Sean had caught sight of him through the front window. He hadn't said anything. Auntie Vivvy hated when Hugh climbed her trees.

One-year-old Deirdre had sat on the floor nearby, babbling and clapping to herself. Sean remembered wishing he were little, like her, and didn't have to hear all this Huntington's crap.

"Each of you has a fifty percent chance of carrying the gene," Auntie Vivvy had said matter-of-factly, the way she said most things. But it had delivered a jolt of understanding—Sean realized what she was *really* saying was they could all end up like their mother—twitchy and weird, saying things that didn't make sense. "There's no way to know until symptoms emerge," said his aunt. "But that wouldn't be until you're older, so you don't need to worry about it now."

Right, he remembered thinking at the time. *I'm twelve, but I'm not a frickin' idiot.*

There in her bedroom, Aunt Vivvy was remembering this scene, too. "He never said a word. I had to do everything. Such a big strong man," she scoffed, "weak as a baby."

"He was heartbroken!"

"We all were."

"It was his wife, for godsake. The love of his life."

"And what would you know about that, Sean Patrick? You've never allowed love into *your* life."

"Neither have you!"

Her face softened slightly, a shadow of a smile, and he realized that she had. Somewhere, at some point, she'd had love. But Sean wasn't interested in his maiden aunt's now-defunct love life. "What made him leave?" he demanded.

"How old were you when she died?"

"Just turned fifteen."

"And Deirdre would've been . . . approximately four."

"What does that have to do with anything?"

Aunt Vivvy's gnarled hands laced together in her lap. "When your mother died, he broke. I've never seen anything quite like it before or since. Possibly it was because his family had scattered to the winds when they'd immigrated to America, and he had no one to turn to. I've thought about it many times. He had planted all his potatoes in one garden bed, as it were, and when the crop failed, he had nothing."

"He had three children."

Her eyes went half-lidded in disgust. "And don't think I didn't remind him of that. Often. Moving here was intended to be a temporary measure. I told him he had to stop the infernal sailor business and get a job that would have him home every night."

"But he didn't."

"I suppose it was some solace to him—the sea. He was raised on an island. He kept threatening to take the three of you and go back to it. But there was nothing there anymore. It had been abandoned in the 1950s, I believe."

"Great Blasket. I remember him talking about it."

"Yes." She sighed. "Ad infinitum."

"You haven't told me when or why he left."

"The crying and the drinking, Sean. The drinking and the crying. My *God*, but it was annoying! After a while I told him I'd had enough. He had one more trip scheduled, and I informed him that when he returned, he'd have to take the three of you and move out."

"Well, we know *that* never happened, so what was it?"

"He hit Deirdre."

"He hit her?" Sean could remember getting cuffed from time to time, and Hugh got spanked regularly. But he never remembered Deirdre being on the business end of those enormous hands.

"He was packing to go, drinking as if every port would be a dry town, and she was pestering him about something. I can't remember what, and it certainly doesn't matter. You know how Deirdre can be—every little thing an opportunity for a scene." Aunt Vivvy's eyes went a little unfocused as the memory came to her, her faced pinched in residual horror. "They were at the top of the stairs. He hit her so hard with the back of his hand that she flew up against the railing. She would have gone over if I hadn't caught her leg."

"Holy *shit*," he murmured. The image of four-year-old Deirdre falling headfirst into the foyer below was a grim one.

"Indeed."

"What did you do?"

She took a breath and let it out slowly. "I told him the truth."

"Which was . . . ?"

"That he was worthless and weak, and didn't deserve to be a father."

Sean felt the blow as if he'd received it himself. "And he believed you," he breathed. "*Jesus,* Vivian."

A mirthless smile rose on her face. "Yes, well, he had the last laugh, didn't he?"

"He never came back," said Sean. "And you were stuck with us."

CHAPTER 29

In the morning, Chrissy came over for another dog training session, and Sean could feel the difference immediately. She was trying. It was not the Chrissy he was used to, always so sure of herself and her place at the fine-grain top of the social sediment. She'd only ever needed to smile or to breathe to confirm her status, and others had always smiled back, hoping to be anointed—at least until the end of lunch period—by the high priestess at the altar of popularity.

"So, Kevin," she said. "How do you feel it's going?" Kevin shrugged, of course, so Chrissy pressed further. "Come on," she said, "you're a pretty astute guy. I know you've seen some things George could improve on." Sean noticed the subtle shift toward George as the student, rather than Kevin.

"Well, she's pretty good at letting me be the boss. But she gets kinda mad when other dogs walk by. She growls and tugs at the leash like she's ready for a smack-down."

"Wow." Chrissy nodded as if he'd just identified a previously unnoticed geological fault line. "I am so glad you pointed that out. We'll definitely need to work on that one, won't we?" She asked further questions about exactly how far the other dogs were when George started to growl and what kinds of dogs, and the like, treating Kevin like an expert witness.

"Okay, so this is a perfect example of what I call a Broken Window. Did you ever hear of the Broken Window Theory?" Kevin shook his head, but his gaze locked on hers waiting for her explanation. She told him how little things like broken windows or graffiti in a neighborhood often led to bigger crimes, because criminals could see that the residents didn't care enough to maintain things. "So we've got to fix any of George's broken windows before they turn into vandalism and car theft. Get it?"

Kevin nodded solemnly. The image of George joyriding behind the wheel of a stolen Beemer almost made Sean laugh out loud, but he was able to maintain a veneer of seriousness.

Chrissy's eyes shifted toward Sean. "I do this with my girls all the time. They start to whine about something, or get sloppy about keeping their rooms clean, and I'm on them like a lightning strike!" She snapped her fingers. She turned back to Kevin. "Let's take George where you've seen other dog walkers, and help her learn to control herself a little more, okay?" She gave Sean a quick sparkle of a smile and set off with Kevin and George.

Sean was giving the porch a much-needed good hard sweep when they returned, and he could hear Chrissy explaining to Kevin, "She growls because she's so protective—that's in her nature, and we don't want to change who she *is*. We just want her to know that not everything is a threat. She'll actually be happier knowing that you can take care of your*self* most of the time."

Kevin nodded, and Sean could see him thinking this through. The boy might not be able to be less fearful for his own benefit, Sean considered, but he might be able to do it for the dog he now loved. It was an odd motivator, but it just might work, and he felt his gratitude and affection for Chrissy rising in response.

When the dog training session ended and Kevin went inside to get George some water, Chrissy said, "So . . . um . . . are you hungry? I was going to get some lunch before the girls get home from field hockey camp."

Milano was her favorite restaurant, and they sat at a little round café table draped in pale green damask cloth and ate their sandwiches filled with high-end deli meat, thickly sliced cheese, and condiments like pesto and roasted red peppers. Chrissy chatted about her girls and her gym schedule and her occasional struggles with Rick, her ex-husband.

"He just doesn't *get* me anymore," she said. "He used to understand me like on this sort of cellular level? But now when I say something as simple as . . . I don't know . . . the accountant says you have too many write-offs and you're going to get audited again—he looks at me like I'm speaking Swahili or something."

"Actually, I'm not sure there's a translation for that in Swahili," said Sean.

She grinned. "Like you speak Swahili."

"Well, I lived in Africa—couple years in Kenya, couple in Democratic Republic of Congo—so, yeah, I really do."

"Say something, then."

He thought for a minute. At first he was going to tell her that she had a little drip of red pepper juice on her chin, but considered she might not take it kindly. *"Wewe ni mrembo."*

"Which means?"

"You're beautiful."

Her smile filled with buttery satisfaction. She made him say it several more times so she could repeat it to her daughters. One in particular was having a little self-esteem problem.

As they walked back out to the parking lot, she slid her hand into his, and it felt smooth and warm, a strangely new experience. Sex was one thing, but hand-holding was something else entirely. It indicated an attachment, and done publicly it was practically a blinking neon sign: WE ARE TOGETHER. Sean had always avoided it more assiduously than exposure to tuberculosis.

But it felt kind of good—as did the kiss she gave him when she dropped him off. In a funny way both felt weirdly more intimate than sex, and the thought that two such apparently innocent acts could start to seem like a contract of some kind tumbled around in his brain.

At eleven that night, the phone rang. It was Da. "Will you see me?" he asked.

"So much for giving me some time to think about it."

"I gave you a whole day."

Sean chuckled. "A whole day," he said drily. "Generous after being gone for almost thirty years. And how come you keep calling so late at night?"

"Because I don't want to talk to your aunt, and I remember she favors an early bedtime."

"You seem to remember a lot."

"Too much," he said. "I remember everything."

There was a silence then, the two of them listening to each other breathe into their respective receivers, like animals circling, each waiting for the other to make the first move.

"Have you told Hugh and Deirdre?" Da asked finally.

There was a momentary temptation to say, *Hugh's dead and you nearly killed Deirdre.* But the seesaw of anger and longing tipped toward the latter. "No," he said. "I haven't."

"You're still very protective of them. I'm glad of that."

"Someone had to be."

The older man was silent. Then he said, "I don't like the phone."

"Neither do I." They'd both spent the majority of their lives beyond the reach of a phone line, Sean realized. But he certainly wasn't going to dwell on their similarities.

"Will you meet me then, and I can beg your forgiveness in person?"

Sean felt the succubus again. He did not want to be begged for anything. "Wait a minute," he said. "Where are you?"

"The Comfort Inn."

"The Comfort Inn *where*?"

"On Route 9."

Jesus, Mary, and Joseph—he was three minutes away! "Did you drive by the house a couple of days ago?"

"I saw you up on the veranda. That's how I knew you still lived there."

Sean felt woozy and thought he might faint. In three minutes, he could see his da. And then what? Weep? Punch him? Tell him one of his children is dead?

"I can't . . . I don't . . ."

"Shall I give you more time?"

"Yeah," Sean said, his throat feeling tight and painful.

"I'll give you the telephone number of the hotel. You can call when you're ready."

After the call, Sean sat in the kitchen. The rain had stopped, and the silence was punctuated by moisture dripping out of the downspouts. More time. Would it help? Would there ever be enough of it to sort out nearly thirty years of absence? Did he even feel like trying?

"Uncle Sean." There was pressure at his shoulder, and pain in his back. He felt sticky and hot, the sheets clinging to him like cellophane. He fluttered his eyes against the brightness in the room. "Uncle Sean." Another poke at his shoulder.

"For the love of God, *what*?"

"I think I'll stay home."

Sean lifted his face off the pillow. "What are you talking about?"

"Boy Scout camp. I think I won't go."

Sean twisted and groaned, hoisting himself up to a sitting position. "And you're telling me at such an ungodly hour, why?"

"It's nine-thirty. You have to call Mr. Quentzer as soon as possible, since it starts tomorrow."

Sean scrubbed his hands over his face. He'd had a beer last night after the phone call from his father. Okay, maybe two or three. He hadn't been able to sleep, and couldn't stop his brain from spinning around and around on this problem of what to do about Martin Doran, ghost father, recently come to life at the Comfort freaking Inn on Route freaking 9.

"Wait a minute. Back up. Why aren't you going to Boy Scout camp?"

The sleep-blur was starting to clear from his eyes, and Sean saw Kevin biting at the inside of his cheek. "I can't do it. I'm too worried."

"What are you worried about?"

"What if it's not good? What if there's a ton of kids there, and it's like middle school?"

"I told you, I'll come get you."

Kevin looked away and muttered, "What if I *cry*?"

"Kev, you gotta go. You can't not do stuff because of a bunch of what-ifs."

"That's easy for *you*. You don't cry."

Hard to argue with that one. Sean scratched his neck and thought for a moment. "Hey, did I tell you I got a tape player? My friend Becky had one. Now you can play your tape."

"Really?"

"Yeah. Maybe if you still like it, you could bring it to camp."

Sean threw on some shorts and a T-shirt while Kevin got the tape from his room. He put the headphones on and adjusted the volume. Sean watched the boy's face pass through a range of expressions: the inner cheek biting stopped, and his eyebrows unfurrowed. His lips parted slightly as a look of recognition spread across his features. Then his eyes rested on Sean. He nodded slowly. "I remember him."

"Remember . . . ?"

"My dad. I didn't think I remembered him, but I do."

Sean didn't know what to say.

"He kinda looked like you, right?" said Kevin. "But his eyes were different."

"They were green. Like yours."

"Yeah!" Kevin nodded. "Like mine . . . I remember." He studied Sean for a moment. "You remember him, too, right?"

"Yeah, Kev," he said, gazing at the boy with his brother's eyes. "I do."

It took all day and several trips to REI, the Scout Store, and Target to get Kevin packed. There always seemed to be one more thing he needed—mosquito netting and sunscreen, hiking boots and official scout socks. They decided that Rebecca's tape player was too big and heavy and bought a compact version.

Kevin's tape was called *Sounds of Acadia*. It was a series of instrumental pieces put out by Acadia National Park that incorporated the calls of birds and rush of streams, breaking waves and horses' hoof steps. Sean vaguely remembered Hugh talking about camping there once. The tape was old, and Sean worried that it would break in the not-too-distant future. He used Deirdre's laptop to locate the Acadia Web site and called to order another, just in case.

"I'm sorry," said the clerk at the park gift shop. "Your credit card has been declined."

Declined? Sean told her he'd call back and called the credit card company. Apparently he'd maxed out his very low credit limit; all that camping stuff had cost more than he'd realized.

"We can easily raise your limit, Mr. Doran," said the overly helpful customer service rep.

Sean hesitated. The limit was low on purpose—if it was stolen while he was overseas, thieves wouldn't be able to rack up much in charges. But if he didn't raise the limit, he'd have to wait until another payment cleared before he could make any further purchases—including a backup for the all-important *Sounds of Acadia* tape.

"Yeah, okay," he said. "But not too high."

The customer service rep laughed a little longer than necessary about this. "My goodness!" she said. "Most people want it as high as they can possibly get it!"

"Sorry to disappoint," Sean responded drily.

The next morning Sean made a breakfast of eggs, sausages, and thick slices of toast with jelly. "Are you sure you had enough?" he asked when Kevin laid his fork and knife down.

"Yeah, I'm stuffed."

"Are you sure? I don't want you to get hungry."

"I'm pretty sure they have food at camp, Uncle Sean. And if they don't, another slice of toast isn't going to help."

Sean laughed. "Stop hovering, is what you're telling me."

"Yeah." Kevin grinned. "Pretty much."

They loaded Kevin's duffel bag into the car, and Kevin said good-bye to Auntie Vivvy and George. He squatted down to scratch behind the dog's ears. "Be good," he told her. "Uncle Sean is the vice prime minister, so let him be the boss." He stood up and addressed Sean. "You'll walk her every day, right?"

"Scout's honor."

"You're not a scout."

"Okay, uncle's honor."

Kevin squinted skeptically.

"I'll walk the dog, Kev, I promise!"

They drove over to the Scout House. The parking lot swarmed with boys. Kevin started to chew the inside of his cheek.

"I think it's going to be okay," Sean told him. "You've got your tape, and there are some good guys here. If you have a problem, talk to Mr. Quentzer."

When they got out of the car, Ivan ran over to show Kevin his new jackknife. Sean hauled the duffel over to the growing pile by Frank Quentzer's SUV. He caught Frank's eye.

"How's he doing?" asked Frank.

"A little nervous. I know the packet said they're not supposed to bring electronics, but he's got this tape he likes . . ."

Frank nodded. "No problem. And don't worry, I'll keep an eye on him. He'll be fine."

As Sean drove out of the parking lot, he saw Kevin standing with a group of boys, admiring Ivan's jackknife. Kevin glanced up and raised a hand as the Caprice passed. Sean waved back.

As he drove home Sean prayed hard, as hard as he had in a long time. *Please let him be okay, please let him have fun, please watch over him and don't let him get overwhelmed or feel sad . . . please. . . .*

CHAPTER 30

Unexpectedly, Deirdre showed up for dinner.

"To what do we owe the pleasure?" asked Sean, as he set another place at the table.

"He's been working us so hard," said Deirdre. "He gave us the afternoon off and said we should all go home and *relax*." She gave a little eye-roll at the ridiculousness of that idea.

Aunt Vivvy sat quietly at the table, gazing out the window. "Windy," she said.

It was, in fact, somewhat more breezy than usual, and the air made the leaves of the red maple in the backyard do a little staccato dance. Sean and Deirdre glanced at each other.

"So . . ." said Sean, ladling chili into Deirdre's bowl. "You feel it's going pretty well?"

"No. It's not. I'm just barely getting in stride, and everyone else has had months to prepare." She stared down at her meal. "I'm the weak link."

"Come on," Sean gently chided. "You've never been weak at anything. You'll do fine."

She glanced up at him. "Don't," she warned.

"Don't what? I'm being supportive."

She snorted derisively. "No, you're being patronizing and clueless. You don't know anything about the pressure I'm under, so don't act like you do."

Sean was slightly stunned by this declaration but recovered quickly. "You're right," he said. "I don't. What I do know is that I've made it possible for you to do nothing but work and rehearse for the past two months. If that comes off as patronizing, I can stop right now."

She glowered at him for a moment, then lifted a spoonful of chili to her mouth and ate. "Pretty good," she said.

Sean nodded, accepting the apology. "In the developing world you get to know your way around a can of beans." He glanced at his aunt, still staring out the window. "I think the chili's cool enough now, Auntie." She looked over at him as if he were speaking another language. He picked up her spoon, handed it to her, and indicated her bowl.

"Ah," she said, nodding, and dipped the spoon in. They ate for some time in silence, Deirdre's gaze unfocused and slightly perturbed-looking.

"Dee," said Sean. "I know it's a bad time to tell you, but there's something I think you should know."

"Oh, God," she said. "What."

"I got a phone call the other night. From Da."

She blinked at him a moment. "*Our* da?"

Aunt Vivvy looked up from her meal.

"Yeah."

"He's still alive?"

"Apparently. And he wants to see us."

Deirdre shook her head. "No."

"No," Aunt Vivvy echoed. "I won't let him hurt you."

Deirdre squinted at her uncomprehendingly, then turned back to her brother. "I don't even know him," she said. "And I sure as hell don't want to get into it *now*. You know what this means to me, Sean—I can't afford to lose one ounce of focus." She scooped another spoonful of chili, but set it down in the bowl without eating it. "Are you going to see him?"

"I don't know."

"Why would you? He dumped us."

Sean was reminded that over the years Deirdre had felt the

repercussions of that blow more than anyone, raised from early childhood only by their stoic aunt. He glanced at Aunt Vivvy, who was staring out the window again. "Yeah," he said. "And that wasn't exactly agreed upon. Apparently the homeowner never wanted the package."

Deirdre smirked. "And you're just figuring that out now?"

The next day was too quiet, especially since Sean had no interest in being alone with his thoughts and the quandary about his father. Cormac didn't need any help at the Confectionary, and Deirdre had left early for a double shift at the diner. Aunt Vivvy came down for a cup of tea and a piece of toast. She ate silently, then went back to her room for a rest.

Kevin was notably absent.

Sean looked at George and let out a resigned sigh. "Where's your leash?" This caused a surprising round of tail wagging. They were almost out the door when Rebecca called.

"Hey," she said. "I'm about to go for a run—want to join me?"

Sean hung the leash back on its hook, grabbed the car keys, and headed out to meet her at The Pal parking lot by Lake Pequot. When he pulled in, she was a couple of spaces down, wearing a pair of black running shorts and a pale blue tank top. Her hands were pressed against the trunk of her car, one leg behind her to stretch her calf. She switched legs and stretched the other, her movement graceful and decisive.

She looked up when he approached. "I don't run that fast. I hope you don't mind."

"I'm pretty sure my aunt could beat me," he said, "so you're gonna kick my ass."

She smiled at him, mouth lopsided, eyes crinkling unevenly, and he felt a quick little intake of air, as if his oxygen supply wasn't quite prepared for the beauty of her expression.

They set off around the lake, their pace easy and relaxed. "How did it go with Kevin and the tape?" she asked.

"Perfect," he said. "He practically went into a trance."

"Sean, that's great! I'm so glad for both of you."

"Yeah, it's a huge relief. And it'll make it easier when I leave, knowing he has that to help him."

Rebecca's head turned to look out over the lake; they ran for a few minutes in silence.

"So, I don't think my adoption's going to go through," he said, but still she didn't turn back. Sean raised his voice a little. "My father called."

Her head snapped toward him. "What? You're kidding! What did he say?"

Sean relayed the gist of the two conversations. "Deirdre won't see him. She's too wrapped up in her play, and she doesn't even remember him. And he doesn't know about Hugh."

Rebecca's hand came out and rested on his shoulder for a few strides.

"Yeah," said Sean. "How do you tell a guy his kid's been dead for six years?"

"Oh, Sean," she sighed. "So you're going to see him?"

"Jesus, I don't know. I really don't want to. It'll be so awkward . . . and then what? He goes back to wherever, and I take off for the next place, and we send postcards a couple times a year? Why bother?"

"Maybe he just wants to explain."

He considered this for a few strides. "Maybe. But is there anything he could possibly say that would justify it? And does it even matter anymore? I'm going to be forty-four in a couple of months. I'm not looking for a daddy."

"So he'll never know about Hugh."

"What do you mean?"

"If you don't see him, he won't know. You'd never say something like that over the phone."

Actually, it was exactly what he'd been thinking he'd do. But when she put it that way, he knew the option was gone.

The houses they passed were small former camps that had been weatherized for year-round residency. They approached a couple standing on the front step of one of the houses. The woman's hair was dark and curly, the man slightly balding; she had her arms crossed, his hands were in his pockets. The casual-seeming stances were belied by the looks of intensity on both faces. It was only when Sean drew closer that he realized the woman was Cormac's cousin Janie, and the man her new love. Sean was about to call out to her but sensed he'd be intruding. She never glanced up, locked as she seemed to be in a war of wills.

Wonder what that's about, thought Sean.

"Hey," said Rebecca. "I've been doing a little research on sensory integration, and wanted to send you some links. You don't have an e-mail account, though, do you?"

Sean chuckled and shook his head. "Is there some organized campaign to get me on e-mail, or is this just a coincidence?"

"I'm not part of a coordinated effort," she said. "But I wouldn't be surprised if there was one. Not having e-mail is pretty last-century, pal."

"In America, maybe."

She glanced up toward a hawk circling the shoreline. "Well, I may be wrong," she said, "but it looks like that's where you happen to be at the moment."

When they had completed the loop around Lake Pequot, Rebecca opened her car and pulled out a water bottle. Sean bent over, resting his hands on his knees. She held out the water to him; he took a couple of gulps and handed it back. "Thanks," he said. "So what's next? You feel like grabbing some lunch or something?"

"Well, I was planning to do a little yoga, then meditate. Want to join me, Swami?"

"I follow my guru wherever she goes."

When they got to her house, he said, "Okay, one little chore first."

"Look, I know how much you love redecorating, but can we give it a rest just this once?"

"We can rest all day—after we pull the desk out of that room."

She narrowed her eyes at him. “Okay. But first we sign you up for an e-mail account.”

“No dice.”

“No dice, no desk.”

He shook his head. She shrugged. “Okay, just so long as you understand it’s a deal breaker. Not one stick of furniture moves until you have e-mail.”

“Give me one good reason.”

She gazed at him, and he sensed she was trying to decide which of several good reasons to mention first. “Kevin,” she said.

“Nice try. Kevin doesn’t have e-mail.”

“No, but you told me there’s nobody on the parents’ listserv from the school for him. This way you could keep up with what’s going on. You could e-mail his teachers if you needed to. And, you could get him an account, too. Kids don’t talk anymore. They text and e-mail and Facebook.” She smiled. “And it’s just a hunch, but I’m betting you’re not quite up to dealing with Facebook.”

CHAPTER 31

They spent the rest of the day together. Sean signed up for a free e-mail account and persuaded Rebecca to move the desk *and* the bed out of the room, leaving it empty of everything but the massage table. They also cleared off a small bookshelf in the basement and brought it up so she would have somewhere to keep massage oil and the CD player.

"Next time, we pull down the wallpaper."

"Ha! Right," she said. "Sol and Betty would have a cow."

Sean made a show of looking around. "No Sol and Betty," he said. "No cow."

"You are really pushing it."

"Yeah, I *am* really pushing it. Because you deserve to work somewhere that's actually conducive to your business and your general mental health. You could make a go of it on your own, you know. Think how great it would be to leave Eden and the Tree of Life in the dust of your highly stable energy."

She sighed. "Pretty darn great."

"That's what I'm saying."

"Ugh!" she groaned suddenly.

"What?"

"It's so easy for you! You're an on-your-own kind of person. You just get on a plane and go to the next place and meet a whole bunch of new people—and you don't worry! It's not *like* that for me. Change is hard. *People* are hard. You never know what they're thinking, or who's going to turn out to be a jerk."

"Everybody's got stuff that's hard, Beck."

"Yeah, I know—of *course* I know. But you having stuff that's hard doesn't make my stuff any easier. It actually makes it *harder*." She shook her head, as if it might help her thoughts sift into a more comprehensible order. "Look," she said. "I hate that you have all this crap to deal with. Why can't life just be easy sometimes? If not for me, for somebody I care about!"

Her exasperation had put color in her cheeks and passion in her voice, and he felt an almost undeniable urge to wrap his arms around her and feel all that energy up against him. He wanted to be in her stratosphere, held there by the gravity of her warmth and generosity. It scared him how much he wanted it, and the fear helped him curb the wanting.

He only put a hand on her shoulder. "Hey, somewhere out there is somebody with no problems at all," he said. "And he's probably annoying as hell."

She kicked him out before dinner, though. She had plans. With "a friend." No further details were offered. Sean didn't like that at all. But even more, he didn't like that he didn't like it. Why should he care? But still he found himself saying in a teasing way, "Sounds like a date."

She looked mildly startled. "Not really," she said.

Not really? Not *really*?

He drove home vaguely annoyed. It was sort of like when a new volunteer came to the hospital or clinic and, through no fault of their own, they just didn't do things the way you wanted them to. But you couldn't be angry because they were thousands of miles from home, enduring the heat or the rain, the flies and the bad food, the cot or the lumpy ancient mattress, doing their best for nothing. Just to help out. You had no right to be annoyed. And yet you were.

Wanting to think about anything other than his own baseless irritability, his mind landed on Chrissy, and he realized he hadn't seen her in a few days. Now that Kevin was at camp, he supposed she had no dog-training-related excuse to pop over. She'd always been the one to initiate getting together. Maybe she was waiting for him to call now? Because he was pretty sure women did that—waited for the guy to call. Or was that considered old-fashioned these days?

He dialed her up when he got home, relieved that neither of her daughters answered. What would he have said—"Please tell her Sean called"?

Sean who? And what business do you have with my mother? Oh, I've heard about you—the guy in the bleachers trying to move in on my mom while my dad was busy scoring touchdowns. He decked you, didn't he?

Yes. Yes, he certainly did.

But Chrissy answered, and though he'd only had a fuzzy idea of maybe getting coffee or taking a walk, their plan soon grew like fast-multiplying cells into dinner and a movie and possibly a nightcap at her house afterward. The girls were staying with their father.

Sean's visceral reaction to this last little firecracker of a revelation was a combination of *Yippee!* and *Yikes!* But he'd worry about that later.

The night seemed to buzz by, except during the movie, *The Bouquet Catcher,* a romantic comedy so cloyingly sweet that Sean thought he might need insulin injections by the time the credits rolled. He focused on consuming his extra large popcorn fast enough to qualify for the free refill before the movie was over. After this personal success, he fell into a drooling, head-bobbing doze. He woke up as the violins were cued, feeling like he'd eaten a bag of rock salt.

"I need water," he told her.

"Great! Let's have a drink at my house."

As they exited the theater, her hand slid once again into his, and pleasant as the physical sensation was, alarm bells began to ring in his mind as he imagined the WE ARE TOGETHER sign flashing garishly over their heads.

Are we together?

Together with Chrissy Stillman, he tried to tell himself. *Way to go!* But somehow it didn't feel the way he'd fantasized it would. Actually, it felt a little like handcuffs. He'd been handcuffed once in India, mistakenly identified as having run out on his bill at a teahouse. It was sorted out fairly quickly. He suspected this situation would definitely take more sorting than that.

At her house, they were soon snuggled on the enormous burgundy leather couch with the beaten metal tacks, glasses of Cabernet cradled between their fingers. He liked the smell of the leather and the wine and her perfume, the feel of her closeness, and the way her perfectly symmetrical eyes sparkled at him.

Symmetrical?

He realized that at the back of his brain was the image of Rebecca's eyes, perfectly *un*symmetrical, as if God's level had been a bit off plumb as he'd made her. She was out with "a friend" tonight, he reminded himself.

Well, so am I.

He kissed Chrissy, and the kissing soon turned passionate, hands passing over backs and then over fronts, Chrissy's lovely half-cantaloupe-shaped breasts rising to the occasion, her nipples erect through her shirt. They went on like this for a bit, and he definitely wanted to have sex with her. But something kept stopping him from pressing forward. It was the hand-holding. He just wasn't sure if he was ready for that.

She didn't ask him to stay, but he got the feeling she would have liked him to. He could always stay another time, he figured. He wasn't burning any bridges. He was just . . . *balking* was the first word that came to mind, but that wasn't right. He was being considerate, waiting until he'd sorted out that hand-holding/handcuff thing. It seemed like the right thing to do.

When he got home that night, there was a glow coming from the den. Since Dee's computer had been left on, he decided to check his e-mail account. There was one e-mail waiting for him from Rebecca Feingold. She had forwarded the links to the sensory integration sites she'd found. Then she'd written a couple of lines.

I'm glad you crumbled so quickly to my e-mail ultimatum. I'll miss you when you're gone, and it's nice to know that now I'll be able to find you from time to time. You never know when another interior decorating emergency might pop up out of nowhere. :)

R

He smiled at this, thinking of receiving news of her ongoing furniture crises at an Internet café in some decrepit third world city. He wouldn't be around to do the actual moving, of course, but he could badger her until she found someone else to help. Someone with a strong back . . . maybe whoever she was with tonight . . .

Don't be an idiot, he told himself, and responded:

Doran Furniture Removal, always at your service, ma'am.

S

CHAPTER 32

After breakfast the next morning, Aunt Vivvy went out to the backyard and slowly snipped at an overgrown bush of some kind, while George patrolled the perimeter of the property as if she were on duty at a maximum security prison. Sean had second thoughts about his aunt's using the pruning shears, but he knew George would get his attention if things went awry.

He went into the den, powered up Deirdre's laptop, and opened up Rebecca's e-mail again. He clicked through to the Web sites on sensory integration, sometimes called sensory processing disorder. It was described as a neurological dysfunction in processing information from the five senses: taste, touch, smell, sound, and sight. Though doctors had been noting and theorizing about the symptoms for approximately forty years, it had only recently coalesced into a definitive condition—one which the medical community was still coming to terms with.

In the "Sensory Modulation" section, Sean found Kevin.

This group over- or underresponded to sensory input, meaning that they might experience a normal sound as too loud or not loud enough, a neutral food to be terrible-tasting or tasteless. The input was the same, but the person's neurons weren't making sense of it at the appropriate level. There was a checklist with symptoms that included:

"Uncomfortable being touched, especially if unexpected . . . avoids certain materials or fabrics . . . distressed by sock seams or clothing tags . . . needs heavy blankets to sleep . . . repeatedly touches objects that are soothing . . ."

Sean thought of Kevin's stubborn refusal to wear the latex gloves at Cormac's Confectionary, and how he now always seemed to have his hand in George's fur.

"Excessively bothered by normal sounds like loud laughter or lawn-mowing . . ."

Lawn-mowing, thought Sean, slumping in shame. *Jesus Christ.*

"Overreacts to bad smells, such as bathrooms, but also to an overabundance of pleasant smells such as perfume or food . . .

"May seem intensely stubborn or easily upset about small things . . ."

"Tends to prefer being alone rather than risking the discomfort of sensory overload . . ."

It was Kevin to a T.

Sean had a thought and went upstairs to Kevin's bedroom. There were no fewer than seven blankets on the kid's bed. Sean opened the dresser drawers—there were pairs of underwear, shorts, pants, T-shirts . . . but no socks. There was not one pair of socks anywhere in the room. Evidently Kevin did not wear socks, a fact that Sean had completely overlooked. He pulled out shirts and underwear. Each and every one had had its tag carefully snipped out. In fact, there was a pair of scissors sitting on the dresser, apparently kept there for just that purpose.

Sean sat down on the heavily blanketed bed. He wondered what it was like to feel as if you were under assault by things that everyone else thought were normal. And to have no one to talk to about it.

Sadness hit Sean like a body slam. But it quickly turned to anger. Why had no one been there for Kevin? Had his teacher, Ms. Lindquist, seen this and done nothing? What about Deirdre or his aunt? There were things that would have helped—Hugh's soothing music, for one. But there were many other suggestions for helping an overly sensitized child learn to manage the perceived mayhem around him. Why had no one helped Kevin?

Sean glanced out the bedroom window and saw Aunt Vivvy sitting on the wrought-iron gardening bench in the backyard. He went down to the kitchen, filled two glasses with water and brought them out, sat down next to her, and handed her a glass.

She took a sip. "It's summer," she said with a hint of disgust.

"Is that a problem?"

"Only with regard to pruning," she responded drily, "properly conducted in the early spring or late fall."

"At least you only did one bush."

"Which has now been carelessly thrown into biological confusion."

Sean wondered how she could find such compassion for plants when she evidenced so little for other living things that had actual feelings.

"It's happening more and more, isn't it?" he said.

"You tell me. I'm hardly aware of it."

"What does it feel like when you are?"

She stared fiercely at the newly shorn bush. "It's much like when you're falling asleep and a dream begins. You know you're lying in bed, but then you sense that you're being pulled toward some greater reality. And you go."

A trickle of sympathy hydrated his parched anger toward her, and he reached over and took her hand. She quickly disengaged it. "The only unpleasantness is when you return and see that everyone is staring at you and behaving as if you were a hallucinating child."

He put his hand back in his lap. "I need to ask you about Kevin."

She sighed. "Proceed."

He summarized the information he'd learned about sensory processing, and what he'd noticed about Kevin's difficulties. "How long has he been avoiding socks?"

"Since he was old enough to pull them off."

"That young? Did Hugh know about it?"

"Know about it? How could anyone within a quarter mile miss the crying and screaming? 'No sock! No sock!' Practically his first words." Aunt Vivvy rested her glass on the arm of the bench. "I told

Hugh he needed to take control, but that was about as effective as telling a street sweeper to run for president."

"How did he handle it?"

"In warm weather, the child wore no socks. In cold weather, Hugh bought every different kind of sock he could find. He must have spent a small fortune trying to find a pair that wouldn't send the boy into paroxysms, all to no avail."

"So he just doesn't wear them. Ever."

"Correct."

Sean considered this—not the sock aversion; that was completely consistent with everything he'd just learned about the disorder. What fascinated him was Hugh's response: a Holy Grail–like quest for the perfect sock. It was another example of Hugh's fatherly dedication.

"And he tossed the boy constantly," Aunt Vivvy interjected suddenly. "It was very irritating."

"Tossed him how?"

"Into the air. Onto the couch. Over his shoulder. The man was a human trampoline. It's a wonder the child hasn't joined the circus."

A trampoline . . . thought Sean. *Hanging upside down* . . . These were on the list of suggestions for parents with oversensitized children. Somehow Hugh had figured out activities that would help Kevin and had used his own body to provide them.

"He must have gotten very strong," said Sean.

Aunt Vivvy's eyes cut toward him. "He was always complaining of back pain."

Sean left his aunt to contemplate what further gardening blunders she might commit, worried that he might start saying things he'd later regret. *Cold-hearted witch,* he thought, returning to the den. *Uncaring, miserable tyrant . . .*

He'd seen the postings of parents who'd been told by relatives and professionals alike that their child was simply manipulating them, and that the correct course of action was to be firm, to punish them if need be. Tragically, Aunt Vivvy's take on it was quite commonplace.

And yet what made Sean's own back ache all the more, like some sort of delayed sympathy pain, was the fact that he hadn't known. Or more specifically, hadn't lifted a finger to find out. Hugh had been a single father whose child had an unknown, untreated condition, muddling through as best he could, tossing the kid into the air by the hour and buying socks by the dozen . . . and his own brother hadn't picked up on it during the one brief visit while all three of them were alive. Had never written a letter to say, "How's it going with you and the kid?"

Something Deirdre had said when he'd first gotten home came back to him. *You've been all about you,* she'd said. *You haven't given a shit about anyone else your whole life.*

It wasn't true.

He had cared deeply about many people—the embattled indigenous Indians of Guatemala, the de facto slaves in the Dominican Republic, the unthinkably poor of India, the wounded and abused of Africa. He thought of conversations with people like Yasmin Chaudhry, the few who understood what it meant to live as they did, to sacrifice so much, to see things no one else wanted to see—and to try and be that drop of water in the desert.

Bullshit, said the Deirdre in his head. *You did what you wanted to do.*

And that *was* true.

More than anything he had wanted to leave Belham. And he had wanted to believe that his screwed-up life had a purpose. He had wanted something to feel good about, instead of feeling shitty all the time. He had saved lives and healed people and brought babies safely into the world—he had made the difference he'd wanted to make.

But in doing so he'd neglected his own sister and brother, his aunt (though God knows she never wanted any help, and a case could be made that she hardly deserved any), and his nephew. And knowing that he'd missed his chance to be there for Hugh, through what were likely his toughest times, Sean felt more committed than ever to helping Kevin now. He would get things on track, and he wouldn't leave until he knew Kevin was okay.

In the spirit of his newfound commitment to Kevin's health and happiness, Sean turned to Deirdre's laptop, his fingers hunting and pecking across the keyboard like a kind of therapy. He entered the Belham Middle School Web site and got himself on the parent e-mail list; he clicked over to Juniper Hill School and sent an e-mail to Ms. Lindquist. And then he made a few purchases.

CHAPTER 33

Sean couldn't have been happier to spend the day at the Confectionary if it had been a swimming pool and he'd been on fire. It was a relief to attend only to people's baked-good needs, spar with the ever-sardonic Tree, and help out his old friend. Besides, the money would come in handy.

It was late morning, the slowest part of the day, and Cormac told him to take his break.

"Hey," he said to Cormac, pulling off his apron. "Think I could borrow your father again next week? Something I ordered requires assembly."

"Heck, yeah!" Cormac turned toward the kitchen and raised his voice. "You want Pop? He's all yours."

A loud grumble replied, "Nothing I'd like better than getting sprung from this sweatshop! Especially with Goliath for a boss."

"Kinda makes you yearn for a slingshot, right, Uncle Charlie?" Cormac's cousin Janie said, approaching the counter.

"Ain't *that* the truth!" called Mr. McGrath.

Sean took a bottle of water for his break and Janie got her coffee and joined him at a seat by the window.

"I saw you the other day," Sean said. "I was jogging around the lake and you and the guy you're with, you were standing on the front step of a house. Looked like a serious conversation, so I didn't want to interrupt."

Janie thought for a moment. "Yeah, that."

His eyebrows rose a little, inviting further comment, but not wanting to pry.

She shrugged. "Just trying to figure it all out," she said. "It's not like when you're in your twenties and you love someone and that's all you need to know. Now there are kids and houses, and potential kids and potential houses. . . ."

"Complicated."

"*Way* too complicated. And me personally? I just don't think I'm that complicated."

"Me either."

"Wanna get married?" she said, deadpan, and they both burst out laughing.

"Okay, how's this for complicated," he said. "My father, who dumped us with my aunt almost thirty years ago and never came back? He's back."

Janie's face dropped. "No way."

"Yeah, he's holed up at the Comfort Inn out on Route 9, waiting for me to decide whether I want to see him again. Beat that."

"I can't," she said. "Wow, Spinster. What're you going to do?"

He shrugged. "Half of me wants to go just to tell him how badly he screwed us all up. Half of me wants to say, 'Sorry, that door's closed.'"

Janie nodded. "I have no idea what I'd do if my father showed up out of nowhere." She looked up at Sean and there was a melancholy behind her eyes.

"You'd see him," he said.

"Yeah. I probably would. I don't know what Cormac told you, but my husband was killed in a bike accident almost two years ago. I met the old guy who hit him, and he was out of his mind with regret. Gave me a new perspective on forgiveness."

"My father says he just wants to apologize."

They sat there for a moment. "Maybe you should see him, Sean," she said gently. It was the only time he could remember her using his actual name.

After work, he walked. He started off heading for home, but then decided to see if Rebecca was back from the spa yet. Her house was in the opposite direction, but it felt good to move after standing in one place all day.

Janie's words bobbed around in his head. There were as many reasons to see Da as there were not to. Sean was coming to the conclusion that the dilemma defied analysis when he turned onto Rebecca's street. The house was dark. He rang the doorbell anyway. No one came. He considered waiting, but she could be taking the later shift and have clients until eight. Or she could have plans after work. With someone other than him. If he'd had a cell phone, he would have called, but he didn't, so he turned back down her street and began the long walk home.

He was tired and hungry when he arrived, and made sandwiches for himself and his aunt. Deirdre's sticky work sneakers had been left in the front hallway, but she was gone now. The dog paced around the kitchen as Sean spread mustard over the slices of deli turkey. The dinner was quiet until Aunt Vivvy said, "Please remind me of Kevin's whereabouts."

"He went to Boy Scout camp. He'll be back at the end of the week."

"Boy Scout camp—the only participants being boys, I assume?"

"That's how it works."

"Sounds noisy. Are you sure he wanted to go?"

"Are you suggesting that I *made* him go?"

"I'm suggesting that living with a bunch of rowdy boys for a week doesn't strike me as Kevin's cup of tea. He likes you very much. He might have done it to please you."

A prickle of anxiety ran across Sean's scalp. He had pushed the idea, and Kevin had certainly been ambivalent about it. But he seemed okay when Sean dropped him off.

"No, he definitely wanted to go," said Sean. "He loves the outdoors."

Aunt Vivvy took another bite of her sandwich and declined to comment further.

That night, with the house dark and quiet, Sean called the Comfort Inn. He waited while the desk clerk connected him to his father's room.

"Okay," he said. "I'll meet you."

Da sighed. "I appreciate it, son. I know it's not easy."

"Where do you want to go?"

"I had it in mind that we might try the old IHOP over by the post office."

"Fine. How's eight?"

"Of course. I'll be there waiting. I've got gray hair now."

"I've got a bit of gray myself."

"Don't you worry, lad. I'd know you with my eyes closed."

The next morning Sean pulled into the IHOP parking lot, but he could not make himself get out of the car. He could feel his pulse racing and counted it just to be sure. Ninety beats per minute. High, but not heart-attack high. Apparently he would survive this.

Still he couldn't get his legs to move, and he suddenly had a desperate wish not to be facing it—him—alone. Deirdre had made her intentions clear, but even if she had agreed to come, she probably would've made it harder. Her temper was a lit fuse these days. Aunt Vivvy was unthinkable. And Hugh probably would've arrived stoned. A reunion with the man who abandoned you as a child—what better excuse to smoke a bone? The idea did have some appeal.

But that was pothead Hugh. What about sock-buying Hugh? For the hundredth time, Sean felt the regret of never having known that side of his brother. The strange thing was that he could almost imagine it. There had always been a patience and a generosity to Hugh that outshone even his worst tendencies.

Sean had never prayed to his brother—a more unlikely saint there never was. But he found himself thinking of him now, praying for guidance, and for the strength Hugh had obviously shown in the face of Kevin's difficulties. Sean closed his eyes, and he could almost feel Hugh sitting in the car with him.

It's all good, man, said St. Hugh. *Loosen up.*

Easy for you, you dead bastard.

A saintly laugh. *Breathe. You're up to this.*

No, I'm really not. What if he falls apart?

Toss him in the air a few times—works like a charm.

What if I *fall apart?*

Then I'll *toss* you.

CHAPTER 34

Martin Doran sat at a booth, back straight, wearing a button-down blue shirt. His hair was, in fact, completely gray. It had been tar black the last time Sean had seen him.

He stood when Sean approached, chest up, shoulders broad, as if Sean were the captain of the SS *IHOP* and his father one of the crew. His eyelids flickered nervously, and he thrust out his hand for Sean to shake. Sean looked down at it. There was a thick scar across the first knuckle that Sean had never noticed before. *Must be new,* he thought. *In the last thirty years, anyway.*

He reached out and took his father's hand for a quick shake, but it was long enough to become reacquainted with the worn-leather feel of it. The only difference was that his own hand was no longer dwarfed in size. He looked up and saw the older man's relief. A handshake. As good a start as any.

"Sean." He studied his son's face as if he might catalogue every freckle.

"Da." Sean looked away and sat down.

The waitress bustled quickly over with a plastic jug of coffee.

"I'd prefer tea, if you don't mind," said Da.

"Orange juice, please," said Sean.

After she left, Sean took a closer look at his father. Tiny capillaries had broken under the skin of his cheeks, like hairsbreadth red spiders scattering into the crevices of his wrinkles.

"So," said Da. "A bit of a quandary knowing where to start."

Well, don't look at me, thought Sean.

"I want to know all about you and Hugh and Deirdre, everything

I missed. But the fault is mine that I missed it in the first place, so I know I've no right to it."

He straightened the knife and fork on his napkin. Right angles. A compulsive habit Sean remembered from childhood. "I've no desire to talk about myself," Da went on. "I'm guessing you might not care all that much. But please let me begin to apologize." His gaze went hard into Sean. "Words may mean nothing at this point, but Sean Patrick, *I'm sorry.* I never should have stayed away as I did. It was weak and shameful, and even if the three of you find it in your hearts to forgive me someday, I shall never forgive myself."

A painful ache started behind Sean's eyes, and his throat tightened like a clamp. If he had known what to say, he wouldn't have been able to say it.

The waitress returned with the tea and orange juice. "Have you decided?"

"I don't believe we have," said Da. "Give us a quick minute, will you?" When she left, Da asked, "Can you eat?" Sean shook his head. "Shall I talk or shall I shut up and let you talk?"

Sean could feel tears like a pinhole leak threatening to burst, and he tightened his molars against it. His words came out in a guttural surge. "Where've you been?"

Da wrapped his thick hands around his mug of tea. The steam curled into the air-conditioned air between them. "At sea mostly," he said. "Container ships. I tried to spend as little time on land as possible. I fell into the bottle between runs." He took a sip of his tea. "Shame and loneliness," he said. "A man's best drinking mates.

"Aboard," he went on, "your mind is always busy, doing things proper, avoiding trouble. The danger is a blessing." He was quiet for a moment, and it seemed he was waiting for Sean to comment. "I had a little flat in Tacoma, Washington, for a bit. Good place for a mariner. Lots of ships. But then my hand got smashed—a chain snapped and flew out like a cobra. Nearly took off my arm." He turned the wrist of the scarred hand, and Sean could see that the knuckles were slightly misaligned. "If it had hit me in the head, I'd have gone to my reward." Da gave a mirthless little snort. "Such as it may be."

The waitress circled back, pad in hand. "Two short stacks, please," said Da. When she left he turned back to Sean. "I didn't want to disappoint her. You don't have to eat it."

The interruption helped Sean settle down a little. "You were working until a couple of years ago?" he asked. This was hard to believe. The man was over seventy.

Da nodded. "An able-bodied seaman can sail as long as he's able-bodied. I was known to be a hard worker. It kept the demons away." He flexed the hand and then clenched it. The index and middle fingers didn't curl as tightly as the others did, Sean noticed. Someone had done a very patchy job on those tendons, but there was clearly some nerve damage, too.

"No more runs," said Da, "no more hiding from the demons." In a drunken haze one night he'd left his hot plate on, he told Sean. A dish towel caught fire and then the curtains. He might have killed everyone in the building if a couple of passing skateboarders hadn't seen the flames and called the fire department. "The neighborhood pests," Da said. "Always whizzing by and giving you a heart attack. These were my saviors."

The landlord evicted him, and he drank himself into a stupor of undetermined duration—he didn't remember much other than getting kicked repeatedly when he slept behind a Dumpster down at the port. He wandered into a place called Nativity House that offers services and meals to the homeless. "At first it was just a warm place to be during the day. The staff were kind, some of them young people, just out of university. One of them—his name was Declan Kelly—he reminded me of you and Hugh. A funny, freckled boy who played backgammon with me and annoyed me to no end with his talk of detox and the AA. That's Alcoholics Anonymous." The young man had slowly chipped away at Martin's resolve to drink himself to death, found a treatment program for him and a halfway house after that.

The pancakes arrived, and with his good hand Da slowly slathered his with butter and jam. Sean's stomach was in no mood for visitors, and his pancakes remained untouched.

"It was the AA that got me thinking of finding you," said Da. "They have a program with twelve steps. One of the steps is making amends to those you've hurt or wronged."

Sean's anger surged. Apparently this was just an item to check off on some drunkard list. "So that's what you're doing," he said drily. "Making amends."

Martin laid his knife on the side of his plate. "No. As I told my sponsor, there's no such thing when the wrong is as wrong as this. I came for two things only. To tell you face-to-face how sorry I am; and to give you a chance to scream or yell or punch me in the nose, if you've a mind to. You must be carrying quite a burden of anger, the three of you, and the least I can do is provide an opportunity to vent it a little."

The old man picked up the knife again and resumed his careful spreading of butter and jam, as if it were an art project of some kind, or possibly occupational therapy for his remaining good hand. Sean considered his offer. He had no urge to punch his father, or to scream and yell. He knew the story, understood the series of events. There was just one thing he wanted to say.

"You left us with Aunt Vivvy."

The knife went still. "Aye," he murmured.

"She didn't want us."

Da let out a sigh. "That woman is a cold bit of mackerel, and don't think it didn't trouble me greatly. But she *did* want you. It was *me* she didn't want."

"She said she told you to take us and leave."

"Which she did. But you're Lila's children, and she loved her sister. She loved *you*, in her bloody arctic way. And she was a damn sight better at caring for you than I was at the time. I was drinking and dreadful depressed. I was out of control, Sean. Vivvy's no Mary Poppins, but she was better than me. 'Tisn't the leaving I regret. It's the not coming back."

Da ate a bite or two of his pancakes and asked the waitress for more tea. He wanted to know about Sean's life, and Sean gave him an overview, albeit brief. "This is the longest I've been back in twenty years," he said.

"And you never married?"

"No."

Da nodded thoughtfully. "Didn't want to do to your own family what was done to you."

"Right."

"And Deirdre? I'll bet she's married. That girl was as fanciful and romantic as any I've seen."

"No, she isn't, either. But she's an actress now. Well, trying to be. She's in a play out in Worcester, and planning to give it a go in New York if things go well."

"Ha!" Da chortled. "Of *course* she is. Brilliant!"

It was startling to see his Da grin so broadly. Sean wasn't sure if he remembered ever seeing such a look on his father's face. It had always had a slightly stony composition, as if anger, worry, and grief had been part of its skeletal structure.

"And Hugh?" Da asked, still smiling. "Don't tell me—he never married, the rascal. He's probably a ski bum. Or a skydiver."

"No, he never married."

"And what's his line of work?"

Help me, Hugh.

"Unemployed?" asked Da. "Well, that's all right. It's a down economy."

"No, uh . . ."

Da waited, but Sean couldn't find the words. He knew this was why he was here—to tell Da about Hugh. But it seemed cruel, and Sean wondered if it would drive him back to the bottle.

The older man became concerned. "Jail?"

"No. Nothing like that." Sean took a breath. "He passed, Da."

The scarred hand went up to his face. "Oh, Jesus, no."

"Six years ago."

"Was it the Huntington's?"

"Pneumonia."

"Pneumonia?"

"I wasn't here. I don't know much more than that." Sean shook his head. "I guess Kevin had it, and Hugh picked it up but didn't get it treated in time."

Da's face went from grief to confusion. "Who's Kevin?"

"Hugh had a son," Sean explained. "He's eleven now."

"A son." Da's eyes filled. "A son with no da." Tears spilled down the wrinkled, spider-veined cheeks. "Jesussufferingchrist," he whispered. "I should have been here."

Sean waited for the old man to collect himself, but there was no sign of it, and Sean began to get worried. The irony was not lost on either of them. So many fatherless sons. Generations of loss. Da's tears continued to flow.

Toss him in the air a few times, came the words in Sean's mind. *Works like a charm.*

His hand slid out across the table and into his father's battered one. He squeezed it, and his father squeezed back. Sean could feel the slackness in the index and middle fingers, and he felt sympathy for his da—for the ruined hand, and the weakness that kept him so far from his family, and for the heartbreak of losing his wife. The shame and the loneliness.

Da's crying quieted then. "Thank you," he said.

CHAPTER 35

They talked a while longer, the melted butter on Da's pancakes congealing into the jam. Sean was exhausted. He felt as if he'd been through Hugh's funeral all over again. He wanted to go home and get back into bed. And from bed he would call Rebecca and report that he had done it. He had told Da in person about his son's death and the existence of his grandson.

"So when do you go back to Tacoma?" he asked Da, politely trying to wrap up the breakfast.

"I've no plans to go back there," said Da.

Sean felt the hairs go up on the back of his neck. "No?" he said.

"There's nothing for me there."

"What about Declan Kelly?" Sean was grasping at straws, but panic was setting in.

"He's gone to California. Law school."

"Oh."

"Actually," Da offered hesitantly, "I'd like to move to Ireland."

"Wow. Do you still know anyone there?" Sean felt as if he'd dodged a familial bullet.

"None I've kept up with. But you know, it's not people I want to see. It's the island."

"Blasket? But there's nothing there anymore, is there? Everyone moved to the mainland."

"Yes, well, some went more happily than others." He tipped his head, a little self-scoffing gesture. "It's silly, really. But I need to. I have to get back there while I've still time."

"Well, I hope you have a great trip."

"Yes," he said, digging a wallet out of his pocket. "So do I." He tossed a twenty on the table. Sean went for his own wallet, but Da's stronger hand went out. "Wouldn't hear of it," he said, and Sean didn't have the energy to disagree.

They walked out to the parking lot—his father to a nondescript compact rental car. Sean put his hand out to shake, and Da took it in both of his own. "God bless and keep you, lad," he said. "And thank you."

Sean sat in the Caprice and watched his father pull out onto the roadway. When the small car disappeared from view, Sean had the strange feeling that maybe the breakfast hadn't happened at all, that it was some sort of fever dream, and when his temperature came down he'd see that it hadn't been real. In fact, at the moment none of it—IHOP, Belham, his prolonged stay in the States—seemed entirely plausible. A Talking Heads song from his high school days started to play in his brain. Something about suddenly being in another part of the world . . . driving a large automobile . . . *You may ask yourself, well, how did I get here?*

Holy shit, he thought. *How* did *I get here?*

Going back to Aunt Vivvy's felt entirely wrong—like it would compound his disorientation. The Tree of Life Spa was just down the road. Sean drove over to see if he could catch Rebecca between clients. He just wanted to see someone real.

Cleopatra sat on her ergonomic throne behind the reception desk. When she saw him, a look came over her face as if someone had just passed some particularly bad gas.

"Just tell me where she is," said Sean.

"Uh, this is a *spa*? So she's, like, giving a *spa* treatment?"

"I'll leave her a note."

Cleopatra pushed a pen and piece of paper toward him. He scribbled on it and handed it back. She pinched it between her finger and thumb, dropping it onto the desk like a used tissue.

Sean got back in the Caprice and started driving east down Route 9, for no other reason than that Tree of Life Spa was on the eastbound side, and it was illegal to make a left turn and go west. The road took him through Natick and into Wellesley. His mother had gone to Wellesley College, though she'd told him once that it hadn't been her first choice. She would have preferred to go to a co-ed school in a city. Wellesley had been her parents' first choice for just the opposite reasons: close to home, no boys.

Route 9 took Sean through Newton and into Chestnut Hill, not far from Boston College. His mother had often visited a high school friend who'd gone to BC. At the same time, his father had lived in Brighton with a guy who also went there. Martin had joined the merchant marine by then, but didn't miss the chance to go to college parties between runs. That's how they met.

The BC Mods were townhouse-style apartments with small adjoining yards that created the perfect venue for multiunit bashes. Martin and Lila had each come with their friends and gotten separated from them in the happy, raucous confusion of the party. Lila was standing next to the keg on the patio, knowing her friend would eventually turn up there, when Martin thrust his plastic cup at her for a refill. She had never used a keg tap before and ended up dousing a boy standing next to her, who was inebriated enough to consider this a kindness.

"Your poor mother was mortified," Martin had told Sean when he was a boy. "I fell in love with her on the spot."

Sean veered off Route 9 onto Hammond Street toward BC. He circled down past lower campus and pulled over where he could glimpse the Mods behind the newer high-rise dorms.

That's where it started, he thought. *This whole godforsaken mess.*

His anger surged at a God who would set in motion such a series of heartbreaks—a God Sean barely believed in anymore, yet who was still real enough to be furious with. He slammed the gearshift into drive and pulled out, coming quickly to Commonwealth Avenue. If he turned left, it would eventually take him directly into Belham.

Hell no, he thought, and turned right.

Comm Ave had plenty of traffic lights, giving Sean ample time to stare out the window, stewing on his family history. A domino effect of misfortune had been set up on the day his parents met, one tile toppling into another over the course of the next forty-five years.

The Caprice seemed to make its way down Comm Ave of its own accord. In Allston the graffiti on the side of a building said, GOD IS LOVE.

"You idiot," Sean told the graffiti. "God is a cruel son of a bitch with a twisted sense of humor. And by the way, you defaced a fucking building with that crap." His vitriol surprised even him. For so many years, God had been the loving parent he'd so desperately wanted and missed, a guide and protector through all that was sad and frightening about his life.

And now he saw it differently: God had tricked him into doing the hardest kind of work, in sort of a protracted practical joke. It was embarrassing to realize he'd been gullible enough to fall for it. Pranked by God

Wanting to get off the city streets and drive hard and fast, Sean pulled onto the Massachusetts Turnpike at the Allston tolls. He got confused at the point where it goes into the tunnel toward the airport and several other exit ramps spin off in various directions. Somehow he ended up in South Boston. And then he was headed up Broadway out toward the ocean.

Castle Island is the easternmost point in South Boston, and his mother had loved the place. She'd taken her children there often, especially when Da was at sea. Jutting out into Boston Harbor, it was a gorgeous vantage point for both the ocean and the airport across the water in East Boston. "Look," she'd say as they stood along the fence that ringed the promontory, "we're as close to Da as we can get right now. And when his run is over, he'll either be sailing back into this harbor, or landing right over there at the airport."

She also loved listening to the occasional brogue that could be heard from the newly arrived Irish in South Boston. "You don't get to hear a brogue very often when Da's not home, now do you?" she'd remind them.

Sean got out of the Caprice and walked. To his left was Fort Independence, a site that had been used for coastal defense for as long as Boston had been a city. To his right was Castle Island Park, where picnicking families laid out their lunches and children skittered around the playground. He followed the walkway out until it turned north along the seawall.

It was a hot August day, and the sun had burned the haze out of the sky. Gulls swooped and screamed, diving down on the occasional dropped hot dog or bag of chips. Bare-chested young men grasped the hands of their tank-topped girlfriends; an elderly couple in matching jogging suits walked purposefully by.

Sean sat down on the grassy lawn and stared out to sea. What if just one of those dominoes had somehow failed to knock the next one over? What if his parents had gotten married, but his mother hadn't had Huntington's after all, or she had, but his father hadn't left, or his father had left, but Aunt Vivvy had been warm and loving? What if they hadn't each been driven to escape—Deirdre into the imaginary world of drama, Hugh into drugs, and Sean to any corner of the world that wasn't home? What if Hugh had gone to the hospital sooner?

What if Sean had made different choices himself—had taken up his career at one of the numerous Boston hospitals, had married someone who didn't mind not having kids and was willing to take a chance on his odds of living to a ripe old age?

The test for the Huntington's gene had become available in the late 1980s when Sean was in nursing school, and he'd decided not to take it. He didn't want to know when and how he would die.

But what if he *had* taken it?

CHAPTER 36

Sean woke up to an unpleasant tickling feeling around his nose and chin.

"Rowdy, come!" he heard someone call. "Leave that poor man alone!"

Sean sat up quickly, and saw a large, short-haired dog with no tail and huge testicles trot away from him. He wiped his face with his arm and spit a few times.

His cheeks felt tight and sore. Sunburned. How long had he been lying there?

The sun was behind him now, so it had to be well past noon. He was starving, and went into Sullivan's, the same little eatery by the parking lot that had been there when he was a kid. He ordered fish and chips; they tasted exactly the same as they had thirty-some-odd years ago: fishy-salty, as if they were the tactile manifestation of the sea air.

He sat down at one of the picnic benches and watched a couple of little brown birds peck at crumbs, scattering whenever someone walked near. In all his ruminations about his family, there was one strange fact that he kept coming back to, questioning it, puzzling at it. . . .

His mother had been happy.

Certainly there must have been things that she'd kept from him as a child, things she'd worried about or fought over with his father. When her mind started to go and her movements got jerky, he saw her fear and anger and sadness. But up until that time, she seemed as happy as anyone he knew. She laughed and joked; she did as she liked. She always seemed delighted and proud of her children. And there had been a strong affection between his parents, simmering below the surface of their casual gestures and comments. It used to give Sean a slightly queasy feeling, once he'd learned about sex, and made him suspect that they might even do it sometimes when they weren't trying to have another baby.

Based on what he knew of the history of Huntington's research, it was likely that his parents didn't know the 50 percent likelihood of her carrying the gene when they were married in the 1960s, nor when Sean was born in 1968. But they almost certainly would have known by the time Deirdre was conceived.

They rolled the dice and hoped for the best, thought Sean. *And they lost.*

It was late afternoon by the time he pulled into Aunt Vivvy's driveway. The house was quiet, and for this he was grateful. As he stood in the foyer, a thought popped into his head: the note from his mother about mowing the lawn—the last thing she'd given him before her mind had been hijacked by Huntington's. He'd kept it in a box in the basement; suddenly he needed to see it.

Rushing down the stairs, the same ones on which she'd fallen and later died, he panicked that the box was gone. Aunt Vivvy would have thrown it away without a second thought. But on the far side of the basement, on the shelf behind Hugh's old tent, he found it. His box of treasures.

He dumped it out searching for the note and rifled through old report cards, his high school yearbook, his driving learner's permit. There was the picture of him and Cormac holding their tennis trophy. He slid that into his breast pocket. And there was Hugh's fishing lure, which he also put aside. There was a pink glove and a signed baseball, and finally there was the note.

Sean, I'm taking Deirdre for her one-year checkup. Auntie Vivvy is watching Hugh. Would you please mow the lawn? Love, M.

Hi Mom, he thought. And he sat down on the damp cement floor and wept.

A little while later he loaded everything but the note, the picture, and the fishing lure back into the box. When he picked up the pink glove, he remembered it was Chrissy's. She'd left it in the bleachers that time he'd put his arm around her, shortly before her future ex-husband popped him one. He pitched it into the box with the rest of his ancient history and put the box on the shelf, no longer worried about hiding it. Aunt Vivvy didn't come down here anymore, and even if she did and decided to get rid of it, there was nothing in it that meant that much to him.

Walking up the stairs, he realized that included the pink glove.

Exhausted, he wandered into the den in search of his book. He was up to *The Last Battle* in *The Chronicles of Narnia* series, and the thought of immersing himself in a mythic kingdom where good always prevailed seemed like a balm to his frayed emotions. He couldn't immediately locate the book, so when he saw Deirdre's laptop sitting there, he absently clicked into his new e-mail account and found a message from Claire Lindquist, Kevin's teacher.

> Hi Sean,
> I was very happy to get your note. I assumed you would have returned to Africa by now. It's great that you're staying and taking an interest in Kevin's education.
>
> Kevin's a wonderful boy, a pleasure to have in class, but he does have his challenges. I'm very concerned about

Before Sean could read any more, he was distracted by the slam of the front door and footsteps coming quickly toward him.

"Hey," said Deirdre breathlessly, appearing in the den and reaching for the laptop. "I need that."

"Sure, can I—"

"I'm in a wicked hurry. Can you just get off?"

"Yeah, but this e-mail is from—"

She gave her head an annoyed shake. "Jesus, Sean, I really don't care. I have to go!"

"Dee, it's from Kevin's teacher."

"Okay, last I checked, it's summer and he doesn't actually *have* a teacher at the moment, so it can't be all that critical." She leaned over him and hit the little X at the top of the screen.

"Christ, are you really that self-centered?"

"Whoa, little pot. You are at least as black as me," she said, clicking the Shut Down function. "So fuck off."

"Fuck off yourself, you raving bitch!"

Aunt Vivvy appeared in the doorway. "What on earth is going on in here?" she demanded. George was at her side, ears standing straight up and twitching agitatedly.

"Nothing, Auntie," said Deirdre breezily. "Sean just needs to come down off his high horse, stop mooching off other people, and get his own stuff." She yanked the cord, grabbed the laptop, and sailed out of the room, the front door slamming moments later.

"I don't appreciate that kind of language, Sean Patrick," said Aunt Vivvy. "And I'll thank you to conduct yourself with some consideration for other people and their belongings."

"Hold on a second." Sean stood up. "Consideration for other people was in short supply around this house long before *I* got home."

"And what is that supposed to mean?"

Her scathing tone rattled him as it always had—as it was meant to. But his anger, stoking all day and fueled by Deirdre's attack, seemed to rise out of his belly like some sort of volcanic eruption. He blazed back at her, "It means that you drove my father out of here, for one thing."

"How dare you," she growled.

"I was with him today. And I can see a little more clearly how it went down. You never liked him. And when he started falling apart, you said exactly what you knew would make him leave—that we'd be better off without him."

She smiled coldly. "And you were."

"Christ, how can you *say* that? Look around!" His finger flew out in front of him, indicting her. The dog started to bark, and Sean turned up the volume to be heard. "Deirdre has the interpersonal skills of a rattlesnake! Kevin's practically raising himself—small wonder Social Services hasn't yanked him out of here! And you! You won't even go to the damned doctor. You're just as happy to lose your mind and leave me with the whole freaking mess!" He was yelling now, and the dog's barking ramped up in response.

"I've had enough of your childish vitriol," Aunt Vivvy said, and turned to walk out. She stumbled against the door and nearly fell. Sean caught her elbow. "Leave me be!" she commanded. But raising her voice—something she almost never did—seemed to increase her instability, and Sean didn't dare let her go.

"Just sit down on the couch," he said as he followed her through the living room. But she was determined to go up the stairs, and he wasn't about to release her so she could fall and break a hip. The dog lunged, nipping at Sean's calves as he buttressed his aunt's ascent.

"Stop!" yelled Sean. "Make her stop!"

"Make her stop yourself," she muttered at him. "You're her master now."

Aunt Vivvy pulled away from him at the top landing, and shuffled down the hallway to her room. The dog continued to nip and bark. Sean grabbed her by the collar and dragged her toward Kevin's room, bracing all his weight against her as her paws slid across the oak floorboards. With one final heave he got her into the room and shut her in.

His back . . . that unhitching feeling, as if the pieces of his spine were railway cars that had suddenly become uncoupled . . . The ibuprofen was in the kitchen, and he clutched the banister as he made his way down the stairs, every movement stabbing at him.

He made it to the foyer, but lay down for a moment in hopes the spasm would subside. Prostrate on the floor, listening to the dog bark rabidly from Kevin's room, back throbbing like hammer blows, he felt despondence fill his head like acrid smoke.

This is hopeless, he thought.

If there had been a wound to suture or a med bag to hang, it would've been so much simpler. But here in this house, with this family, there wasn't even a diagnosis. Just a seemingly unending stream of ever-worsening symptoms. And the impact of his efforts seemed negligible. At what point did you stop fighting and let the situation run its course?

Lying there in the fog of pain, he heard a knock on the front door. He didn't answer. Another knock, slightly louder. He waited for the person to give up. *For the love of God,* he thought, *just go away.*

The knob turned, and the door opened slowly. In his peripheral vision, Sean could see the outline of a face peeking in. "Hello?" it called. "Sean?" Then the voice was coming toward him. "What happened?"

Rebecca's face came into view, and he started to laugh a little—not at her, but at the absurdity of the picture before her: him lying in the middle of the floor with the damned dog going mental upstairs. He shook his head, unsure of where to start. Aunt Vivvy and her hellhound? Deirdre and the computer? His trip to Castle Island? Breakfast with his father?

She stood there for a moment waiting. When no explanation appeared forthcoming, she came down next to him, lay on her side, and propped her head against her hand. "Got your note," she said. And she smiled.

He could've kissed her. And he might have actually done it, if he could've turned toward her without what felt like shards of glass twisting further into his back. A confusing rush of urges that ranged from deeply emotional to highly sexual to desperately painful ran through him. But none of that seemed to matter. She was here. Somehow it would be okay.

"Should I let the dog out?" she asked.

"Hell no."

"Tough day?"

"Nah," he said, grimacing. "What makes you say that?"

She grinned appreciatively and said, "Okay, tell me."

So he gave her all of it. She didn't say much, just the occasional "Wow," or "Oh, how sad." He watched her intently as he talked, trying to gauge her reaction as her eyes squinted in concentration, or her brows went up in surprise, or her lips tightened in commiseration.

"So," he said. "How's that for a day."

"That's some day," she nodded.

"Not much of an opinion." He'd expected a bigger reaction.

"Well . . . I guess I don't really have an opinion. I'm just sorry everything has to be so difficult and complicated."

He nodded. "To put it mildly."

"Um . . . no . . ."

"What, you think this stuff is *normal*?"

"Not normal, exactly." She put her hand on his shoulder and started to pulse her fingers against the edges of his pain. "But Sean, you have to realize—this is life. This is how most people our age live: with the younger and older generations relying on them, and needing things, and driving them crazy sometimes. You and I don't really have that—or you didn't until now. But see, *that's* what's unusual. Not the other stuff."

Her fingers made their way up to his neck, and he could feel his muscles throbbing against them, as if to defy their peaceful mission. *Maybe all this crap is normal for other people,* he thought, *but I built my life differently. I didn't get the bennies of marriage and kids and a comfortable bed and regular sex, so how come I still have to pay the price?*

Rebecca got up and asked him where the ibuprofen was. She returned with the tablets and a glass of water. He turned over, slowly, gingerly, and she worked on him while the medication took effect. Soon he was feeling semifunctional again.

"How come you got off work so early?" he asked.

"One client canceled and Missy's schedule was open for the last one, and she said she needed the money, so I gave him to her."

Sean smiled. "Poor slob."

"Hey, she's actually a pretty good massage therapist," said Rebecca, "when she's not hormonal, or pissed at her boyfriend, or the moon's not full . . ."

"It's funny to think that if she'd been having a good day two months ago, when I first came in, I never would've found you."

She didn't say anything for a moment, and Sean got nervous. Maybe she was getting sick of all his problems and complaints. Maybe *he'd* become a complication for *her*. . . .

"Yeah," she said finally. "We're lucky she's such a nut, huh?"

Crazy lucky, he found himself thinking. But he didn't say it out loud.

CHAPTER 37

Sean was anxious to see the e-mail from Kevin's teacher, so they went to Rebecca's house. First he released the dog from solitary confinement and let her outside to do her business. The hair was up on the back of her neck until she got into the yard.

"That dog does not like you," said Rebecca.

"Yeah, I'm pretty sure she thinks I'm a cross between Ted Bundy and Michael Vick."

"Have you been walking her?"

"Oh, God," he said. "I completely forgot."

"Sean, you promised Kevin."

"I know! It's just been so crazy around here."

"We could take her now."

"With the mood she's in and the state of my back, one good yank on the leash, and she'd put me in traction." Rebecca gave him a look. "I'll walk her tomorrow," he said. "I swear."

As they drove in her car, she said, "So I had kind of an unusual thing happen yesterday."

"Yeah?"

"I have an elderly client that I see in her home. She's an artist—kind of funky for her age. Unfortunately, she doesn't get around very well anymore. Anyway, her house is gorgeous. It's decorated with this really beautiful furniture. Lots of natural wood and warm colors. Just the kind of stuff I would buy if I had the money . . . and a house to decorate."

"Sounds nice."

"It's lovely." Rebecca pulled into her driveway and turned the motor off. "And now she's moving into an assisted living condo with much less room."

"And you want to buy her furniture?"

"No." She looked at Sean. "She wants to give it to me."

"Great! When does the moving van get here?"

"I can't *take* it," she said, annoyed. "You know there isn't an inch of space left in my house for more furniture. And I'd feel bad, like I was taking advantage of a sweet old lady."

"Why does she want to give it to you in the first place?" said Sean. Then he held up a hand. "No, let me guess. First, you don't charge her extra for the house call." Rebecca made a no-big-deal face. "And second, you listen to her and sympathize and make her feel like she's sixty again. Am I right?"

Rebecca looked away and gave a little shrug.

"Becky . . ." said Sean, but she didn't face him.

She got out of the car, and he followed her into the house. "You're *taking* that furniture, so help me," he warned idly. "I'll make the call myself. I'll say I'm the moving company and I'm arranging a pickup. Then I'll call your parents and say . . . uh . . . I'll say there was a small fire and the house is fine, but all the furniture got smoke damaged and had to be thrown out."

She sat down on the couch and folded her arms. He lowered himself gingerly next to her. "That could work, actually," he said.

"I am not going to *lie* to my parents, Sean. That is some seriously bad karma."

"Then for crying out loud, just tell them the truth! This is a perfect opportunity and you're throwing up all kinds of ridiculous roadblocks. What the hell kind of karma is *that*?"

She scowled at him. "I really dislike you."

He grinned. "No, you don't."

He watched her face soften from aggravation to a barely perceptible smile. And parts of him began to throb, none of which were in his back. If she held his gaze a moment longer, he was pretty sure things would start happening that he wasn't entirely in control of.

She ran her hand through her hair and glanced at the hulking furniture pieces. “I need to get out of this room,” she said. “And I could really stand to meditate.”

He followed her downstairs, knowing he would have followed her pretty much anywhere—a bridal shower, a group therapy session, the mall—just to maintain physical proximity. She spread out a cotton blanket for him, knowing he’d be more comfortable lying flat.

And then the soft, atonal gonging music started, and she was saying something about sitting in the center of all things, and other stuff that had made a lot of sense the last time they meditated. But all he could really focus on was the occasional whiff of her scent—not perfume, he decided, more like really nice-smelling soap. And the way her legs had looked in those running shorts a few days ago. And that surging feeling between his legs.

Cut it out, he told his crotch. *This is not good.* He tried to think about patients he’d treated, emaciated babies and AIDS-infected mothers, but inevitably the train of thought veered off to the med student or volunteer doctor who’d helped him treat the patients, all of whom he’d later slept with.

Sex.

Such a good thing. A necessary thing for most people. And it sure had been a while since he’d had any. Was it that USAID worker who’d toured the area when the rainy season had turned the fields into swampland and they’d spent so much time indoors? Or maybe the assistant to that minor celebrity who had “worked” at the clinic for a couple of weeks?

He wanted Rebecca. It was pretty clear. But how badly would that screw things up—everything would get weird. She would feel hurt when he left. He cared so much about that, he realized—about not hurting her. The thought of his guilt and her sadness dialed back the activity down below. He could still feel it, but it was less like a steaming locomotive, more like the hum of distant traffic.

He opened his eyes and looked up at her sitting a few feet away, her eyes closed, her back straight. She had taken off her cotton jacket when they sat down, and her hair concealed the straps of her tank top. If he looked only at her shoulders and head, it was as if she were topless. . . .

Sean shut his eyes. *What are you—sixteen?* he chastised himself. She was beautiful, though. In a sort of an understated, easy-to-miss way. Not like Chrissy, who had that obvious, lingerie model, you-know-you-want-me thing going for her.

Oh, yeah. Chrissy.

It had been two days since their date, and he realized he was probably supposed to call her again. The idea evoked about as much interest as making a haircut appointment. How had that happened? How had the pinnacle of all fantasies been reduced to a maintenance task? She was as attractive as ever, but other than that . . . no juice. She was actually a little boring. And if he had to sit through one more stupid movie . . . Would things have been different if they'd had sex? Maybe. But then what? He'd be in even deeper, with those handcuffs getting tighter. . . .

Nah. He was glad he'd left early. So much simpler. So much less to regret. In fact, he was proud of himself that his head had won out over its downstairs neighbor. A sign of maturity. And it would be the same with Rebecca. A month or two from now, when he was at his next foreign post, he'd be glad he hadn't screwed things up with her. Because she was beautiful and kind and smart and good. And he wanted her in his life. More than anything, he wanted to be able to come back here and hang out with her and know things were okay between them.

As she meditated Rebecca had occasionally murmured a comment or suggestion, such as returning to the sensation of breathing when the mind began to wander. This was clearly for his benefit, though his mind had wandered like a frustrated teenager with a boner for most of the time. Now she began to murmur again, a summation of sorts, or in any case, notice that the meditation was about to end. Sean was fine with that, since his had never actually begun.

She glanced over at him. Her face was serene, glowing like a saint in a medieval painting, and he thought that if he looked hard enough, he might see the aura of a halo around her head.

"Hey," she said.

"Hey," he responded. And the surging and throbbing started up like a band that had come back from a break.

"Can you hand me my jacket," she said. "My cell phone's in the pocket." When he gave it to her, she pulled out the phone and dialed. "Mom, it's me. . . ."

Holy smokes! he thought. *She's doing it!*

Pleasantries were exchanged. Apparently the air conditioning in their condo had been turned off one morning when they'd gone to Sanibel Island for the day. Mom blamed Dad, Dad blamed Mom, but he then admitted it could have been him, however he refused to plead guilty until evidence could be produced. When they came home, the place had smelled like a cave.

"A cave?" said Rebecca. "Oh, mold . . . Are caves moldy? . . . No, I've never been in one, either. . . ." She glanced over at Sean, and he fixed her with a gaze that was meant to imply, *Enough with the moldy cave. Get down to business.*

She took a deep breath and reached her hand out to grasp his.

"So listen," she said into the phone. "I have this really unbelievable opportunity. . . ."

Sean marveled at her diplomacy. While the old furniture had been such a smart buy, she told them, it had probably come to the end of its reasonable usefulness. Her hand gripped his, squeezing occasionally when they balked or came up with yet another reason to keep everything the same. Though quite a bit smaller than his, her hand was strong, and the squeezing sent sensations up his arm. Her olive-toned skin, slightly tan, especially across the knuckles, looked like caramel against his freckled paleness. He wanted to pull her hand up to his face and smell it.

"I was thinking I could store the old furniture in the garage," she said. "And if there are pieces you want, they'd be handy for you. . . . Of course, I'd have to have it all out of there by winter so I can pull my car in."

He nodded at her encouragingly. *Smart thinking!* he mouthed. She squeezed hard and practically broke his pinkie.

"You're sure?" she was saying. "That's so understanding of you . . . no, really, you guys are the best . . . I love you, too . . . so much. . . ."

When she closed the phone, she looked at him, eyes wide, face lit up with surprised joy.

"I am so proud of you!" he said.

She let out a squeal and launched herself at him, hugging him, knocking him over. His back twanged in protest, but every other single part of him welcomed her body like a long-overdue homecoming. He wrapped his arms around her and kissed her cheek, and she kissed his.

"Sean," she whispered in his ear, "Sean, I'm so happy!"

"You deserve it," he murmured back. "You deserve everything."

Sprawled on top of him, she pulled back and looked down into his face. "You do, too," she said.

It should have been impossible for him to lean up to her—his back should have stamped that move "access denied." And it may have tried. But all Sean knew was that he had to have his face near hers, breathing her in, kissing her lips. Had to taste her and smell her and feel her stomach against his.

"Rebecca," he breathed. "Rebecca . . ." Her name felt so good in his mouth. Her real name. How had it taken him this long to use it?

She seemed to hesitate at first, her lips soft but closed, kissing but not pressing. Once he said her name, though, her lips opened and invited him in, and her arms slid behind his neck and cradled his shoulders. Her legs slipped around his hips.

Her legs . . . that was when every nerve ending rose up against his skin, straining to feel every single part of her. His hands moved down her back, around her bottom, down her thighs and back again, and she let out the slenderest moan of agreement.

That sound. Good God.

She was pressing into him, rocking slightly, and he felt as if he might burst the metal fly of his shorts. His hands came up, slipping her tank top off, tugging at her bra clasp until it flew open. He rolled to the side, lowering her to the cotton blanket so he could get rid of the bra completely. Her breasts, several shades lighter than the rest of her, were soft and warm under his hands.

She tugged off his T-shirt and explored him as if she'd never touched him before, and didn't already know the contour of every rib and muscle. Their kissing became needier. The shorts and underwear came off. And they were naked, stroking and pressing and wanting with a desperation Sean couldn't ever remember feeling before.

When he slid inside her, they let out twin moans. "Sean . . ." she murmured in his ear. It sounded like a plea. "Sean . . ."

He was able to hold off until she cried out, but just barely. And then the world exploded in warm and wet and good and release. There were loud sounds—his own, it turned out—and she gripped him harder, rocking against him from below until he was spent and loose, with only enough strength to take in air.

CHAPTER 38

When his limbs could hold him again, he moved off her, but not far, still wanting closeness, the aftershocks of their love-making still sending ripples across the network of his nervous system.

And then worry gripped him. What the hell had he done? This was exactly *not* the plan. Friendship. Hanging out. Not messing it up. What happened to those? What happened to using his head—the guy on the top floor, instead of the guy in the garden apartment?

He was afraid to look at her, but he had to look. Exactly how bad had he screwed up?

It was like glancing in a mirror. She had that same *Holy shit, did that really happen, was it okay, are we okay?* expression that he felt on his own face. She pressed her lips together, and he thought, *Oh no, please don't do that. Please let it be okay.* Her lips pressed tighter, almost disappearing. And then a snort came out of her nose—a laugh that exploded from the only available outlet. She was laughing!

"What?" he demanded to know.

"Oh, my God, Sean. That was . . . it was . . . unbe*liev*able."

He smiled. How could he not?

"I mean . . ." She suddenly looked unsure. "It was, right?"

He gathered her up in his arms, kissing her temple, running his fingers up and down her back, thanking God she was happy. "It was," he murmured against her cheek. "Un. Believable."

She snuggled deeper into his embrace until every possible part of them that could be touching was. And he surrendered to that loose, weak feeling, with the astoundingly comforting knowledge that everything was okay. At least for now.

When he woke, it was dark, and he was freezing. He slowly released one arm from around her back and reached behind him to see if he could pull a corner of the cotton blanket over them. His back registered its extreme displeasure.

Rebecca stirred. "I'm hungry," she whispered.

They put on clothes and went up to the kitchen. Rebecca poured them each a heaping bowl of Raisin Bran. She'd put on her tank top and shorts, but her bra must have been left in the basement, wherever he'd flung it. Her breasts were loose against the fabric of her shirt. He dutifully ate his cereal, all the while wondering how soon he could get his hands on her again.

"How's your back?" she asked with a yawn.

He shrugged. It was killing him, but he didn't want her to know that. Suddenly back pain seemed synonymous with old and decrepit, and that was hardly the look he was going for.

"Are you tired?" he asked.

"Yeah, I guess." She smiled wryly. "It's been an unusually busy day."

"If you're too tired to drive me home . . . I could stay." As soon as he said it, he was sure it sounded desperate. But how did he know? Before now, he'd never really cared all that much whether he stayed or not. Which, of course, meant that he had never sounded desperate.

She crunched on her Raisin Bran for a few chews. "Do you *want* to stay?"

"Do you want me to?"

She studied him, thinking about this. Five seconds of torture. "Yes."

"Okay."

"That doesn't sound very enthusiastic."

How do guys do this? he wondered. *How do* I *do this?*

He stood, came around to her side of the table, took the spoon out of her hand, and slid it into the bowl. Then he gently pulled her up toward him, against him, wrapping his arms around her. "I am very enthusiastic."

"I can feel your enthusiasm," she giggled.

"My enthusiasm likes to make its presence known. And it wouldn't mind feeling a little of yours, in return."

They slept in the twin bed in her room, which was uncomfortable in a very appealing way. He couldn't get enough of feeling her body against his, even when he was spent, and sex wouldn't be happening again anytime soon. And since there was no way for a good portion of her *not* to be in contact with a good portion of him, he spent a very happy, if incommodious, night.

When he woke it was light out, and finding her gone was like getting pencils and Scotch tape in his stocking on Christmas morning. He heard a shower running, and it was tempting to go and join her. He was pretty sure his "enthusiasm" was in need of some time to recharge, but the thought of being naked with her under a stream of warm water was enticing all the same.

Just then the shower shut off. She probably had to get to work.

Work!

He was scheduled at the Confectionary and had forgotten entirely. He looked around for a clock. All the furniture was white with hearts carved into it; it was little girl furniture. The walls were painted blue. He finally spied the clock on the bookcase. It was 8:15.

He jumped out of bed and almost knocked her over as she came into the bedroom wrapped in a towel. That smell—really nice soap. He wanted to rip the towel off and smell every inch of her. But he was so late for work. He grabbed up his boxers. "I'm supposed to be at the Confectionary," he told her, "like two hours ago."

"You're going to shower first, though."

"No, I really gotta go."

"Sean, you have to shower," she said. "You smell like sex."

"Oh."

"Yeah, I would definitely not buy a cruller from you."

"No?" he said, dropping the boxers and putting his arms around her.

"Well . . ." She smiled up at him. "I guess *I* would. But trust me, every other person on the planet will find you offensive."

He called the Confectionary and told Cormac he'd overslept, which was certainly no lie. When they pulled into the Confectionary parking lot, he noticed that she didn't put the car in park, but let it idle in drive with her foot on the brake.

"So, um . . . are you around tonight?" he asked.

"I have plans," she said.

"Plans." One word. With the impact of a gut punch.

"Uh-huh. But let's get together tomorrow, okay? Are you open?"

"Yeah," he said, still slightly stunned. "I'm open."

"Great. Okay, so I'll see you then." She smiled at him, and he didn't see the joy in it. But maybe he was just comparing it to last night. Hard to compete with that kind of joy.

They leaned toward each other for what ended up being a goose-necked awkward kiss. He got out of the car, and she drove away. He felt a weird, gauzy kind of bereavement descend on him, in part because of being separated from her body. And in part, because of her plans.

"Is it possible you've had a minor stroke?" said Tree. "Because you have messed up like eighty percent of the orders since you got here."

"Sorry," he said. "I didn't get much sleep last night."

"Huh," she snorted. "I'm a teenager. We're in a constant state of sleep deprivation, so you aren't scoring any sympathy points with that one."

Cormac came by and clapped a hand on Sean's shoulder. "Seriously," he murmured low enough so no one else could hear. "What the fuck?"

"Complications," muttered Sean.

"Yeah?"

"Like you read about."

"Wanna go for a beer tonight?"

"Yeah, but it's Thursday. Doesn't Barb have her class on Tuesdays?"

"That class ended last week. But, um . . . I'll check in and let you know."

"She could come if she wants," offered Sean. He had a new appreciation for Barb's powers of discernment since that "if you call yourself an old soul, you aren't one" comment. And a woman's perspective might come in especially handy with the Rebecca situation.

"Yeah . . ." said Cormac, scratching the back of his neck and leaving a powdery trail of flour. "She's hanging close to home these days."

"Everything okay?"

"She's on this new fertility drug. Makes her kind of . . . emotional." He gave a humorless chuckle. "Sort of like a weepy grizzly on crack."

Sean nodded sympathetically. "Good times."

"Like you read about."

CHAPTER 39

When Sean got home, all he wanted to do was down a handful of ibuprofen and pass out for about six hours. But Aunt Vivvy was wandering around the house in a semivague state, George stalking by her side on high alert, and Sean was afraid to close his eyes until the two of them settled down some. Also, he remembered that he'd never checked that e-mail from Kevin's teacher, as he'd meant to do at Rebecca's house. Just the briefest thought of exactly how he'd gotten distracted made his nether region start to perk up a little.

He focused on locating Deirdre's laptop and found it in her bedroom under some clothes. He powered up right there in her room, found the e-mail, and skimmed to where it said,

> Kevin's a wonderful boy, a pleasure to have in class, but he does have his challenges. I'm concerned that middle school might be especially tough for him. Would it be possible for us to meet and discuss this? I feel strongly that it's in Kevin's best interest to get some supports in place under the circumstances.
>
> Best,
> Claire Lindquist

He replied that he was free to meet her anytime and thanked her for her concern.

There was another e-mail, this one from the middle school administration, notifying parents "and other guardians" that class schedules for the upcoming school year had been sent to the e-mail address specified. Copies were available in the main office.

He had promised Kevin two things: to walk the dog and pick up the schedule. Since he'd so far failed miserably at the former, he was especially anxious to fulfill the latter. He could walk over to the middle school and take George with him, killing two guilt birds with one stone.

A new e-mail dropped into his in-box. It was from Claire Lindquist, telling him that she would be prepping in her classroom all day tomorrow, and if that was convenient for him, he could come by. He wasn't scheduled to work for Cormac, so he replied that he'd be there at ten.

He got his aunt a cup of tea and some Fig Newtons, fanning them out on a china dessert plate the way she always did.

"How did you know I like these?" she asked.

Because you eat them every day. "Just a guess," he said.

She seemed calmer after that, and decided to go up to her room for a nap. George stood up to escort her. "Oh, no, you don't, beast," muttered Sean. "You're with me."

George allowed herself to be clipped to the leash, but stood immovable as a statue in the foyer until Aunt Vivvy's bedroom door clicked shut. If a canine could be said to feel conflicted, George was the poster dog. She clearly needed a walk, but she didn't want to leave the house.

A thought occurred to Sean as the two of them stepped down off the porch and out toward the street: he and George had the same problem. They both wanted desperately to get out into the world, and they both felt guilty about going.

He stopped for a moment and looked down at the dog. She looked up at him, waiting for his lead. The ibuprofen had kicked in, and Sean's back had downgraded from a high-pitched squeal to a dull roar. Carefully he squatted down and gave the dog's neck a good rough scratch.

"Listen," he told her. "Viv's the queen, and Kevin's the prime minister. But you and me, we're just rank and file. We're on the same team, so let's try to help each other out, okay?"

George turned her muzzle into Sean's hand and gave it a little lick.

When they got to the middle school to pick up Kevin's schedule, Sean looped George's leash through the bike rack and went into the main office. The exterior of the building looked the same as it had thirty years ago, but inside, things were different. The glass trophy case was crowded with art and music awards, in addition to sports trophies. He glanced into the library across the hall and saw that a third of the room was now filled with computer terminals.

In the main office, he told the secretary he was there for Kevin's schedule.

"Great, let me just get you to sign off on this form," she said. "You're his dad, right?"

"His uncle."

"Oh." This seemed to throw her off for a moment. "Um, his legal guardian?"

Having dealt with bureaucrats in every hospital and clinic he'd worked in, Sean could smell a paperwork problem, and he did what he'd learned to do years ago: figure out the right answer and bend the truth to approximate it. "Yeah, I'm his guardian," he said. Not legal, perhaps, but he was "guarding" Kevin a heck of a lot more than anyone else at the moment.

He signed the form and left with the packet, leafing through it as he and George walked down the street. There was a notice on yellow paper that caught his eye: SUBSTITUTE NURSE NEEDED. Apparently the school nurse had recently been in a car accident and was on medical leave. A full recovery was expected, but she wouldn't be able to return to work until October.

School nurse, thought Sean. *Could there* be *a job more boring than that?* It basically amounted to being a human Band-Aid dispenser.

And you'd spend your day sitting in a Petri dish of viruses and flu bugs. He'd take a gangrenous wound over that any day of the week.

As he walked, his mind wandered to Rebecca and the satiny feel of her thighs against his, but then turned quickly to speculating about her plans for tonight. If she was just going out with a friend, why would she be so tight-lipped about it? Maybe it was something she was embarrassed about . . . like a support group of some kind . . . Unhealthily Controlled by My Parents Anonymous? Women on the Verge of a Good Career Move, But Not Quite?

Or maybe it was a support group for women trying not to get into bad relationships with guys who would inevitably leave them. The thought hit him like an electric shock. If he really cared about her—and he did, he knew that without a doubt—he should nip this thing in the bud before she truly *did* need a support group.

He expressed this opinion to Cormac over beers and wings at The Pal.

"Hold up—you finally broke it off with Chrissy?" said Cormac.

"Okay, you don't have to say it like I *finally* realized the world is round or something."

"Touchy!" snorted Cormac.

"And what do you mean 'break it off'? We only went out a couple of times. It wasn't like we were together."

Cormac shrugged. "You brought her to meet your friends. That means something."

"What does it mean?"

"Hell if I know." He laughed. "Jesus, where's Barb when you need her? No, it's like a *thing*. Like you wanted to . . . *include* her. In your life. Which, at the time, you kind of did." Sean squinted skeptically. "Oh, please," said Cormac. "Bullshit yourself if you want to, but don't bullshit me. You were practically wagging your tail, hoping she'd take you home like one of her rescue dogs."

"So now I have to . . . what—say something? Like call her up and tell her it's over?"

"I think you probably should. You know, so she's not waiting around. It sucks when something's over and you don't even know." Cormac took a swig of his beer. "Kind of ironic, though—worrying about her feelings when she certainly never worried about Becky's." He nodded approvingly. "Becky Feingold. I always liked her."

Sean felt a primitive little zing of competition. It must have shown because Cormac said, "Chill out. I don't mean *liked her* liked her. I just mean she was a good egg. A nice person."

"Yeah," said Sean. "Too nice to be screwing around with me, and no chance of a future."

"Hey, you don't know that. Maybe you'll change your tune and stick around. Or maybe she'd go with you."

"I didn't think of that."

"I mean, I don't know how likely it is. The conditions you're talking about are pretty rough. But it's not out of the question, is all I'm saying."

Not out of the question. She could make the choice to be with him. It turned the burner way down under his little pot of conflictedness.

They ordered another round of beers, and Sean told Cormac about seeing Da.

"No wonder you couldn't tell a whoopie pie from a cannoli this morning," said Cormac. "Hell of a day you had."

Sean chuckled. "Yeah, you think?"

Cormac took a swig of beer. "I'm pretty sure this is what those daytime self-help shows call 'a crossroads.'"

"You don't watch daytime self-help shows," scoffed Sean.

"No, but Barb does, and she tells me about it. In between crying at diaper commercials, yelling at me for smelling like old coffee grounds, and jumping me every time her temp goes up a tenth of a degree." Cormac tipped his beer up and finished it. He raised it in the direction of the bartender, who put two more bottles up on the bar for the waitress to bring over.

"Hormones are pretty powerful drugs," said Sean. "She can't help acting crazy."

"Which I remind myself on an hourly basis. But honestly, I'd kinda like my wife back."

"Are you okay with not having biological kids?"

"I'm okay with anything. But she keeps saying that she loves me so much, she wants a baby with my gene pool. A little me." He gazed distractedly out the window into the dark. "What the hell's the comeback for that?"

CHAPTER 40

There were more beers than usual on their tab at the end of the night. Before they parted ways in the parking lot, Cormac pulled Sean into a back-slapping hug. "Keep the faith, brother."

"You, too, man," said Sean. "She's a good girl. Hang in there."

"She is." There was a choky little sound to Cormac's voice, and it caught at Sean.

"You okay walking home?"

"Totally fine. 'Sides, it'll give me a chance to air out a little before I get there. Gotta blow the stink of old coffee grounds off me." They both laughed, though it was not that funny, but knowing they had to part on a lighter note.

Sean walked home thinking, *It never ends. You meet the perfect girl, get married, settle down somewhere you both are happy . . . and shit still happens.*

When he arrived, he went into the kitchen for another round of ibuprofen, now doubly necessary for his back and to stave off the hangover that would surely result from the evening's intake. The phone rang, and it felt like someone was blowing a party horn in his ear. He grabbed it up quickly to make the satanic thing stop.

"Sean," said a gravelly voice. "It's your da."

Oh, for the love of God, thought Sean. *Could I please get a break?*

"I've been thinking so much about all that you told me yesterday. I can't make my mind stop turning it over and over."

Like father, like son, thought Sean. "I can't really talk now," he said. "Can I call you tomorrow?"

"Sure. I'm sorry for bothering you."

"No, it's just I'm unbelievably tired." And a little drunk. And *so* not in the mood for another heart-to-heart.

"I'm a bit of a night owl, so I guess I assumed you were, too. But listen," he said. "Can I just plant a little idea with you and you can see how it sprouts overnight?"

"Sure."

"I keep thinking about Hugh being gone, and Kevin with no da, and you going off to parts unknown. And I was thinking . . . I would really . . . I think it would be good for all of us—"

"What, Da."

"I want you and Kevin to come to Ireland with me. I know Deirdre's busy with her acting career, and she's not ready to see me, but the two of you could go."

"Oh, I don't think so—"

"A short trip. I just want you to *see* it, Sean! I want to get to know you again, and spend time with my grandson. I've never even met him."

With more sleep and less beer under his belt, Sean might have chosen his words more carefully. Or better yet, not said them at all. But that was not the case.

"And whose fault is that?" he said. "Look, you wanted to see me. You saw me. You wanted to open up the whole can of worms to make amends, as you call it. You opened it. Now you have to back off."

Sean could hear a little gasp on the other end, as if he'd punched his father in the stomach. He felt bad for that, until his father said, "Jesussuffering*christ*, but you're bitter! I would have thought that you of all people would understand."

"*Me* of all people? What is that supposed to mean?"

"You've been off on your own journey, too," Da said. "You're a prodigal, like me."

"Pardon me, Da, but 'prodigal' doesn't mean someone who returns after being gone a long time. It means wasteful. I've never wasted anything in my life. I've never had anything to waste."

"I know what 'prodigal' means, son."

You brass-balled bastard! The words were about to come out, so Sean hung up.

He went up to bed but he couldn't sleep. Jesus, the nerve of the man. Go to Ireland with him? No way in hell. Fury slammed around in his beer-addled brain until exhaustion overtook him, and he fell into a restless sleep.

When Sean woke the next morning, he rubbed his eyes. They felt puffy and his tongue felt furry. He thought of Rebecca and experienced that vaguely bereft response to her absence again. He wished he were scheduled for a shift at the Confectionary. It would make the time pass more quickly until he saw her that night.

He went down to the kitchen. Aunt Vivvy was fixing herself a soft-boiled egg. It occurred to him that cooking might not be the wisest activity for her. Even boiling water could have disastrous consequences for someone without a consistent hold on her senses.

"Who is your late-night caller?" she asked him, as he rooted around in the cabinets for something that would settle his stomach.

"Hmm?"

"Who keeps calling here so late at night? It's a bit presumptuous to think calling at that hour is acceptable."

"Da."

She was silent, lifting the egg from the pot with a slotted spoon and depositing it into an eggcup. As a boy, Sean had always thought they looked like miniature thrones for the soon-to-be-decapitated eggs. Humpty Dumpty meets Louis XVI. Aunt Vivvy took the enthroned egg to the kitchen table. "He calls then because he knows I won't answer."

"Yup."

She murmured something under her breath as she elegantly hacked off the top of the egg with a spoon. It was the word *coward*, he realized, and a little part of him rose up to defend his father. But he allowed himself only the satisfaction of slamming down the knob on the toaster a little harder than necessary.

Later, when he took George for a walk to his meeting with Ms. Lindquist, he left Aunt Vivvy sitting at her desk writing a letter. She seemed calm and lucid, and Sean hoped she would remain so in his absence.

Claire Lindquist was on a step stool in her classroom, tacking bright orange letters to the top of a bulletin board. IF YOU HAVE A BOOK, YOU ALWAYS HAVE A FRIEND, they spelled out.

"Hi," he said.

She turned and nearly toppled off the step stool, her glasses going slightly askew on her face. She caught herself and quickly adjusted the glasses, embarrassment coloring her cheeks in splotches.

"I'm sorry," said Sean. "I didn't mean to surprise you."

"Oh, no, I'm fine. Just clumsy." She adjusted her glasses again, though they seemed perfectly straight. After commenting on the heat and the waning days of summer, they sat down in small chairs at a low table to discuss Kevin.

"First, I just want to say that, despite his challenges, he's one of my all-time favorite students," said Claire. Sean wondered how long "all-time" was—maybe five years, tops. "I know I'm not supposed to have favorites, but he's such a special kid."

An unexpected wave of pride rippled through Sean, though of course he knew he'd had absolutely nothing to do with Kevin's specialness. "Yeah." He nodded. "He really is."

"And he's doing *so* much better."

Better? Things had been *worse* than avoiding all situations that are loud and smell bad and make him the least bit anxious? Worse than having no friends?

"Can you tell me about that? From what I'm seeing now, it seems like he has some sensory issues," said Sean. "The last time I saw him was only briefly when he was five, right after my brother died."

"Certainly. I reviewed Kevin's file and talked to his prior teachers. Your brother did a wonderful job of preparing him for kindergarten. They made visits to the school over the summer and met with Kevin's teacher several times to get him used to the new environment."

Another example of how party animal Hugh had found his calling in being a dad. The thought of it made Sean's chest tighten.

Claire went on. "Of course, it was terribly hard for Kevin, losing his father, and the whole school community rallied around him. But you've probably picked up on the fact that being rallied around is not Kevin's favorite thing."

"No, not so much." Sean smiled at the thought.

"Each of his teachers had to find ways to facilitate his learning without crowding him." She looked away for a moment. "Some of us were a little more patient about it than others."

Sean's heart sank. He didn't even want to think about what that meant. "But you say he's gotten better?"

"Absolutely. Usually, as a child's nervous system matures, they get better at managing sensory input. Think about it—little kids get overstimulated much more easily than teenagers. Kevin's gradually learned to hold it together most of the time even without any intervention."

"My aunt isn't much of an intervener. I think she's taken good care of him, but she was never one to get overly involved, even when I was a kid."

"She raised you, too?"

"Yeah. Long story."

"Okay, well . . . Your aunt did come to the school and meet with the guidance people when Kevin was in first grade."

"How did that go?" Sean had a feeling he already knew the answer.

"Well, the file says she agreed that Kevin had some challenges . . ." Claire hesitated a moment and tucked a strand of her thin hair behind her ear. "But she pointed out that Kevin was fine at home. The house was quiet. No one touched him unnecessarily. She seemed to feel that if Kevin struggled at school, it was the school's problem. There were several requests from guidance to have him evaluated, but she wouldn't sign off, saying she wasn't going to waste money to have someone tell her he was sensitive. She already knew that.

Everyone knew it, and everyone knew the only remedy was for Kevin to toughen up."

Sean looked out the window. He had tied George's leash to a handicapped parking signpost, and he could see her lying in the shade of a nearby tree with her head on her paws. When Sean turned toward her, the dog's head came up to look at him through the glass.

"Yeah," he told Claire, still gazing at the dog. "That's my aunt in a nutshell."

They sat there in silence for a moment, and then he said, "So we'll get him evaluated."

"It might be good to see if there are any other learning issues he's handling, aside from the sensory stuff. But I'm guessing that's the main thing."

Sean was surprised she wasn't pushing it more, and asked her why.

"No, I definitely think he should get tested, but you have to understand, it's possible that confirming the diagnosis won't really matter at this point. Despite everything, Kevin's pretty smart, and his grades haven't suffered. He's very conscientious about homework and reviewing for tests—which is terrific since he has a hard time concentrating in school. See, he's developed a successful coping strategy on his own. The public schools only provide services for kids whose learning is affected by their disability. There isn't much evidence of that with Kevin.

"However, they could put him on what's called a 504 plan, which means he doesn't qualify as special needs, but we get it that he needs a little extra help. For instance, they might let him off the hook for gym class, which is loud and smelly and involves a lot of bumping. They might let him eat his lunch somewhere other than the cafeteria. They would keep an eye on him a little more."

"That would be great," said Sean, thinking how much easier it would be to leave knowing the school was giving him the attention he needed. He shook his head. "I can't believe my aunt wouldn't get him tested."

"You know, she's not completely wrong. Obviously, I believe every child with special challenges should be given as much help as possible. But ultimately, Kevin does need to learn to live with a little more noise and physical contact. The world doesn't conform to meet unusual needs very much. And if he builds a life that allows him to avoid everything that's hard for him, he'll be a pretty lonely guy."

She smiled and reached over to the top drawer of her desk. She took out a piece of paper, crisscrossed with fold lines, and handed it to Sean. "This is what makes me know he can do it."

Dear Ms. Lindquist. The writer had clearly taken great care with his penmanship, pressing down hard and purposefully with a sharp pencil.

> *This was a good year. It was the best year I had at Juniper Hill. I am sorry I got mad or cried sometimes when everything got too much. But even when I was mad or sad, I still liked you, and I still knew you were mostly right when you said keep trying.*
>
> *I wish you would be a teacher at the middle school next year. Even if I didn't get to be in your classroom all the time, I would still know you were there. I will miss you. Maybe I will come back and visit but I will be quiet and not distract your class. I'll just stand in the back and listen.*
>
> *Have a nice summer. Thanks.*
>
> *Sincerely,*
> *Your student for one more minute,*
> *Kevin Doran*

"See?" said Claire, and her eyes were just the slightest bit glossy with emotion. "That's what's special about him, too. Not just the sensitivity to noise and smell and touch. The sensitivity to other people. Nothing has ever made me feel better about being a teacher than that note. How many kids would have even thought to write it?"

CHAPTER 41

Claire Lindquist loaned him several books on sensory integration that she'd pulled from the guidance department shelves. They were titles he'd seen referenced online. One was specifically for parents, and after their talk he was anxious to flip through it.

As he walked home with George, he found himself wishing Kevin were there so he could ask him questions—mainly, what does it feel like? What makes it feel better? How can I help?

And he thought about the letter. So earnest and appreciative. Claire had it right—what eleven-year-old would think to write a thank-you note to his teacher? God knew no one had coached him to do it. No one coached him to do anything. And Sean got a little chuckle out of that "Your student for one more minute" line. Kevin had clearly written it ahead of time and carefully considered when he would present it to her. Sean had actually watched him do it just moments before the Clap Out. And then Kevin had let her hug him.

Two priceless gifts. Quite a kid.

Aunt Vivvy had told the guidance people that her house was quiet and no one touched Kevin. No one tossed him or hung him by his ankles, either, which he needed. And yet Kevin had progressed, developing his own set of coping skills—studying at home, spending time in the pleasant-smelling woods, piling his bed with blankets to create the pressure that soothed him. The enormity of these accomplishments began to dawn on Sean as he walked home.

"Did anyone call?" Sean asked his aunt when he got to the house.

"I don't believe so."

"Are you sure?"

"I didn't hear it ring, but I was outside in the yard for a bit."

"How long were you out there?"

She gave him her standard this-has-grown-tiresome look. "My sense of time isn't what it once was," she said wryly.

Had Rebecca called? They'd talked about getting together tonight, but there was no actual game plan. He figured since she had suggested it, she would initiate. Then again, he was the guy—was he supposed to call? Maybe she was annoyed that he hadn't contacted her yet; on the other hand it was entirely possible that his calling would make her feel hounded.

He needed some sort of manual, like *Relationship 101* . . . assuming that's what they were doing now. Having a relationship. Or was this more of a friends-with-benefits thing?

I'm forty-three and I have the dating skills of a twelve-year-old stamp collector.

Paralyzed by indecision, he did nothing. Rebecca eventually called between clients and said she'd be off at nine, could they get a late dinner?

Yes. He was open.

By eight-thirty he was showered and ready. He had taken longer than his usual nanosecond to decide what to wear. He only owned six shirts, so that reduced the decision making somewhat. When he heard a car pull into the driveway he was out the door like a kid after an ice cream truck.

It was not Rebecca. It was Chrissy.

"Hi!" She strode toward him, and he knew she thought the look of anticipation on his face had been for her. She threw her arms around him and when he responded in kind—not knowing what else to do—she actually lifted her feet up so he was carrying her for a few moments. His back twanged indignantly.

"I was going to say I was in the neighborhood." She grinned coyly after he'd nearly dropped her. "But I wasn't. I came over specifically to see you. On purpose."

"Oh, that's so . . . great. I was thinking I should call." In truth he'd been apprehensively avoiding it. In the past, he'd only ever had to remind the woman that he'd been clear it wasn't a relationship. But he didn't have that to fall back on this time.

Chrissy was looking up at him expectantly now, but her smile had dimmed, as if she were just getting the barest whiff of something about to spoil. "What's up?" she said.

He stammered and stumbled through an overgrown forest of words: how great it was to spend time with her, old friends hanging out, so pretty, so smart, such a good mom . . .

At first she affected a slightly perplexed expression. Then she just looked annoyed. "You're breaking it off."

"Well . . . it's not that I don't . . ."

She gave the little head-wag/eye-roll. "Sean Doran is dumping me," she muttered disgustedly to herself.

"No!" he said. "*Dumping* . . . that's . . . such a harsh word."

Then she put her hands up, lacquered nails rising like parapets above her slim fingers. "Please," she said. "Just. Stop. Talking."

Sean stood there stupidly, watching her pull out of his driveway, feeling sick and exuberant all at once. He was still standing there a few minutes later when Rebecca pulled in. He got in the passenger side. "Hey," he said breezily. He hoped it was breezily.

"Hey." She smiled. He leaned over to kiss her, and got her cheek, the one that bulged out a little. She turned to peck him back, but he hadn't actually withdrawn from his peck, letting his lips linger an extra second against the warm satin of her skin. His lips were positioned perfectly for hers. His hand came up to the back of her head and his fingers filtered into the downy hair at the nape of her neck. And then they were making out. Right there in the driveway.

After a few minutes she pulled back, and so he pulled back. Following her lead was so much easier than deciding a course of action for himself. She looked at him and a crooked little smile curled around the corners of her mouth. He smiled, too. She laughed, putting her fingers up to her lips. "This is so *weird*," she said from behind them.

"Yeah?"

"No, I mean good weird. Unexpected. Right? Aren't you surprised?"

"Well, after the other night—"

"No, the whole thing. Did you see it coming? I did not see it coming."

"Not like a month ago . . . but maybe two weeks ago."

"Two whole *weeks*?"

Sean felt like his brain was at warp speed, careening through hyperspace to locate the correct response to each of her questions. "I don't know. Yeah. I mean . . . I'm attracted to you. I guess that's pretty obvious." He watched her face for clues as to whether his spaceship had landed on the right answer planet, or whether he was even in the right galaxy.

"But you didn't used to be." This was a question, too.

"Well, I wasn't *un*-attracted to you, I just didn't . . . I guess I thought of you as a friend . . . and then . . . that . . . changed." It was exhausting, this intergalactic answer-locating business. "How about you?" he said, to take himself off the hot seat.

"Me?"

"Yeah, when did you realize that you were . . . um . . . interested?"

A blush crept out of the top of her peasant blouse and up her neck. The blush said, *always*.

They went to a funky storefront restaurant called Pizza My Heart that had mismatched chairs and Frank Sinatra music playing. Things got a little dicey when they were negotiating pizza toppings—he liked meat and spicy stuff, she was more into broccoli and mushrooms. They had to send the waitress away twice while they were deciding and in the end ordered something that was completely different on one half than it was on the other.

But then, like dance partners who had finally found their mutual tempo, they talked. Sean told her all about the meeting with Claire Lindquist, knowing she'd be interested even though it had nothing to do with her. She told him how her parents were considering leaving their Floridian trailer park paradise to come up and "help" her move the furniture.

"No," Sean told her. "Absolutely not. That is such a bad idea."

"I know, okay? But what do I say—'I don't want you here'? It sounds so ungrateful."

"Listen, I heard you on the phone—you were playing them like violins, saying how considerate they were and everything. You know how to handle them, Rebecca, you just have to *remember* that you know."

She smiled at him, half grateful, half amused. He wanted to crawl over the table and kiss that smile. "Hey," she teased, "if the third-world nurse gig doesn't work out, you'd be an excellent life coach."

No I wouldn't, he almost said. *You have no idea how many answers I don't have.*

After dinner, he put an arm around her as they walked back to the car, and she slid hers around his waist. It felt so good to stroll down the sidewalk, hip to hip, and as they waited at a curb for traffic to pass, he turned and kissed her head. She gave him a little squeeze in response, and he thought, *This is what it would be like, having someone.*

And it did not feel like handcuffs.

When they got in the car she started the motor but didn't pull out. "Um . . ." She cut her eyes toward him. He worried for a moment that she was hesitating before crushing him with the news that he couldn't come over. But then she raised her eyebrows.

He could feel himself grinning like an idiot as they drove to her house.

When they walked through the door she said, "Do you want something to drink?"

"No, thanks." He pulled her up close and kissed her. Her hands slid up under his shirt back, fingernails skimming across the surface of his skin. He ran his hand down the back of her jeans and pulled one of her thighs up to his hip. She let out a soft little sound in the back of her throat, and the blood sluiced through him so that he felt he couldn't press hard enough against her, and so he released her leg and walked her backward to the couch, letting her down onto it and himself down onto her. And for a moment, the relief of pressing against her was so great he was certain his brain would burst into flames, but then it was suddenly desperately unsatisfying to have anything between them, and he rose off her so they could remove their clothes in a flurry of tossed shirts and flung undergarments.

She reached up to stroke him, and he thought his heart would seize. He froze there kneeling over her until he almost lost control, and then he leaned down, stabilizing himself with a hand against the couch, the other reaching between her legs. He kissed her neck and her breasts until she pulled him down onto her, into her, and nothing in the world seemed to exist except her.

"Hey," he whispered into her hair just as her room was starting to become visible around them in the predawn light. "Where were you the other night when you said you had plans?"

He wasn't even sure she was awake, half thinking this was a trial run before he asked for real. But then her finger began to run lightly across his knuckles, fingering them like worry beads. He felt her chest expand. "I had dinner with a guy that I used to be with. We broke up about a year ago, and lately he's been calling because he wants to get back together."

The sudden pounding of Sean's heart was amplified by the fact that he was holding his breath. "Oh," he said. "So . . ."

"So I told him I had reconnected with an old friend, and something was happening but I wasn't sure what, and we could still hang out but I couldn't consider being with him until . . . things resolved."

Sean began to breathe again, because it was good that she'd told the guy no. Temporarily at least. Until things "resolved."

"I'm trying to be honest," she said.

"No, I appreciate it."

"But you're not saying anything."

"I'm not really sure what to say. I guess I'm not clear what you mean by 'resolved.'"

Slowly she rotated toward him so that they faced each other, though it was still too dark to see clearly. "Sean," she murmured, and her voice was soothing, conciliatory. But also a little sad. He was always amazed by what he could hear in her voice when he couldn't see her. "I know you're leaving. Being here in Belham is a temporary detour for you, and I'm fine with that. I'd never ask you to stay because I know you'd just get all conflicted and start to resent me." She kissed him lightly on the chin, as if to prove how fine with it she was. "Let's just enjoy this," she said. "Let's just be together until you leave, and not worry about what happens after."

It was so reasonable. He wanted very much to enjoy this, and not worry about anything. However, he couldn't help but wonder if her enjoyment was made easier by knowing there was another guy waiting in the wings.

By three o'clock he'd shopped for groceries, vacuumed, paid bills, WD-40'd several squeaky door hinges, and blasted the tub grout with some hideous cleaning product that smelled like an atomic bleach bomb. Still three more hours until Rebecca was off work.

He took George for a long walk and ended up in the vicinity of Our Lady Comforter of the Afflicted Church. It was almost four by then, and Mass was about to start. Sean sat down to rest on a bench near a statue of St. Mary.

He did not want to go to Mass. He hated Mass, he reminded himself. It was always a disaster for him these days. God was MIA.

And yet, it was sort of like sticking his tongue into the empty socket of a pulled tooth. For some reason he kept feeling for it to make sure it was still missing. Looping the dog's leash through the arm of the bench, he went inside and sat in the last pew.

The first reading was from Genesis, the story of God evicting Adam and Eve from the Garden of Eden, after they'd eaten from the tree of the knowledge of good and evil. Sean felt an immediate solidarity with poor Adam and Eve. *The Big Guy bailed on you guys, too,* he thought.

It was proclaimed by a teenage boy with a sprinkling of acne across his cheeks and a slight lisp. "By the sweat of your face will you earn your food, until you return to the ground, as you were taken from it." *Sweat* sounded more like *thweat*.

Sean was impressed by the boy's bravery. How much courage must it take to stand up there in front of hundreds of people, knowing you were definitely going to botch it?

Distracted and bored, Sean glanced around, his gaze catching momentarily on the sun shining though a stained glass window of Jesus carrying a lamb, on the cantor flipping nervously through her songbook, on an old man with granite-gray hair sitting alone a few rows up. . . .

Da.

Anxiety rippled through Sean. The last thing he wanted was to see his father again after the fight they'd had the other night. And yet he couldn't take his eyes off the older man. The thick neck and broad shoulders—they were the same as they'd ever been. And when he stood for the reading of the Gospel, he clasped his hands behind his back, the crippled one cradled by the strong one. Sean would know him anywhere.

The young-looking priest was on the altar again and launched into his homily. "The Garden of Eden is probably one of the best-known Bible stories in the world. It comes to us from the Jews, and is part of the Muslim canon as well."

Exactly, thought Sean. *Same old, same old.*

"What's interesting about this story is that it has so many layers," the priest went on. "On the surface, it's the story of a punishment.

Adam and Eve disobeyed God, and from then on, humankind has been paying for it. We have to work to eat, and childbirth is painful.

"But a story doesn't last as long as this one without having a little more to think about, a little more depth. Consider this: we believe in an all-knowing God. If that's true, how could God *not* have known that Adam and Eve would eventually goof up?

"Many of you are parents. Do you expect that because you tell your children not to play with matches, they absolutely won't—or do you understand that all children misbehave from time to time? And do you expect that they'll *never* touch matches—or do you know that once they're old enough, they'll need those matches and will be mature enough to use them wisely?

"Is it possible, then, that just as parents watch their children grow and mature, needing greater challenges, God knew it was time for Adam and Eve to leave the nest? Think about Eden for a moment. It sounds like a pretty great destination. You don't have to work or feel pain. There's no need for compassion or forgiveness because nothing bad ever happens. It's perfect.

"As we all know, real life is *defined* by imperfection. But it is in facing and dealing with those things that are not perfect—with justice, compassion, and forgiveness—that we grow.

"Here's the line that makes me think that God anticipated and even approved of Adam and Eve's leaving the Garden of Eden: 'God made tunics of skins for the man and his wife and clothed them.'

"He knew they would need these in the world, and he gave them as any parent might give their young adult a warm jacket before they leave for college, or a set of dishes before they move into their first apartment.

"God blessed his children, even after they goofed up. Just as he blesses us all."

Sean waited for some sort of rebuttal to commence in his mind, but nothing came. The absence of his own annoyance seemed foreign and slightly suspicious to him. When it was time to take Communion, it still tasted bad, but he was able to make himself return to the pew for the final blessing rather than scurrying out the door like a refugee.

He resigned himself to seeing his father when everyone rose to leave. *What am I going to do—run?* he thought.

The older man stood and turned toward the aisle, spied his son a few rows back, and stopped in his tracks. The people beside him also stopped, waiting for him to exit the pew.

"Come on, Da," said Sean wearily. "You're holding up traffic."

CHAPTER 42

"I'm very sorry about that prodigal comment the other night," Da said, as they walked out into the sunlight. "I had no desire to insult you."

Sean shrugged his acceptance. It still bugged him, but what could he say in the face of such contrition. The older man followed him around to the bench to which George was tied. Da let the dog sniff him, and when she seemed satisfied he gave her a scratch behind her ears. "And who's this beauty, I'd like to know."

"This is George. She's Aunt Vivvy's."

Da's head snapped up, his eyes disbelieving.

"Yeah, I know," said Sean. "I can't really explain it."

They stood there awkwardly for a moment. "I was on my way to get some supper," said Da. "Would you care to join me? We could get a sandwich and sit outside."

Sean was about to say no, he had to get home, but that was a lie. And, like going back to church, there was a little part of him that felt the need to probe at his father's presence, as strangely contradictory as it was to his absence all those years. It was an experiment in proving the reality of a ghost.

They went up the street to a deli and took their food to the Dudley Ball Field. No one was playing. They sat alone on the bleachers and spread their meatball subs and cans of soda on the bench between them.

"You're still at the Comfort Inn?" asked Sean idly.

"Yes, but not for long. I bought my ticket. Flying out of Logan in a little over a week."

"Must have been expensive."

"It was dear, but I have funds. Once I was sober, Declan Kelly, that boy in Tacoma, helped me go after the workman's comp for my hand." He poked a loose meatball back into the recesses of the bun. "I could pay for you and Kevin, too, if that's what's holding you back."

"I can't. I have a million things to figure out. Deirdre's leaving after her show next week, and I have to come up with some sort of plan for Kevin and Aunt Vivvy. He's got some problems, and she's starting to . . . not be quite so sharp."

Da's eyes flicked toward Sean. "She's failing?"

"Not exactly. But she doesn't always know what's what. I think it might be Alzheimer's, but she won't let me take her to a doctor."

"Stubborn old nag," he muttered.

"We've all got our short suits," Sean said, quick to defend her. "Don't we?" Despite her faults, Viv had buckled down and stuck it out. Neither of the two of them could say as much.

Prodigals, thought Sean. He hated to admit it, but maybe the old man had had a point.

"I've no right to speak ill of her," Da conceded.

They ate their meatball subs and sipped their sodas. The wind kicked up a bit, and they had to hold the butcher paper down to keep it from flying away. Sean thought about his father's trip to Ireland. There was something appealing about it. He hadn't been on a plane heading to a foreign country in a long time. Not that Ireland was as foreign as other places he'd been. But the draw of travel—any travel—tugged at him.

But the thought of being separated from Rebecca quelled the daydream like ice water. His need to be back in the fray of disaster would override the attachment to her soon enough. Ireland was not nearly reason enough to leave.

As Sean and George walked Da back to his car in the church parking lot, the older man said, "I'd like to meet Kevin before I go."

Sean's first thought was to deny him. He certainly hadn't earned the right to make demands. But Kevin might want to meet his only grandparent, and Sean didn't want to make the choice for him. "I'll talk to him about it and see how he feels."

"I'm his grandfather."

"I'm aware of that fact, but it's up to Kevin, not me—and not you."

There was a foot nudged up against Sean's groin when he woke on Sunday morning, and a breast by his ear. He smiled and turned his face into it, thinking there could not possibly be a more blissful way for a guy to gain consciousness. Rebecca arched her stomach against his chest. He kissed her ribs.

"Stop—that tickles!" But she didn't sound like she meant it.

Sometime later they got up and showered. Sometime after that they dressed and went down to the kitchen for breakfast.

"I'm picking up Kevin at noon," he told her. "I'll probably sleep at home tonight."

"I'd like to meet him," she said. "I feel like I know him already."

"Yeah, I'd like that, too. Just let me see how he is."

At quarter to noon, Sean was sitting in the Caprice in the parking lot by the Scout House with George in the backseat. Half an hour later he let George out to pee, and the two of them stretched their legs with a walk around the lot. By quarter to one he was starting to get worried. Had Frank Quentzer's car broken down? Had there been an accident?

There were a couple of other people waiting in cars, and he walked up to one with an I'M PROUD OF MY SCOUT bumper sticker on the back and tapped on the window.

"Supposed to be noon, right?" he asked the middle-aged woman with a Red Sox cap.

"Yeah, but that's kind of approximate. They probably called, but my cell phone died. Did you check yours?"

"I don't have one."

The woman blinked at him from under her cap. "You don't have a cell phone?"

"No."

"Then I guess we're both in the dark."

Just then Frank Quentzer's gray Suburban rolled into the parking lot and came to a stop in front of the Scout House. Boys piled out on both sides, and Sean found himself anxiously searching the unruly herd. Kevin was the last to emerge.

It was tempting to run up and say, "Hey! How are you? How'd it go?" But the boys were unloading the rear of the truck, and the other parents were standing around the edges, like wallflowers at a dance waiting to be noticed.

From a distance, Kevin looked sunburned or dirty, or both. His sleek black hair stuck out at weird angles. Sean watched him lug a cooler with another boy. As he held up his end, his gaze scanned the parents until he saw Sean with George on the leash. A little grin lit his face.

Yes! thought Sean. *Happy!*

Eventually the unloading was done and items sorted, and each boy stumbled off with his parents hauling his trunk or duffel. Sean hoisted Kevin's bag and said, "Hey, camper."

"Hey, Uncle Sean." He squatted down next to George and rubbed his hands all over the dog's neck and back. "Hiya, girl," he said. "Did he walk you? Did he take good care of you?" The dog's tail wagged madly.

They got in the car and drove toward home. "So? How was it?"

"Good," said Kevin, head turned toward the window.

"Come on, I need details!"

Kevin didn't answer. He slid down on his seat until the lap belt was across his chest. And then he put a hand up to his eyes and started to sob.

Sean almost crashed into a mailbox. "Whoa! What's going on? What happened?"

Kevin didn't answer. He just kept crying, chest heaving for gulps of air. Sean reached out to put a hand on his shoulder, but the boy flinched away, and Sean silently chastised himself. He knew better than that.

Kevin was still scrunched down on the seat sobbing when they pulled into the driveway.

"Kev," soothed Sean. "Kev, you gotta tell me what happened. Were kids mean? Did somebody do something?"

From under his dirt-streaked hands, Kevin shook his head. The sobbing slowed and shifted toward hiccuppy little gasps.

"Okay," murmured Sean. "Okay, that's it. Breathe, buddy."

Kevin inhaled an enormous sniffle and wiped his drippy hand on his pants. His breathing recalibrated to a more normal pace. Sean waited.

"It was good," Kevin muttered. "Mostly."

"Yeah? Because a minute ago you didn't look like it was all that good."

"No, it's just . . ." He looked exhausted, like he had barely enough energy to form words. "Sometimes it was all . . . you know . . . loud and stuff."

"Like what?"

"Like . . . at meals everyone's jammed into this big room. And they squish into picnic tables. And then they sing these really loud songs."

Camp songs, Sean realized. *I should have thought to warn him.*

"How'd you handle it?"

"I made sure I sat on the end of the bench. And I went outside when they started to sing."

"Good thinking!"

"And I didn't cry." His face got tense. "I didn't cry *all week*." And he burst into tears again.

"Ah, Kev," Sean murmured. "You did great. And now you just have to blow off some steam. You've been holding it all in. Just let that sucker out."

Kevin wept for another few minutes. But he didn't cover his face this time.

Deirdre was home for dinner. "So, how was camp—disgusting?"

"Yeah, really disgusting." Kevin was clean and his still-damp hair was shiny again. He shoveled rotini pasta into his mouth like he was trying to beat the clock.

"What was the most disgusting thing?" she asked with a conspiratorial smile.

Kevin nodded as he chewed and swallowed, as if this were a game the two of them had played before. "The latrines are the worst. But after that comes our tent. This kid William cut the cheese like a hundred times a night. Mr. Quentzer thinks he might be lactose intolerant."

"'Cut the cheese'?" Deirdre said. "I've never heard you use that expression before."

"All the kids say it." Kevin loaded his fork up again and stuffed it in his mouth. Deirdre raised her eyebrows at Sean, amusement playing across her face. Aunt Vivvy's expression was decidedly less amused.

"Must have been hard to sleep," said Sean, "with all that cheese happening."

"Mr. Quentzer gave us little branches of pine needles, and we kept them by our pillows so we could sniff them when William cut one."

"Might we turn the conversation to another topic?" said Aunt Vivvy. "I'm developing indigestion."

"Yeah, okay," said Deirdre. "When do you guys want tickets for *Joseph*? There are shows every night starting Tuesday, and the last show is the Sunday matinee. I get four for free."

She didn't want them to come opening night—she said she'd be too nervous. They decided they would go Wednesday. After dinner, Aunt Vivvy went up to her room, and Kevin said he had a lot of TV watching to catch up on. As Sean cleared the table, Deirdre said, "So I notice you haven't been around as much lately. Like, at night."

Sean handed her a stack of plates. "I've been at a friend's house."

"A friend?" she teased, sliding the dishes into the dishwasher.

He smiled despite himself. "Yeah, a very good friend."

"A *beneficial* one?"

He shot her a look, and she put her hands up in mock surrender. "Hey," she said. "Just asking. It doesn't matter to me—do what you like."

"I will."

"You always do."

That night when the house was quiet, he called Rebecca and gave her the update on Kevin and invited her to come with them to see Deirdre's play. She told him she had hired movers to transfer her parents' furniture to the garage and her elderly client's pieces into the house. Eventually they were talking about almost nothing at all, but the sound of her calm, melodious voice kept him on the phone like a drug addict inhaling all that he could.

CHAPTER 43

Walking through the woods up Jansen Hill with Sean and George the next morning, Kevin said, "I was thinking about something at camp."

"Yeah?"

"Yeah."

"Are you going to tell me, or should I guess?"

Kevin didn't answer for a moment. The three of them were walking single file up the path, Sean bringing up the rear, so he couldn't see the boy's face.

"Um," said Kevin. He picked up his pace and Sean had to hurry to stay close enough to hear him. "I know you like living in other countries and stuff . . . but I wish you would stay."

And there it was.

Sean was caught off guard. It seemed like every time the subject had come up before—with Deirdre or Aunt Vivvy, or even Cormac or Rebecca—no one had actually said the words. They had insinuated or implied. Rebecca had blatantly told him she knew he wouldn't stay. Sean had been able to build a sort of seawall against the lapping waves of their disappointment. This was different.

"Kevin . . ."

"Don't you like it here?"

No! he wanted to say. *I'm a goddamned change maker at my friend's coffee shop. Aunt Vivvy's going crazy, and she wasn't even that nice when she was lucid. I don't want an e-mail account or a cell phone or any of that extraneous crap. I want to go back to my life!*

"I really like being with you," Sean said. And when the words came out, and he heard himself say them, he knew they were true.

"I like being with you, too. A lot."

Sean sighed. "There are a lot of things up in the air right now."

"Yeah, that flux thing."

"I'm trying to work it out so everyone gets what they need. Can you just trust me on that one? That I'm figuring it out?"

"Okay," said Kevin. "I trust you."

The credit card bill came in, and it was much higher than Sean had anticipated. He checked it twice. He had made a lot of purchases. And now that he was doing Aunt Vivvy's bills, he knew that they did not have much of a cushion to play with. She was getting Social Security, which basically covered the house bills, but not much else, and her inheritance had dwindled to the vicinity of an emergency fund. He called Cormac. "Hey, load me up with shifts," he said. "Baby needs a new pair of shoes."

"Bad news, buddy," said Cormac. "All the staff vacations are over, and they're all asking me for extra hours now, too. I can give you some, but I gotta keep my permanent people happy."

"No problem. Let me know if somebody calls in sick or something."

Permanent people. Damn.

Life in the States was ridiculously expensive—and that was with him serving as unpaid housekeeper, cook, errand runner, plumbing fixer . . . he was basically the wife in this situation. And admittedly he'd been avoiding thinking about Deirdre leaving. If he didn't find some sort of caretaker for Kevin and Aunt Vivvy, he'd be trapped in Belham forever.

His aunt had never wandered or left a stove burner on, and she seemed to be fine in the house with only George there. When her memory dimmed she just got quiet and drifted in her own world. It was like a mental brownout. If he could get someone to spend a few hours there in the afternoon, do some housework, make dinner, and help Kevin with homework, that would probably be enough. For now. It depended on how fast Vivvy deteriorated. He could be in touch with Kevin by e-mail to check on how things were going on that score.

There was money left in his trust fund to pay for a caretaker—the question was how long it would last. Sean decided to limit his foreign work search to positions that paid a little more—that is to say, more than virtually nothing.

The other concern was getting Kevin used to the new school. Sean thought of his slacker pothead brother scrupulously preparing Kevin for kindergarten. Kindergarten—where the biggest stressor was whether there'd be enough blocks to go around. Middle school was practically combat by comparison. Sean would have to stay for at least the first few weeks until Kevin made the transition and the school had him on their institutional radar.

A thought flickered in the back of his mind, a memory of junk mail that might, on second thought, have some value . . . He dug through Kevin's school packet and found the flier for the temporary school nurse position. It was short-term—only until October. He could handle doling out ice packs and sanitary pads for that long.

Staying for another six weeks had an added benefit that he didn't like to ponder too deeply. Rebecca. More time with her. He knew the longer they cocooned themselves in the fantasyland of Let's Just Enjoy This, the harder it would be when he left. Already he was in deeper than he'd ever been with anyone. There were women he'd slept with off and on for months at a time . . . but none that made him feel like some pining idiot from a pop song the minute she left for work.

Anxious to solve at least the immediate problem of income, Sean dialed the middle school. He told the secretary that he was interested in the sub nurse position.

"For yourself?"

"Yes."

"You're a registered nurse? Because we can't take an EMT certificate. You have to be an RN."

Sean rolled his eyes. Was a male nurse still such a surprise? "Yes, I'm an RN. I'll submit a copy of my license with the application."

"Okay, then," she said tightly. He heard papers rustling. "The posting says you also need five years of experience, preferably in pediatrics."

"I've been a nurse for twenty years, much of it with children. Can you tell me what the position pays?"

"Fourteen dollars an hour."

Fourteen? That was a 50 percent raise from the Confectionary! Come to think of it, he'd never made that much in his life. "I'd definitely like to apply."

Later that afternoon, a package arrived.

"Kev!" Sean yelled. "Come here a minute!"

They struggled to open the box. "Run and get a knife from the kitchen."

Kevin pulled a jackknife out of his shorts pocket and flipped it open.

"Hey, where'd you get that?"

"Bodie gave it to me. I forgot to tell you—I got my Totin' Chip at camp, so I can use knives and axes now. He has about four of them and he says this one's kinda dull anyway." He slid the knife blade under the box flap to sever the tape. "See, you always cut away from yourself so you don't get hurt," he explained.

"Good to know." Sean made sure Kevin didn't see him smile.

When the contents of the package were revealed, Kevin said, "What is this stuff?"

"Lie down and I'll show you." Kevin flopped onto the living room rug, and Sean gave him a throw pillow to put behind his head. "Close your eyes." Sean gently spread the fleece blanket over the boy. It had rows of enclosed tubelike pockets filled with weights.

Kevin's eyes popped open in surprise, and he ran his hands over the fleecy hills of extra weight. "It's really heavy."

"Too heavy? Do you feel trapped?"

"No . . . it feels good. You try it!"

Sean lay down and Kevin adjusted the blanket over him. To Sean it felt like he was being pinned, like his lungs couldn't quite fully expand.

"Not my thing," he told Kevin. "But I'm glad you like it. It's yours. Now you don't have to sleep like the Princess and the Pea—with you as the pea!"

When Sean took out the other item, Kevin grimaced. "I don't wear socks."

"Yeah, I noticed. Just try these. They don't have a seam across the toe, so they might not bug you as much."

Kevin tried one on and quickly pulled it off again. "Not my thing," he said. He looked up, checking Sean's face for disappointment.

"A long time ago there was this famous baseball player called Shoeless Joe. I'm going to start calling you Sockless Kev."

"No, you aren't," Kevin said knowingly.

"Yeah." Sean chuckled. "Probably not."

Sean set the kitchen table with china for the second time that evening. The first time the delicate dishes had looked incongruous against the old wooden table. Pulling open cabinets and drawers, he found what he was looking for—a nice lace tablecloth.

Kevin came in red-faced, his hair sticking to his forehead in shiny black clumps. He poured water into a bowl for George, who lapped it up eagerly, and then got himself a glass. "Who's coming?" he asked. "The president?"

"No, smart-aleck," said Sean. "A friend of mine."

"The baker guy? Tell him to bring some pie!"

"No, someone else. Her name is Rebecca. She used to go to high school with Cormac and me. She's nice, you'll like her."

"Ohhh," said Kevin with a teasing grin, "a *girl*."

"Yeah, try not to be too jealous."

"Gross!" said Kevin, but there was a little flush behind his freckles.

When Rebecca arrived, she was wearing a pale pink cotton

sundress printed with trails of tiny flowers. Sean had never seen her in anything so feminine, and he thought his heart might stop. It was all he could do to keep himself from going after her right there in the foyer.

He restrained himself to kissing her cheek and murmuring, "You look amazing." When he turned and introduced her to Kevin, he saw a strange, slightly worried look on the boy's face as he held out his left hand to shake, then looked down and quickly switched to the right. "Sorry," he muttered. "That's how we do it in Boy Scouts."

"How was camp?" she asked him. "I heard it was disgusting but fun."

Kevin looked at Sean.

"I told her about it," Sean confessed. "We're friends. We talk."

They went into the kitchen, and while Sean cut up Granny Smith apples for the salad, Rebecca, in her gentle way, got Kevin to talk in more detail about camp. He told them about watching the boys pile into the war canoe, an enormous Indian-looking thing big enough for ten boys and two of the leaders. They paddled out to the middle of the lake for a splash fight with another troop, and Kevin admitted that part of him would've liked to go. "But I don't really do stuff like that," he explained to her. "I'm different from a lot of kids."

"Yeah," she said. "I'm kind of different, too."

"Yeah?"

"Well, I'm pretty shy," she said. "Also, I have this face thing, and kids used to tease me about it, which made me feel even more shy."

"How'd you get it?"

"I was born with it. The doctors said I must have been lying funny in my mom's tummy, and I'd grow out of it, but I never did. In fact it got worse. Nowadays they put helmets on babies who have it to make their heads grow right. But I guess they didn't think of that back then."

"Do people still tease you?"

"No, but sometimes they look at me funny, and I have to remind myself that it just takes people a little while to get used to it."

"I'm getting used to it already," said Kevin.

"Thanks," she said with her lovely crooked smile. "I appreciate it."

When Aunt Vivvy came down for dinner, Sean saw a spark of recognition as he introduced her to Rebecca. She stared an extra moment at the younger woman. Then she nodded with just the barest note of triumph and said, "I take it you've purchased a raincoat since I saw you last."

When your memory kicks in, thought Sean, *why not flaunt it?*

"I'm still grateful to you for that ride home, Miss Preston," said Rebecca.

"Anytime, my dear." And she carefully lowered herself into a kitchen chair.

After dinner, Sean, Rebecca, and Kevin went to Dairy Queen for ice cream. They sat at one of the plastic picnic benches, Kevin on one side, Sean and Rebecca thigh to thigh on the other, holding hands under the table. They chatted, falling into an easy familiarity. Rebecca offered Kevin a taste of her Brownie Batter Blizzard and held out a spoonful for him, which he happily accepted. It reminded Sean of a mother robin feeding her baby a worm, and it squeezed at him in a slightly ecstatic, slightly painful way.

That night after they'd pulled all the extra blankets off Kevin's bed and he was snuggled happily under the new weighted fleece, Sean told him, "So you know my dad left a long time ago, right? When I was a little older than you?"

"Yeah."

"A couple of weeks ago he called me."

"Whoa! Did you freak out?"

Sean chuckled. "Yeah, I was pretty surprised."

"Did you tell him he was a jerk for leaving?"

Sean nodded. "I kinda did. He told me he's really sorry, and explained what happened a little better. I still think it was a pretty awful thing to do, though."

"Did you forgive him?"

"Not totally, I guess. But I'm trying. Sometimes you just have to let things go."

"I don't think I'd let it go. I think I'd still be mad."

Sean considered that Kevin's own father had left, in a sense. "I can see how you'd feel that way. Part of me is still pretty mad. But here's something you hopefully learn when you grow up: it takes a lot of energy to be angry—energy you could use for a better purpose."

Kevin's brows furrowed in thought for a moment. "Like camping?"

Sean smiled. "Exactly. In fact, we should have a bumper sticker made up: DON'T BE MAD—GO CAMPING!"

"No one would get it."

"True." Sean tucked the blanket in a little tighter, and Kevin's face started to get that slack, relaxed look. "So, here's the thing. Your grandfather wants to meet you."

Kevin's half-lidded eyes suddenly went wide. "What?"

"I know, it's a little strange. But he's moving back to Ireland, and he wants to see you before he goes. You'll probably never get a chance to meet him again."

"Do I have to?"

"No, you don't. But maybe you should think about it. He's your only grandfather."

"Will you be there?"

"Absolutely."

"The whole time?"

"Every second."

"Okay," he said, unhappily. "I'll think about it."

CHAPTER 44

The next day, Sean got a letter from Yasmin Chaudhry, the doctor he'd worked with in Kenya. She'd been happy to hear from him, having wondered why a letter she'd sent to the hospital in the Democratic Republic of Congo had elicited no response.

I can only imagine how dislocated you must feel! For people like you and me, our own birthplaces have become the "foreign" countries. Your description of the shop windows had me shaking my head in wonder. A whole display of fancy women's purses—how exotic! At the moment, I'd give anything to see a full display of canned goods and unused syringes.

As you can see from the postmark, I'm in Haiti now. The world seems mostly to have forgotten about the devastation here. Ah, well. The news cycle lasts only so long. And there's no real news—things haven't changed all that dramatically. Still so many homeless and ill.

If, as you say, you are looking for your next "adventure," I could certainly use your help. It would be delightful to work with you again, a trusted comrade, a dear friend.

The letter went on to describe her clinic near Port au Prince. Yasmin was in charge, and he could imagine her competent, no-nonsense approach, a very satisfying person to work for. But he had to secure short-term employment before focusing on the future. He walked his sub nurse application and license copy over to the middle school, leaving Kevin and George throwing a stick in the backyard. He didn't want Kevin to know, in case it didn't work out. He submitted the paperwork to the secretary and asked when they would start interviewing.

"As soon as they feel they have a qualified candidate," she said.

Well, they've got one now, he thought, and hoped they might call by the end of the day. He was anxious to check this off his list.

After dinner, Kevin said, "I guess I'll see him. My grandfather."

"What made you change your mind?" asked Sean.

"Well, it was really fun hanging out with Rebecca last night. I figured maybe it wouldn't be so bad meeting another new person. But you'll be with me, right?"

"I won't even leave to go to the bathroom. I'll just hold it the whole time."

Kevin crossed his eyes and made a pained face.

"That's just how I'll look," said Sean. "By the way, I'm going over to Rebecca's tonight. I might be home late." *Like in the morning.* "You all right with that?"

"Oh. Sure. But why doesn't she just come over here again?"

"Hey—are you trying to steal my girl?"

Kevin giggled. "She did kinda like me. Maybe even better than you!"

Sean was still smiling about that as he drove to Rebecca's. Getting bird-dogged by an eleven-year-old. He told her about it when he got there. She smiled, but he could see it wasn't a real one. "What is it?" he asked.

"Nothing," she said. "It just sounds funny—referring to me as 'your girl.'"

A prickle of anxiety ran up his neck. "It's just an expression."

"I know." She unplugged a huge brown ceramic lamp and brought it down to the garage.

Later, after he'd finished brushing his teeth and checking to make sure he still smelled reasonably good, he came into her room to find her sitting up in the twin bed reading a book.

Should he have brought a book? Is this what couples did after they'd been together a little while—read before sex? If he had known, he would have brought *The Last Battle*. He was almost finished. Now he felt like a kid at a masquerade party who'd forgotten to wear a costume.

She looked up and there was something there, an uncertainty of some kind. Could she possibly be unsure of how absolutely giddy he was to sleep with her? Maybe she was worried that after a week of pouncing on each other every chance they got, he was losing interest. She had no cause for concern. None whatsoever. But was he supposed to come out and say it?

And what was with the book?

She slid over to the wall, as far as she could go in the narrow twin bed. He hesitated. "Are you sleepy?" he asked, wanting to give her a gentle excuse if she wasn't interested in sex. Because if there was some other reason, he didn't want to know it.

"No," she said. "Are you coming?"

He climbed in beside her, every cell rising up to heave itself in her direction. She allowed his arms around her—how else would they fit? And then her hand began its customary migration across the landscape of his chest, and at last he took a normal breath.

Their lovemaking felt self-conscious and frenetic. Rebecca gasped once, then again, and he was relieved that she was climaxing. But it didn't quite sound the same. In fact, it didn't sound the least bit happy or ecstatic. In another moment he realized she was crying.

He quickly pulled back. "Oh, my God," he said. "Did I hurt you?"

"No." In the dark he could hear that the pain she was feeling was worse than physical.

"Tell me . . ." he said, though part of him absolutely did not want to know—would have paid good money to avoid hearing whatever it was she might say.

"I thought I could do this," she whispered, "but I can't. I feel like I'm falling into a hole I might never climb out of." She rolled away from him and off the bed, grabbing up a blanket that had fallen on the floor to wrap around herself.

He sat up in bed. "What did I do?"

"Nothing. It's fine. You're just you. It's not like you ever tried to hide it."

"Hide what?"

"That you like me, but not enough."

"Enough for what? To want to be with you every second of the day? Because I do."

"Enough to do more than hang out and have sex, Sean. Enough to stay."

Which of course silenced him. He thought of Cormac talking about Barb's desire for a child with his genes and asking, *What's the comeback for that?* Absolutely nothing.

"This isn't healthy for me, Sean. I thought it was—like it might be some kind of closure for how in love with you I was in high school. But it's not. I'm thinking crazy thoughts, like, 'Maybe if I were more like Chrissy . . .' Or 'Maybe if my face—'"

"No!" he said, standing up and coming toward her. "That's not—"

But she backed away from him. "I *know.* But don't you see why that makes it worse? I know it's crazy, but I'm thinking it anyway."

He stood there stunned. Because he did see why that made it worse. And he couldn't believe he could cause someone that kind of pain. He wasn't used to . . . *affecting* people like this.

"I'm sorry." He meant it so sincerely, but knowing, too, how meager a response it was.

"*I'm* sorry," she said. "I wish I were so much . . . cooler than this."

"Rebecca, you're perfect. I'm the—"

"Oh, my God, please don't do the 'It's not you, it's me' line. We both know it's you. But it's also me for knowing you so well and wanting you anyway. So let's just not say it."

They stared at each other in the dimness, and he could see the reflection of light from a streetlamp on her dampened face. He knew that if he offered the only kind of comfort that he had ever been good at—physical comfort, palliative care—she was likely to reject it. But he did it anyway, because how much worse could it get than this?

He put his arms around her and was surprised when she didn't pull away. He held her as close as he dared and said, "You are everything that's good."

"Please shut up," she whispered. And he knew that at least it was better than the other thing she could have said, which was *But still not good enough*.

CHAPTER 45

Sean came to consciousness in his own bed like a man suddenly dropping through the ice of a frozen pond. The memory of the previous night hit him before he'd even opened his eyes. It was over with Rebecca. In every way. She had told him she couldn't see him until she got herself back on solid ground. That's how she'd put it. As if his very presence were a kind of emotional tar pit, sucking her down into some dark lifeless place.

She hadn't blamed him. And yet she'd called their relationship "unhealthy." It was only a whisper away from saying that he was bad for her. He had never been The Bad Guy before. Certainly he'd disappointed women occasionally. There had been one or two, prone to drama, who'd professed their love for him, demanding to know why he wouldn't return it. And he'd felt sorry for them, despite what he'd known to be a very clear message: This is casual. It is not love.

Rebecca had demanded nothing. And he'd given her everything he had. His innermost thoughts. His worship of her body. His utter admiration and pride in her. He'd loved her and it showed. He had to admit that now. The fact that he'd never said the words seemed now to be as relevant as making a promise with your fingers crossed behind your back. A technicality that counted only among children.

And there was that guy—the old boyfriend. Maybe now that Sean was The Bad Guy, this jerk had been promoted to The Good Guy. Gainfully employed, centrally located, saying all the right things simply because he knew how. He'd been in an *actual normal relationship* with her, for godsake—he had the edge!

But she was too smart to go out with some loser who didn't appreciate her, wasn't she? He couldn't be all that bad, because at some point Rebecca had chosen him. But why did they break up? It was hard enough to be without her, but he found it unbearable to lose her to someone who might not get how great she was. As if he had a choice.

Why he had agreed to take Kevin to meet his father at IHOP, he couldn't for the life of him recall. Just pulling into the parking lot, remembering the dread he'd felt only a week ago when he'd faced his father the first time, compounded that drowning-in-ice-water feeling he'd been having all morning. He was grateful that Kevin was too anxious to notice.

Da was too excited to notice, at first. He reached his hand out to shake Kevin's, grinning, studying every hair, every freckle. As Kevin slid into the booth, Da gestured surreptitiously to his eyes and murmured, "Just like . . ."

Hugh.

"Yeah." Sean nodded and sat beside Kevin.

The older man asked his grandson about school and camp and the dog. Sean monitored this interaction as if he were sitting in a high school English composition class, struggling to focus on what he knew he would be tested on later, but unable to keep his mind from wandering out the window, across the sports fields and over the trees.

"And your Aunt Deirdre," he heard Da say. "I understand she's to be in a play."

"Yeah, we're going to see her tonight. She's got a really big part. But not the biggest part. That has to be a guy, because the play is called *Joseph and* . . . something about a jacket."

"Where is the theater?"

"In Worcester. She practically lives there."

Sean studied his father, who was assiduously avoiding eye contact as he stirred sugar into his tea. Kevin excused himself to go to the bathroom.

"You can't go," Sean told Da. "Deirdre's already freaked out enough. If you show up, she'll blow a gasket."

"She said she didn't want to see *me*. She never said I couldn't see *her*."

Sean squinted at him, annoyed. "You're kidding me with this. Really? You want to play semantics with the grown daughter you haven't seen since she was in preschool?"

When Da looked up, his gaze was lit with anger. "No, I want to *see* her. I want to lay eyes on my baby girl before I move across the ocean and die."

"Don't be dramatic. You could have seen her anytime in the last twenty-eight years. And don't pull the old man stuff on me, either. We're all going to die."

Da scrutinized him. "Rough night?" he said.

He thinks I'm hungover. Sean let out a bitter snort. "You could say."

Da studied him a moment longer. "Well," he concluded, "not from drinking. Bad news of some kind?"

Oh, what the hell, thought Sean. He could play twenty questions or he could just say it.

"I was seeing someone. She broke it off last night."

Da nodded, his face softening slightly, but thankfully not to the point of pity. "I'm sorry."

Sean shrugged, but he supposed that Da knew better than to believe the matter was shrug-able.

When Kevin returned, Da shifted the conversation to his upcoming trip. "It's a beautiful place, really," he told Kevin. "Great rolling hills and green pastures. A place that heals the soul."

"What's the highest point?" Kevin asked, his lips sticky from syrup.

"That would be Carrauntoohil, in County Kerry, where I was born. It's a great one for climbing."

Kevin's eyes shone with interest. "What makes it so great?"

"Ah, you have to scramble up the Devil's Ladder to get to the top."

"Why do they call it that?"

"Well, not for being a stroll in the garden, lad, that's for sure!"

"Have you done it?"

"Once. Just before I came to America when I was nineteen. I wanted to go to the very top of Ireland before I left it, so me and some of the lads hitchhiked down and made the climb. The weather turned sour at the peak and we very nearly froze to death—even though it was May!"

"That's *awe*some," breathed Kevin.

"You'll have to see it yourself someday."

As the boy's questioning gaze turned to him, Sean realized a campaign had been waged by the wily old man. Waged and practically won.

"Could we go?" asked Kevin.

"Ah, Kev," Sean said wearily. "It's not exactly like going to Connecticut."

"The highest point in Ireland, Uncle Sean. The Devil's Ladder!"

Sean looked at his father, the man's eyes wide with false innocence.

"Don't give me that," Sean told him. "You're sinking pretty low, turning the kid on me."

"I've done no such thing, and I resent the implication."

Sean snorted. "Right!"

"Just think for a moment," said his father. "Think of the boy and yourself, traveling the land of the faeries with me. It'd be grand!"

"And don't turn on the Irish charm. I'm half Irish—it doesn't work on me."

Kevin watched this sparring intently, as if the outcome had significance far beyond vacation plans. Sean looked at him, at Hugh's eyes silently hoping.

"It might do you good to get away for a bit," Da said, his tone mild, his meaning clear.

Yes, indeed it might. In fact there was nothing Sean wanted more at the moment than to go far away. "School starts in two weeks," he relented. "We could do one week, tops."

Kevin and Da let out simultaneous whoops of joy that made pancake eaters at other booths turn their heads and smile.

They went straight to the Belham library, got onto a computer, and filled out the online passport forms for Kevin. Then they stopped off at the house for Kevin's birth certificate, went to the post office, submitted the forms, and had his picture taken. For a steep fee, the passport would arrive in two days.

When Sean saw the cost of the expedited passport and then the airline tickets, he murmured to his father, "Are you sure you can cover all this? I can help, but money's tight on our end. I'm working at a coffee shop at the moment."

"I was never happier to pay a bill in all my life" was all he said.

Later that afternoon, after Da had gone back to his hotel and Sean and Kevin had returned to the house, the phone rang. "Is Kevin there?" asked a boy's voice.

Sean handed it over and dawdled in the kitchen, constructing his turkey sandwich with unnecessary care. The caller apparently asked what classes Kevin would have, and the two of them determined they would have science and drama together. Then the conversation circled around to a tent full of farts, and Sean quickly determined that the kid on the other end was Ivan from Boy Scouts.

"Sure, I can hang out," said Kevin. "But it'll have to be in the next couple days." He waited for the obvious question this begged, a proud little smile playing around his cheeks. "I'm leaving on Sunday for a week. Me and my uncle and my grandfather are going to Ireland."

CHAPTER 46

Sean assumed that Deirdre was working at Carey's Diner, but when she came downstairs, auburn locks still sticky with hair-spray, vestiges of stage makeup around her eyes and hairline, he realized she'd been sleeping all day.

"How'd opening night go?" he asked.

"I didn't suck," she said, slumping into a kitchen chair.

"Good girl." Sean poured a glass of orange juice and set it on the table in front of her.

She squinted up at him. "Is this for me?"

"Yeah, you look like you could use some sugar and vitamin C."

"Thanks," she murmured. "No one gets me juice."

Maybe it was a commiserating response to his own recent reminder of being alone in the world, but Sean felt a surge of sympathy for his sister in that moment. No one got her juice . . . or anything else. As little parenting as Sean had had, Deirdre'd had virtually none. And for all the grief she'd given him over the last two months, he felt forgiveness descend on him like an unexpected blessing.

"How about an egg?" he said.

"Really?"

"Yeah, how do you like them? I'll make you any kind you want."

"Scrambled," she said. "Geez, I didn't realize how hungry I was till you said that. I'm freaking *starving*."

Sean started to laugh. It was so . . . Deirdre.

"Yeah, I know." She chuckled. "Drama, drama, drama."

He pulled out a pan and she told him about last night, about how her heart had pounded so hard before her entrance she thought she'd need a defibrillator, about that ecstatic feeling of wanting to give everything to the audience—*everything.* To rock their world with her voice and body and emotion. To knock it out of the park.

They had clapped after her number—hard, she thought, but not so hard that their palms hurt. Enthusiastically, but not wildly. And she had been thrilled and relieved that they hadn't given her golf claps, polite but subdued. But at the same time disappointed that they hadn't stood on their seats, screaming and crying and throwing roses onstage.

"Have you ever felt like crazy happy and deeply depressed at the same time?"

"Yeah," he said. "At work. You're living in these horrible conditions, and your patients are living in even worse. But then you do something—clean out an infected gash or give some antibiotics, and you know without it they would've eventually died, but since you were there, they won't. And they know it, too, and they are so grateful, Dee. So joyful to live another day. It's inspiring and heartbreaking all rolled up in one."

Deirdre nodded. And she smiled at him—a real, loving, sisterly smile. And his heart opened to her all over again.

He set the plate of eggs down before her with a fork and a napkin, and sat down, too. "Listen," he said. "I should've talked to you about this before. I'll be honest, I'm a little whacked out because I just got dumped last night."

"You liked her, huh."

"Yeah. A lot. Too much, if you know what I'm saying."

"Been there," she said, nodding, and he wondered about it. Of course she'd been with guys, he figured. He was about to ask her how she'd handled it, but she cut in first with, "So what'd you neglect to tell me, in your kicked-to-the-curb state?"

"I took Kevin to see Da yesterday."

Her eyes went half-lidded with false disinterest. "That has nothing to do with me."

"Yeah, okay, let me finish. So they kind of hit it off. And Da's been bugging me to go to Ireland with him. I said absolutely not about ten different times, and then the two of them wore me down."

"You're *leaving*? Goddamn it, Sean, you can't just fucking—"

"Whoa, I know, okay, I *know*. So here's my proposal, and you can accept or reject it, but just hear me out first. Kevin and Da and I leave for Ireland on Sunday, the day your show ends. Would you be willing to stay for one week, look after Viv and the dog, and then you can sail off into the sunset when we get back?"

She stewed on this, eyes simmering with suspicion. "So what does that mean, exactly? I can leave because you're staying?"

"Yeah. I'll stay until I figure out what to do. I'm going to try and hire some kind of housekeeper-caretaker."

"Someone good, Sean. Someone who can really deal with all of it, not just toss groceries in the fridge and keep the bathroom clean. You have to *promise*."

"Jesus, I promise, okay?"

"And if it doesn't work out it's on you," she said. "You won't call me in a month and say I have to come back because you're jetting off to Siberia?"

He sighed. Jesus, what was he agreeing to—and what choice did he have? "Yeah," he said. "I won't call you."

"Holy shit," she whispered. "I feel like I just got released from a Turkish prison."

He chuckled. So dramatic. "One thing," he said. "When you make it big, *you're* footing the bill for the hired help. Because we both know I'm never going to make any money."

"Type up the contract, Mr. Ziegfeld, I'm ready to sign."

Sean called Cormac to see if he'd wanted the extra ticket to Deirdre's show—Rebecca's ticket—and caught him up on the latest developments. "Wow," Cormac said. "For a guy who hates complications . . ."

"Yeah, I know, you practically need Cliff's Notes to follow them all."

Cormac laughed out loud, and Sean was grateful. At least his sense of humor kicked in sporadically. It was the only relief he got. And it was fleeting.

Cormac called the theater and was able to get another ticket for Barb. They would drive on their own in case Barb wanted to leave. "Still a little up and down," he explained.

The Worcester Footlight Theatre was a hundred years old. It had recently been completely renovated, every fleur-de-lis and winged cherub replastered and regilded.

"Pretty fancy," said Kevin.

"Worth wearing a button-down shirt for?" said Sean, holding Aunt Vivvy's elbow as they climbed the polished marble steps.

"I guess," grumbled Kevin. The shirt collar bugged him, and they'd butted heads about it. Sean had won out, saying Kevin should show respect for Aunt Deirdre, and make himself get used to things a little. Kevin had thrown the tie on the floor. It was a compromise.

When they reached their seats, Cormac and Barb were already there. Cormac greeted Aunt Vivvy with a respectful handshake and Kevin with a high five. Sean gave Barb a hug, and she gripped him tightly. "I'm praying for you, Sean," she whispered in his ear.

"I'm praying for you, too, picture taker," he said, and sent one up right there on the spot.

"Thanks," she said. "Thanks *so much*."

The hug had gone on for a few moments now, and Cormac said, "Dude!" playing the jealous husband. But when Barb let him go, Sean could see the gratitude behind his friend's posturing. *Hug my wife*, his faux-indignation seemed to say. *She needs it.*

As they waited for the curtain to go up, Sean gave Kevin an overview of the story. Joseph was one of the twelve sons of Jacob, he explained. Jacob loved Joseph so much that he gave him a really expensive coat. The other brothers were jealous, especially when Joseph started having dreams that he would rule over them one day. They were so angry they sold him into slavery.

"Slavery?" Kevin was skeptical.

"Yeah, slaves were pretty common back then. This is a story from the Bible—you knew that, right?"

"How would I know that?"

Sean smiled. "Sorry, I forgot to mention it. So he ends up being a slave for a guy named Potiphar. Then Mrs. Potiphar . . ." How did you explain seduction to an eleven-year-old? Sean decided it wasn't a good idea to go into it. "Well, she had kind of a crush on Joseph, and Mr. Potiphar got mad and sent Joseph to jail."

"Aunt Deirdre plays the guy's wife, right, so she's the one who gets Joseph in trouble?"

"Yeah."

Kevin grinned. "This'll be good. Aunt Deirdre's good at acting mean."

When Deirdre made her entrance, she was dressed in a tight black sequined gown and headdress. It was glamorous, but also somehow lewd. It wasn't the dress, Sean realized. Though her movements were minimal, smoking a cigarette from a long holder and leaning back sensuously, Deirdre exuded a persona that was half starlet, half dominatrix.

The chorus sang, "She was beautiful, but—"

"Evil," Deirdre replied. And she was.

When she began to force herself on poor Joseph—who didn't look as horrified by the proposition as he was supposed to, in Sean's opinion—running her hands over his bare chest and squeezing his buttocks, Kevin's eyebrows went up so high they almost met his hairline. He glanced over at Sean, who had no idea how to react. The boy's aunt was acting like a millionaire porn star, for godsake. He decided to go with a look of shock. Kevin giggled silently at this and went back to watching the show.

When Deirdre's scene was over, the audience clapped enthusiastically. Sean let out a whoop and Cormac whistled loudly, which served to extend the applause. Kevin clapped hard and fast, his small hands a blur. They grinned triumphantly at each other for their small part in Deirdre's success. Sean found himself hoping there was some Broadway bigwig in the audience noticing the unfettered appreciation of her performance.

At intermission they all got up to stretch, and Aunt Vivvy murmured to Sean that a trip to the powder room might be in order. The two of them shuffled toward the lobby with the rest of the crowd. As they approached the back of the theater, Sean saw him—Da, dressed in a suit jacket, a bouquet of pink roses in his lap. Sean didn't know what to say. On the one hand Da had been told in no uncertain terms not to come. On the other, it was his one chance to see his daughter. "Enjoying the show?" Sean asked him when their eyes met.

"Very much," said Da. "She's brilliant." He glanced to Aunt Vivvy, whose grip on Sean's arm was starting to leave marks. "Vivian," said Da. "Faith, you're a sight altogether." It was clear to Sean he was taunting her, his brogue harsher, his phrasing distinctly Irish. He sounded like the Lucky Charms leprechaun.

"Martin," she replied coldly. "You've returned."

His jaw tightened at her parry.

"Okay," said Sean, briskly. "We're off to the powder room."

"Would you give these to your sister?" Da asked him. "I won't be here at the end of the show. Tell her they're from you." Sean took the flowers and guided his aunt out to the lobby.

"The unmitigated gall," she muttered. "You throw those weeds directly into the trash." And she released him as she entered the ladies' room.

When she returned she gazed pointedly at the bouquet in his hands. "You'll do his bidding." It was as close to a sneer as he'd ever heard from his aunt.

"Someday Deirdre might like to know that he gave her something," said Sean quietly. "And one thing I won't do is get in the middle of your grudge match. It's almost thirty years now, Auntie. Enough is enough."

After the show, they made their way backstage and found Deirdre. She had changed out of the slinky sequined dress, but her stage makeup remained, her face still resembling something from an Egyptian tomb. They congratulated her, grinning awkwardly, feeling like star-struck fans. Even Aunt Vivvy said, "Brava, my dear."

Sean presented the roses, saying only, "These are for you."

Deirdre accepted the flowers and compliments graciously. "It was such a great crowd tonight," she said. "The whole cast could feel it. I'm going to miss that in New York—audiences are so much tougher there."

"You're going to New York?" said Kevin.

"Um, yeah," said Deirdre, glancing at Sean. "But not till you get back from Ireland, so I'll definitely see you."

"Oh, okay," he said, clearly uncertain as to why this was so important.

The cast was being called for director's notes; Deirdre said goodbye and hurried off.

Later, when they pulled into the driveway, Kevin scrambled out of the car to reassure George that she hadn't been left for good. Aunt Vivvy turned to Sean. "Please don't keep Kevin in the dark about Deirdre's departure," she said. "He needs to be prepared for what's to come."

As Sean and Aunt Vivvy made their way up the walk, they could hear George barking maniacally. "I'm coming!" Kevin called, as he heaved himself against the uncooperative door. When it popped open the dog jumped up, and Kevin stumbled back onto the porch. "Whoa! Hey!" he yelled, batting her down. "No jumping!" She obeyed, but continued her loud barking. *"Chtch!"* he told her. She barked once and then soothed herself by circling him several times.

He could barely take a step. "I know!" He laughed. "You missed me—I get it!"

Aunt Vivvy gave Sean a look. *I know,* he almost told her. *I get it.*

Before bed, Sean went to say good night to Kevin. He sat down on the edge of the bed and straightened out the weighted blanket, which tended to get bunched up if Kevin moved around too much. "So, what did you think of Aunt Deirdre tonight?"

"She's pretty good at getting all creepy and weird." Kevin grinned.

"True." Sean smiled. "So, there's something I need to tell you. You know how much Aunt Dee loves being onstage."

"Like crazy."

"Yeah. And the best place to try and be a stage actor is New York City."

"She said she was going down there when we get back from our trip."

"She is. Actually . . . she's moving there."

Kevin's eyes blinked, calculating the implications. "For how long?"

"For a while. Like maybe years."

A look of horror grew on Kevin's face. "Am I going with her?"

"No! You're staying right here."

"Okay." He sighed, relieved. "Because I've seen TV shows that're in New York City, and it looks really loud and crammed in."

"That's an accurate description." Sean nodded, enjoying the brief calm before what he knew would be Kevin's next realization.

"Wait, but who's going to be here? I mean, when you leave. Aunt Vivvy's not very . . . she can't do a lot of stuff. There won't be anyone . . . like, responsible."

"Well, I'm going to stay until I can hire someone to come and help out. Someone who could do housework and help you with homework and stuff. How does that sound?"

"So, like, when?"

"Maybe a month or so."

"That's right after school starts."

"Yeah, we'll get you settled, and things should work out pretty well." It sounded weak, even to Sean. "I'll come back and visit, too," he insisted. "I'm not going as far as Africa this time."

"Where are you going?"

"I've got an offer in Haiti—that's a lot closer."

"Haiti? Where they had that earthquake and all the buildings fell down?"

"Well, a lot of them did, but not all. Hey, how about if I plan to come back for Christmas? That's only a couple of months away."

Kevin stared at him. "Four," he said finally. And he began to snuggle deeper beneath the covers, curling his body until every limb was pinned down under the heavy blanket.

"Four?"

"Four *months*," he said, and closed his eyes.

CHAPTER 47

Hi Rebecca,

I hope this is okay that I'm e-mailing you. I know you were looking for a little space, but I'm hoping you meant physical rather than electronic. Is there such a thing as electronic space?

I wanted to let you know a couple of things, just in case anything changed on your end, so you'd know where I was. I'd hate for you to try and get in touch and think I wasn't responding on purpose. Because I don't think I could ever not respond to you.

Apparently meeting you gave Kevin the courage to meet my father. Thanks for that. It's no surprise that he would feel comfortable with you, but seeing as he's not a kid who generally feels comfortable anywhere, it actually was a surprise to him. My father was good, didn't overwhelm him, seemed to get it that he was on thin ice and better not stomp too hard.

He spread that Irish charm pretty thick, though, and got Kevin interested in a trip to the old sod. Totally manipulated me, which pissed me off at first. But as things stand at the moment, I thought it might be good to take off for a little while. Locational therapy. The three of us leave Sunday, and Kevin and I will be gone for a week. I just wanted you to know.

Also, I've applied for a temporary sub nurse position at Belham Middle School. It's just till October, by which point I plan to have things set up for Kevin and my aunt. I heard from a colleague from my days in Kenya who wants me to work at her clinic in Haiti. She's an older woman, really smart, and I think it would be a good gig. Also, it's much closer than a lot of other needy places in the world. I've already promised Kevin I'd be home for Christmas.

I have kind of a crazy suggestion, and you might hate it, but I'm just going to put it out there. Would you ever have any interest in coming with me to Haiti?

You could work in the clinic, or any one of a hundred volunteer projects in the area. The conditions would be pretty rustic. Actually I have no idea what the details are, but the conditions are always "rustic." Or worse. But you don't strike me as a girl who can't travel without a blow dryer, and I can guarantee it would be a hell of an experience. It always is. And I would really love to share it with you.

Just a thought.

I miss you. Maybe I'm not supposed to say that, but it can't be too much of a surprise, so I'm going to chance it. It's been a day and a half and I feel like it's been a year.

But I want you to know that I get it, and you had every right. Part of me is proud of you for taking care of yourself. And I'll admit, part of me selfishly wishes that you would just throw caution to the wind. That's the selfish part, did I mention that?

Hope you're well. Hope the furniture moving is quick and easy. Sorry I'm not there to help. Think about Haiti, okay?

Love,

Sean

After he hit Send, Sean wondered if it was okay that he'd signed it "Love." Maybe he should have used "affectionately" or "fondly" or just his name alone. Did "love" seem like a taunt—like "I love you, but not enough," or "I love you, but only on my terms"?

Jesus Christ, I am SO BAD at this!

He turned his attention to something he might actually be able to succeed at: nailing the sub nurse position. Especially with the Ireland trip, the added income would really come in handy. He called the middle school and spoke to the secretary, who passed him on to the assistant principal, who passed him on to the principal, a Mr. Girardi.

"So you're interested in the sub nurse position?" He inhaled noisily. Sean diagnosed him as asthmatic, a smoker, or morbidly obese. Possibly all three. "We're waiting for a few more applications before we start interviewing."

"Well, I just wanted to let you know that I'll be out of town next week on some family business. Would it be possible for me to interview tomorrow? Otherwise I could be available the following Monday. But I know that's getting close to the start of school."

"Huh," said Mr. Girardi, and then there was only the sound of his juicy inhalations.

"Can I ask a question?"

"Shoot."

"Are you hesitant to hire a man?"

"Not at all! That would be discrimination." His breathing got heavier. Sean could imagine the beads of perspiration on Mr. Girardi's upper lip. "But lemme ask you . . . in middle school some girls are menstruating, and some are even involved in sexual activity. How comfortable would you feel talking about this stuff? And more important, are they gonna feel comfortable talking to you?"

Sean smiled. Menstruation? Sex? Mr. Girardi was in for a surprise. "Well, that's a very reasonable concern," he said. "Some guys wouldn't know how to handle it. For myself, a good portion of my career has been in poverty-stricken areas, working with refugees from natural disasters and wars. I've treated and counseled girls dealing with terrible trauma. Rape and childbirth complications are common, unfortunately. So I'd be pretty comfortable talking about tampons and STDs. I think when you're comfortable, the patient feels better about opening up."

"Huh," said Mr. Girardi, practically wheezing now. "You've got a point there." After a laborious sigh, he conceded. "Well, I suppose we should get you in here ASAP."

Arrangements were made for an interview the following morning. Sean hung up knowing he'd better have very good answers to all of their questions. He booted up Deirdre's laptop and surfed nursing sites on pediatrics and working in schools, jotting down notes on whatever he needed to brush up on.

Every half hour or so he'd check his e-mail. *Oh, let's be honest,* he thought, *it's more like every five minutes.* So far Rebecca hadn't responded. It was Thursday, and she'd be at work, he told himself. But like an allergic sneeze or a facial tic, the checking felt beyond his control.

He wanted more information about Yasmin's clinic and sent off a note to the e-mail address she'd included in her letter. Maybe there was something particularly appealing about it. Maybe they used massage for the really traumatized patients.

Unlikely. But it was worth a try.

The next day an enormous box arrived.

"What's in it? Where'd it come from?" Kevin was dying to know.

"It's a surprise," said Sean. "We'll open it when I get back from an appointment I have."

"What appointment?"

"Nothing. Just something I have to do." He didn't want Kevin to get his hopes up about the sub nurse position, especially after talking with the less-than-enthusiastic Mr. Girardi.

"Why is everything a secret?" Kevin whined.

"Because it is. Now go walk the dog, and I'll be back in an hour."

Sean drove over to the middle school with his pile of notes on the passenger seat. At stoplights he glanced over them and gave them one last look-through in the parking lot.

There were two people waiting for him in the main office. One was Mr. Girardi, who was about a head shorter than Sean and had a torso like a beach ball. His thick glasses needed a good wipe.

"This is Penny Coyne," he said, indicating a tiny woman with short black hair and a sharp beak of a nose. "She'll be taking the lead nurse position while Kelly Krasmus is out on medical leave. When

Kelly comes back, Penny will return to the part-time position we're hiring for now."

The interview proceeded through Sean's qualifications and experience. Penny was particularly interested in his work with refugees, asking about how he'd dealt with the emotional trauma of his patients. The depth and thoughtfulness of her questions were impressive, given that she'd never worked anywhere but suburban Boston.

Mr. Girardi checked his watch several times. "Penny, I think we should move on to talking about Mr. Doran's knowledge of *school* populations."

"Just one more thing," she said. "Why do you want this job?"

Sean had prepared a response to this very question that involved his respect for the important work of school nurses, blah, blah blah . . . But he liked Penny, and he didn't want to dish off some brown-nose baloney. So he told her about Kevin not having parents around, needing moral support for the transition to middle school. He also mentioned his plan to go to Haiti. "Kevin should be pretty well settled by October. The timing's perfect."

They discussed the job, which appeared to consist of an extra set of hands for Penny, who would be doing all the administrative work. Sean wouldn't even have access to computer files. As far as he could see, he just had to show up, help triage the real medical issues from the get-out-of-class scams, apply common sense and the occasional ice pack to each, and keep his hands washed. A heck of a lot easier than remembering the "extra hot" at the end of "half-caf skinny latte, shot of sugar-free caramel, two Splendas."

On his way home, he stopped by the Confectionary and picked up Mr. McGrath, Cormac's father. They had a job to do.

"What's in it?" Kevin begged as the three of them carried the enormous box around to the backyard. "What is this thing? Tell me!"

"It's a trampoline," said Sean, grinning at him.

"No. Way."

"Way."

They dropped the box in the desired spot just in time for Kevin to do a goofy little happy dance. "I *love* those!" he yelled.

It was no small task setting it up, and Sean was grateful for Mr. McGrath's savantlike expertise at assembly, even if it did come with a bit of under-breath muttering of "Jesus, Mary, and Joseph!" After a lot of sorting pieces, attaching things, hoisting this, and holding that for Mr. McGrath, Sean and Kevin took the trampoline for a test bounce.

"THIS . . . IS . . . SO . . . AWESOME!" Kevin sang out, one bounce to every word. Sean didn't think he'd ever heard the boy be so loud. "Come on, Mr. McGrath, you have to try it!"

Sean wasn't sure of the wisdom of this, but Mr. McGrath was apparently unencumbered by such concerns. In moments he was climbing the short ladder and sliding in through the slit in the net. He was careful at first but then caught his stride, a wide grin gracing his face as his round belly shifted up and down with each bounce. "Good-bye gravity!" he called out.

After a little while Mr. McGrath got tired and Sean drove him home. On his way back he was thinking about Kevin screaming on the trampoline and smiling to himself. So satisfying. Such joy. And it was a relief to discover that even when you felt heartbroken and raw, the joy of someone you loved could still make you feel almost okay.

As he passed back through Belham Center he saw her car parked in front of the hardware store. He slowed to look at it, Rebecca's car, imbued with Rebecca-ness, and narrowly avoided slamming into the pickup stopped in front of him at the light. When he turned back, Rebecca was coming out of the store with a bag in her arms. The door was being held from behind, and then a man emerged carrying a can of paint. Medium height, light brown hair. And smiling, the bastard.

Sean was pretty sure he had a minor stroke at that moment because the whole way home his brain felt like it was melting. The rest of him just felt numb. He wasn't entirely sure how he got back, but when he did, Kevin was still bouncing and Sean slumped down onto the garden bench to watch him. Kevin entertained him with different poses for each jump, his skinny limbs curling up or striking out with wanton grace, and Sean could feel his vitals starting to normalize a little. The boy's unabashed grin made him look much younger. Sean could imagine a three-year-old Kevin beaming just as happily when his father threw him into the air.

Look, Hugh. Sean sent the thought out to the cosmos. *I found a way to toss him.*

At least he had that.

Later that evening Sean checked his e-mail and found one message in his in-box. The sender was Rebecca Feingold.

> Hi Sean,
> Thanks for letting me know about your trip. I think it's great that you're going, and I'm glad Kevin likes his grandfather. Have a wonderful time.
> Rebecca

No love.

CHAPTER 48

The flight to Ireland felt strange to Sean. He'd never sat on an airplane with anyone he actually knew before. He'd always loved the *idea* of flying—that you could get so quickly to a location that was radically different from the one you just left. He was not a souvenir guy, never kept anything from one experience to bring to the new one. There was enormous freedom in that.

Kevin had never been on a plane before, and was completely enthralled by the spaciousness of the terminal and the cacophony of color pulsing from the shops and food stalls. But once they were on board, he started to get that irritated look.

"I can't sit here," he murmured to Sean. "It's too squished." He was wedged between Sean in the aisle seat and Da by the window. Sean switched with him. But when people started brushing by him he didn't like that, either. The flight attendant's cart was the last straw. They switched again, putting him by the window and Sean in the middle.

It was an overnight flight, and Sean hoped the boy would fall asleep, but he was too distracted. "It smells so bad in here," he kept telling Sean. "Like plastic and metal and old rugs."

"Well, basically, that's what it is." This did not help matters.

When someone nearby began to eat something that smelled like a dead animal—Sean guessed liverwurst—Kevin panicked. "I have to get out!" he muttered furtively. Sean grabbed a bag of honeyed peanuts the flight attendants had delivered. "Smell these," he said.

"I'm not gonna stick my nose in a snack bag for the whole trip!"

They took walks, which helped, but neither of them got any sleep. After watching the sun rise through the tiny window of one of the hatches, they returned to see that Da had taken the window seat. "I want to see my home from the air," he said. A skirmish ensued.

"Da," Sean said wearily, "please just give me a break here." With thirty minutes left to the flight, the boy finally fell asleep, his grandfather leaning across him to look out the window.

Da was teary, Kevin was cranky, and Sean was wondering what the hell he'd been thinking as they went to find their rental car. But once they'd left the airport and made their way past Limerick and onto the N-21, Kevin conked out again and Da busied himself with serving as navigator. He marveled at the spread of the towns and the wind turbines that now spiked the ridges of Stack's Mountains. As they passed on to the Dingle Peninsula, there was a shift in Da, a skittishness as he neared the land of his boyhood. He muttered things Sean couldn't understand. Then he let out a groan. "I've lost it," he said.

"What?"

"The Irish. I can read it—there, that one?" He pointed to a road sign that said TÓG GO BOG É. "That says 'Take it easy.' Not a bad suggestion, by the way. You're driving awful fast." He sighed. "But I don't know if I can make conversation."

Da had chosen the Beiginis Bed & Breakfast in Dunquin for its proximity to the Blasket Ferry and for a note on its Web site: *Fáilte faoi Leith roimh Gaeilgeóirí.* He'd proudly translated this for Sean: "Irish speakers particularly welcome." But now he wasn't so certain he qualified.

"Well, I'm sure you don't *have* to speak Irish," Sean reassured him.

"It's a matter of pride!"

For Sean it was only a matter of not driving off the side of the narrow mountainous road. He didn't care if they spoke Martian when he got there, as long as he could sleep for a couple of hours. He was just grateful to keep his wits about him and remember to drive on the left.

Da had fully given up on navigating by the time they hit Ventry. He couldn't take his eyes off the landscape, head swinging back and forth like a metronome, trying to absorb every detail. "All so different," he mumbled intermittently with, "That's just as I remember it."

Mount Eagle rose brown and bare on their left as they traveled down into the town of Dunquin. A twinkle of light, like a flash from a signal mirror, made Da cry out, "Stop!" Sean hit the brakes. With no cars in sight, there was no reason not to stop right there in the middle of the road. Then he realized that what he saw was the sunlight glinting off water in the distance.

"There!" said Da. "That's the island."

Sean squinted his sleep-starved eyes. "Oh, yes," he said, only because he knew the old man so desperately needed him to. He let the car move forward again. Kevin stirred in the back.

"Are we there?" he yawned.

"Very soon, *cuisle mo chroí*."

"What's 'cushla macree'?"

"Just an endearment," Da explained. He pointed things out to them: that shuttered building had been a pub; the small house over there had been a store.

"A *store*?" said Kevin.

"Well, not a Stop and Shop, lad. It was just a place for supplies."

"Like a convenience store?"

"Exactly like!" Da laughed. "Except it only carried about ten items—and from the island, wasn't terribly convenient!"

In another minute they were pulling onto a smaller uphill road and then into a driveway. The house was a mustard yellow in color, tidily kept with flower boxes adorning the front windows. When they got out of the car and turned to look downhill, their eyes followed squares of pastures in differing shades of green out to the glinting iron blue of the sea. They stared at the several islands that rose out of the waves. Kevin murmured, "Which one?"

"The biggest," said Da. "That's where I was born."

"There was a hospital out there?"

"Not even a doctor. That was the way of it."

"Are you coming in, at all?" asked a voice with a smile in it. They turned to see a woman in the doorway, dark hair striated with gray, extra padding under the chin. "You're the Dorans?"

They assured her that they were and hauled their bags out of the car. Orla Dunleavy introduced herself as the proprietress and showed them in.

"Dunleavy?" said Da. "Are you an islander?"

"Oh, yes," said Orla. "Well, I never lived there, of course. By the time I came along, my people had moved here to Dunquin." Sean could sense his father's disappointment immediately. "Were your people islanders?" she asked.

"Yes," he said. "I am. We were evacuated in fifty-three."

"Oh!" she exclaimed, opening a door to a room with a twin bed and a set of bunks. A soft stream of words came out of her mouth, none of which made the least bit of sense to Sean. All that made sense to him was the horizontal surface of the lower bunk. The bags were dropped and he mumbled something about taking a little rest. The door closed and he was asleep in moments.

When Sean woke it was late afternoon, and the three of them strolled down to the Blasket Island Ferry. There was a little wooden shed with times posted for crossings. They walked down toward the boat landing, to where the steep cement walkway took a hairpin turn, and from there the view of the islands was panoramic, the tiny village on Great Blasket Island just visible in the waning light. Then the clouds on the horizon churned closer, cloaking it in shadow.

"Ah, the rain." Da chuckled to himself. "Sweet Mary, I'd almost forgotten."

They went to Kruger's Pub on Orla's advice. "It's the furthest west you can go in Europe to get a meal and a pint. You shouldn't miss it." There were several families and couples eating at the polished wooden tables. One loud bunch was clearly American. New York, Sean guessed.

"Oh, my gawd, Jimmy, just *eat* it," said the mother to one of the boys. "We're not stopping again for you."

"I want a Happy Meal," he said sulkily.

"Here's your meal," she said, nudging the plate closer to him. "Be happy, already."

At the bar, three or four older men nursed their pints while a young couple smiled secret smiles, their faces close, murmuring to each other. It hit Sean like an anvil. Rebecca had smiled up at him in just that way, reflecting back his own contentment, her face telling his story.

He looked away. "Here's a table," he said, and took the seat facing the window.

The waitress came over. Da greeted her with *"Dia dhuit,"* and Kevin echoed a sloppy but well-meaning "Dee-a wit."

"Nicely done!" she told him. "You'll soon be speaking Irish as well as your older brother here!" Da let out a guffaw and slapped the table.

Kevin looked confused. "He's my grandfather."

"You don't say!" She murmured something to Da, and he nodded, though his smile dimmed just a little. They ordered their drinks, ginger ale all around.

"What did she say?" Sean asked.

"Something about teaching the next generation, I think." He shook his head. "It's not coming back as I thought it would. Bits and pieces, but not the whole pie."

"Be patient," Sean told him. "In a month you'll be having pie à la mode."

Da shrugged, not completely convinced. He tipped his head toward the bar. "You could have a pint of something, you know. It won't bother me."

"Soda's good for now," Sean said. "I'm still pretty tired."

Da studied him for a moment. "I'm glad you don't seem to have my . . . proclivity."

"I think Hugh may have had that department covered for both of us."

At his father's name, Kevin's gaze broke away from the Gaelic football match on the television over the bar. "What department?" he said.

Sean couldn't think of an answer quickly enough. Da came in for the save. "The department of fun," he said. "Your da was the laughingest little boy I ever did see."

"He was?"

"Oh, yes. He was a wiggler and a giggler."

Kevin digested this for a moment. "I'm not like that."

"Not so much," conceded Da. "But you do have an excellent sense of humor, and you'll learn to speak Irish before your uncle here, I can guarantee it."

"Guh rou mah a-gut!" Kevin said proudly.

Da slapped the table again, *"Tá fáilte romhat!"* he crowed. "You are very welcome!" He jerked a thumb at Sean and told Kevin, "See, he hasn't a clue what we've said."

Sean feigned annoyance. "Apparently there was an Irish lesson while I was sleeping."

"That's right," Kevin teased. "And you're miles behind."

Sean woke in the morning to the sound of rain tap-dancing on the patio stones. He got dressed and found his family in the dining room, eating their "Full Irish" breakfast—eggs, baked beans, fried tomatoes, toasted brown bread, black and white "pudding," a rasher of Irish bacon, and a couple of sausages. "I've been a lot of places," Sean said, rubbing the sleep from his eyes. "But Ireland's the only place I know that serves four kinds of meat with breakfast."

"Four?" said Kevin. "There's only sausage and bacon."

"The pudding isn't the kind you're used to," said Da. "More like a meat muffin."

Soon Orla had a Full Irish in front of Sean, too. "So," he said. "I guess we should make our ferry reservations."

"They won't go this morning," said Da. "Too stormy."

"It's just a little sprinkle."

"The water'll be rough," said Da. "That current is a bully even on a good day."

"Let's just call," said Sean. "We're not going in a canoe."

"It's called a *naomhóg,* smarty," Da chided. "But go on and call if it suits you."

"Too rough," the ferry operator told Sean after breakfast. "Maybe tomorrow."

So they set out to do "a bit of looking around," as Da put it. They drove south toward Slea Head and stopped at Dunbeg Fort, a stronghold built on the cliff's edge more than a thousand years ago. Kevin scrambled around the thick stone walls, worrying his uncle and grandfather for a moment when he crawled into a small cavern and disappeared. When he poked his head out again, Da said, "Come out of there."

"I can't, I'm a prisoner!"

Da looked past him into the dark. "Snakes!" he said, and Kevin was out like a rocket.

They continued on toward Dingle. "The Big City." Da chuckled. "I only went once, after we'd moved off the island. We were living with my aunt in Dunquin, but the place was small. I was soon sent to an uncle in Springfield, Mass. And that's how I came to America."

"How old were you then?"

"Sixteen. Just five years older than this one." He poked his thumb to the backseat. "I never saw my parents again, God rest them. My mother died of cancer, and my father went soon after. I always thought I'd be back, but they passed before I had the chance." He was quiet then, looking out over the sea, whitecaps playing tag with each other across the chop. "They were never sick on the island," he added. "Never once, in my memory."

"Did they want to leave?"

"They were of two minds," Da explained. "They were island people so they loved the place. But that life requires people to work together—the young rising up to take the place of their elders. Our lives stayed the same as they had been for hundreds of years, while the rest of the world was changing so fast. Electricity and television and new opportunities no one had dreamed of! The young people started leaving, and there weren't enough strong backs to do the work anymore." He looked down at his hands. "So the government moved us off. And that was supposed to be a good thing." He glanced over to Sean. "But think how much was lost."

In Dingle, they parked the car and walked along the harbor, past brightly painted storefronts. There was a small carnival set up in a lot by the harbor, and they let Kevin ride the rides and play games in the arcade. Da placed a call at a payphone. "I'll leave you to yourselves for a bit," he said. Sean and Kevin walked up the hill to the sports field and watched a rugby match.

"Where'd he go?" asked Kevin.

"To a meeting, I'm guessing." This, of course, prompted a litany of questions about where and with whom, and why anyone would drink so much alcohol if it made them do dumb stuff.

"There are a whole lot of things people do that just don't make a ton of sense to the rest of us," Sean said finally. "Like you don't like to be bumped, but look at these guys." He indicated the mud-spattered men in striped shirts, tangled into a tight scrum.

"What about you?" Kevin asked. "What do you do that doesn't make sense?"

Sean chuckled. "What I do makes sense to *me*, at least while I'm doing it. Maybe I should ask what *you* think I do that doesn't make sense."

The comment was meant rhetorically, but Kevin clearly didn't get that part. "That's easy," he said. "You go far away to help people you don't even know."

CHAPTER 49

The next day the clouds receded into clumps of cotton batting, but the sea was still too rough to cross. Da was not happy. Sean suggested they visit the nearby Blasket Island Centre.

"I don't want to see any dusty old museum on what I already know," Da grumped, but he allowed Sean to prod him along.

The Centre itself was surprisingly modern for a museum about a bygone culture. There were interactive displays and enlarged photographs of inhabitants. Da studied each of them. "I knew him, of course," he'd say, and then offer a tidbit, such as how the man was known for being the most nimble in a *naomhóg* ("he could dance a reel and never tip into the water"); or how that woman could carry more turf in her creel basket than half the men on the island.

Kevin got antsy after a while, and they got back in the car and traveled northeast, stopping at Gallarus Oratory, a church likely built in the 700s. Shaped like an upturned boat and built entirely of mortarless stone, it remained as tight and dry as the day it was completed.

Standing inside the single room on the dirt floor, Sean wondered at the countless prayers that had been sent up from that very spot over hundreds and hundreds of years. Had the senders ever questioned? Had they ever felt fury at a God who would submit them to barely sufferable lives of hard labor, foreign attack, and death as common as a cut finger?

Sean could easily imagine it, having spent most of his adult life in similar settings. Except the faces here would've been white. Actually, they would've looked a lot like his, he realized; they'd possibly been his own ancestors. He sent up a prayer—not to the God who watched such suffering, but to the sufferers themselves. *Strengthen the hearts of all those in need,* he asked, *and guide the hands of those who aim to help them.* And he felt a little buzz of connection, a lightness that had often come to him when he'd prayed in the past. But maybe it was just the setting—one of the world's oldest intact churches. Maybe he was kidding himself. Maybe he'd been kidding himself all along.

They picked up sandwiches and headed to the northern side of the Dingle Peninsula, where Mount Brandon rose gently skyward, grassy and treeless. Sheep grazed lazily, as if the world were their luncheon buffet. They hiked up the trail toward the peak, but Da soon got tired, and they sat down and ate their sandwiches, looking out across the bay.

"Is that a beach?" Kevin asked Da, squinting into the distance.

"I don't know," he admitted. "I've never been up this way."

Sean pulled out the map Orla had given them and determined they were looking at The Maharees, a spit of land that jutted out into Brandon Bay. The sun shone onto it, illuminating the long crescent of sand that faced them. "It says you can swim there. Also surf, apparently."

"Surf?" Kevin's eyes lit up.

"You interested?" asked Sean.

"I'm *definitely* interested. I saw this surfing competition on TV, and it was in Australia or someplace? And it was so cool, it was like—" He jumped up to show them, stance wide, arms out for balance. "There was this huge wave, and it was like the guy was *skating* through it—"

"Okay, but look," Sean said, interrupting Kevin's rapture. "You understand it doesn't start out like that, right? The waves are small and you fall off a lot. You still want to?"

"Definitely," said Kevin. "No doubt in my mind."

Doubt came by the bucketload, however, when they drove up to the surf school—which was more like a surf shed—and found that wetsuits were required. To Kevin it was like wearing the latex gloves at the Confectionary, times about a hundred. He decided he'd be fine without it.

"You'll freeze, man," said the surf instructor, a slim twenty-something with wild sun-bleached hair. "The water's sixteen degrees today. I can't recommend it."

"That's about sixty Fahrenheit," Da said. "Pretty cold, lad, especially with this stiff breeze. You won't last twenty minutes, much less two hours."

Sean told the surf instructor, "We'll get back to you." They went down to the water's edge, Kevin insisting he was *not* cold, he would be *fine*, he didn't *care* what that surf guy said.

"No wetsuit, no surf lesson," said Sean. "I'm not wasting the instructor's time and that much money so you can get hypothermic." Kevin stormed off down the beach.

"He can be a bit of a fussbudget," said Da.

"Ya think?" Sean murmured sarcastically, for which his father rightly cuffed him.

Kevin came back. "*Fine*, I'll wear it," he said murderously. "If I cry, I can duck underwater, and he won't know."

Sean helped Kevin change in the shed. Even with a bigger size, Kevin pulled the legs on and off three times before he could stand to tug the top part up. "If you can't do it, you can't do it," Sean said, trying to calm him. "It's not the worst thing in the world."

"Yes," Kevin said through gritted teeth, as he wrangled the wetsuit over his hips. "It is."

Finally the suit was on. Sean zipped up the back and Kevin stood there for a moment with his arms sticking out from his body, his eyes closed. "Are you going to be okay?" Sean asked.

"I don't know," murmured Kevin. Then he walked out of the shed.

"Good man," Donal the surf instructor said. "I'm not such a fan of these seal suits, either." Sean almost slipped the guy a twenty for his compassion.

Donal and Kevin dragged their big yellow surfboards out to the beach, and Sean and Da followed at a distance. They sat in the sand and watched as Donal and Kevin started by kneeling on all fours on the board. Sean told his father about Kevin's sensory issues.

"Hugh hated socks," Da said. "Never wore them. That's why his feet always stank."

Sean laughed, remembering Hugh's stinky feet. "I didn't know he hated socks. Aunt Vivvy told me he spent a small fortune trying to find socks Kevin would wear."

Da got a little choked up then. "I keep forgetting Kevin's his," he said. "It's like he's off with his friends somewhere, and the boy just fell out of the sky."

They watched as Kevin worked to conquer the unwieldy piece of fiberglass. As soon as he stood upright, he'd fall into the waves. But when he bobbed up again, Donal would high-five him as if he'd surfed like a pro. Eventually Kevin was up for a few seconds at a time. And then suddenly he seemed to hit everything right and surfed all the way in to shore, arms outstretched, face wide with happy surprise. Sean and Da leaped to their feet, cheering and clapping.

"I surfed!" Kevin yelled to them, and they howled back their congratulations.

When the lesson was over, they drove out toward the end of the point and happened upon Spillane's Pub. Inside, they were seated beneath an upturned *naomhóg*. Wider and longer than a modern canoe, it could carry entire families and their possessions across a lake or a bay. "That's very like the one we had," Da pointed out. "I'd go out with my own da, and we'd pull in mackerel or lobsters. Sometimes we even took cows and sheep back and forth to Dunquin."

"A *cow* could fit in that?" Kevin was skeptical.

"Well, yes," Da said with a grin, "but not happily."

The waitress came to take their drink orders. Sean asked for a pint of Smithwick's. When Kevin ordered ginger ale, Da said, "You'll need a better drink than that to celebrate your triumph, lad!" He turned to the waitress. "Can the barman make a Shirley Temple, d'you think?"

"Come 'round to the bar," she said, "and you'll tell him how it's done." Da gave them a wink as he left.

"So," Sean said to Kevin. "I expect you're feeling pretty big on yourself, now that you're an official surfer dude."

Kevin grinned. "Yeah, now I'll have two big things I did on this trip."

"What's the other?"

A glimmer of doubt traced over Kevin's face. "Carantoo-something. The highest point." He watched Sean remember this, and rightly took his silence to be a bad sign. "You promised!"

"Yeah, I know, buddy, but I thought we would've been out to Blasket by now. It's already Wednesday, and if your grandfather doesn't get us out there before we leave on Sunday, he's gonna have a fit. We'll check the weather when we get back tonight."

Da came back carrying a bar tray with Sean's beer and two glasses of pink soda with maraschino cherries bobbing in them. "Once we got the recipe right, it looked so gorgeous I decided to have one myself!"

The meal was leisurely, and as the sun dangled lower over Mount Brandon to the west, Da reminisced about his early days on the island—about the all-night parties they would have the day before one of their own left to cross the Atlantic. "An American Wake, we called it, and we stayed up all night with 'the body' just as we would have done if they'd died."

"That's a little morose, isn't it?" Sean asked.

"No, just realistic. We knew we'd likely never see the departed again, and it was only right to give them a good send-off."

"With a heck of a hangover to start the journey."

Da smiled. "That and a piece of the place." He dug into his pocket and pulled out a little stone painted white. "The traveler would take a chink of the whitewash from his house on the way out as a keepsake. I took this the day we were evacuated and kept it with me ever since." He studied it for a moment. "Maybe tomorrow I'll be able to put it back."

CHAPTER 50

Da was up early. Sean found him sitting with a cup of tea, staring out the window at the clouds as if he could vaporize them by force of will. "Too rough" was all he said.

"It doesn't look that bad," said Sean.

"It's fine *inland*," Da said with disgust. "Only *out there* is it . . . what's the word . . ."

The word came to Sean—in his mind he heard Rebecca's voice. "Unstable."

He was hesitant to broach the subject, but it looked to be the perfect day for the highest point. Da conceded that it was, and besides, he wanted to do some poking around, see if he could find any relatives or old friends. He'd been an only child, but there had been a cousin or two. . . .

Orla found a hiking book with directions to the base of Carrauntoohil and information about the climb. The text noted that at approximately 3,400 feet above sea level, it was not an especially high mountain, but erosion and loose stones along the path required caution. The drive would take about an hour and a half each way, and the hike up and back could take as many as six hours. They would stop in Dingle on the way to buy food and bottles of water.

"Please be careful," said Da. "The weather can change in a heartbeat."

"Enjoy the day to yourself, and don't worry about us," said Sean. "We'll be fine."

Da was standing sentry at the door when Sean and Kevin straggled in late that night. "Is he all right? What happened!" he demanded. "I was out of my wits!"

"He's fine, Da. Just a little scraped up. And very tired."

Kevin allowed himself to be guided to bed, and Da hovered as Sean pulled his shoes and jacket off. "Where did he get that cut on his cheek?"

"Devil's Ladder," said Kevin, though he was half-asleep. "The rocks are loose and I slipped. But it was awesome! Uncle Sean got a disposable camera in Dingle and took pictures."

Once Kevin was tucked in, Sean went back out to the dining room with Da, who was peppering him with questions. "Did you have it looked at? What took so long?"

"Da, I'm a nurse. *I* looked at it. It's just a big abrasion—wide but not deep. We went to a pub afterward because we were starving and they had a tube of antibiotic cream behind the bar." He slumped wearily in his seat. "What did you do today? Find any relatives?"

Da sighed. "I found some people who'd known some people. . . . And I found my parents' gravestones. Gone fifty years now. Strange to say, but in my mind they were still on the island."

"Any leads on a place to stay?"

"A few. They all look nice." He didn't sound enthusiastic, but his eyes brightened when he added, "There's some land for sale on the island, and a building, though I suspect it's in pretty poor repair. I know it's mad, but it would be a dream to live there again."

The next morning clumps of clouds still trundled across the sky, and Sean braced himself for Da to sulk. But when the older man joined them at breakfast he was grinning broadly.

"It's all set," he told them. "We're to go on the ten o'clock departure."

"Are you sure?" said Sean. "The weather doesn't look any different."

"It's not the skies we care about—it's the seas, boyo!"

Apparently Blasket Sound had calmed enough for a crossing, and soon they were descending the winding cement walkway to the boat landing, along with a few other families and older couples vacationing together. The trip took a little longer than usual, about twenty minutes, the captain explained, because there was still a bit of chop. Da didn't talk once they were about halfway across the sound. He stared at the village nestled against the leeward side of the island.

A hundred feet or so from shore, the captain anchored the boat, and his crewman began to help people into a motorized rubber dinghy. The landing was hidden behind an outcropping, in a narrow, rocky harbor. When they climbed to the top of the steep cement walkway, Da stopped.

"Are you tired?" asked Kevin.

"You okay, Da?"

"I'm . . . a might flabbergasted."

From a distance, the shapes of the houses and stone walls seemed deceptively intact. Closer vantage told a different story. The village was in utter ruins.

There were a few houses farther up the hill that still had whitewash, one or two of which seemed to be used for storage or for rustic overnights. But the great majority of the former homes were roofless and overgrown with weeds. Da was unprepared for the sight of it.

"These were thick walls," he murmured to himself. "Never a drop of rain came through."

"Not quite what you expected," Sean murmured. "Which house was yours?"

"I'm not entirely sure."

On his opposite side stood Kevin. Sean saw the boy slide his hand into his grandfather's. The three of them stood there surveying the remains of Da's boyhood. Sheep grazed across the hillside. The sun shone, bleaching the white of the few standing cottages, supersaturating the green of the grass. It was breathtakingly beautiful . . . and devastatingly sad, all at once.

"Let's go to the top where we can see better," said Kevin. "I bet you'll find your house then."

So they climbed, and as they did, Da was able to get his bearings. "This was the schoolhouse," he told Kevin. "But we didn't even have a teacher those last years. Most of the children went to Dunquin for school, but my parents didn't want me to go. I was their only child, and *mamaí* wanted me with her, so she taught me herself."

"You called her mommy? What did you call your grandfather?"

"Mine had died before I was old enough to address them. But I would have called them *daideó*." It sounded like "daddo." "In Dunquin the English-speaking kids used 'gran-da.'"

Sean realized he'd never heard the boy call Da anything at all. They wandered uphill, and Da pointed out different houses and who had lived in them. Finally they came to the one he remembered best of all. "This is it," he said. "Here's my home."

The back wall, what was left of it, was set against the hill. One side wall had held a door with two windows on either side. Remnants of the fireplace were barely visible behind the weeds that sprouted out of the dirt floor. Da described the contents as if it were a litany of sacred objects. "This was my parents' bed," he said, pointing to one corner, "and here's mine over here. Here's the table and chairs, and the cabinet for the dishes." His hands made the shapes as he trod through the weeds. "The roof was very sturdy—my da made sure of that. We used to dry the fish up there on sunny days to cure it for the winter. But you couldn't smell it in the house. That's how tight that roof was."

And now it was made of sunlight and salt air.

Da took the little whitewashed stone out of his pocket. "I had the idea that the divot I made when I took it would still be here, and it would fit right in." But there was no whitewash left, nothing but rain-battered stones ready to topple at the next stiff wind.

Kevin made a loop with his thumb and forefinger and rested it on a rock in the doorway. "Here," he said. "Try it out."

Da set the little stone into the well of the boy's fingers. He laid his hand lightly on his grandson's head and gazed at his scraped face. "You're a keeper, *cuisle mo chroí*."

Kevin wanted to get a closer look at the seals on the beach. About forty of them were nestled together at the far end of the sandy spit, like an enormous lumpy gray blanket. Sean, Kevin, and Da sat a respectful distance away and pulled out the sandwiches and drinks they'd brought. Kevin ate his quickly and went down to the water's edge to skip stones.

"Our name in Irish," said Da, "it means either exile or pilgrim."

"Doran? I didn't know that."

"There's some irony in it. It's the same word whether you're coming or going. Whether you're being kicked out or drawn toward a place." He glanced back toward the village. "I've felt like an exile ever since I left here. Except with your mother, of course. That woman had a way of making me feel so at home. You know how that feels? Like you're in exactly the right place?"

"Yeah," said Sean. "I used to feel that way when I was up to my armpits in a medical crisis—a birth gone wrong or a bad burn. The worse it was, the surer I was."

"Admirable."

"Maybe. Or maybe it's just my drug of choice—other people's medical problems."

"Ha!" Da laughed. "Either way, it's a damn sight better than pickling your own liver and puking in your bed!" He clapped a hand on his son's shoulder and Sean allowed it. "Doing good for the wrong reason is still doing good. Who's to say anyone's motives are completely pure?"

"I guess I was more of a pilgrim, then. I never felt kicked out. I always wanted to go."

"It gets to be a bit of a habit, doesn't it? The leaving." He picked up a handful of sand and let it slip through his fingers, studying it as if to gauge it against memory. "You said you *were* a pilgrim. Are you still?"

"I don't know. I certainly don't have the religious fervor. At least not anymore."

"But you did at one time."

"Yeah, it was . . . you know . . . my purpose. God's plan. Go patch up a bunch of people."

"What changed?"

Sean shrugged. "I guess I thought Huntington's gave me some sort of special status, turned me from a pumpkin into a golden carriage." He gave a self-deprecating little snort. "Now I know I was just a pumpkin all along."

Kevin ran toward them. "Can I go in?" he called. "It's getting hot!"

"Okay," said Sean. "But you'll have to go in your boxers. We didn't bring extra clothes."

"You can't go deep," Da warned. "That current will take you out to sea like a rocket." Kevin pulled off his shirt and pants and ran back to the water. "You have to watch him," said Da.

"I'm watching him." Kevin waded slowly into the water, holding his arms out.

"Does he know about the Huntington's?" Da asked.

The question caught Sean off guard. "What? I . . . I have no idea."

"You were about this age when we told you. He should know."

"We don't know if Hugh had it. It's very possible Kevin's not even at risk."

"Yes, but we'll *never* know if Hugh had it. We have to assume he's at risk."

"I've assumed that all my life. It didn't do me any good."

"The doctor told us we should tell you. He said it gets harder as the child gets older."

"I can't think about that now, Da." Sean watched the boy hop a little deeper. "I don't even know who's going to take care of him when I leave, I can't exactly—*Oh, Jesus!*"

Kevin seemed to lose his footing, and suddenly his head bobbed under. Sean was racing toward the shore in an instant. "Kevin!" he yelled. Though it was only about a hundred feet, it seemed to take ages to cover the distance, and the boy still hadn't come up. *"Kevin!"*

Sean dashed into the cold water and immediately felt the pull of the current—it was much stronger than it seemed from the surface. He spun around, arms carving through the water to search out and grab hold of the boy. But they found nothing.

Da ran into the water, but Sean called to him to stay shallow. All he needed was for the old man to go under, too. They screamed and screamed for Kevin, scrambling back and forth in the waves, Sean's legs aching against the grip of the current.

Seconds ticked by, and Sean's medical brain began spinning through the possible outcomes of oxygen deprivation . . . loss of consciousness . . . brain damage . . . death. "KEVIN!" His voice intertwined with his father's broken cries and the raw wind.

Finally, a few yards to the right, Kevin's black hair parted the waves and he came up sputtering. He went under again before Sean could get to him, but Sean dove in his direction and was able to grab an arm and haul him up to the surface. He pulled the boy close and struggled against the current as he carried him toward the shore. As the last wave licked at his ankles, he stumbled and they both fell onto the sand.

"Are you all right?" Sean grabbed his face to look at him. "Are you okay?"

"Yeah," Kevin choked out. "But you're hurting my scrape."

Da was kneeling over them, "Kevin! *Jesussufferingchrist,* boy!"

"Sorry," he coughed, sitting up. "It got deep faster than I thought."

"You nearly gave me a heart attack!" Sean panted raggedly. Then he felt his father's arms come around his shoulders, steadying him, comforting him, and he thought he might cry from the relief—not just for Kevin's safety, but for his father's embrace, something he realized he'd longed for for almost thirty years.

"I didn't mean to scare you," said Kevin.

"I know, it's okay." Sean rested his head against his father's shoulder, took a deep breath, and let it out slowly. "If you're okay, everything's okay."

CHAPTER 51

"Your last full day in Ireland," Da said to Sean and Kevin over breakfast the next morning. "What do you want to do?"

Kevin said, "I want to know why one meat muffin's black and the other one's white."

"Ah, the black one has a secret ingredient I dare not reveal!"

"What is it?"

"Da . . ." Sean shook his head. "Trust me, Kev, you don't want to know."

"Tell me!"

"It's blood!"

"Gross!" said Kevin, stabbing the dark pudding with his fork and flicking it onto Sean's plate. "That's disgusting! Why would anyone put blood in food?"

"Because it's full of nutrients, lad! If you've precious little to eat, you'll get your nutrition where and how you can." Da laughed. "Now it's just tradition. Eat the white one. It's got no bodily fluids that I know of." Not surprisingly, Kevin was done with breakfast.

In Dunquin, Da showed them his parents' gravestones and took them over to see the small apartment he planned to rent, tacked onto the back of one of the newer homes.

"In America they call it an in-law apartment," he told Sean, "though the only in-law I have is your aunt Vivvy. But then she's more than enough—quite a bit more!"

The next day they rose early for the long car ride back to Shannon Airport.

"It's weird that you're not coming with us, Granda," Kevin said disconcertedly.

"I feel a bit discombobulated about it myself."

"Da, think about coming back for Christmas. Then we'll all be there together."

"I'll do that." Da extended his hand to shake and Sean took it. But then his father pulled him in for a hug. "You're a good boy," Da murmured in his ear, and squeezed him a little tighter, as if he could embed a reminder of himself in Sean's skin.

"Love you, Da," said Sean. Because he did.

"Love *you*." He released Sean, took a breath, and stuck his strong hand out to his grandson. Kevin moved forward hesitantly and put his arms around his grandfather's waist. Da gently laid his hands on Kevin's back. He whispered something down to the boy.

"What does it mean?" Kevin whispered back.

"Pulse of my heart."

When they got back to Belham after the long flight, Deirdre was packed and ready to go. She would be staying with an old friend in Brooklyn, and said how anxious she was to get there . . . and yet she kept not leaving. "Seriously, how was it?" she asked Kevin, studying him as closely as if he were the basis for a part she might play someday.

"Great!" He told her about surfing and climbing Carrauntoohil, and nearly drowning, and taught her how to say *dia dhuit*, in case she met any Irishmen in New York. She listened raptly to his stories and practiced her Irish hello with him until she could say it as well as he could.

"And what was the most annoying thing—the worst bad smell or sound?" she asked him with a sly smile.

"That's easy," he said. "Uncle Sean and Granda snoring together. It was like sleeping with a cave full of bears."

When Kevin took George outside to play, she asked Sean, "Was it weird with Da?"

"A little at first. But we got used to him pretty fast. Do you wish you'd seen him?"

"No," she said quickly. "I mean, really, what's the point? But he was good with Kevin?"

"Actually he was pretty terrific."

"Huh," she snorted. "Making up for lost time."

"I suppose he was," Sean conceded. *Aren't we all,* he thought.

The sound of Kevin jabbering to George filtered in through the kitchen windows, filling the silence between them. "How's Viv been?" he asked.

"Same," said Deirdre, poking around in her purse to find her sunglasses. "By the way, the school called. You got that job."

After a loving but not-too-tight hug for Kevin, including a kiss that he promptly wiped off, and an admonishment to Sean to get the kid an e-mail account so she could communicate with him, Deirdre was backing out of the driveway, her little car packed to the roof. Sean and Kevin waved from the porch; Aunt Vivvy stood stone-faced, and Sean wondered if she understood that Deirdre wouldn't be back—or if she understood all too well.

"That's a lot of good-byes for one day," said Kevin.

Too true, thought Sean. Deirdre's departure officially certified that they were all irrevocably his responsibility. He wished he could talk to Rebecca about it—this and a million other things. His need to see her had been rising in pitch like an oncoming train all day. In Ireland it had been easier to accept their separation—or perhaps to deny it. Across an entire ocean, there was no question of access. Now the distance was easily walkable. It was killing him.

This must be how alcoholics feel, he thought, the hundredth time he considered calling her and convinced himself not to. He suddenly had a greater respect for his father, watching his son have a pint, while he himself drank ginger ale.

That night, as he was turning off lights and locking up, he passed the phone. *Ginger ale,* he tried to tell himself, but this time it didn't work. He picked up the receiver and dialed.

"Hi," she said, and by the way she said it, he knew she'd checked the caller ID first. The fact that she'd decided to answer anyway made him anxious not to make her regret it.

"Hey," he said, and he hoped it was with just the right tone—enthusiastic but not giddy, warm but not stalkerish.

"How was your trip?"

"It was pretty great, actually. We got back a couple of hours ago. How was your week?"

"Um, good. I'm painting so it's kind of a mess. But it's coming together."

"That's great!"

"Thanks."

There were a couple of beats of silence, and he started to panic just a little. "So, listen, I was going to e-mail you instead of call, but Deirdre left for New York right after we got home, and she took her laptop with her, so I couldn't get online, but since I'm going to be here awhile I'm thinking I should probably pick one up." *Nice going,* he told himself. *Way to babble.*

"Yeah," she said. "They're pretty handy." He could hear the smile in her voice, which was mortifying in a thrilling kind of way.

"So, it's okay I called?"

Another few beats of silence. *Don't talk,* he commanded himself. *For chrissake, just shut up and let her answer.*

"Yeah." It wasn't an open-arms response. But he felt she meant it, and that was enough.

"I got that job," he said. "The sub-nurse thing at Kevin's school."

"Is that what you wanted?"

"I think it'll help him, having me nearby. Also, I could use the money."

"Is Haiti expensive?"

"No. I mean, I have no idea, but it's not like you spend a lot of money doing that kind of work. Are you . . . um . . . maybe thinking about what I said? About coming with me?"

He could hear a little puff of a sigh. *Don't sigh!* he wanted to tell her. *Just say yes!*

"I thought about it," she said. "I really did. And it means so much to me that you asked, Sean. It kind of blew me away."

"I meant it. I want you to come. It'd be amazing."

"I don't . . . I think it's not . . ." Her voice was shaky, and it hurt him to hear her that way. "I'm trying really hard to live my own life, Sean. You know how I am—you know better than anyone. I get pulled into the slipstream of other people's ideas so fast. You were the one who kept pushing me to stop following everyone else's agenda and do what *I* want to do."

"Yeah, but if you want to come to Haiti with me, that's doing what you want to do! It doesn't matter if it was my idea."

"But I don't."

In the seconds that followed, he could feel his chest expanding and contracting. It was sort of like meditating, feeling the breath, his mind empty. And yet it was the opposite of meditating. There was no floating. Only crashing.

"I want to be with you," she whispered, her voice weak with emotion. "But I don't want to live in Haiti."

"Rebecca—"

"I have to go now, Sean." Then there was a soft click.

For the briefest moment he had this crazy thought that as long as he held on to the receiver, she might still come back on the line. Once he hung up, he would lose her completely.

No . . . Hell, no. He hung up the phone and got the car keys.

CHAPTER 52

"Who is it?" she said when he knocked on the door. He could tell she'd been crying, and that she was pretty sure who it was.

"It's me," he said through the door.

"If you came over here to try and change my mind—"

"No, I didn't, I swear."

"I'm finally getting it right. You *made* me, Sean. I didn't even want to at first."

"I know."

"I ordered business cards . . ." He could tell she was starting to cry.

"Show them to me."

"Go home, Sean. Really."

"I'm not going home. Please just let me come in."

"No." She was really crying now.

A sick, hopeless feeling grew in his gut. And guilt. He had pestered and cajoled her into pulling her life together on her own terms. But that seemed like a hollow offering, now that she was sobbing behind a door he couldn't open. In frustration he grabbed the knob and twisted. It turned easily.

He came in and put his arms around her, and she continued to cry. He found himself rocking her. And though she still cried, he didn't feel sick anymore. He felt enormous relief and even a little bit of hope. He kissed the top of her head and gently brushed her teary cheek. *Holding her is like a drug,* he thought. *And I am an addict.*

The sex was tender and sad, and neither of them could sleep afterward. She lay on her back and he on his side, head propped on one arm, the other arm around her waist. They looked at each other for some minutes. And then she smiled and said, “It’s kind of like watching something fall, and you know it’s going to shatter, but it hasn’t yet, and you keep hoping it can defy gravity somehow.”

“So that’s a definite no to Haiti, right?”

She punched him, but she was laughing.

“Seriously,” he said. “What if we just hung in there? I mean . . . unless you’re with . . .”

“No,” she said. “I’ve spent time with him, but at this point I’m just seeing if we even have a friendship.”

Sean nodded. It was all he could do not to pump his fist in the air and yell *Woo-hoo!*

“Listen,” he said, when he felt like he could talk without a victorious giggle sneaking out. “I’m not going anywhere for at least another six weeks—that’s October. I already promised Kevin I’d come back for Christmas. Long distance sucks, I know, but it’s not impossible. Maybe you’d even come down to Haiti and visit.”

The smile on her face receded again. The obvious question hung in the air, unspoken.

And then what?

He slunk back into the house like a cat burglar just as the sky was starting to lighten. George growled from her post by Aunt Vivvy’s bedroom door and then put her head back down, too sleepy for a full-scale rebuke.

When he woke up, the sun was dappling through the leaves, and the breeze coming through the window felt crisp and dry. Autumn air. Sean hadn’t experienced a New England fall in twenty years, but he recognized it before he even opened his eyes, the August Autumn Appetizer. It would get hot and muggy again, of course, before the cooler weather set in for good. But lying there in bed, he was thrown back to his childhood, and he could feel school coming, as unstoppable as the changing of the leaves.

He got up and called the middle school, and they put him

through to Penny Coyne, who was getting the nurse's office ready for the first day. "You're definitely coming, right?" she said.

"Absolutely," he told her. "Did you think I was iffy about it?"

"Not at all," she said quickly. "I just didn't know if . . . your plans might've changed."

"Nope, I'm ready to report for duty."

"Any chance you can come down today?"

Mondays were Rebecca's day off, and he had hoped to spend it with her, but what was he going to say, "Ready to report for duty . . . but not really"?

Kevin padded barefoot and pajama-clad into the kitchen just as Sean was hanging up. The outer edges of the scrape on his cheek had begun to fleck off, leaving spots of tender pink. "Who was that?" he asked.

"That was my new boss." Sean told him about the six-week sub-nurse assignment. He never bargained for the look of horror on Kevin's face.

"You're going to be there? At my *school*? Like, every *day*?"

"Geez, I thought you'd be glad!"

"Why would I be *glad*? Everyone'll know we're related—it's weird!"

"Oh, for crying out loud," said Sean. "I'm sorry to be such an embarrassment."

"It's not *you*. It's just, you're like a . . . a parent or something. Nobody wants their parent at school. It's creepy!"

Sean drove to the middle school, muttering to himself. What the hell had he gotten himself into? He didn't want this stinking job, he'd only done it for Kevin, and the kid was acting like he'd be showing up to work in a Speedo and high heels.

He found tiny Penny Coyne dwarfed even further by teetering mountains of files. Though it was only ten-thirty, she looked as if she'd accept a cocktail if someone offered. Sean felt a momentary temptation to walk out and never come back. "How can I help?" he said.

"Oh, you can't do anything," Penny sighed. "Subs can't touch the files, it's a confidentiality thing. But thanks," she added. "They just wanted me to get your paperwork started and give you a little run-through on protocol before school starts on Wednesday."

She gave him the work forms to fill out and toured him through the supplies and the emergency card drawer. "This is the only file you'll have access to. When a kid comes in with any kind of allergic reaction, or, say, if a parent needs to be called, you pull his card. All the information you need should be right on there."

Around noon, Penny slid some files onto the floor and spread out her lunch on the desk. She handed him half her tuna sandwich. He politely declined, but then she said, "Seriously, take it. I rarely eat a whole sandwich even on a good day."

"So," said Sean, after he'd polished off the half sandwich, most of her cucumber slices, and all of her cookies. "What do I really need to know?" She glanced at him. "Come on," he said. "There's official protocol, and then there's all the little unwritten shortcuts. I won't be here long enough to figure them out myself, and it looks like your hands will be pretty full."

She smiled and nodded. "Okay. The real job? It's about figuring out what's true and what's adolescent BS. Does the kid have conjunctivitis or is he high? Are the girl's cramps really a ten on the pain scale, or is there a French test she's blowing off? And then there are the frequent flyers—the kids who don't even have much of an excuse, they just need a dose of nurse attention to make it through the day."

"That's kind of a drag, huh?"

"Yeah, but think of it this way—they could stop in here, or they could go smoke cigarettes behind the cafeteria Dumpster. Personally, I'd prefer to have the nurse's office be their drug of choice." She nibbled at a cucumber slice. "Can I tell you something?"

"Sure."

"Stan Girardi was worried about hiring you because you're a man. We've never had a male nurse before. You can see how parents might feel a little funny about their sweet innocent daughters getting their spines checked for scoliosis by a guy."

Sean nodded. "I get it. And not like this means anything, but just for the record, I like adult women. Period."

"It would help if you were married and had kids of your own."

"Hey, plenty of pedophiles are—"

"I know. I'm just saying what makes people feel more comfortable. I don't get a sketchy vibe from you, otherwise I wouldn't have pushed for the hire. But please, for everyone's sake—yours most of all—keep the door open, and don't have physical contact with a student unless you absolutely have to."

"But you're around most of the time, right? It's not like I'd be alone with kids that often."

"Lead nurse is an administrative position. I'll be going to meetings and chasing paperwork around the main office a lot of the time. Believe me when I say, of the two of us, you've got the better job."

On Wednesday, Kevin took the bus to school.

"This is silly," Sean told him. "I'm driving right there."

Kevin refused even to consider it. As Sean pulled into the parking lot, he saw Kevin step off the bus he'd boarded forty minutes earlier. Kids were hanging out the windows calling to one another. Kevin had that squinched-up, pre-freak-out look on his face. He'd never ridden a bus to school before—he lived close enough to Juniper Hill Elementary to walk.

Poor kid, thought Sean. It was tempting to catch up with him and say something encouraging, but Sean knew it would only make things worse. *Hang in there, buddy!* he called out silently. And to his brother he prayed, *Toss him a few times. He's going to need it.*

The nurse's office looked like a ticket window at a Red Sox game, with kids lined up out the door, and Penny Coyne standing behind the desk collecting emergency cards and medication forms. The crowd cleared by the time the first-period bell rang. There was a brief lull, and then kids began to trickle in again. A nosebleed, a stomachache, a weird pinching feeling at the back of the neck that turned out to be the kid's shirt tag. Sean snipped it out with scissors and sent him on his way.

"The kid's got sensory issues," he murmured to Penny.

"Don't we all," she told him.

A girl came in with the most gorgeous pale blond hair and light blue eyes Sean had ever seen. "Frequent flyer," Penny whispered as the girl approached the desk. "Hi, Amber," she said.

"Hi, Ms. Coyne. I don't feel that good."

"This is Mr. Doran. He's the new me and I'm the new Ms. Krasmus until she gets back."

"Uh, okay."

"Mr. Doran, can you help Amber? I have to run these forms over to the office."

"Sure thing," said Sean. "Amber, why don't you tell me what's up."

The girl took a moment to look him over, and when she was done, he felt as if he'd been taken apart, inspected for parasites, and put back together again. "I don't feel that good," she said, as if this were new information.

For the next five minutes, Sean asked questions about where the pain was and how it felt, and Amber gave answers like "kind of" and "a little." Finally, she said, "Can I just lie down?"

"Should I call your parents?"

"No." And she went to one of the sick bays—a vinyl-upholstered cot with a sheet of exam paper over the pillow area—and pulled the curtain closed. At one point, he peeked in to check on her and she was just staring straight ahead.

Three headaches and a kicked shin later, Amber got up, signed out, and left.

When the last bell rang, Sean could say this for his new job: the time passed quickly and it was, in fact, easier than filling complicated drink orders at the Confectionary. At least for him.

When he got home he changed into shorts, checked on Aunt

Vivvy, left a message for Rebecca inviting her over for dinner, and went out on the porch to wait for Kevin. He put his feet up on the railing and paged through the latest edition of *The Journal of School Nursing* Penny had given him. He'd read the articles on trichotillomania (pulling out one's own hair), identifying lice, and the signs and symptoms of sexual abuse by the time the bus stopped up the street. When the engine idled, Sean could hear the yelling and horseplay reverberating out the bus windows. Kevin got out and trudged up to the house; when his foot hit the first stair, tears came leaking down his face. Sean followed him up to his room.

Kevin lay on his bed with the pillow over his head, weeping. Sean spread the weighted blanket over him and sat in the desk chair. After a few minutes, Kevin quieted a little and took the pillow off his face.

"Anything super awful, or just the usual?" Sean asked.

Kevin inhaled a juicy sniffle. "My English teacher, Ms. Crosby, has this really loud high-pitched voice."

"Do it for me," said Sean.

Kevin screeched, "PLEASE SIT IN THE SEAT ASSIGNED TO YOU!"

"Ouch!" Sean laughed.

"And there's this kid, Davis Dixon. He's like a human Ping-Pong ball."

"Bump into you?"

"Four times. The last time, I shoved him away and said, 'Dude! Seriously!' Then he went off and bounced into someone else."

"Excellent strategy."

There was no hope for the lunchroom with its constant roar of voices and hideous scrap heap of smells, but he sat with Ivan from Boy Scouts and they talked about knives, which distracted him a little. When Kevin was done off-loading his school day, they went out and jumped on the trampoline for a little while. Then Kevin returned to his room to do homework, and Sean made dinner while he waited for Rebecca to come over after work.

Aunt Vivvy walked slowly into the kitchen with George.

"What did you do today?" asked Sean.

"I was about to ask you that very question," she said.

"I went to work in the nurse's office at Kevin's school. Remember how I told you I'm subbing in for a while?"

"No, I do not remember that. And that was not my question. My question was, what did *I* do today?"

CHAPTER 53

No amount of talking would convince Aunt Vivvy to go to a doctor. Sean went so far as to threaten to have her declared legally incompetent, to which she replied that she understood it to be an arduous process, one that would likely delay his departure for weeks, possibly months. And what if he was successful? Wouldn't it require far greater responsibility on his part? Game, set, match. She was still sharp as a tack—when she was mentally in the building.

"Okay, well, here's another item for the Aunt Vivvy agenda," Sean said peevishly.

Eyes blazing, she waited for him to draw.

"Kevin needs a special ed evaluation for sensory processing issues. I'll get the forms. As his legal guardian, you'll sign them."

"Agreed," she said, smiling pleasantly. "I'll also call my lawyer and initiate the process to have guardianship of Kevin transferred to you."

Game, set, match.

Later, after Kevin and Aunt Vivvy had gone to bed, Rebecca headed home and Sean followed her in the Caprice. Her living room was full of drop-cloth-covered furniture and paint cans. One wall was painted a sage color she said was called "folklore green."

"Folklore has a color?"

"Yes," she said. "Apparently this is it."

He offered to help her paint for a little while, but she slipped her arms around his waist. "You want to paint?" she said, smiling up at him. "That's what you really want to do?"

"It's not my first choice," he admitted, pulling her in tight. "I'd say it's a distant second."

They walked up the half flight to her bedroom, and while she went to brush her teeth, he undressed and settled into her twin bed. When she came back he watched her take off her clothes, admiring her subtle musculature. *A strong, healthy female body,* he thought. He'd seen relatively few of them over the course of his life.

"Kevin seems good," she said, snuggling into the crook of his arm.

"Yeah, Ireland really built up his confidence. He got along well with my father, too. I was thinking maybe he could go over there next summer for a couple of weeks." Sean shifted toward her and reached up to brush a lock of hair away from her face. "I'd have to lay down some rules, though. Sometimes Da wants to talk about stuff that's not necessarily helpful."

"Like?"

"Like he was practically giddy to tell Kevin about the blood in black pudding."

"Ew!"

"Yeah, and he thinks I should tell Kevin about Huntington's. We don't even know if he's at risk, because we don't know about Hugh. If you don't have it you can't pass it on."

"It might be worth talking about it in general terms," said Rebecca. "Like about your mother. Just so it's not out of the blue when the time comes."

"When the time comes for what?"

"To talk about getting tested."

"Jesus, he's just a kid—he's not getting tested! Every major medical organization advises against it. Kids can't handle a bad diagnosis, and it's not like there's anything medical science can do for him if he's positive."

"I'm not saying to test him *now*," she said quietly. "But at some point when he's older he'll have to at least consider it." She took a breath as if to say something else, but then didn't.

"What?" Sean demanded.

"You're not going to want to hear this."

"Say it anyway."

"If you're going to be his legal guardian . . ." It was her soothing voice, he realized. ". . . you might want to consider getting tested yourself."

"Christ, where is this coming from? I told you I'm almost sure I don't have it. My mother was ten years younger than I am now when she first had symptoms."

"Sean." She put her hand on his chest, and he could feel his heart revving just beneath it. "It's less likely as you get older, but it *is* possible to have a late-onset case. When you're responsible for another person, that could be important to know."

"Someone's been doing research," he muttered. He felt her body receive the gibe. "I'm sorry," he said. "It's just stuff I don't like to think about."

"I'm on your side, Sean."

"It sure didn't feel like it, for a minute there."

"Being on your side doesn't mean I won't ever talk about things you don't want to talk about. It just means I'm with you."

With me. It sounded nice the way she said it, but there was a downside, wasn't there? It wasn't all hot sex and witty banter. They lay there quietly, and when his pounding heart decided it wasn't actually under attack after all, he turned and kissed her. And she kissed him back.

Kevin was already up and dressed when Sean's alarm went off at 6:20. He threw on shorts and went to have breakfast with Kevin, though he could have used a few more winks of sleep. Being in his own bed for a mere four hours was no easy way to start the day.

School woke him up pretty fast, however. Fifteen minutes into first block, two boys came in from phys ed. They had collided playing kickball and it soon became apparent that Alejandro with the split lip laid the blame squarely on Davis, who had a growing lump on his forehead.

By the time Sean had cleaned up the lip and given Alejandro an ice pack, Davis was breathing fast, and when Sean applied ice to his head, he burst into tears.

"Maricón," Alejandro muttered at him.

"Hey," said Sean. "None of that!"

Penny looked up from the desk. Sean mouthed the translation, *faggot*, behind the boys' heads.

"Alejandro," said Penny. "Do you need to spend a little time with Mr. Girardi? I'm sure he'd be very interested to know what you just said."

"No, Ms. Coyne."

Alejandro left with his ice pack, but Penny told Davis to stay for a moment. "You didn't come in for your Ritalin yesterday," she said. "What's going on?"

"Yes, I did!" he said quickly.

"No, Davis, you didn't. What's the deal?"

"I just forgot. I'll come in today, I promise."

When he left, Penny explained that Davis had attention-deficit/hyperactivity disorder—"emphasis on hyperactivity"—and was supposed to take a dose of Ritalin every four hours. "Judging by his behavior, I don't think his mom made him take it this morning."

"I don't think she made him take it yesterday, either." Sean told her about Kevin's account of Davis bouncing into people.

"She may have ADHD herself—it runs in families," Penny said. "By the way, you speak Spanish?"

Sean shrugged. "Not fluently. At least not anymore."

The reference to unfortunate family inheritances had reminded him of his late-night talk with Rebecca. But then three girls came in, two leading one in the middle. "She has a migraine—it really hurts—she might throw up—" They talked over each other, faces grave, competing to show the most concern. And Sean was back in work mode.

Around lunchtime, Davis came back. Penny was at a meeting, so

Sean pulled his meds. Davis took the pill and turned to leave. Sean held out a paper cup. "Here's some water."

"I can take it in the cafeteria."

"How about you just take it here?"

"I don't like water." Davis's eyes darted from the cup to Sean and back to the cup. "I have a Coke in my lunch."

Amber came in, pale blond hair spread like a silken shawl around her shoulders. Davis stared at her, and she silently rebuked him with a look of disgust. His gaze dropped to the floor.

"Mr. Doran, I don't feel that good," she said.

As soon as Sean turned to her, Davis slipped out the door. Sean sighed. "What's up, Amber?" He went through a slightly shorter round of questions this time, none of which she answered with any actual information, and she went to lie down on the same vinyl cot as before.

After school, Sean waited on the porch for Kevin, reading an article on ADHD in *The Journal of School Nursing*. Kevin walked directly past him, and Sean let him be for a few minutes while he finished the article. Kevin's face was red and damp when Sean went up to his room, but he wasn't crying anymore. The bus was loud and the lunchroom disgusting, he said. But the worst part of the day was science. "I had to be lab partners with Davis Dixon! And he just kept *breathing*—like he was running a race or something! It was so loud and annoying."

"Was this after lunch or before?"

"After. Alejandro Ramirez is really pissed at him for crashing into him in gym, and every time Alejandro walked by him in science, the breathing got louder. I could barely stand it!"

"Sounds like he was worried Alejandro might clock him one."

"Yeah, he's scared of, like, *everything*."

"You know," said Sean. "Davis might be dealing with some things he can't control."

"Right, like he can't control bouncing around all the time?" Kevin scoffed. "I doubt it."

Sean didn't want to use Kevin's own idiosyncrasies against him, but he was surprised at his insensitivity. "Kev," he said. "*Everyone* has stuff that's hard for them. And sometimes it isn't the same stuff that's hard for everyone else. You see what I'm getting at?"

"No," said Kevin, petulantly.

"What's hard for *you*?" Sean watched as the point hit home. "I'm not saying you have to like him or be best pals or anything. But don't be mean to him. Life's hard enough."

The next day it was as if the entire school decided to pay a visit to the nurse's office. Fevers, headaches, cramps. Sean wondered if every menstruating female in the building had spontaneously gotten her period. Even the teachers needed supplies. "Where's Penny?" one asked, eyes casting furtively around the room. When he told her Penny was at a meeting in another building, a blush rose up her cheeks. "I need a . . . a . . ." she murmured.

"Tampon?" whispered Sean. He slipped her a couple surreptitiously, like a drug dealer.

A sprained ankle, a case of lice, a broken tooth. Emergency forms were pulled from the file like cards from the deck in a gin game. Parents were called. Notes were written. Forms filled out. Sean was sweating by the time things slowed down a little before lunch.

Two kids were waiting in the sick bays for parents to pick them up when Davis arrived for his Ritalin. Sean took him out to the hallway to talk privately. "You're not taking your medicine, are you?" Davis looked away. "When you do take it, does it help?" Sean asked.

"A little."

"So why not take it?"

"It makes me feel weird. Like something's gonna get me."

"It makes you anxious?"

"More anxious," Davis clarified. "My mother says I'm a born worrywart."

"Who prescribed the Ritalin?" Sean asked.

Davis glanced down the hallway, which was empty. "My psychiatrist," he murmured.

"Does he know about the anxiety?"

"Yeah, but he says we have to deal with the ADHD first. He says for the anxiety I should *meditate*." Davis rolled his eyes. "I have an *attention* problem," he said. "How'm I supposed to sit still and clear my mind? If I could do that, I wouldn't need a psychiatrist, would I?"

Dual diagnosis. Sean had read about this in the *School Nursing* article. It wasn't uncommon for kids with ADHD to be anxiety-prone. This made it difficult to get the medication right because ADHD drugs tend to have a revving effect that can help with concentration but increase anxiety.

Sean said, "I'll talk to Ms. Coyne about this," and let him leave without taking the pill. After school, when the nurse's office cleared out, Sean broached the subject with Penny. "The kid has a point," he said. "So I let him off the hook with the Ritalin."

"We can't make those decisions, Sean." She shook her head wearily. "In fact we could get in a lot of hot water for it. I'm handing this over to guidance." And she typed up an e-mail on the spot, with Sean's input. "Let's see what they say."

CHAPTER 54

On Saturday, Sean and Kevin went computer shopping.

"That one has no speed," the salesclerk warned them. "They stopped making that processor like six months ago and the RAM's low. That's why we're selling it so cheap."

"We'll take it," said Sean.

They looked at cell phones, but there were so many plans and models and accessories to consider, Sean got overwhelmed and anxious about the expense. *This must be what Davis feels like all the time,* he thought.

On Sunday, Sean went to Rebecca's to help her paint. He found an eighties radio station, and they laughed and sang along to forgotten superstars like Frankie Goes to Hollywood. Katrina and the Waves came on with "Walking on Sunshine," and Rebecca dropped her brush into the paint can. "This was my favorite!" She began to dance around the room and Sean jumped up to join her. Rebecca knew all the words and sang them with abandon, even the part that went, "Baby I just want you back and I want you to stay!" Sean felt a little funny about that.

When the song was over, she leaned breathless against an unpainted wall. He grinned at her. "I'm pretty positive I never saw you dance like that in high school," he said.

"No," she sighed and slid to the floor. "I only did it in the privacy of my own basement. I wasn't exactly the bouncy, wild-dancing type. People would've thought I was trying too hard."

He went and sat next to her. "So you're a secret sunshine walker."

She smiled. "Still respect me?"

He hung an arm around her. "More than ever."

The thought of her melodious voice and secret inner happiness reminded him of something. "Hey," he said. "Can you make a recording of your voice on your laptop?"

Monday was Labor Day, and Cormac's family was having their annual, semilegendary party to celebrate not working. Sean had gone every year in high school. "Bring the family," Cormac had said. "Bring Rebecca, too!"

Aunt Vivvy didn't want to go. She was lucid enough that morning to explain that she was vexed by the possibility of embarrassing herself.

"Mrs. McGrath would love to see you," said Sean. "You could catch up on Garden Club news. I'll take you home if you start getting foggy." He could see the temptation this presented and pressed his point. "Auntie, you haven't been out of the house in months. Aren't you bored?"

She sighed. "Terribly."

All Kevin wanted to know was would the big guy be there, and would there be pie. Sean assured him there'd be plenty of desserts, including the all-important Labor Day cake designed by Cormac himself. George made it clear that she did not want to be left home alone, barking and whining when she saw them all getting ready to leave. "Absolutely not," Sean told Kevin.

When they went to pick up Rebecca, she was wearing that pale pink dress with the tiny flowers. He felt a secret little gasp erupt in his chest. Aunt Vivvy glanced over at him. Perhaps not entirely secret. He got out to greet her with a peck on the cheek and opened the back door.

She greeted everyone and said, "Hey there, George. Are you coming to the party, too?"

"Don't ask," Sean grumbled.

When they arrived at the McGraths' there was music playing in the backyard, and voices and laughter. Cormac was the first person they saw, and he greeted them with his characteristic enthusiasm, high-fiving Kevin and beckoning his mother over to help Aunt Vivvy to a chair. "Rebecca," he said. "Man, the years have been good to you!"

She smiled. "I hear you kept Sean out of trouble at your bakery this summer."

"Actually, he was the worst cashier I ever hired."

"Hey!" Sean said, mock-indignantly.

"Sure, the guy can sew a head wound," Cormac went on, "but he doesn't know a half-caf macchiato from his elbow, let me tell you *that*."

Cormac suggested to Kevin that he take a look at the cake, but Kevin was a little iffy about the crowd. Rebecca volunteered to go with him.

"First get George's bowl and fill it with water," Sean told him. "Even with the windows down she'll get hot."

They went off to do so, and Cormac said, "The responsible dog owner!"

"Let's get one thing straight: I do not own that dog."

"Got it." Cormac nodded sarcastically.

"Where's Barb?"

Cormac's joviality faded, and he took a few steps away from the crowd. "Upstairs in my old bedroom," he murmured. "Having a nervous breakdown."

"What? Why?"

"My cousin Janie's pregnant."

"Oh, God, buddy. I'm so sorry. Janie's not even married to the guy, right?"

"They will be in about a month." Cormac shrugged. "In the end it's a good thing. Tug's dying for more kids, and in my personal opinion, Janie needed a kick in the ass. 'Where will we live?'" he mimicked. "Who freaking cares? What a stupid thing to stop you from being with someone who's really right for you."

Sean felt the zing of this comment, though he knew Cormac hadn't meant it for him. *Spoken like a man who's never had a location problem,* he thought. But his sympathy for his old friend returned a moment later. "Shouldn't you be up there with her?" he asked.

"No, she's pissed at me. Not entirely sure why, of course . . ."

"It's the hormones," said Sean. "And you're the husband."

Cormac nodded. "So," he said after a moment. "You neglected to mention that your girlfriend is smokin' hot."

Sean laughed. "She's pretty great, huh?"

"It's funny, because she doesn't actually look that different. It's like she's grown into herself or something. Plus she looks happy, which she never did in high school." He smirked at Sean. "I suppose you might be marginally responsible for that."

"We school nurses do have a way with the ladies."

Kevin and Rebecca made their way back, and Kevin was mightily impressed with the cake. "It's this enormous flower!" he said, holding his arms wide. "With Mrs. McGrath's face in the middle! And it says 'The President'!"

"Because she's the president of the Garden Club now," Cormac explained. "Your aunt used to be, you know."

Kevin grinned at Sean. "She must have graduated, because now she's the queen."

Sean laughed. To Cormac, he said, "Inside joke."

"Spinster!" Cormac's cousin Janie came over with her son Dylan. "How's everything?"

Sean introduced her to Rebecca, and Janie remembered her from high school. The women chatted as Kevin and Dylan eyed each other. Finally, Kevin said, "Wanna see my dog?" Dylan looked to his mother, who wanted to know where the dog was and how long they'd be gone, and whether the dog was friendly. "He's only in first grade," she murmured to Sean.

"Kevin's in sixth grade, and he's a Boy Scout, so he's pretty responsible, right Kev?" Kevin responded with a shrug-nod. "Don't worry," Sean told Janie. "It's safe."

"'Don't worry,'" she said wryly. "Not sure I know that tune."

Sean nodded. "Yeah, just when it seems like the coast is clear, some other danger pops up." He told them about Kevin going under the waves when they were in Ireland. "I nearly lost my mind!" They both looked at him for a moment without responding. It seemed strange to Sean, and he said, "Well, wouldn't you?" Yes, they both nodded. Absolutely.

There was an awkward silence. Sean said, "So, Janie, I hear you've got good news."

"Cormac told you."

"Yeah, I hope that's okay."

"No, it's fine," she said. "I'm just trying to keep it on the down low until after the wedding. And I'm *really* hoping Cormac and Barb will have some good news of their own by then." She told Rebecca about the pregnancy and impending wedding, and then she heard her daughter start to cry from the opposite side of the yard and hurried off.

The boys came back and wandered around the party together. Aunt Vivvy truly was the queen, surrounded by Garden Club members who stopped to pay homage to her past leadership. Sean and Rebecca talked to the McGraths and various other party-goers. Sean always introduced her as "my friend, Rebecca," but they stood too close for their relationship to be mistaken as platonic. Mr. McGrath and Cormac bantered at the grill.

And Barb stayed upstairs.

After a while, Sean asked Cormac, "How about if I take a plate up to her?"

"Are you packing heat? You might need it."

"I'll take my chances." Sean loaded a plate and went upstairs.

Cormac's childhood bedroom still had a shelf full of trophies from their high school days and a poster of tennis great Boris Becker. Barb was curled into an overstuffed chair in the corner.

"Missed you out there, picture taker," Sean said. "Thought I'd bring the party to you."

"Oh, Sean, that's so sweet of you. I keep hoping I can get calm enough to face it."

"Cormac told me."

The circles under Barb's eyes were darker than ever. "I'm happy for them," she said dully. Then a flash of anger: "But she wasn't even trying! And she's just such a *smartass*!"

"A total smartass." Sean nodded sympathetically. "But she's family—what can you do?"

"Not a damn thing," she muttered, staring out the window.

Cormac had warned him, but Sean was still surprised by this uncharacteristic bleakness.

Then she turned to him. "Look," she said, "you've been through a lot, and you have a right to build your life however you like. But I just want to know: would you stay if he was your biological child?"

"Kevin?" Sean said, a vague panic dulling his comprehension skills.

"Of course, Kevin. Who else?"

"Um . . ." Sean hadn't really considered the question of biology before, because there'd never been a possibility of his having *any* kind of child, biological or otherwise.

"I've been thinking about it a lot," she said. "How much it matters . . . whether it matters at all."

"I guess maybe it's just personal preference," he offered. "Some people care about having the same genetic makeup, some don't."

"And what if you don't get a choice?" she said quietly.

They sat there, with the implications of her question hanging in the air around them.

She went on staring out the window. "I've been so determined to have a biological child, and I really want the experience of being pregnant. But that's over in nine months." She turned to look at Sean. "At which point, what does it matter where the kid came from?"

It seemed like sound logic. And yet he sensed something beyond it, something more than whether she'd decided to give up the hormone treatments and contact an adoption agency.

Her gaze softened. "I don't think either of us has a choice, Sean," she said, gently. "I think you and I are both going to raise and love other people's children."

She took a long slow breath and let it out with a sigh. Her shoulders, which had been stiff and ready for a fight, relaxed. Something seemed to change for her then, a perspective shift, a letting go. "It's an honor, really," she said, "don't you think?"

Without waiting for him to answer, she rose and went down to the party.

The rest of the day was surreal to Sean. His legs felt as if they might go out from under him at any time and he would sink into the ground and disappear without anyone noticing.

"Have you had anything to eat?" Rebecca asked at one point. She seemed to be studying him. He turned away, pretending to see someone he knew.

Eventually they left, and he dropped her off with a tepid peck on the cheek. At home, he helped Aunt Vivvy up to her room and told Kevin to take a shower and make sure his backpack was ready for school tomorrow. All of this was automatic now. He did it without a thought.

Other people's children. Had he somehow become a parent without his consent? Had the choice been made for him?

Later when the house was quiet, he was restless, and his shock turned to indignation. Who was Barb to make pronouncements about what choices he did or didn't have? He hardly knew her. Cormac must have told her about their conversations at The Pal—conversations he thought were just between them.

He paced around the kitchen, his back throbbing, which was strange because it hadn't bothered him for a while. He threw down four ibuprofen and opened a beer, hoping it would ease his restlessness. A massage would help, he thought, or, even better, sex. Anything that would take him out of his spinning thoughts. He grabbed the car keys and went out the door, telling himself he was not going to Rebecca's to lose himself in her body. He just wanted a change of venue. If sex happened, that would be nice, too.

When she opened the door she was wearing pajamas, faded and

stretched out, a seam popping at the shoulder. He'd never seen her in pajamas before. If she had to wear them, why couldn't they be nice ones, at least?

"Well?" she said.

"Well, what? I can't just come by?"

She squinted at him, baffled. Then she held out her arms, indicating the room. He looked around. They had finished painting the day before. She must have moved all the furniture herself, because the room was completely set up. Or maybe she'd had help. Maybe that old boyfriend.

"It looks great," he said.

"Is everything okay?"

"Yeah, fine. I just couldn't sleep."

"You seemed a little . . . funny after you talked to Barb."

Sometimes he loved how perceptive she was. This was not one of those times.

He lifted a shoulder dismissively and dropped onto the new couch, which was not as squishy as the old leather one. It jarred his back.

"So," she said, when it was clear he wasn't starting the conversation. "The party was nice. I remember Cormac as being sort of this funny giant in high school, but he's got a very sweet side, too, doesn't he?"

Sean shrugged. He did not particularly care to talk about the "sweet side" of his traitorous friend at the moment.

"And Janie's just how I remember her," Rebecca went on, "nice, but a little edgy."

"Yeah, what was that weird look you two gave me when I told you about Kevin almost drowning? It was like in stereo."

"Um . . . I don't know if Janie was thinking the same thing . . ."

"It certainly looked like it."

"Well, I don't know. It wasn't really what you were saying, but how you were saying it."

"How was I saying it?"

"You just sounded very . . ." She hesitated. "Parental."

This was exactly *not* what he'd come here to talk about. It was what he'd come here to *avoid*. And here she was sitting in her ratty pajamas, hitting the sore spot.

"This is about getting tested, isn't it?" he said, knowing he was being irrational, but not able to stop himself, now that his building agitation had finally been unleashed.

"What?" Her eyes were wide with concern. "I never said anything about—"

"No, but the other night you implied it—that I'm like his parent now, so I should suddenly jump to do something I've always been completely against doing."

"Sean, that is not what I—"

"You know what I think? I think all this concern for Kevin is really self-interest. You want me to get tested for *you*."

For a moment she looked as if he'd slapped her, and somewhere down deep he knew that in a sense he had, and the resulting guilt made him even angrier. But then her eyes lit in just the same way Aunt Vivvy's did, and he realized he'd started a much bigger fight than he'd intended.

"Do I want you to get tested?" she said, her voice low but furious. "Of *course* I do. I can't put it out of my mind like you do. And how could I not want to know what I'm in for? Because whether we're together or not, Sean, if you have Huntington's, I'll be devastated."

"I could get hit by a bus and the outcome's the same."

"Yes," she said, nodding hard. "That would devastate me, too. Because that's what it means to live in the world, Sean—not on the edge of it." She crossed her arms. "And what if *I* get hit by a bus? A change of scenery won't help. The fact is, it *never* really helped. It just gave you a way to hide from yourself."

"Oh, my God, *you're* lecturing *me* about hiding? You've been peeking out from behind your parents your whole life. You're forty-three freaking years old and I practically needed a crowbar to get you to separate!"

"Okay," she said, standing up. "Time for you to go."

"You're kicking me out. What—is my energy destabilizing you?"

"Your energy is practically radioactive right now, and I want it—and you—out of here."

"Fine." In three long strides he was at the door. "But this conversation is not over."

"You're damn straight it's not over." She twisted the knob and held the door wide. "We'll finish it when you can stop being such a jackass. And next time? Call first."

CHAPTER 55

Sean went to school early on Tuesday morning to get his mind off the previous night and found Penny with a shopping bag full of clothes. "Running away from home?" he teased.

The bag belonged to an eighth grader. "His father left, and he says his mom's sad and doesn't get out of bed much. He and his older sister are managing, but the washing machine broke, and he was starting to smell bad. The other kids were calling him 'Stink Bomb.'"

"So you're doing his laundry *here*?" Sean was shocked. Nurses didn't do laundry.

"There's a washer and dryer in the janitor's closet. We're working on getting a new machine donated to the family, but until then—"

"Shouldn't you call Social Services?"

"I think guidance made a call. But DCF has much bigger fish to fry. The kids are holding it together and they don't want to leave her, so it's pretty low priority."

"Any word on Davis?"

She sighed. "That could take weeks to get sorted out. We have to give the meds until the order changes, okay? So please don't let him off the hook again, or it's my neck on the block."

He took the bag from her and said, "Point me to the janitor's closet."

"You don't have to do that."

He patted her shoulder. "Least I can do for the patron saint of Belham Middle School."

The day brought its usual host of cuts, lumps, and fevers, and an impressive parade of weekend-related maladies: several third-degree sunburns with blisters popping and oozing, a handful of sports-related wounds that required dressing changes, and nine cases of poison ivy. Sean's fingernails turned pink from all the calamine. It was fairly monotonous, but Sean found he liked joking with the kids, keeping them calm as he pulled out a particularly deep splinter or tugged at a stuck wound dressing. He was starting to know the frequent flyers on sight.

Amber came in, and it was so busy Sean didn't even bother to question her. She went to her usual bed by the door. Later he realized she'd signed herself out and left without a word.

Davis came in at lunchtime. "Please don't make me take it," he said.

"Have to, pal. I got in trouble for letting you off last time."

"I'll be good," he pleaded. "I'll stay in my seat the whole—or at least *most* of the time."

"If you take it, I'll give you a special prize."

Davis rolled his eyes. "What, like a sticker? Been there, done that, torched the chart."

Sean handed him a CD. "A friend of mine made it. It's for meditating—"

"I told you I can't—"

"It's *guided* meditation. You listen to words. She has a really nice voice." He thought of Rebecca's voice, the anger in it last night, and guilt pinched at him.

"It's a girl?" Davis looked at the CD. "Is she cute?"

"She's beautiful."

Davis gave him a sly-dog smile. "Way to go, Mr. D."

He was long gone by the time Sean realized he was still holding the pill.

When Penny came back, Sean told her what happened. "I'm like the loser nurse," he said. "Seriously, why did you hire me?"

"To be honest," she said, "you were the only one who applied."

The day got worse from there. When he got home, he heard the dog barking upstairs and ran up to see if Aunt Vivvy was okay. When he opened her bedroom door, the dog lunged out and down the stairs. Aunt Vivvy was not in her room, or anywhere else in the house. Sean took George and searched the neighborhood, knocking on doors, but no one had seen her, so he went home and called the police. He heard Kevin crying in his room, but assumed it was just the usual. When Sean went out again to search the woods behind the house, George wouldn't go. She barked at Kevin's door until Kevin let her in, and Sean had to go on his own.

As he trudged through the woods, the sick feeling in his gut rose up into his chest. Aunt Vivvy was stubborn and hard-hearted and . . . well, stubborn. But no one deserved an end like this. She would hate it more than anyone, he realized. It was so undignified.

Jesus, Viv, where the hell are you? And he found himself praying for Hugh's help.

When he circled back to the house, Kevin was still up in his room, and Sean decided to look in on him. "Whoa!" he said. "How in the world did *that* happen?"

Kevin's eye was purple and swollen shut. "In gym," he whimpered. "Last period."

Sean went down to the kitchen and wrapped some ice in a paper towel and went back up. "What happened?" he said, laying the ice pack against the eye.

They had been playing dodgeball and Keri Franzenburg, "who's about nine feet tall," elbowed him in the face. "I *hate* dodgeball," he cried. "It's such a *stupid game*."

That special ed evaluation can't come soon enough, thought Sean. "Why didn't you come to me?"

"Because some of the guys in the locker room were calling me baby, and why didn't I just go cry to my uncle. And then they started saying that you must be stupid because you're not a doctor, and you probably like to look at naked little girls, or something."

Sean's eyebrows went up. "Wow," he said. "Those kids are jerks. Who was it?"

"I'm not *telling* you!"

The doorbell rang and Sean went to answer it. Officer Dougie Shaw was standing there with Aunt Vivvy, who was clearly so angry she practically had steam coming out of her ears.

"Thank God!" said Sean. "Where've you been?!"

Officer Dougie walked her into the living room and they all sat down on the couch. "I was in the cemetery," she said, biting at every word. "I wasn't aware there had been an ordinance passed against visiting graves."

Dougie smiled. "She did not come along quietly . . . but we'll spare her the jail time."

"I would like to lie down," she spat out. "I have had a very trying ordeal."

Sean helped her upstairs and noticed a piece of paper gripped in her hand. George bounded out to greet her and then stood in the hallway whining, looking from Kevin's room to Aunt Vivvy's. "Go on," Kevin called, and the dog ran in behind her before the door shut.

Sean went back downstairs. "Jesus, Dougie," he breathed.

"You got your hands full," he said. "Alzheimer's? It can't be Huntington's this late in life, right?"

"You know about that?"

"Sure. Hugh told me."

"You were friends?"

"Well . . ." Dougie chuckled. "Your brother was 'known to the police,' as they say. But once Kevin's mother blew town, he pretty much stopped partying and buckled down. I used to come by and check up on him, and we'd get talking."

"What did he tell you?"

"All kinds of stuff. He was real worried about Kevin and how everything bothered him. He did a lot of reading up on it. The pediatrician was no help—just kept telling him Kevin would grow out of it. Hugh always blamed the girl, you know, for all the drugs she did when she was pregnant. But then he was doing them, too, so he felt bad about that."

"The last time I saw you, you said something about him being such a good dad, and that's why the pneumonia got him."

Dougie shook his head. "Terrible, really. Kevin had it first, and it was so bad Hugh was worried he'd lose him. He was so little. And even when he turned the corner, he didn't want Hugh to leave the room. So Hugh stayed and just kept getting sicker. Your aunt hounded him to see a doctor, but you know, whatever she said, Hugh would do the opposite. That part of him never changed. Finally he collapsed and she called the ambulance. I was on duty that night, and it killed me to see him like that. Such a damned shame."

The two men stood silently in the foyer. After a few moments, Dougie said, "You might want to think about alarming the doors. If she wanders like that in the winter, it'll be all over."

After Dougie left, Sean went up to Aunt Vivvy's room. She was sitting on the side of the bed, clutching the paper to her chest. As soon as he sat down next to her, she turned on him. "You had to call the *police*? Have you no respect for me at *all*?"

"Auntie, I . . . I love you. You took care of us when everything else fell apart. Now *I* have to take care of *you*."

"I wasn't doing anything that required your intervention!"

"Auntie. Look down."

She lowered her gaze to her lap, and then to her feet. "Oh, dear God," she murmured. She was wearing nothing but her nightgown and slippers.

"Why did you go to the cemetery?" he asked gently.

"I had to find him," she said, and handed Sean the crumpled paper. It was actually a letter, addressed in her fastidious handwriting to someone named George Gardner. Across the top a shaky hand had scrawled, *DECEASED—RETURN TO SENDER*.

"Is he the George you named the dog after?"

"Yes. When we were young, he asked me to marry him."

This was him, thought Sean. *The man she loved. And now he's dead.*

"But you turned him down," he said.

"My father was sick with Huntington's—we didn't know what it was back then. And my mother was frail, and rather . . . flighty. Lila was so young. I couldn't leave them. I told myself I'd have other chances, once my parents had passed and Lila was grown. But I never found anyone I loved as much as him." She sighed. "And then we learned that the Huntington's was genetic, and I told myself I was glad I'd never had children . . . and then I had children anyway, didn't I? I had all of *you*, and you were just as much at risk as if I'd borne you myself, so there I was with the same problem, after all." Slowly she leaned toward him and rested her head against his shoulder, and he put his arm around her. "I'm so glad you don't seem to have it, Sean. But I can't stop worrying about Deirdre and Kevin."

He looked at the address on the envelope. If it was correct, George Gardner had lived in Ashburnham, Massachusetts, about an hour's drive from Belham. "I'll see if I can find out where he was buried, Auntie. And then I'll take you to say good-bye."

He got her settled for a nap and went to check on Kevin. The ice had reduced the swelling a bit, and they went downstairs. Kevin started his homework in the den and Sean set up his new low-speed laptop to search for George Gardner. He hadn't checked his e-mail since Deirdre had left. When he opened it, there was an e-mail from Yasmin Chaudhry.

> Sean, I'm so glad you'll be joining me here. You're going to love it!

CHAPTER 56

The next day, during lunch period, Davis stopped in for his pill. Sean asked him about the CD. "It was okay," said Davis. "I still don't want to take the pill."

"You've slimed out of it so many times, Davis, you owe me this one."

"Okay, but can I keep the CD?"

"Absolutely."

Just before the end of school, Amber came in, but this time she looked different—paler, blue eyes a little too shiny. "I don't feel that good," she said.

Story of your life, Sean thought, and reminded himself to be patient. "What's up?"

"I'm, like, freezing." Her chin clenched and her teeth began to chatter.

Sean checked her temperature. "Wow, Amber," he said, smiling. "A hundred and two point six. You win the prize—that's the highest temp I've seen since I started here."

She looked at him blankly. "Can you call my mom?" She went to lie down in her usual spot. Sean pulled her emergency contact card and called her mother's work, cell, and home numbers, but only got voice mail. He went back to check on Amber. She was curled up, arms wrapped around herself, but this time she wasn't staring at the curtain. She was snoring.

The next name on Amber's card was her father's. Sean called him and got through. "I'll be right there," he said.

"Okay, thanks," said Sean. But the guy had already hung up.

About ten minutes later, a man walked into the office, short and stocky, looking like a fire hydrant dressed in a business suit. It was clear he worked out fairly obsessively—his short arms were so muscle-bound they stuck out from his body on both sides.

"Where's Amber?" was all he said.

Sean handed him the sign-out clipboard and suddenly got a distinctly creepy feeling. The guy didn't seem aggressive or angry in any way, but his energy was somehow menacing.

Menacing energy. He would have to tell Rebecca that one. But then he remembered their fight, and her calling him a jackass. In the light of day he had to agree with her. She'd been right about a lot of things. And he'd countered with that nasty crowbar comment. He wondered if she'd ever forgive him.

"Where is she?" said the suit-wearing hydrant.

Sean drew the curtain back and murmured, "Amber, your dad's here."

The girl was upright by the time he'd finished the sentence.

"Let's go," her father said.

The look on her face was surprisingly familiar to Sean. It was the war-torn face. It was the I've-seen-more-hell-than-you'll-ever-know face. But what Sean realized in that moment was that he'd never seen it with blue eyes before. All the war-torn faces he'd seen had had brown eyes. And yet it was the same. Blue-eyed terror was just the same as brown-eyed terror.

"I'm not supposed to go with him," she told Sean, never taking those eyes off her father.

"Let's *go*, Amber."

"I'm not supposed to," she whispered to Sean. "The court said."

"Are you sure?" Sean asked her. "Because he's listed on your emergency card."

"I'm sure."

"Look," said the guy. "You called *me,* remember?"

"Yeah . . . but I think maybe we should check with the main office first."

"I'm her father. I don't need permission to take my sick kid home." He took a step toward Amber, who crouched back to the far corner of the vinyl bed.

Instinctively, Sean stepped into his path. And the guy smiled, a sneer really, as if the very idea of Sean were ridiculous. "I could kick your ass," he said with sociopathic calmness.

No doubt, thought Sean. But what could he do in the face of blue-eyed terror?

"Well, kick it then, asshole," he said. "Because that's the only way you're getting her."

The guy clenched his fist and Sean thought, *Shit, I am about to get punched.*

But a strange thought came to him in that moment, that maybe getting clocked wasn't such a terrible thing. Maybe he kind of deserved it in a cosmic, karmic kind of way. He wasn't always such a great guy.

In fact, there was a tiny part of him that was just as much of an angry, selfish jerk as the fireplug now raising a fist to him. And that tiny part had convinced itself that it had a right to have what it wanted, no matter the cost to others, because of the bum deal he'd been handed. That tiny part of him was just like this guy.

So hit me, already, thought Sean. *It'd be a relief.*

There was a sound behind them, and they both turned. Amber had squeezed into the corner of the sick bay, knees up in front of her, arms covering her head. She was the smallest possible version of herself, emitting the softest possible whimper of fear.

Sean glanced back at the guy and watched him deflate. The fist came down, and the menacing energy he'd emanated from the moment he'd walked into the office was gone. Replaced by shame.

Shame energy, Sean learned, had a whole different feel. He would have to tell Rebecca.

The guy left.

"It's okay," Sean said, and sat down on the vinyl bed next to Amber, in part because he wanted to make sure she'd heard him, and in part because he was suddenly so exhausted he couldn't stand upright any longer. And even though Penny had warned him against it, he reached out and laid his hand on her shoulder. "You're safe, Amber."

Things happened after that. Amber's mother came in, having gotten one of Sean's messages, and Amber told her that Sean had called her father, and he had tried to take her. The mother flipped out quite a bit, yelling at Sean for calling him, and why didn't he know he wasn't supposed to call that bastard, she'd told the school a week ago about the court order, and she'd worked so hard to get it, and what use was it if the school completely disregarded it.

Sean was really too tired to defend himself. Clearly the guy shouldn't have been called. But he was pretty sure he'd followed protocol, except for the part where he put a hand on Amber's shoulder. He didn't mention that, but he almost did.

Because this weird thing was happening. He was realizing things about himself. Things he'd been blind to. The angry, selfish jerk part, mostly. The guy who thought he was entitled just to play the game for himself, without any concern for his team. Also, blind to the fact that he *had* a team. But he did, he could see that now. And blind to the possibility that God's idea of Sean might not be limited to a guy who patches up poor people. God's plan for Sean might be evolving.

Sean himself might be evolving, too.

CHAPTER 57

On the drive home, Sean considered that he might lose his job. Amber's mother had vowed to get to the bottom of the disregard of the court order. Heads were going to roll. As she left with her mother, Sean heard Amber trying to defend him through chattering teeth, recounting how Sean had been ready to get into a fistfight. This had only served to enrage her mother further.

Yeah, he could definitely be fired.

And he realized he was disappointed. A week ago he probably wouldn't have cared. But now he saw there was more to it than splinter removal and lice checks—quite a bit more—and he would miss it. The nurse's office wasn't a war zone or a disaster area . . . except when it was.

It was a quiet night. Sean's thoughts continued to swirl. He considered calling Rebecca to apologize, but with his mind swimming in uncharted waters, he felt like he would botch the job. He made dinner. He checked Kevin's eye, which seemed to be healing nicely, though it was still purple. Kevin said he kind of liked it. It made him look tough.

He did get a call from someone late at night, as he sat in the kitchen watching the wind dance with the curtains. It was Da. Ireland wasn't working out.

"As a boy I was ashamed that I only spoke Irish. Now I'm ashamed that I don't speak it well enough. I miss Kevin. And you. I'm going to come back and rent a little apartment in the area so I can visit."

Of course you are, thought Sean, shaking his head in wonder at the uncanny convergence of needy family members. "I'll help you find a spot," he said.

It was no surprise to Sean that both he and Penny were pulled into the principal's office as soon as they got to work the next morning. Stan Girardi was not a happy man. It was seven-thirty and he was already sweating. "Sean, what the hell happened yesterday afternoon," he demanded.

Sean recounted the series of events, leaving nothing out, not even inviting Amber's father to fight him, or putting his hand on Amber's shoulder. It felt good to come clean.

"Oh, my God," breathed Penny, looking pale. "It's my fault."

"What?" said Sean. "You weren't even there."

"I got the notice to take Amber's father off her emergency card and I didn't do it. So many other things were piling up, and I just hadn't gotten to it yet."

"Jesus, Penny," said Stan. "If he'd actually taken the kid, we could have been sued!"

Not to mention the kid getting hurt, thought Sean. "Penny's been working so hard," he said. "She's killing herself—no one could do a better job."

"I'm going to have to reprimand you both," said Stan. "Penny for the paperwork failure, and you, Sean, for baiting a parent to a physical confrontation." He stared down at his desk and moved a pen into his pencil can. He took off his glasses and wiped them. "Consider yourselves reprimanded." And that was it.

The day was a little strange. The office was flooded with kids who didn't seem to have that much wrong—a headache or a funny feeling in their stomachs—but wanted nonetheless to hang out for a little while. Teachers stopped by to murmur their thanks for protecting Amber.

And strangest of all: at the end of the day, Kevin came in for a ride home.

"So," said Sean as they pulled out of the parking lot, "to what do I owe the honor?"

"That thing where you practically took that girl's father out? It's all over school. You're like a hero now."

"What? Who told you?"

"Amber texted a bunch of her friends and it spread like crazy. All the kids are writing *KITA* on their notebooks." He showed Sean his.

"What's *KITA*?"

"It stands for 'Kick It Then, Asshole.' Did you really say that?"

Sean shook his head, embarrassed. "I . . . I don't remember the exact words."

"I bet you did. Anyway, Amber says so. You should just agree with her."

When they got home, Sean checked on Aunt Vivvy, and then he and Kevin took George for a walk in the woods. As they passed the graveyard, Sean stopped for a moment and looked over.

"Do you want to go?" said Kevin.

Sean hadn't really thought about it, but he wasn't averse to the idea. Somehow it didn't seem as depressing as it used to. They walked through the brush and over the old stone wall surrounding the cemetery. Kevin knew where the headstones were and headed right for them.

They stood there looking at the two graves—one for Lila and the other for Hugh. Then Kevin went over and sat at the base of a nearby maple, and George lay down next to him.

"Looks like you've been here before," said Sean.

"Sometimes," said Kevin. "Not that often."

Sean sat down next to him, and they looked at the stones some more. Sean had always dreaded this very thing, but it wasn't so bad. His mother and Hugh were dead. It was part of living in the world—not on the edge of it, as Rebecca had said.

"So," he said to Kevin, "I've made a decision."

"What decision?"

"I'm not going to Haiti. I'm going to stay here with you and Aunt Vivvy."

Kevin's face went wide with joy, and it reminded Sean of the trampoline and how utterly blissful it made him. But then the boy seemed to reconsider his good fortune, and his expression turned stoic. "Thanks," he said. "That's really nice of you."

Sean was stunned. "What's the matter?"

"Um," said Kevin. "Well, that means I have to be good all the time, right?"

"Why do you say that?"

"Because I know you really wanted to go, and you're just staying because there's no one to take care of me. So that's like a . . . something you have to give up that you don't want to—it's a . . ."

"A sacrifice?"

"Yeah. So I have to be, like, really good so you're not sorry you did the sacrifice."

Sean gazed at him. "You don't have to be really good. Don't get me wrong, I'm in favor of good behavior. But you can just be yourself. And you're right, I used to think it would be a big sacrifice—you probably picked up on that."

Kevin raised his eyebrows and nodded.

Sean laughed. "Well, I realized something. It isn't. Actually I think it'll be really good."

"Are you going to keep working at my school?"

"No, that job's over at the end of the month. But I'll find something."

"Are you and Rebecca going to get married?"

"Not sure. I really care about her a lot, but we're still working things out."

Kevin nodded sagely, and Sean suppressed a smile.

"What about Aunt Vivvy? What if she takes off again?"

"Yeah, that's a tough one. We're going to have to figure out a way to keep her safe while you and I are out of the house."

"So," said Kevin. "There's still a lot of flux."

Sean nodded. "A ton. But that's kind of how it goes. You get one thing nailed down, something else pops up."

"But you staying—that's nailed down?"

"Completely."

A grin bloomed on Kevin's face again, like he was just now believing it. He gave Sean a nudge with his shoulder, and Sean nudged him back. He patted the dog and looked up at the trees. He took a deep breath and let it out.

"Smells good," he said.

Yeah, thought Sean. *It does.*

CHAPTER 58

After a bit they hiked back home, and Kevin pulled out his homework. Sean told him he'd be back before dinner. There was something he needed to take care of. He drove over to Belham Center, looking for a florist. But then something in the hardware store window caught his eye. *A little unorthodox,* he thought, *so I guess it's fitting.*

At home again, he set a salmon fillet in the broiler and put some rice on to cook. He was just snapping the ends off the green beans when Aunt Vivvy came into the kitchen and sat down. Without a word he filled the teakettle and put it on the burner. They listened to the *sproinging* sound of Kevin bouncing on the trampoline. Sean finished the green beans and made the tea. He sat down as he set it in front of her. "I'm not leaving," he said.

She cut her eyes toward him, then took a sip of her tea. "For now," she said.

"Everything's 'for now.'"

"True."

"This 'for now' should be a while, though."

"That's very dutiful of you."

"Yes," he said. "It also happens to be what I want."

"You'll get bored."

"I'm sure I will—there's no place on the planet that isn't boring from time to time. But that's my problem, not yours."

Aunt Vivvy sipped her tea. *Sproing, sproing* went the trampoline.

"I like that Rebecca," she said. "Don't make the same mistake I made. I find you very unpleasant when you're heartbroken."

He laughed. "I'll do my best, Auntie." And he leaned over and kissed her soft wrinkled cheek.

After dinner, he powered up his laptop. There were three messages in his in-box—a flood by his standards. The first was from the middle school reminding sixth-grade parents about the upcoming bike trip to Walden Pond. The next, from Cormac, had the subject line "KITA."

> Tree just told me. Apparently you're a legend in the whole school system now. I hear they're going to make a TV movie about it. Who do you want to play you—Chuck Norris or Jean-Claude Van Damme? Bah ha ha!

The final e-mail was from someone named Lorianna offering enhancement products that Sean was pretty sure weren't based on medical science. He chuckled. *My first spam.*

He sent a message to Yasmin Chaudhry, saying that although he'd love to work with her again, his family needed him, and it just wasn't in the cards right now. He found himself telling her about his school nurse work, his experience with Amber and how familiar it had seemed.

> She's not the kind of refugee you and I are used to, but she's a refugee all the same. I'm thinking I'll look into Emergency Department positions, maybe in Boston, where my language skills would be useful. Even if I end up as a school nurse, there's good work to do anywhere.

He asked if there might be an opportunity for short-term stints at her clinic—a week or so—and whether he could bring some non-medical volunteers with him.

Then he picked up the phone and dialed. "Hey," he said, "I'm calling first."

"How's your energy?" Rebecca asked drily.

"Stable as the Rock of Gibraltar."

When she opened the door her face was composed, but he could tell she was wary, her sensors scanning him for hidden pockets of irrational anger.

He held out his peace offering, a doormat. "For your new-old house." He pointed to the pumpkin-colored sun printed on the brown fibers. "When you use it, you'll be . . ." he prompted.

She thought for a minute. "Walking on sunshine?"

He smiled, gratified that she got the joke. She pursed her lips, but a hint of a reciprocal smile broke through anyway. She let him in.

In daylight, and without the toxic veil of his guilt and anger, he could appreciate what she'd accomplished with the room. The soothing cream-colored walls were the perfect canvas for the warm wood and jewel tones of the furniture. It was a room you could sit in all day long and never wish for something better. "Wow," he said appreciatively.

"Yeah, I'm pretty happy with it."

"Sorry I didn't notice it the other night when I was here."

She crossed her arms. "You weren't in a particularly noticing mood."

"I was pretty busy," he said. "Being a jackass takes a lot of focus."

She let out a little chuckle of agreement and sat down on the couch, which he took as permission to do the same. "I'm really sorry," he said. "A whole ocean of sorry for the way I acted."

She nodded, accepting it, and the simple gesture sent a warm wave of relief through him.

"There's no excuse," he went on, "but here's why." He told her about how Barb had cornered him about raising Kevin, and his guilt rising to new heights, and how crazy it had made him feel. "So of course, I came here because you always make me feel better about everything, and I ended up taking it out on you." He grinned at her. "And you *threw me out*!"

"You were awful!"

"Okay, well, let me ask you this: have you ever done that before—shown someone the door like that?"

"Wait a minute," she warned. "If you're making some point about how you *once again* taught me to stand up for myself—"

"No! I wasn't teaching you anything other than what a jerk I can be. But I have to tell you, it was kind of . . . I don't know, impressive. Like we must be pretty solid if you're comfortable enough to chuck me when I'm being an idiot."

She gazed at him, contemplating their solidity, and he could see the pain behind her eyes. "I'm not going to Haiti," he said. "I'm staying here."

Her face went wide with disbelief. "Sean, you can't give up the one thing that makes you really happy. It'll crush us. It'll crush everything."

"My God, Rebecca, do you think that's the only thing that makes me happy? You make me *crazy* happy. Kevin, for all his little quirks, makes me unbelievably happy. I'd be miserable so far away from you two. I'm just sorry it took me so long to get that."

Rebecca watched him intently as he spoke, slowly absorbing the here-ness of him.

"There's something else," he said. "I've been thinking about what you said about getting tested, and I'm going to look into it. I think I'm ready to know."

She was still for a moment. Then she launched herself into his arms, hugging him so tightly he could barely take a full breath. He held her and stroked her hair, still a little surprised by how much he could affect her. He was used to saving people's lives, but he still wasn't entirely accustomed to making this kind of personal impact. He would have to get used to that, he told himself, now that he no longer lived on the edges of the world, but right in the heart of it.

Read on for the first chapter of

CHAPTER 1

In jeans that fit four pounds ago but now squeezed her in a mildly intrusive manner, Dana stood at her kitchen counter pinching foil over a tray of lasagna and waiting on hold, the phone wedged against her shoulder. Her gaze skimmed the obituaries in the local paper, but Dermott McPherson's name did not appear—not this time anyway. Mr. McPherson was the reason she'd made the lasagna, though it wasn't actually for him. He probably wasn't eating much. It was for his family, who were understandably distraught over their loved one's terminal illness. Dana didn't know them. She belonged to Comfort Food, a group who cooked for families in crisis.

When it was her turn, Dana prepared meals that would, she hoped, sustain them as hands were held and medication dispensed, bedding changed and phone calls placed. She often thought of her own mother's quick descent into a gray, fetid-smelling infirmity, with lungs that seemed to shrivel almost visibly. Dana would have appreciated a well-made meal. Nothing fancy, just something better than rubbery pizza and half-flat soda. A small connection to a world outside the thick humidity of death.

Her father's exit had been swift and clean by comparison. There'd been no hospital stays or grieving friends, or even a casket to choose. But Dana didn't like to think about that.

"Cotters Rock Dental Center," said a voice in her ear. "May I—"

Startled from her somber reverie, Dana flinched, and the phone clattered to the floor. She grabbed it up quickly. "Kendra, I'm so sorry! I hope that didn't make an awful noise in your ear."

"That's all right," said the receptionist.

"I'm so embarrassed. I really apologize."

"I'm fine. May I help you?"

"This is Dana Stellgarten. Morgan and Grady's mom? I need to make appointments for their checkups, if that's okay."

Out in the mudroom, there was a squeak of the door and the thud of a backpack dropping onto the tiles. "Excuse me for just a minute, please," Dana murmured into the phone, then covered the mouthpiece with her palm. "Morgan?" she called.

"Yeah."

"I thought you were going to Darby's."

"Well, now I'm not." Morgan appeared in the kitchen and opened the refrigerator door. She stood staring in, as if there were some movie playing that only preteens could see, in among the condiments and containers of yogurt.

"I'm so sorry, I'll have to call back," Dana said into the phone. She focused on her daughter, backlit by the refrigerator light. "The plans changed?" she asked.

"Darby didn't *feel* well." Morgan's fingers twitched abruptly into little quote marks.

"Did you reschedule for another day?"

Morgan twisted toward her mother. "No, Mom, we didn't *reschedule*. It's just hanging out. You don't reschedule hanging out."

"You seem . . . Are you angry with Darby?"

Morgan closed the refrigerator door with a thump. "I don't *get* to be angry. She didn't do anything wrong."

"How did she tell you?" Now that Morgan was in sixth grade, Dana had learned it wasn't *what* girls said to each other anymore. All the real information came from *how* they said it.

Morgan slumped into a kitchen chair, picked up a napkin, and twisted it into the shape and density of a swizzle stick. "She was standing with Kimmi, and I was like, 'Hey, I'll meet you after last period.' And she looked at Kimmi."

This was bad, Dana knew. Their eyes were their weapons now. "She looked at her?"

"Yeah. And she was like, 'Oh, yeah, um, I don't feel good. I think I should go home.' So I said, 'Are you sick?' Then she looked at Kimmi *again* and said, 'I'm fine. I just need some downtime.'"

She would rather be alone than with Morgan? thought Dana. A wave of protective anger swept over her, but she didn't show it, knowing that it would confirm Morgan's suspicions and make her feel even worse. Dana herself often needed to cling to the slim chance that things weren't quite as disheartening as they seemed. "Honey, maybe she's just overscheduled," she offered.

"We're not preschoolers, Mom." Morgan rose and went up to her room. Dana let her alone. She knew that Morgan would open a textbook and curl over the page, narrowing her focus until all that existed in the world were Figure A and Subsection B.

"I'm taking Grady to practice!" Dana called up to Morgan a little while later. She loaded Grady and all his gear into the minivan and made a detour to drop off the lasagna, Caesar salad, Italian bread, and brownies at the McPhersons' house.

"Ca' I shay inna car?" asked seven-year-old Grady, sucking on his mouth guard.

"What?" Dana struggled to pick up all the containers of food. "I could use some help here."

He yanked out the mouth guard. "I don't wanna go to the door with you. It's all, like, *sad* in there. And if a kid answers, he's gonna hate me because *my* dad's not sick and *I* don't have to wait for some lady to dump off my dinner."

Dana sighed and went to the door. No one answered. She placed the food on the front step in the cooler labeled COMFORT FOOD and went back to the car. As she was pulling away, a woman in jeans and a T-shirt came out with a toddler on her hip, glanced down at the cooler and then out toward the street. For a brief moment, she met Dana's eyes and raised a hand in thanks. Dana waved back.

So young . . . she thought as she drove away.

Dana tried to attend as many of Grady's football practices as she could. The coach scared her. He yelled at the unruly posse of second-graders as if they were candidates for the Navy SEALS. Dana wasn't used to this. Until football, Grady had been coached mostly by weary fathers who sped down Interstate 84 removing their ties as they drove, trying to get to practice on time. They had no interest in yelling at other people's children—they yelled enough at their own. They just wanted the kids to learn a few skills, have fun, and avoid bloodying each other.

Coach Roburtin—Coach Ro, as the kids called him—espoused a less limited philosophy. Football practice doubled as his own workout, and he charged around the field running laps with the boys and doing push-ups. He slapped the tops of their helmets when they weren't listening, their little heads bobbing into their shoulder pads, a sight that made Dana's own neck hurt. She'd heard he was unmarried and childless, had grown up in town and played football for Cotters Rock High. He was now a car salesman in nearby Manchester.

"Stelly! Where's Stelly? Get your butt over here, son! Did you come to play or knit mittens?"

"Mitten knitting" was a catchall phrase for Coach Ro, indicating anything that wasn't football. A boy ran over, his bright blue T-shirt dangling down from under his practice jersey. That was Grady's shirt, Dana was sure of it. Coach Ro was so busy roaring at the boys he hadn't learned their names! Maybe Coach Ro had had his *own* helmet thumped a few too many times. Then it occurred to her—Stelly was short for Stellgarten.

"All RIGHT, now." He grabbed Grady's face mask and positioned him next to the quarterback. "Timmy's gonna take the snap. And he's gonna hand it off to YOU, and you are NOT going to drop it. You are going to run like your PANTS are on fire to the end zone! You with me?" Grady's helmet bobbed up and down. "Lemmehearyousay YES!" bawled the coach.

"YES!" came Grady's high-pitched howl.

Then the play was in motion, and the disorderly gaggle of youngsters suddenly transformed into two focused, goal-driven teams. For about six seconds. And then Grady's blockers seemed to forget they had anything else to do but ram their friends or straggle toward their water bottles. The opposing team swarmed toward Grady, who'd been running back toward his own team's goal line. One boy yanked at his practice jersey, pulling him down from behind. Then boys from both teams began leaping on top of them until there was a pile of bodies about three feet high. With Grady at the bottom. Dana let out a panicked, "Oh, my God!"

"Get up, you baboons! Get off him!" boomed Coach Ro, grabbing players by their shoulder pads and heaving them to the side. "Stelly, you okay? You're fine, right?"

Dana began to rush toward Grady but got only a step or two before a hand grasped her forearm. "You *know* you can't go to him," said the voice behind her. Dana turned to see Amy Koljian, Timmy the quarterback's mother. "Coach will wave you over if it's bad," Amy said with a knowing nod.

"But he could be hurt!" Easy for Amy to be calm. Her son was now sitting off to the side, chewing on his mouth guard like he hadn't been fed in a week.

"No parents on the field unless Coach says," Amy chided. "Grady'll be embarrassed if you go."

"Coach says?" said Dana. "Coach doesn't even know his first name!"

Amy motioned toward them. "See?" she said smugly. "He's fine." Grady was sitting up now, air heaving in and out of his little body. Dana willed him to look at her, to assure him of her presence. His helmet turned in her direction, and then he slowly got up. Coach thumped him on the shoulder. "All right, you knuckleheads, what the heck was THAT?" he yelled.

"God, I hate football," Dana breathed.

Amy chuckled beside her. "New football moms are always so

skittish." Timmy was the youngest of Amy's boys, and Amy enjoyed being the superior, experienced mother.

Dana attempted a grateful smile. Grady certainly would have been embarrassed, and in the end he hadn't been terribly hurt. His spine was still intact, his teeth still fit snugly in their gums. And yet Amy's self-satisfaction made Dana want to wring her neck—or, better yet, mention the girls' night out her friend Polly was throwing, knowing that Amy was not invited.

This uncharacteristic surge of vindictiveness surprised Dana. This was not her. She never purposely hurt people's feelings. And it was the very thing she'd drilled into her children since the formation of their first friendships: Do not discuss invitations. Do not mention that Cassandra is having you over after preschool today and you might finger-paint with chocolate pudding if her mother remembered to buy some. Do not announce that you're going to Owen's birthday party at Laser Tag Rumble and you thought all the boys were asked. Don't even squeeze your host's hand behind the monkey bars at recess and whisper, "I can't wait!"

Practice was over, and Grady walked toward her—was that a limp?—grabbed her thumb, and began towing her toward the car. "Are you okay?" she asked him. "That was a heck of a pileup."

"Yeah," said Grady. "Can Travis come over tomorrow?"

"Sure, I'll call his mom when we get home."

"TRAVIS!" bellowed Grady across the parking lot. "WANNA—"

Dana clamped her hand over Grady's mouth, a lightning strike of parental correction. "What have I *told* you about that?" she murmured at him tightly.

"No one cares, Mom," he insisted, squirming away from her.

Everyone cares, she thought. *Even if they don't want to go, everyone wants to be asked.*

A PENGUIN READERS GUIDE TO

THE SHORTEST WAY HOME

Juliette Fay

Sean Doran has spent the last twenty years as a nurse in war zones and natural disaster areas around the world. His mission has always been to help the poorest of the poor, and the work has allowed him to escape his own painful memories, which include a mother who died young of Huntington's disease and the sneaking suspicion that the genetically passed disease might get him next.

After twenty years, he's burned out, so he decides to go home to Belham, Massachusetts, for a short interlude between assignments. Soon after he arrives, he realizes that the household is barely functioning. His iron-willed Aunt Vivvy, who raised him in his parents' absence, is showing signs of dementia, which may or may not be related to Huntington's. His late brother's son, Kevin, appears to have behavioral problems. And his sister, Deirdre, is embittered that Sean has left her to take care of the family when she desperately wants to go off and pursue an acting career. Reluctantly, Sean starts to build a closer relationship with his orphaned nephew and to take on more responsibility around the house. Meanwhile, he and Deirdre must decide what to do about their ailing but still coolly stubborn aunt.

Luckily, Sean's two closest friends from high school are also in Belham. His buddy Cormac McGrath hires Sean at the family bakery. He accidentally encounters Rebecca Feingold, the class wallflower, and they quickly resume the candid conversations they had as teenagers. And then there's Chrissy Stillman, Sean's onetime crush who's recently divorced and unexpectedly showing interest in him.

As the days pass, the unencumbered life Sean has so carefully built is becoming increasingly complicated. He must decide whether he's ready to take on the family responsibilities and emotional commitments he's successfully avoided so far, or go back to jetting across the world to help less demanding strangers.

Juliette Fay's third novel captures the joy and pain of everyday life with a relatable cast of characters and pitch-perfect storytelling. Earnest, funny, and heartfelt, *The Shortest Way Home* is about healing old wounds, redefining familial roles, and finding yourself where you least expect to.

About Juliette Fay

Juliette Fay's first novel, *Shelter Me*, was a 2009 Massachusetts Book Award Book of the Year nominee. Her second novel, *Deep Down True*, was shortlisted for the Women's Fiction Award by the American Library Association. She received a bachelor's degree from Boston College and a master's degree from Harvard University. She lives in Massachusetts with her husband and four children.

A Conversation with Juliette Fay

The Shortest Way Home centers around a family afflicted with Huntington's disease, a condition that is often diagnosed by middle adulthood. By the time the novel begins, Sean seems to have dodged the bullet. How did you decide when to start this story?

I became fascinated by Huntington's years ago when the mother of a close friend had the disease. I remember listening to a radio program that aired in the late '80s around the time that the genetic test for Huntington's first became available. Medical professionals were stunned by how few people wanted to take the test. (This is my memory of the radio piece, which I've unfortunately never been able to find again.) Of the three people who had taken it, one tested positive. His reaction was resignation, something along the lines of "I always thought I had it and now I know for sure." The other two people tested negative . . . and they were angry! They had spent their whole lives with Huntington's looming in the background, only to find out they could have lived without all that stress and uncertainty.

That really grabbed me. What do you do when the worst *doesn't* happen? How do you move forward when a defining factor in your life turns out never to have been there in the first place? I wanted to start the story asking that question. The basis for Sean's whole vision of his life appears to be evaporating. What now?

Sean's return after so many years away is a wonderful catalyst for the Doran family to begin to heal old wounds and reconfigure their respective individual roles. How did you develop the arc for each of these characters? Did any of their journeys surprise you?

I decided that if I was going to give Sean an identity crisis, I would give everybody else one, too! Each character is at a point of enormous personal change. Aunt Vivvy has always been intellectually sharp and in control. Now she's losing the part of herself she values most. Kevin is the quiet kid who won't join in, but he's heading off to middle school, and he's going to have to face his issues. Deirdre is trying to launch herself toward the one thing she's always wanted—and she may have only a narrow window to enjoy it, if it turns out she has Huntington's. Rebecca has spent her entire life under her parents' thumb, but now she's trying to bust free and follow her own agenda. Da is the absent father, but after almost thirty years he wants to be a part of his family's life again, if they'll let him. Cormac and Barb want to have a baby, but that's not working out as planned, so they have to consider new options. Even George the dog is undergoing big changes in her role—from aggressive beast to obedient protector.

There were no big surprises in character arc for me, but there are always little ones, which make it a pleasure for me as their creator. I loved when Sean was a jerk to Rebecca and she threw him out. I didn't see that coming until it "happened," and I was saying "Go, girl!" to the computer screen.

You capture the subtle mood shifts in conversations between characters so elegantly. What is your technique for tuning in to their emotional lives?

For me, writing each character is a little like method acting. I have to know a whole lot more about them than the reader will see on the page. I have to feel how they feel and be empathetic with even the most hard to like characters. This helps me give depth to each one.

I've always been fascinated by how people talk—or don't talk—to each other. So much in life is communicated nonverbally, and that can be hard to get into print. It's easy to fall back on making characters overly verbose when a look or a gesture or tone of voice will get the point across much more authentically. I often act it out so I can feel the movements and hear the tone and try to incorporate these clues into the exchange. Then I aim to have every single word they do actually say mean something. If it doesn't, it's out.

This is your first novel from a man's point of view. Can you talk about how it changed the writing process for you?

It was a challenge, but also so much fun! The protagonists of my two previous novels, *Shelter Me* and *Deep Down True*, are suburban moms who are newly single. That's me (although I'm still married). Sean Doran is a man with no kids, who's never been married—never even been in a relationship. Other than volunteer work in a third world country, Sean and I have virtually nothing in common, right down to that pesky Y chromosome. It was a blast.

The love scenes were a real challenge. I came at them from the premise that men tend to be more physical and less analytical than women in the heat of the moment. They are—on the whole—less likely to be asking themselves "Do I really like this person? Where is this going?" even as passion flares. This of course is somewhat stereotypical, but I had to start somewhere.

The scenes between Sean and Cormac were also tricky. How do men talk to each other with no women around? How do they express their appreciation and concerns? Men don't always come out and say that stuff to each other (and I certainly wasn't going with the clichéd "I love you, man!"). These two have a longstanding and deep friendship. But they're also regular guys. There's a lot of support and compassion between them, but Sean and Cormac don't express these feelings as explicitly as women tend to.

By the way, my husband was my go-to in this area. I was so relieved when he read those scenes and said, "Yeah, that's pretty much how it is."

The issue of sensory processing disorder and how it affects children is a fascinating one. What made you want to write about it?

Sensory processing is interesting because it's often misunderstood and it wouldn't be something Sean would know about from his own work. If Kevin had been a generally happy, well-adjusted kid, it would have been easier for Sean to leave. I liked the idea of Sean becoming more compassionate and attached to Kevin as he gets more drawn into the mystery of Kevin's behavior issues.

Abandoned by his own father, Sean nonetheless wrestles throughout the book with the question of whether to stay and be a parent to Kevin. How did you bring him to this decision?

One of the big questions this story raises is: What binds us to one another when the responsibility isn't clear? Is Sean duty-bound to stay? It's not his kid, it's not his life, and in fact he's worked really hard to set things up so he has no permanent responsibilities. Until now, he could come and go as he pleased. But as he grows closer to Kevin, he has a harder and harder time figuring out how to leave. Falling in love with Rebecca compounds the problem even further. We've all had those "Should I Stay or Should I Go?" moments. For Sean, the answer to that question will have a drastic impact on everyone he loves.

There is an almost deceptive simplicity to your writing style—it's so clear and seamless. How do you achieve this effect? Who are your favorite authors, and who has inspired your work?

I try to keep the writing free of anything that isn't absolutely necessary, first because it decelerates the forward motion of the story, and second because I think readers are generally pretty intuitive. They can infer most of what they need from characters' actions and don't always want as much exposition and explanation as we sometimes think they do. Personally, I like to figure things out when I'm reading, and I'm more engaged if the writer doesn't detail every last motivation or stick of furniture for me.

Some of my favorite authors are Dennis Lehane (*The Given Day*), Zora Neale Hurston (*Their Eyes Were Watching God*), Malcolm Gladwell (*Blink* and *Outliers*), Vanessa Diffenbaugh (*The Language of Flowers*), Jonathan Tropper (*This is Where I Leave You* and *Everything Changes*), Marilynne Robinson (*Gilead* and *Home*), and so many others.

Sean's father coming back into the picture toward the end of the book is something of a surprise. How did you make the decision to bring him into the story?

There were two reasons, really. Throughout his adulthood Sean has more or less steeled himself against missing his father. And yet it's a wound that never quite healed. I wanted him to experience having a father again to help him relate more deeply to Kevin's loss. Bringing Da back puts that right in Sean's face.

Second, through research for a family trip to Ireland, I became fascinated with the history of Great Blasket Island. I decided to incorporate it into the story I was working on, which became *The Shortest Way Home*. And there you have it—the randomness with which authors sometimes choose their plot threads.

Your novels seem to have a common theme of people at a crossroads forced to redefine their lives. What draws you to this theme?

I guess it's because the unexpected turn of events that force us to change course are what make life so endlessly interesting. You're going along, thinking you've got things in hand, or are at least moderately comfortable in your rut, and something falls out of the sky. I like to start stories there, or shortly thereafter, because the event is usually not as interesting as how we react and how the flow chart of possibilities careens from one repercussion to the next.

What's the most important feedback you've ever gotten from readers? What do you hope readers will take away from this book?

The most meaningful feedback has always been, "This book helped me." As a fiction writer I never anticipated that people would get anything other than a good story from my books. But when someone writes to say something like, "Now I understand my widowed sister better" or, "Now I appreciate my husband more" or, "Now I'm more compassionate with my middle schooler who's driving me crazy," it's like winning the lottery.

From *The Shortest Way Home*, I hope readers will feel that they've gotten a good story and some things to chew on even after the book is over. Some of those might include: What is family, and to whom are we bound? How do we find redemption amid suffering? How do we step up to the plate and hit those curve balls life inevitably pitches at us? And do fruit, sugar, and a flaky crust really make the world a sweeter place?

Yes, I think they do.

Questions for Discussion

1. After spending most of his adult life as a nurse in developing countries, Sean returns home to reconnect with what's left of his family. How might things have turned out differently if he'd gone home more often?

2. The Doran family has dealt with enormous loss. How does each member of the family cope, and how well are these coping methods working?

3. When he first comes home, Sean falls into some old habits, including his teenage crush on Chrissy Stillman. In what ways is Sean stuck in his adolescence? What events help him grow up a bit over the course of the story?

4. What does Sean learn about his brother Hugh through other characters in this book? How does this affect Sean's decisions

about his own future? Do you think Sean will be a good parent? What will his shortcomings be?

5. Outwardly Aunt Vivvy displays mixed emotions about her role as sudden parent to the Doran kids. What do you think her true feelings are? Why does she hide them?

6. Sean's relationship with God shifts over the course of this book. How does it evolve and why? Is destiny a permanent thing or can it change?

7. What was the saddest moment of the story for you? The funniest? The most surprising?

8. Which character are you most like? How did you relate to that character's learning curve over the course of the story?

9. Though he has only ever worked in extremely impoverished communities, Sean takes a temporary job as a school nurse. Were you surprised by what Sean learns from this experience?

10. At the end of the book, Sean and Rebecca have some decisions to make about their future. What do you think their life will look like? What advice would you give them?

11. What character would you most like to have lunch with and why? What questions would you ask? What would you like to tell him or her?

12. If you were at risk for a genetic disease, would you get tested?